While I Was Gone

While I Was Gone

SUE MILLER

Alfred A. Knopf   New York   1999

for Ben

Acknowledgments

I am indebted to Detectives Brian P. Branley and John F. Fulkerson, and to Sergeant Joseph J. McSweeney, all of the Cambridge Police Department, for taking time to imagine my story with me; and to my brother, David Beach Nichols, D.V.M., animal lover extraordinaire, for his resourceful and painstaking help—though I alone am to blame for any inaccuracies or unlikely details.

Cedar waxwings dart among the swallows
Iridescent fish with wings,
Layers of life above the water.
Under, the trout.

JUDITH BEACH NICHOLS (1919–1979)

While I Was Gone

1

I T'S ODD, I SUPPOSE, THAT WHEN I THINK BACK OVER ALL that happened in that terrible time, one of my sharpest memories should be of some few moments the day before everything began. Seemingly unconnected to what followed, this memory is often one of the first things that comes to me when I call up those weeks, those months—the prelude, the long, beautiful, somber note I heard but chose to disregard.

This is it: silence between us. The only sounds the noises of the boat—the squeal of the oarlocks when my husband pulled on the oars, the almost inaudible creak of the wooden seat with his slight motion, and then the glip and liquid swirl of the oars through the water, and the sound of the boat rushing forward.

My husband's back was to me as I lay in the hard curve of the bow. He sat still a long time between each pull. The oars dripped and then slowly stopped dripping. Everything quieted. Sometimes he picked up his fishing rod and reeled it in a bit, pulling it one way or another. Sometimes he recast, standing high above me in the boat, the light line whipping wider and wider, whistling faintly in its looping arc across the sky before he let it go.

It was a day in mid-fall, well after the turning of the leaves. The weather was glorious. We always took one day a week off together, and if the weather was good, we often went fishing. Or my husband went fishing and I went along, usually with a book to read. Even when the girls were small and it was harder to arrange, we managed at least part of the day alone together. In those early years we sometimes made love in the boat when we were fishing, or in the woods—we had so little time and privacy at home.

It was a Monday. The day off was always Monday, because Sunday was Daniel's busiest day at work and Saturday was mine. Monday was our day of rest. And what I recollect of that Monday, that fine fall day, is that for some long moments in the boat, I was suddenly aware of my *state*, in a way we aren't often. That is, I was abruptly and most intensely, sharply aware of all the aspects of life surrounding me, and yet of feeling neither part of it nor truly separated from it. Somehow impartial, unattached—an observer. Yet sentient of it all. Deeply sentient, in fact. But to no apparent purpose.

If I were trying to account for this feeling, I might say that it had something to do with the way I was half lying, half sitting on several pillows in the bow, the way the curving walls of the old rowboat framed a foreground for my view as they rose away from me. I saw them, these peeling wooden inner walls, and then my husband's familiar shape. Above him there was the flat, milky-blue sky and sometimes, when we were close enough to shore, the furred, nearly black line of the spruces and pines against it. In the air above us swallows darted—dark, quick silhouettes—and once a cedar waxwing moved smoothly through them. Layers of life above me. Below, I could hear the lap of the deep water through the walls of the boat.

As a result, let's say, I felt suspended, waiting. Between all these worlds and part of none of them.

But this isn't what I really believe; I think the sensation came from somewhere within me.

We feel this way sometimes in adolescence, too, surely most of us can call it up. But then there's the burning impatience for the next thing to take shape, for whatever it is we are about to become and be to announce itself. This was different: there was, I supposed, no next thing.

I had felt something like this every now and then in the last year or so, sometimes at work as I tightened a stitch or gave an injection: the awareness of having done this a thousand times before, of surely having a thousand times left to do it again. Of doing it well and thoroughly and neatly, as I liked to do things, and simultaneously of being at a great distance from my own actions.

Or at home, setting the table, sitting down with my husband to another meal, beginning our friendly evening conversation about the day—the house quiet around us, the old dogs dozing under the table or occasionally nuzzling our feet. A sense suddenly of being utterly present and also, simultaneously, far, far away.

Now I stirred, shifted my weight. My husband turned, no aspect of his face not dear to me. "Hurting?" he asked.

And with that, as quickly as it had come over me, the moment ended. I was back, solidly in time, exactly where we were. It was getting chilly. I had been lying in the wooden boat for several hours now, and even though I had the pillows under me, I was stiff. I had a bad hip. Replacement had been discussed, though everyone said I was young for it. I liked only that part of the problem, being too young for something.

"A little," I said.

"We'll head back."

"Are you sure?"

"I've got two reasonable ones. I'm a happy man." He began to reel his line in.

I turned and stretched. "How nice, to be a happy man," I said.

He looked over his shoulder at me, to get my tone. "It *is* nice," he said.

"And I meant it," I answered.

As we rowed back, as we drove home, I found myself wanting to tell my husband about my feeling, but then not knowing what to call it. The shadow of it lingered with me, but I didn't say anything to Daniel. He would hear it as a want, a need. He would feel called upon to offer comfort. Daniel is a minister, a preacher, a pastor. His business is the care of his flock, his medium is words—thrilling words, admonishing or consoling words. I knew he could console me, but consolation wasn't what I felt I wanted. And so we drove along in silence, too, and I looked out the window at the back roads that sometimes seemed utterly rural, part of the nineteenth century, and sometimes seemed abruptly the worst of contemporary suburban life: the sere, beautiful old fields carved up to accommodate the too-wide circular asphalt driveways, the too-grand fake-garrison-colonial houses.

We lived in the center of town, an old, old town—Adams Mills, the Adamses long dead, the mills long burned down. Our house was a simple square farmhouse, added on to repeatedly at the back of the

first floor over the years, as was the custom then with these old
New England homes. We had an unpainted barn behind it, and
behind that was a small meadow which turned to pinewoods at the far
edge, woods that hid our neighbors to the rear, though in the summer
we could hear them fighting, calling each other things that used to
make the girls laugh with joy. "You fat-ass pig!" they'd imitate. "You
stupid shithead!"—which for some years they had, uncorrected, as
"shiphead."

We used the barn as a garage now, and Daniel had his study out
there, in a small heated room at the back. When we'd moved in, it was
still full of rusting old tools and implements, the kinds of things people clean up and hang on their walls as folk art. There were still mason
jars of unidentifiable fruits and vegetables in the old root cellar, a dark
earthen space you entered by lifting a sort of trapdoor in the kitchen
yard. Because of all this, we felt connected to the house's life as part of
a farm.

Yet at the front of the house we were townsfolk, connected to the
village. Our view was across the old common to the big Congregational church. Not Daniel's church, it's true, and we looked at its back
side—its *rump*, the girls had called it—but it was a splendid civic vista
nonetheless. Beyond the church, we could see the row of grand Georgian houses lined up face-to-face with its front.

Along one side of the green was an inn, where we could get a fancy
and tasteless meal in the main dining room, or a beer and a good ham-
burger in the bar, with its large-screen TV always tuned to the sports
network. Along the other side of the green there were shops: a small,
expensive grocery, a video store, a store with high-quality kitsch—
stoneware, cute gardening tools, stationery, rubber stamps, coffee-
table books, Venetian-glass paperweights. Everything in town was
clapboard, painted white with green or black trim. If you tried another
color, the historical commission descended on you and made you very,
very sorry you had.

We turned into our drive now and pulled up next to the horse
chestnut that shaded the dooryard. It dropped its leaves early every
year. They littered the yard now, and our feet made a crunching noise
on them as we crossed to the back door. The nearly bare ancient
branches, twisted blackly above us in the dusky light, made me think
of winter. When we opened the door, the house was silent. Daniel
began to put his gear away in the spare room off the hall, speaking

loudly as he clattered around. "Boy, it is sure nice to have dogs! Dogs are so great, how they come running to greet you when you get home, how they make you feel like you count, even when you don't." This was a familiar riff, and as I headed to the john, I threw back my contribution: "Dogs! Dogs! Man's best friend!"

When I came out, a few minutes later, all three dogs had finally bestirred themselves from wherever they'd been nesting and were whacking their happy tails around the kitchen. Daniel was cleaning his fish at the sink—the smell already suffused the air—and there was hope of food for them. Nothing excited them more. They barely greeted me.

The answering machine was blinking. I turned it on. There were three messages, all for Daniel, which was the way it usually went, except when I was on call. I'm a veterinarian, and the crises among animals are less complex, more manageable, than those of humans—actually very much a part of my choice of profession.

Daniel had turned slightly from the counter to listen to the calls, and I watched his face as he took them in—one about relocating a confirmation class because of a scheduling conflict; one from Mortie, his assistant pastor, reporting on the worsening state of a dying parishioner Daniel was very fond of, a young mother with cancer; one from another minister, suggesting he and Daniel try to "pull something together" among their colleagues about some racial incidents in the three closely adjoining towns around us. Daniel's face was thin and sharp and intelligent, his eyes a pale gray-blue, his skin white and taut. I'd always loved looking at him. He registered everything quickly, transparently—with these calls first annoyance, then the sag of sorrow, then a nod of judicious agreement—but there was something finally self-contained about him too. I'd often thought this was what made him so good at what he did, that he held on to some part of himself through everything. That he could hear three calls like this and be utterly responsive to each of them, and then turn back and finish cleaning his trout. As he did now.

"Will you go and visit Amy?" I asked.

His plaid shirt pulled and puckered across his shoulder blades with his motion. His head was bent in concentration. "I don't know," he said without looking at me. "I'll call Mortie back and see when I'm done here."

I refilled the dogs' bowl with water and poured some more dry food for them. Daniel worked silently at the sink, his thoughts elsewhere. I went out the front door and got the mail from the box at the road. The air was getting chilly, darkness was gathering around the house. I turned on the living room lights and sat down. I sorted through the circulars, the bills, I threw away the junk. While I was working, I heard Daniel leave the kitchen, headed across the yard to his office in the barn to make his calls.

WITH THE CLOSING OF THE DOOR I FELT RELEASED FROM THE awareness of his sorrow that had held me in his orbit. I began to roam the house, with the dogs as my entourage, feeling restless, a feeling that seemed connected, somehow, to that moment in the boat, and maybe also to Daniel's sad news. I went up the steep, narrow stairs to the second floor, where the girls' rooms were.

All the doors were shut up there, and I opened them, standing in each doorway in turn. The sloped-ceiling rooms were deeply shadowed. Light from the hall fell in long rectangles on the old painted pine floors. In the older girls' rooms the beds were made, the junk was gone—boxed in the attic or thrown away forever. Only Sadie's room still spoke of her. One wall was completely covered with pictures she'd cut out of magazines. There were stark photos of dancers in radical poses, of nearly naked models in perfume or liquor ads, engaged in moments of stylized passion, there were romantic and soft-focus views of places she dreamed of going to—Cuzco, Venice, Zanzibar. There were guys: Daniel Day-Lewis, Denzel Washington, Brad Pitt. In the corner of the room where the ceiling sloped nearly to the floor, all the stuffed animals and dolls she'd ever owned were standing wide-eyed in rows by height, like some bizarre crowd in the bleachers at a high-school event.

I went into Cass's blank room and lay down across her bed. Maybe it was the girls I wanted. Maybe I just missed the comfort of their noise, of their smells and music and flesh.

And then I laughed out loud, thinking of how angry I'd gotten at them, and how often, for these very things. Allie, our old retriever, barked at me, for my odd sudden noise. "Sorry," I said, and dangled my hand off the edge of the bed so she could lick it. "Sorry, old girl."

Suddenly I was thinking of a morning years before when all three girls had climbed into bed with me and Daniel. I kept trying to get up to make breakfast, and this became the game. The twins held me in their bony hard arms, they wrapped their long stringy bare legs around me. They were shrieking, "No! No breakfast! You must stay in the nest! You must!" Sadie, sleepy, plump, all our baby, lay in front of Daniel in the curve of his arm, her pink, wet thumb resting at her lip. The two of them—Daniel and Sadie—were turned to watch us wild wrestlers, but they had moved out to the edge of the bed, trying to avoid the odd knee or elbow.

I reached over, making my hand a desperate claw. "Help me, Sadie," I croaked dramatically from the flailing mound of bony flesh. "Help, help!"

Sadie sobered and looked for a moment up at her father. Was it real? She believed in everything. He made a face that put her at ease. She laughed.

She lay thoughtfully still for just a few seconds more, before she, too, threw herself forward into the fray—my rescuer. And then Daniel's arms were encircling all of us, and he grabbed somebody from behind—Nora, I think—and swung her up. I felt his legs push powerfully against me.

It lasted only a minute or so, the shrieking, the laughter, everyone's nightie hiking up, all the bare flesh, the bones and angles, feet big and small, soft parts, damp parts. Our familiar smells.

Ordinary life. Flesh. It was my world then. I was wrapped in it, held in it, I thought. And now I'm not. Now I float.

Allie was steadily licking my hand. I turned, and she stopped and smiled at me, panting, her long curled tongue flicking upward slightly with each breath. "Laughing Allegra" we had named her, because her face fell into this happy, dopey grin when her mouth opened.

"It was fun, wasn't it, Allie?" I said. She thrust her head forward and licked my face, once.

I got up and went downstairs, into our bedroom. At one time it had been the front parlor of the house. It had a working fireplace with a painted wooden mantel, but no closet, so we'd mounted a row of hooks on the wall and hung them with what we most frequently wore—Daniel's slacks and jackets, jeans and scrubs for me and one or two nighties; both our bathrobes, homely, wrinkled shapes. A motorcycle blatted rudely past on the town road, only a dozen yards or so from our bed. We had talked about moving upstairs to the back of the house now that the girls were gone, but we hadn't done anything about it yet.

I stood for a long time in front of the mirror. Flesh, indeed. From time to time Daniel felt moved to say to me, "God, you're a beautiful woman," but this was kindness, or love. I examined myself objectively, clinically now. I saw a nice-looking middle-aged person, someone you wouldn't look at twice if you passed her on the street. And I'd never been beautiful, in fact. I'd been attractive, tall and blond and strong-looking. I'd had a notable kind of energy, and people—men—were drawn to it.

Now, though, when my face was in repose, I looked tired. The downcurving lines at the corners of my mouth made me seem judgmental and stern, even a little pissed off. Sometimes my receptionist, Beattie, a woman I'd known and loved for twenty years, would ask me—out of the blue, from my perspective—"What's wrong?" and I'd realize my face had fallen into those lines again. "Nothing," I'd say. And then consciously try to open my face, to make it pleasant. To make it, I suppose, younger.

Here's what else I knew: I was no longer sure exactly what color my hair would be if I didn't regularly rinse it a color called Silver Ash. I was about an inch shorter than I'd been in youth, and had earned at least that much more waistline as my body had compressed. I had arthritis in my hips, and it was starting a little in my back.

And I was lucky, I knew this too. There was no cancer in my family, there were no blood pressure or cholesterol problems. Though my father had died when I was small, it had been an accident of nature—a quick, brutal case of hepatitis. No, I was a good specimen, from good stock. My mother, eighty, still worked part time as a secretary, typing articles and papers for two or three retired professors who'd known her since she was a young woman. She still lived by herself in the house where I'd grown up—though I suppose she was technically not alone, since she rented rooms to students at the university, and I suspected that more and more they did the work of keeping the house up. Still, she managed it all. She managed it well, she kept herself going through the long Maine winters.

Thinking of her, looking at myself, I wondered if she'd ever felt this sense of dislocation from her past, from her present, from her own reflection in the mirror. This empty unease. And then I smiled at myself, remembering her answer to questions of this nature. "Now, why would I bother to do that?" she'd say. She wouldn't stop what she was doing, she wouldn't turn to look at the eight-year-old, or ten-year-old, or thirteen-year-old girl who stood next to her, asking. She wouldn't wonder where the question had come from or what its deeper meaning was. She'd slap the sifter to loose the flour, she'd slam the iron down on the shirt under attack, she'd rat-tat-tat even harder on the typewriter and violently fling the return across. "Now, why would I bother to do that?"

"Just *'cause*, Ma," I said out loud now. And then I turned and said it to the dogs, who'd gathered in a circle behind me and were staring up, pondering my immobility. "Just 'cause, guys and gals." Their tails thudded the floor. The little one, Shorty, growled in pleasure just at being spoken to. I felt, somehow, comforted. This was all of it, no doubt, the strange passing feeling that had come to me in the boat. Age. Vanity. The impossibility of accepting the new versions of oneself that life kept offering. The impossibility of the old version's vanishing.

Ah, well, it had vanished, hadn't it? As surely as the rooms upstairs stood empty and neat in the dark.

I washed my face and put on fresh makeup. Daniel came back from the barn and we began to move around the kitchen, making dinner. He hadn't been able to reach Mortie, but he'd talked to everyone else he needed to talk to. Now he turned the radio on to the news. As we did our separate chores, we listened and commented idly to each other on what we heard—the politics, the plane crashes and crimes, the large disasters of the day, which we all use to keep the smaller, more long-term sorrows at bay.

When we were sitting at last at the kitchen table, with a curry I'd quickly put together and a salad he'd made, he looked over at me and frowned. "What's wrong?" he said.

Beattie's question. I laughed.

"What's so funny?" he asked.

"Now, wait a minute," I said. "It's either 'What's wrong?' or 'What's so funny?' It can't possibly be both."

"But it *is* both. I can't keep up with what goes on in your face, it changes so fast."

"Well, nothing's *wrong*," I said.

"Aha! But *something*"—he lifted his fork and waved it in rhythm—
" 'is not right.' " And we smiled at each other, in honor of Sadie's
favorite book. We began to eat.

"That's about it, I guess," I said after a moment. "The unnameable
something."

"Give it a shot," he said. "Name it."

I took a breath. And then, abruptly, I had the sense of how much I
loved this, this conversation freed of the reports of what one or
another of the girls had done in school that day, of what she needed,
wanted, *had to have* before the junior prom or the class day or the party
at Sarah Malone's. We'd had five months of it, alone together, and
there were times like this moment, Daniel pushing me, wanting to
know me again, that made me feel it would be enough, more than
enough. That it would call forth all that was in me. Later I would
remember this moment, too, and wish I'd held on to that feeling of
possibility.

"I don't know," I said. I shrugged. "Earlier, in the boat today, I was
feeling odd. Just a sense of . . . dislocation, I guess, in my life."

"From what?" And when I didn't answer right away: "Dislocation
from what?"

"From . . . just one thing from another, I guess. I don't know." I
looked at him and made a face. It seemed, suddenly, an embarrassing,
even a foolish feeling to have indulged. I settled for an easy answer.
"It's probably a little bit about the girls, actually. In a way, missing
them. But more . . . just all that energy, all that work and closeness.
Where did it go?"

"It went into making them wonderful. Making them who they are."

I made a noise, and he frowned, which with Daniel was the tensing
of a single faint line between his brows. "Don't go *pfft*. It's true," he
said. "I'm not consoling you, Joey. I'm not humoring you, so don't act
as though I am."

"Ach. I know," I said. "I know."

More gently, he said, "You always go *pfft* when I say something
good. You should let me be loving to you."

"I know," I said again. "I need to learn to just say thank you." I
reached over and rested my hand on his arm. I could feel the wires
under his skin. "Thank you," I said.

"Thank *you*," he said. "And you're welcome." After a minute, "But
name it better than that."

"Oh, Daniel!" I cried.

Still, I stopped and thought for a moment. "I really don't know. I don't. I've just felt . . . creepy. Crepuscular? Weird, anyway, all day. It feels . . . admonitory or premonitory or something."

"Which?"

"What's the difference, exactly?"

And he explained, Latin-lover that he was, the derivation of each. "But I don't believe in premonitions," he said thoughtfully, after a moment's silence.

"I don't either, really." And then I remembered. "Except, remember the time that Cass and Nora got up on the roof?"

"That wasn't really a premonition, though."

"I *saw* them. In my mind's eye, I saw them there, with the sky behind them, toddling around."

"But that was the result of thinking. You hadn't heard them in a while, your brain ran through a few options, the kind of stuff they might be up to. You thought of the ladder and the skylight—"

"I didn't, Daniel. That's not the way it happened. I just saw them in my mind and ran upstairs. I *knew*. I knew where they were, and I knew I needed to get to them."

Daniel was helping himself to more curry. He looked over at me. "Yeah, but I bet that somehow, maybe so quickly you never remembered it discretely, you went through those steps."

"I suppose I might have. But that's not what I remember. What I remember is popping up through the skylight and seeing them just as I'd seen them mentally, staggering around, happy as larks. As close to death"—I held my fingers an inch apart—"as that." I remembered their faces lifting in delight at the sight of me, just my head sticking up through the open skylight at first, then my hands rising too. They laughed, as though I were doing a kind of magic trick, conjuring myself out of thin air. I stayed right where I was, on the ladder, so they wouldn't be tempted to tease me by running away, a favorite game. So they wouldn't step back, back over the edge and down. I made my voice as richly cozy and seductive and welcoming and calm as I could through my panic. I spoke as slowly as ooze. "*Hi!* Hi, you cuties. Come here and tell me what you been doing. I didn't see you for a *long* time. Come right here by me, come by Mumma. Come for smoochies, sillies. Come right here"—and as they ran forward into my grip, "Oh, my good girls, my loves."

"But you know," Daniel was saying, "the way memory works, you might have attached that image—the real image, the way they truly looked—to your earlier thinking."

"Which *was* premonitory."

"Yeah, but maybe not in that exact, image-based way."

I stopped and looked at him. "Why are you arguing endlessly with me, Daniel?"

"I'm not. I don't mean to be." He looked sheepish suddenly. "I just think it's interesting. I've been doing all this reading about memory, how it actually gets laid down and altered over time. It's fascinating. 'Memory,' " he sang suddenly in his light tenor, " 'lights the corners of my mind . . .' " He let the song trail off. I was smiling at him. "Plus, of course"—he smiled back quickly—"I do like to talk. Talking is life. Right?"

"For you, yes."

"So what was this feeling? Today. Talk. Talk to me."

"Oh, I don't know. It was silly." I leaned back. "No. Here's what it was. I was looking at myself in the mirror, and I *saw* myself, and I don't know how I got this way." I made a dramatic gesture down my body. I wanted to amuse him. He had amused me.

He looked me up and down. "What way?"

"Older. Not young. Not what I once was."

"Ah, but which of us is?" He grinned, a flash of dry pleasure.

"Of course. It's silly. But just, from time to time, don't you kind of get *swept* by it? By the sense of separation between the parts of life. Don't you? Doesn't the part that was crazy and doing drugs and having random sex in the sixties sometimes sit up and wonder what you're doing here? Look at that," I said. I pointed to the counter. "There's a Cuisinart there. There's a dishwasher. That's indefensible."

He laughed. And then he said, "People change, my Jo. That's all you're saying."

"No it isn't. I don't think it is. What I'm saying is I don't like this business of whole lives being taken from me."

"Who's taking? Who's taking anything from you? *'Whole lives.'* " He made a face. "Too melodramatic. It's just life."

For a few moments we ate, we talked about the food, I poured myself more wine. Daniel wasn't drinking, because he thought he might be going out later.

Then, abruptly, he pointed at me with his fork. "I mean, Jo, look at my parents. Born on farms, raised on farms, both of them. Farming, raising their kids on a farm. And lo and behold, the kids don't want to farm, so they sell it. They move to town, they grow old looking out at the parking lot by Meadow Glen Acres. That's disjunctive as hell. But that's the way life goes."

"See, I don't think it has to. I think it can feel more connected. I bet it used to. I bet this has something to do with goddamned *modernity*."

"Could be," he said.

I sighed. I drank more of my wine.

"It's life, Jo," he said after a few moments of silence.

"It isn't," I said.

We both laughed, small, rueful laughs.

"Ready to clean up?" he asked.

After dinner, Mortie called back. Daniel turned his back to me while he talked. His voice was grave, a series of quick, short responses. Okay, okay. Yes. Okay.

When he hung up, I said, "She's dying."

"Yes," he said.

"I'm so sorry."

"I know." He went to change, and I moved more slowly now around the kitchen. The windows had gone black, they were steamy with our life. I was thinking of Amy, his parishioner. I'd met her only a few times. She'd been pregnant the last time I'd seen her, singing in the choir. Her hands, holding the music, had rested on the shelf formed by her big belly in the maroon robe.

When he came back, he said, "I'm not sure how late I'll be." His face was stricken, frightened-looking, and I thought about how difficult his job was.

"I know," I said.

"Don't wait up."

"I want to," I said.

He nodded, and gripped my arm for a second, and left.

A WHILE AFTER HE'D GONE, SADIE CALLED, AND HER SMALL, light voice made me see her and yearn for her. She was the youngest of my daughters, the easiest, and my love for her was the least complicated.

The twins had always been much more difficult. Unplanned,

they'd come at the wrong time in our marriage, just when I was starting out as a vet, needing to put in long hours of scutwork as the junior
partner in a practice. Daniel had their care more than I did, and I
sometimes felt shut out from their life together. And from the two of
them, too, their mysterious dark twinniness. They cared most about
each other.

And then suddenly, when they were two or so, they began to fight.
Within seconds they could move from a wild mutual joy to murderous
violence. They left the tracks of their tiny fingernails on each other's
faces, the beautiful, even, red circlet of their teeth marks in each
other's soft flesh. They pulled out clutches of each other's wispy black
hair. They pushed and scratched and grabbed and would not let go,
and woe unto him who tried to separate them. We rarely got through
a meal without one of them attacking the other, without wails and
shrieks and inconsolable sorrow.

Intermittently they'd be best friends again for a while. *Oh, maybe
it's over,* we'd tell each other. *Oh, thank God.* But at the slightest
offense, the mildest difference, they'd start again. "Why must we live
like this?" Daniel and I would ask each other. I sometimes wept, it was
so different from what I'd hoped for or imagined when they were
born, these two perfect, helpless creatures nested bonelessly side by
side.

And then, when they were five, along came Sadie. Planned for,
adored by us all, pliable, sweet, she sat like a small Caucasian Buddha
in our midst. I was able to take a maternity leave of three months this
time, and I lay in bed long mornings, nursing her and sleeping, while
the twins were off at kindergarten and then their after-school program. When they came home, they swarmed her. They carried her
everywhere with them. She was their doll, their toy, their beloved. She
walked and talked late because they were so eager to serve her, to
anticipate her every need.

They vied for her affection, and Nora, finally, was the winner, the
one Sadie began to gravitate toward most often. I think that for Nora,
Sadie may have offered a way of escaping from the demands of
her bond to Cass—from the wild love, the maddened jealousy. At
any rate, she became a kind of second mother to Sadie, and as Sadie
got older, she often turned to her before me or Daniel for help and
information.

Cass was angry, she felt left out. She wanted to go on fighting. And that's what she *did*, really—with herself, with us, with the world. Dukes up, she charged at everyone and everything. She became the outsider, the tough one, the one we worried about. Even now. Here was Nora, living in New York with a young man we genuinely liked, going to film school. Sadie had just started college in western Massachusetts, still loving, still easy, voluntarily in touch all the time. And Cass?

Well, Cass played guitar in a band. The last time I'd seen her, her hair was dyed a plummy black that rose around her head in a wildly teased tangle, and she was wearing lipstick so dark it seemed the color of violence itself—it put you in mind of bruises, of dried blood. The band made no money to speak of. Who knows what they ate? A lot of the time they all slept together in their van in parking lots along the highway, on derelict empty streets in faraway cities. Sometimes we didn't know where she was for two or three months at a time. Then one of us would pick up the phone in the middle of the night and it would be Cass, collect, from a pay phone in Louisiana, or North Dakota, saying she could talk only a minute, they were about to go on, there's more snow here than I've ever seen in my fucking life, I dyed my hair blond, the van broke down, I broke up with Tod, now I'm with Raimondo, oops, they're calling me, love ya, gotta go.

Not Sadie. Sadie called and lazily talked and talked. What's new? she'd ask. What have you guys been doing? Though all she wanted to hear was that everything was the same.

"Hi, Mom, it's Sade," is what she said tonight in her little voice. (*If it isn't Betty Boop,* Cass used to tease.)

"Oh!" I cried in pleasure. "Sadie, Sadie, my shady lady."

There was a second of silence. Then she said, "God, isn't it bad enough to give me the *name?*"

"It's a beautiful name." It was Daniel's mother's name. She'd wept when we told her, though she warned us, too, that it was a hard one to live with.

Sadie snorted now.

"What's up?" I asked. I could hear background noises—music, a muted conversation. She had a roommate, she had a boyfriend, she had a whole life, only fifty or so miles away.

"Yeah, well. I had this kind of, like, favor to ask."

"Okay," I said. "I'll try anyway."

"I've got this professor in my poli sci class? You know, I told you about her—Jean Bennett? She's just so *brilliant*. And it turns out she lives in *Adams Mills*! I mean, she's new. She just moved there."

"Hey," I said.

"So after I made that connection, I was mentioning you guys to her. Like if she ever needed re*lig*ion, she could call Dad, and if she ever needed a vet, she could call you. Which I assume was fine."

"Of course."

"Though actually, you know, it was really just, like, being polite or something. The way you do. But today. After class? She mentioned to me that her dog is having some kind of trouble. She actually told me, but I forget what she said it was. Anyway. She wanted your name, and I gave it to her."

"Okay," I said.

"Which means, I assume, that she's going to call you. So . . . I wanted you to know."

"Okay," I said again.

"Mom, she is *so* amazing. She is just so extraordinary."

"Well, I'll try not to embarrass you, dear."

"You think I'm exaggerating, but it's true, Mom. It's true. You will love her."

"And what is her name again? This paragon."

"Jean Bennett. Jean. That's one of the cool things, that we call her by her first name."

"But you've always called everyone by their first name, haven't you? I mean, grown-ups."

"Not around here, Mom. Not professors. Everyone is Dr. This or Professor That."

"I see. Well, I'll look forward to meeting her," I said. "Jean Bennett, right?" She made a noise of assent. "And what's new with you, sweetheart?" I asked.

Suddenly a deep sigh. "*That's* my problem, I bet," she said. "There's absolutely nothing new."

"But every little thing you do is new to us."

"*Mother.*"

"I mean it, hon." I allowed a beat of silence. "And then, of course, I don't."

She laughed. And then she sighed again, less dramatically. "Well, if you must know, I'm really stressed. I've got papers, I've got this *dance* thing"—a recital she was in. Daniel and I were planning to attend.

We'd have a fancy dinner at an inn we knew on the way, and then get to see Sadie in motion. "I've got tons of reading I'm so behind on. And I've been having those dreams, you know, where you're taking some test you're not ready for."

"Ugh," I said.

She began to tell me how unfair her humanities teacher was, not to grant her an extension.

As I listened and commiserated, I could hear the dogs stirring at some noise in the living room. Sadie's voice, her own sweet voice combined with all the standardized cadences and phrasing of adolescence, rattled on in her world. The dishwasher sloshed in the kitchen. Daniel's clothes hung touching mine on the rows of hooks. I was alive, I was in all these worlds at once. *A finger in every pie*, I thought. This, *this* is what we grow old for.

Sadie asked me our news, and I reported it as blandly as I could. No need to mention Amy, no point in trying to describe my odd feeling of the afternoon. It was gone now anyway.

Finally she said she had to get off. "Oh! But, Mom . . . just, when Jean comes, *if* she comes, *don't* talk about me, okay?"

"Never in a million years."

"And don't dare tell her how *enthralled* I am. Swoon, swoon."

"Well, now, that would be talking about you, Sade."

"Right, Mom." Her voice had dried.

"Good night, sweetie."

"Night."

WHEN DANIEL WASN'T BACK BY ELEVEN, I TOOK THE DOGS out for their walk. The air was cool, and I pulled my jacket tight. Light fell from the windows behind me into the yard, and the world disappeared beyond its touch. I stepped forward, into it.

Often Daniel and I had done the dogs' walk together when the girls were still home, happy just to be alone with each other at the end of the long day, to escape from them and the phone and the duties of the house. We'd stumble through the dark, reviewing our separate days for one another, ignoring the dogs, who ran ahead or trailed behind. We'd walk past the stores, the fancy houses, looking in at other people's lives like strolling gods, commenting. We'd wander into the unlighted streets off the common that turned gradually into knotted paths, into fields. We'd walk slower and slower as we wound down, bumping into each other more, unmoored and dizzy in the dark. And then finally Daniel would say, "Well, we better head home and see if anyone's still alive." Reluctantly, yet eagerly now, we'd whistle for the dogs in the soft night air and turn to start back.

That's what I was thinking of that Monday night before everything changed, before my other life caught up with me. I'd pushed aside that moment in the boat, I was thinking only of Daniel trying to offer comfort in the face of death, of Sadie turning back to her world, and Cass and Nora moving around in theirs; even of the dogs, running after each other through the dark village to sounds and smells I couldn't guess at. And I was remembering that time in our lives together, the time of those ritual walks. I was remembering the way it feels at just that moment when you begin to turn, when you're poised exactly between the things in life you want to do and those you need to do, and it seems for a few blessed seconds that they are all going to be the same.

WHEN I ARRIVED AT WORK THE NEXT DAY, BEATTIE was already behind the counter, with three dogs moving excitedly around her feet. We let the good-natured boarders loose for company for each other during the day, so there were almost always three or four of them nosing about officiously or sleeping under Beattie's desk. "The supervisors" she called them. The barkers, the fighters, we kept in the runs in the back, and the cats had their own room, so they wouldn't be in perpetual panic at the dogs' noise.

Beattie was on the phone, making reassuring, motherly sounds to someone. She would be on the phone fairly steadily through the morning. Tuesday was my day to catch up with all the bad things that had happened to my people's pets while I had my two days off. My partner, Mary Ellen, handled the worst of it on Mondays, the real emergencies left over from the weekend: fights, traumas, difficult births, the sudden onset of skin problems, unexplained loss of appetite or other gastrointestinal issues. "Party time" was what Beattie called Monday. Mary Ellen always said she loved it.

Even on Tuesdays, though, we tried to hold up to two hours empty in the afternoon for the unscheduled visits of clients who'd waited to see me, and we kept the rest of the appointments the equivalent of well-baby care, so we could flex around the odd disaster.

This was ample random excitement for me. I took my deepest pleasure in the ordinary: in simply reentering the office with its familiar animal and medicinal smell, in giving what comfort and help I could to the animals and their owners, in just moving around among the polite and curious boarding dogs. I even enjoyed the way Beattie's loud, clucking voice threaded through my day. Now I waved to her and went back down the hall to my exam room to see who my first clients were and what I'd be asked to do for their pets.

ANIMALS HAD COME INTO MY LIFE ALMOST BY ACCIDENT, when I was twenty-three. I'd just separated from my first husband, and for this and other reasons, I felt that my life was ruined—I didn't believe then in second chances. Broke and full of despair, I retreated from everything and went home to Maine, to my mother's house. There I wouldn't have to worry about rent or food for a while.

But I still needed a job. Any job. Any job but waitressing, I told myself. I was done with that. What I had in mind was some mindless secretarial position, and that's what I got. I thought. I was hired as a receptionist-assistant in a veterinarian's office.

And so it began before I recognized it—my second chance.

Dr. Moran, my boss, was about sixty-five then, I suppose. Of course, he seemed ancient to me. He was unsentimental, but gentle and slow-spoken. He called the animals we saw—the cats, the dogs, even the snakes and guinea pigs and gerbils—"our friends" or "our silent friends." He was fairly silent himself, but I learned to watch the way his hands did his talking for him with the animals. He was small, portly and neat and almost completely bald, but he had large square hands, the hands of a young, strong man. As they moved over the pets, the animals gentled and stilled. He used his voice, too, but only a little. It was his hands that did the trick, and it was the way he used his hands that I imitated when I began to work with the animals.

I worked seven days a week, including the cleanup and feedings on Sundays, and I was grateful for every minute of it, every minute away from the consciousness of my own failures, away from my misery. Gradually Dr. Moran trained me to take over more responsibility in the clinic, though the chores were still menial—giving medications, changing dressings, removing sutures, preparing injections. I'd never had pets as a kid—my father, plant-lover that he was, didn't believe in it—so I was startled at how easy I felt with the animals, even when, at first, they were aggressive. I learned to touch them, to move with confidence around them. I was surprised at how much their need and trust affected me. I was surprised when they touched me back— the unexpected flick of a rough, warm tongue, the deliberate gentle nudge of a wet nose. The first time it happened, I started, and then had to swallow several times to keep from crying, I was so oddly moved.

Slowly, then, over the first weeks and months of my life in the clinic, I began to believe again in the possibility of a simple kind of goodness, the goodness of the animals' dependency and trust. In response to it, I felt some shift, some opening up, in what I'd thought of as my hardened self. I remember the first time I woke in the morning and was aware of *anticipation*, of eagerly looking forward to getting up, going to work: just to take care of, to be touching again, a young hunting dog I'd nursed through a chest injury—he'd been ripped open by a barbed-wire fence he tried to jump. A few months after I'd started the job, I signed up at the university for the first of the science courses I'd need for vet school, and a year and a half later I was enrolled and beginning my training.

Even now, at this point in my life, when much of what I did at work was routine, when very little could happen to the primarily dogs and cats I had in my suburban practice that I hadn't seen and dealt with dozens of times before; even now I enjoyed it, enjoyed the falling away of other concerns when I came into the office, enjoyed the differences among our "silent friends." I took delight in the humor in much of what went on, and felt grieved, but enlarged, too, by what was sad or painful in the powerful bonds between animals and humans.

That Tuesday morning I had some puppy shots, a suture removal, two rabies vaccines, a dog who needed his anal sacs emptied, a cat catheterization, and an abscess to clean on a cat named Henry, who was entirely too familiar to me. I tried, for the sixth or seventh time, to persuade his owner that he should be neutered.

"Neutralized" she insisted on calling it, as though it were some science fiction fate I'd inflict on him with a ray gun. She was young, what we might have called a hippie thirty years ago. The flannel shirt rather than the pierced nostril kind. She always turned me down about Henry. "I like him to know he's a boy," she said to me coyly today.

"Louise, he has absolutely no *doubt* that he's a boy!" I said. "He's tormented by being a boy. How many times have I treated him for abscesses? Do you think he enjoys that? Do you think he enjoys the fights? It's not *dating* when you're a cat, Louise."

She stroked his scarred orange head. He'd lost a good chunk of ear long ago. He looked tired today. Tired and dusty. "We don't know what it's like for him," she said.

"I think it's fair to say that this stuff hurts. I would venture that."

"But you can't say he'd choose not to do it."

"It's *your* choice, Louise. Not his."

"Well, I like him just the way he is." She put her face down next to his head. He squinted his eyes shut in pleasure. His tail whipped, once, on the table.

I heaved a sigh. "Well, I have to accede to that, but I also have to say I don't like to. It's against medical advice, and it's contrary to common sense. And it's not too responsible either." I pointed at her. "All those kittens and no child support."

She laughed gaily and carried Henry out.

Over lunch, Beattie talked about her older sister, who had lived with her since her retirement and who was addicted to the shopping network. It made her mad, Beattie said. "It should be like gambling," she announced. "You should have to go someplace special to do it, like Atlantic City, so's you'd notice it more, what you were up to." She said her sister often didn't even bother to open the cartons and packages when they came now. They were stacked in the hall, or behind the couch her sister pulled out to sleep on.

When she said this, Beattie gestured over her shoulder, where, as it happened, the dog runs were. We were sitting at a picnic table out back in the weak sunlight, wearing sweaters against the fall chill and listening to the intermittent barking. Our office was in one of the tiny malls that had sprung up everywhere around these old towns as quickly as mushroom patches after rain. It was next to a bagel shop and a dry cleaner, and the land behind us rolled slowly down to a brook whose name I loved: Brother Brook. When the dogs were quiet, you could hear its steady rush.

"Isn't there something like TV Shoppers Anonymous?" I asked. "Some group cure?"

She made a snorting sound. "Should be, if there isn't," she said. She took a tiny bite from her sandwich and chewed, daintily. "And how's *your* family?" she asked after a moment, as though it were all part of the same enterprise, from her perspective. Beattie was white-haired, small, with a birdlike quick delicacy. She'd known the girls since they were babies.

"Good," I said. "We never hear from Cass, but Nora and Sadie are well. Thriving, I'd say."

"And how's my boy?" she asked, grinning. The wind puffed her thin hair strangely around her ears, and I looked away.

"Daniel? He's fine. He caught two trout yesterday, and he said he was happy."

"Happy," she said in a faraway voice, as though it were an emotion she could only vaguely recollect. "Lovely."

The afternoon jammed up and was crazy, as often happened. I had a cat who'd been hit by a car and needed a bone set. A dog who'd gotten into a fight with some kind of wild animal. A boa constrictor who seemed "depressed," according to his worried teenage owner—he had, I thought, a cold. It wasn't until after four that Beattie tossed a folder labeled *Jean Bennett* onto the steel examining table, and I remembered Sadie's call from the night before.

I glanced through the information quickly. The dog's name was Arthur. A mutt. He was nine. He'd been experiencing trouble walking for a while, most acutely for the last couple of days. I stepped into the hallway and called the woman's last name: "Bennett?"

To my surprise as she appeared around the corner—I'd assumed glamorous youth—Jean Bennett was close to my age. I would have said forty-six or -seven to my fifty-two. A different type, though. Exotic. Long, frizzing gray hair was set free around her head and shoulders. I watched her approach down the hallway. She was carrying the dog, who was medium-sized—mostly cocker spaniel, I thought. Jean Bennett wore dangly earrings and several loops of beaded necklace. Black leather pants with a long knitted tunic top over them. Expensive leather boots.

"Hello," she said as she moved toward me.

I said, "Hi," and stood back to let her enter the room. She moved awkwardly past me to the table, where she set the whimpering dog. He lay down immediately.

"I'm Jean Bennett," she said, turning. She made a quick pass at smoothing her hair down.

"Well, I'm awfully glad to meet you," I said. "I'm Dr. Becker, the famous Sadie's mom."

We shook hands. Her bracelets clashed metallically. She had smooth olive skin, dark brows.

"I'm strictly forbidden on pain of death to talk about Sadie with you"—I drew my finger across my throat, and she smiled—"so let's move right in on our friend Arthur here. Tell me what's going on with him." I moved to my side of the table and put my hand on his back. He was trembling with fear, long shudders every few seconds. He was short-haired, mostly a marmalade color, with a cocker's sweet, reproachful eyes. His ears were flat to his head.

"Well, *Arthur*." She shrugged, an exaggerated helplessness. "What can I tell you? His story is, all of a sudden he seems not to be able to walk. But just in his hindquarters. He's mostly just been dragging himself around by his front legs."

"For how long?"

"Well. He's been like this for a couple of days now. Actually, he's had arthritis for a couple of years—he's on medication for that—and it's been lots worse this fall. Worse than ever. So that's what I was thinking this was. And all fall, really, it would get worse for a few days, and then it would get better. And honestly, my life is so crazy right now that I just kind of ignored it, I guess, thinking the same thing would happen. And now it's somehow over the edge. I feel terribly guilty. *Mea culpa*." She patted her chest.

"Has he lost bladder control? Bowels?"

Now her hand rose to her throat. "Well, it's hard to know, exactly, since he can't get himself to the *door* anymore."

"So he has had accidents."

"Oh, yes. Plenty of those." She sounded grimly amused.

"And was there any trauma that you know of? Did he have a fall or get struck by a car? Something like that. Even a glancing blow?"

"No, no. Nothing. Nothing that I know of. Arthur has what you might call a quiet life. He's inside by himself all day. And I probably don't walk him enough at night either. He just got up Friday and . . . well, he *couldn't* get up on Friday, actually. But I thought maybe it was just one of these temporary crises—something that would get better by itself. So I went to work. And then I was in and out over the weekend and not paying him enough attention. I did have to carry him back and forth, you know, because he didn't want to move himself. But sometimes we've had to do that when his arthritis was bad. And he didn't seem to be in pain, so I just waited. And now it seems clear that something is really wrong." While she talked, her hands moved nervously, expressively, in front of her. She was plainly upset.

I turned to the dog. "Well, let's check you out, Arthur," I said. I stroked him a moment, scratched his silky ears gently. He looked at me dubiously. Then I lifted the front part of his body so that he was sitting. He growled at me. "I know, I know," I said to him. "It isn't fun, is it?"

"He doesn't much *like* to be moved," Jean Bennett said.

Arthur's hind legs made no accommodation to the sitting posture, and he lay down again as soon as I released him. I came around by his hind legs and manipulated them gently. They were utterly limp. He turned to watch me, perhaps thinking about warning me off. But clearly nothing hurt him. "Good boy," I said.

I did a couple of other tests on him—a few needle sticks for superficial pain, with no result until I was halfway up his back. I was explaining things to Jean Bennett as I went along, that it seemed Arthur had a spinal injury that was causing paralysis. I talked about the levels of pain response in the spinal column. She winced when I pinched his toe with a hemostat, but Arthur just watched. His ears were down, he was nervous still, but he didn't cry or try to bite.

Jean Bennett was sitting by now, in the client chair. I asked her again when Arthur had gone down.

"Go down?" she said.

"When did he stop being able to walk?"

"Well, he had pain all week, I think. But on Friday he just wouldn't walk. Or couldn't. But he did seem more comfortable, so I thought . . . I thought, Well, this is bad, but it's a good sign he's not in so much pain, and anyway . . ." Her voice trailed off. "I blew it, didn't I?"

"Well, it's not good that he's been like this for so long. If we'd gotten to him right away—if he'd come in on Friday—I would have sent you immediately to Angell Memorial for surgery. Back surgery."

"And Angell Memorial is . . . ?"

"It's a big, very complete animal hospital in Boston, where they do this kind of thing. I do more or less just routine surgeries here. But it's not anything I'd recommend now. At this point, I'm afraid it really wouldn't make any difference."

"So what you're saying is the damage is done."

"I'm afraid so." She looked shocked, defeated. I made my voice gentle. "This was a tough, tough call for you to make, because of the arthritis. That meant you were balancing pain against mobility, and it's always harder on us when an animal's in pain, so we're relieved when it stops. But in this case, unfortunately, it's the absence of pain that's the bad sign."

She sat still a moment, looking at Arthur. Then her fists balled and she punched her thighs. "Shit! Shit! Shit!" she said fiercely.

I had stepped over closer to her, and now I put my hand on her shoulder.

She leaned back and looked up at me. "No, I'm okay," she said. She smiled wearily. After a few seconds, she sat up and said, "So where do we go from here?"

I stepped back and rested my hands on Arthur. "Well, I'm afraid that in the end you're probably going to have a choice of whether to keep this guy alive in a pretty compromised way or not. And there'll be a lot of care if you do, cleanups and changing bedding and whatnot." I could see she was pained. "We could, if you want to, try a round of steroids," I offered.

"Would that help?"

"It's a very long shot, actually. But there's a possibility. Remote, but possible."

"Well, I want to do whatever I can. So let's. Let's try them." She clutched her hair back from her face, held it there. "Christ, I feel so *guilty*."

"You shouldn't." I tried to make my voice reassuring. "When a dog is so incapacitated anyway, it's sometimes hard to tell what's going on."

She released her hair—it burst out around her face—and shook her head. "No. No, I think it's more what you said earlier. That I was just relieved he wasn't in pain." Her lips firmed bitterly. "Cowardly," she said.

"So we'll try the steroids," I said gently. I didn't really think they would help the dog, but I felt they might help her—or at least give her time to adjust to what had happened.

She seemed to pull herself up taller. "Yes," she said. "Yes, let's go ahead with that, certainly. And then, if it doesn't work . . ."

"Then we'll talk about what comes next," I said.

"Yes," she said. She stood up. "Poor old Arthur indeed." She reached over and patted him, so I let my hands fall away.

She frowned suddenly and looked at me. "Actually, the thing is," she said, "you won't be talking to me. It won't even be my decision."

"Oh?"

"No. Arthur's my husband's dog." She produced a low, throaty, sorrowful laugh, her face stricken. "They've been married much longer than we have. I'm handling all this just for now while he's traveling a lot—or not handling it, I guess I should say. But he should be home by Friday. So he'll have to decide, if a decision becomes necessary. And in fact"—she pointed—"you should probably change the name on the folder. Take mine off. He'll be the one you'll need to contact about anything that happens."

I picked up a marker and crossed out her name. My hand was poised. "So he's . . . ?"

"Mayhew. Eli Mayhew."

It took a second or two to register. Then I looked up at her. "Really!" I said. "Eli Mayhew?"

She nodded.

"I knew someone with that name once."

"Did you? It's kind of an unusual name."

"Yes. It is." I wrote it now on the folder, under the crossed-out *Jean Bennett*. I looked at her again. "I wonder if it could be the same Eli Mayhew. This guy went to graduate school at Harvard. We lived together. I mean, in a group. In a kind of commune, I guess."

"This is so strange." She shook her head, and the mass of her wild hair swayed slightly. "I think it probably *is*. My husband did go to Harvard. He did do his graduate work there. He was a biochemist."

"That's it. It was a lab science anyway, I know that. Though I was pretty out of it at the time. He'd be maybe in his mid-fifties now?"

She smiled quickly. "Amazing! The world is a smaller and smaller place all the time, isn't it?"

"Well, please tell him hello from me. I'm Jo. Joey Becker. Give him my warm greetings." I looked at Eli's name on the folder, the big black letters, trying to call up his face. Instead I was seeing others in the house—Dana, and Larry. And then it occurred to me: "Actually, he knows me as Licia, come to think of it. Felicia. I suppose what you should tell him is that Licia Stead said hello."

"Oh!" she said. She looked quizzical. "A nom de plume?"

"It's complicated." I looked up at her and smiled ruefully. "More like . . . a kind of alias, I guess. Another life anyway." My hands were trembling, I noticed. I reached over and stroked Arthur's head to steady myself as much as to comfort him. "What's he doing now?" I asked. "Eli."

"Well, *right* now he's on a sabbatical. We've both just left jobs on the West Coast, but he hasn't started his new one yet. He's got the semester off, so he's in and out of town, lecturing. But he starts in January at Beth Israel in Boston, teaching and doing research. He's mostly a research scientist. Sort of well known in his field, actually. I thought for a second maybe you were recognizing his name because you'd heard of his work."

"No. To me he's just old Eli." Arthur lay passive under my hands. I felt almost dizzy with the rush of memories.

"Well, I'll certainly tell him I ran into you," she said.

"Do. Please," I said.

I picked up the folder for a moment, I made a note or two on Arthur, mostly to gather myself in, to make myself think again about him. Then I turned back to Jean, and we talked about how to handle the steroids. She wanted to administer the pills at home. "It's the least I can do for Eli," she said. We agreed that I'd start him on an IV injection right away, that she'd bring him in the next day and leave him for two shots, and that he'd be home then for the oral sequence. I explained to her that he was basically incontinent now and showed her how to express his bladder, instructed her on keeping him clean. They had a crate "somewhere in the house," she said, and I told her Arthur would need to be confined except when she carried him outside.

When she seemed comfortable that she knew what to do, I went into the hallway and prepared the steroid shot under the boarders' watchful eyes. Jean Bennett was bent over Arthur's head when I returned, and I felt the pang I always did at a client's pain. I injected Arthur quickly—he was uncomplaining—and we agreed on a time for her to drop him off in the morning. I followed Jean to the front door and opened it for her. I followed her to her car, too, and held Arthur while she got her keys out. There was an old flowered bedspread in the back seat, and she set him gently on it. I told her to call if anything came up in the night.

"I will," she said. And then she shook her head again. "See you tomorrow," she said finally.

I nodded and went back to the office as she started the car.

Inside, I slowed down. I felt numbed. I had two last patients, and then I told Beattie to go home, that I'd close up. Ned, the lanky high-school student who cleaned the cages and fed the animals morning and evening, had come in and led the boarders out. Now he was bagging all the garbage and trash, wailing occasionally along with whatever was playing on his Walkman. I refiled the last charts, sprayed and wiped the examining table. I reviewed my list of routine surgeries for Wednesday. All the while I was thinking of Eli Mayhew, and of Dana and Larry and Duncan and me, and our lives in the house. Of the horrible way it had all ended. Did Jean Bennett know any of that? It seemed not.

I tried again to call up Eli's face. And thought suddenly of a moment at dinner one night when he was laughing and telling all of us about a dream he'd had in which he was a component of a machine—a machine whose function was to excrete small, square, metallic turds. We were laughing with him because we recognized Eli's orderliness, his anality, in the dream, and this was kind of a joke among us, a joke he was playing to.

We all had our roles in the house. The rest of us were bohemians of one sort or another, lefties, druggies, deviants, *artistes*. This, anyway, was how we understood ourselves. Eli was the only scientist, gone for long hours daily in the lab. We saw him—and he saw himself—as straight, as rigid. Unfairly, we poked fun at him, often in his presence. We imagined great things for ourselves, *other* things. For Eli, we imagined simply *more of the same*. And yet he seemed grateful to be among us. He sat, usually silently, listening as we floated our theories—about life, about art, about music, about politics. He watched as we flirted with each other, as we danced. And very occasionally he said something, he risked something, as he did that night, by playing the nerd.

We had set candles out, as we often did for these group meals, scented candles whose sweet vanilla smell I can still recall. Friends were over, so there was a crowd, all the young faces circling the table in the mellow light. Sara was stoned—she usually was, from the time she arrived home from work—and Dana and Duncan had smoked some too. Eli's dream made them shriek with laughter until their faces were red and wet with tears, until Sara had to stand and pace the room to calm down. Eli, meanwhile, elaborated, went on in his earnest, pressured voice, trying to keep the laughter going, even imitating the way his dream machine worked, his elbows squared up, his head sunk between his shoulders, weird mechanical noises emerging from him—"Kkkkkk, *punk*! Kkkkkk, *punk*!"—as he stiffly moved.

I remembered being surprised by him that night, surprised and delighted by his willingness to laugh at himself, by his evident pleasure in making us laugh. And I remembered that when I saw him for the first time after Dana's death, he wept. His face—which I recalled now was quite handsome—crumpled up like a child's, and he wept.

I MET ELI—ELI AND DANA AND THE OTHERS—DURING A TIME when I was running away from my life. I had never done such a thing before, and I haven't since, which makes it hard to remember what it was to be *me* at that time. *Another me* is how I think of it. Another life.

I was in my first marriage then, an auspicious marriage, actually, to a medical student. Ted. Ted Norris was his name. I could have been said to be doing quite well. I was going to be a doctor's wife and a high-school teacher. But here's how I saw my future: a long, narrow tunnel. A house. Children. Dogs. Money. Lovingly furnished rooms. Everything I'd wanted, of course, when I got married. Everything that made me happy when I actually had it years later, with Daniel. But at this time the thought of it felt like the end of hope, like the closing down of all expectation. I think I realized I couldn't do it the first day I was practice-teaching in high school, when someone—I can still remember his pimply, hangdog face, but not his name—raised his hand and called out, "Mrs. Norris?" He was all of three or four years younger than I was.

That was me. Mrs. Norris. Josephine Norris. Josephine Becker Norris. He might as well have taken out a gun and shot me. "Yes?" I said, but I was thinking, *Get me out of here.*

So that was step one, quitting my hard-won teaching job.

Step two was taking the first job I spotted in the help-wanted ads: as a waitress in a seedy bar in a marginal neighborhood near our apartment in Philadelphia. I wore a kind of third-rate Playboy bunny costume to work in: very high heels, mesh tights, a short tunic over a leotard. When I peeled all this off at the end of the evening, it reeked of nicotine. I reeked of nicotine, too, though I rarely bothered to shower before bed. It was late, too late, when I got home, one-thirty or two in the morning. Ted was usually asleep anyway, and I was always tired from teetering on those heels all night. I turned my face into my long, teased, stinking hair and tumbled heavily into dreams haunted by liquor orders.

You might have thought I was slumming, taking such a job, and of course, in a way, that would be fair. I was a college graduate, from a good school. I'd taken courses after college to prepare myself to teach high school. I'd married my promising husband. He certainly thought I was slumming. But he saw my job as a kind of perverse joke, too, and took a malicious pride in it. That was fine with me. Whatever he thought. Whatever anyone thought. The point for me was that for once I didn't have any idea what it would lead to. Some of the point anyway. The job was also a claim on my time from five or so in the afternoon until well after midnight nearly every day, time I might have spent cooking a nice meal, grading papers, making curtains, talking to my husband. All the things I'd prepared myself to do and promised others I would do.

The Ace of Spades was a world I didn't know. A side step. It was sexualized, exciting. On a busy night, the waitresses were always brushing past each other, touching each other, like lovers, a casual kind of touching among women that I'd never experienced. It thrilled me. And there was a thing I loved that used to happen just after we'd closed. It would be twelve-thirty or one o'clock. The customers would all be gone. We'd finished our workday, we were ready for a little fun, but everyplace else in town was closed, too, so we'd sit around and have a drink with the owners, the boys in the band. Nobody wanted to go home. The drinks were on the house. Everybody was a little bit on the make. Like me, most of them had husbands or wives waiting in bed, but it didn't matter for the moment. A lot of fingers were busily trailing over wherever there was bare flesh. I stayed clear of it, I always left alone, but I loved to feel the tension in the air, to watch the shifting couples form and re-form over the months.

The attraction was that none of the rules from my world applied. With everything I saw, everything I did, I felt that doors were opening. My life had been so orderly, such a careful, responsible progression, one polite step leading logically to the next. In this crummy, second-rate world, I had a sense of liberation, of possibility, and I embraced even its most tawdry aspects. I once complained to the genial, barrel-bodied bartender, Eddie, about the language a few of my customers were using in addressing me. He was silent a minute, pouring my shots, filling my chaser glasses with ice in a fixed and elegant rhythm. When he handed me back my check, he met my eyes and said, "Grow up, sweetheart." I was shocked for only a few seconds, and then I laughed—*Of course!* I thought—and he grinned back at me.

There was a fight at the bar one night just as we were closing. I'd never witnessed a fight among adult men before. I was handing over the last of my checks at the cash register when it started. From time to time as the evening had worn on I'd noticed the raised voices among the men sitting to my left. Now there was a kind of explosion over there, and someone slammed into my back. Eddie dropped his shaker and was on top of the bar within a second, pulling at a huge man who was bent over the harmless old regular we called the Judge. It was he who had fallen against me, and he was lying on the floor now, under the big guy—you could hear the dull wet whumps as he hit the Judge's head over and over.

Almost as soon as it had begun, it was finished. The men were in motion everywhere, violently pulling the big man away and out of the bar, bending his arms behind him with unnecessary force. Eddie was helping the Judge up, then getting him ice as he sat bleeding on a barstool in cheerful drunken amazement. Already everyone was laughing, talking excitedly. It was becoming a *story*.

I stood there dumbfounded for a minute, and then I felt I had to sit down immediately. When I looked at myself in the mirror in the ladies' room, I saw that I was covered with dark, spreading freckles. It took me a moment to recognize them as blood, the Judge's blood, sprayed all over me when he got hit.

I was perversely excited. I decided to wear it home. I wanted to scare my husband, to make him see something—I couldn't have said what—about the world I was moving in now. I wanted a witness. I hoped a policeman would notice me and stop me.

But it was dead in the city. At a red light, a car pulled up beside mine. A couple. She looked over. She turned to him. He bent forward and looked over too. Then the light changed and they took off, speeding to cut in front of me on the narrow street.

Ted was asleep when I got home. We had pink bathroom fixtures in that apartment, and I remember watching the blood purl an odd rusty color in the water against the pink basin as I washed it off.

IT WAS THERE, AT THE ACE OF SPADES, THAT I GOT THE IDEA to leave. Step three. I was substituting on a Wednesday for another waitress, Judy. Anita, the headwaitress, had called me that afternoon and asked me to cover as a favor. She'd pitched her voice dramatically low on the phone: "If anyone asks, you don't know anything about why Judy's not there."

I was about to point out to her that as a matter of fact I didn't know anything about why Judy wouldn't be there, but I checked myself, as I often did with my coworkers, afraid I might sound snotty or smart-ass. Afraid I might sound like myself.

The night was easy and slow. So slow that the band barely bothered to perform, instead sitting around in the bar, "drinking their paycheck," as Eddie said. At ten-thirty or so, Tony Zadra—Tony Z, we called him—arrived. He was one of the owners and also Judy's lover. He saw me and came right over. "Where's Judy?" he asked.

I was standing at the bar, filling chaser glasses. Ginger. Soda with a twist. "I don't know," I said.

"You don't know," he said.

"Right," I said. I looked at him. He was a small man with a thick neck and a big pompadour. He needed to be smiling to be attractive in any way, and he wasn't smiling.

"She call you?" he asked. I noticed a little dab of shaving foam on the curve of his ear.

"No." I gestured toward the back of the bar. "Anita asked me to fill in for her."

He turned and went toward the kitchen, where Anita was taking a cigarette break.

They were in there awhile. I had to cover a couple of Anita's tables for a round or two, and I was relieved enough when she emerged to be incurious for the moment.

But then Tony Z came up to me again. I was resting by the waitress station. My tables were happy.

"So I suppose you didn't talk to Judy."

"No," I said.

"You don't have any idea where she is."

"I told you. No."

"What bullshit," he said. He pointed his finger at me. I saw the cords stiffen in his neck. "What complete bullshit that is, Jo."

She'd run away, of course. She'd vanished. And now, now that she was gone, we began to get the explanations. Every day, there was new gossip. Tony Z was so jealous that she couldn't even go shopping with a friend. He'd monitored her phone calls. He'd had her followed. He'd sometimes parked all night outside her house; when she looked out she could see his cigarette glowing in the car. He'd hit her a few times.

And now she was gone. She'd escaped.

This was like sirens singing me away. It was, suddenly, all I could think of. The job at the Ace of Spades had been a foot out the door of my ordinary life, but I saw now what it could lead to. *All* of me out the door.

I wanted to go as much as I'd ever wanted anything. Suddenly I saw the paltriness, the temporizing quality, of everything I'd done so far. At night I'd lie awake next to my innocent, dreaming husband and imagine it: where I'd vanish to, the note I'd leave behind.

You might have thought I'd worry about him, about causing him pain or at least embarrassment. I simply didn't. I felt the kind of desperation, I think, that cancels the possibility of empathy. That makes you unkind. When I described myself as I was at that time to Daniel, I often said to him, "You wouldn't have liked me then."

He'd shake his head. "Not possible."

"I wouldn't have liked *you*," I said once, just to startle him, to show him how mean I might have been.

It worked. His face shifted, a hurt he was trying not to show. And then he said, "Well, that's different, isn't it?"

I think, too, that by then, by the time I was getting ready to leave, I understood how shallow, how inconsequential, Ted's and my attachment to each other was. We had married through innocent stupidity, through a pure lack of imagination. We had gone to college together and had furtive sex for a year. He was accepted to medical school. We wanted to go on having sex, we wanted to live together, but in the world we'd grown up in, you couldn't do that without love, without marriage. So, trapped already by our desires, we made it happen—we fell willfully in love, we got married.

It seems to me that Ted was probably not unhappy. He had his work, which he liked, and which kept him too busy to think about the shape of his life, his *destiny*—as I did, constantly. And my strange job gave his life a certain kinkiness that the other medical students couldn't claim. They came home to wives who *were* teachers. Or social workers, or nurses, or graduate students. Or to their dorm rooms—a bed, a desk. They came home to dinner, to studying deep into the evening, the night. Ted might have felt he was unusual, having a wife with such an intriguingly unwholesome job. I think I imagined my disappearing as something he might even, in some sense, be grateful for. Another story he could tell to make himself interesting.

I left on a Monday. I'd called Anita a day or two before and told her that my mother was ill, that I had to go to Maine and didn't know when I'd be back. I told Ted I was going to Washington for a few days to see a friend from college who'd ended up there. I got on a bus for Boston with a one-way ticket. I was familiar with the city from college visits, but I wasn't aware of knowing anyone who actually lived there. I thought I could find my way around easily and also be completely anonymous.

I didn't see my husband again for seven months.

I arrived with one bag on a rainy evening in May. Within three days, I was sitting in a bright, sparsely furnished living room in Cambridge, being interviewed by four people as a potential roommate for a group house. One of them was Dana, whom I came to love. One was Duncan, another was Larry. And one of them, a tall, slightly slouched man in his mid-twenties, with worried brown eyes and curling dark hair that came down just over the rim of his collar—I remembered him clearly now—was Eli Mayhew.

CHAPTER

3

THE FIRST LIE I TOLD WAS MY NAME. "FELICIA," I SAID. And then, because this was, I suddenly realized, a seriously ridiculous name, I also said, "As in 'happy to be here,'" and dipped my head slightly. "But my friends call me Licia. Or Lish." I don't know where any of this came from. I certainly hadn't planned it. It just seemed suddenly the wisest course, to be someone else.

After that, the other lies seemed easy. Seemed to be not so much lies as *the story of Licia Stead*. And some of it *was* true. I had just gotten a job at Red Brown's Blues, a bar in Inman Square. I was living temporarily at the YWCA. And if I wasn't from Montpelier, if I hadn't gone to school at the University of Vermont, well, Licia Stead might have.

I'd found the house advertised on the bulletin board at a dusty bicycle repair shop I'd gone into, searching for cheap transportation. It was next to ads for used furniture, typists, and three or four other housing options. I tore off one of the little fringed tags with a phone number and made my appointment, along with several other appointments, from a pay phone at the Y.

The room I was sitting in for my interview was large and squarish— the living room. It was a sunny day, light was pouring in at the two tall windows that ran from ceiling to floor on the wall that faced the street, and lying brightly across the bare floor, which was stained dark toward the corners of the room and worn to a scratchy grayish white in the traffic patterns. There was a large mantelpiece, whose fireplace, if there had ever been one, was plastered over. There were two sagging couches covered with Indian-print spreads, facing each other over a wooden box that seemed to serve as a kind of combined coffee table and footrest. My interviewers were sitting on these couches—had the air, actually, of having been swallowed by them. For this reason I had perched myself on one of the two metal folding chairs set up next to them, facing the mantel. As I talked, I felt awkwardly and intensely visible, and very tall.

The girl asked most of the questions. Dana. At first glance I'd been startled by her—she could have been my twin. Like me, she was big-boned, with straight blond hair worn long, below her shoulders, the way everyone wore it then. The way I was wearing mine. It's true she was more solid than I was, more bosomy. Still, I thought, there was even a facial resemblance: the long oval, the just-slightly-too-big nose, the dark brows. But Dana had freckles, which I didn't. And she frowned earnestly in concentration when she spoke—or smiled, or grimaced; whereas my face, I knew, was more masked, more careful.

Did I smoke? Oh. How much? (The house allowed smoking; I had checked, because I did smoke then, sporadically.) What would my hours at work be? While I was talking, she smiled steadily at me, an extraordinary, warm, encouraging smile. And then she'd fire away again. Did I like to cook? Did I like movies? What movies?

Every now and then after one of these questions, one or the other of the men in the room would groan audibly, or say, "Jesus, Dana." Once, one of them—Duncan—said in a singsong voice, "What's your favorite color? What's your favorite food?"

Dana gave him the finger, then turned to me. "I know they're dumb questions, but we just need to hear you *talk*. Maybe you have questions for us?"

I had been to two other houses before this. The gravity of my interviews in them had intimidated me. Now I realized that I just hadn't liked the people I met.

I liked this. I liked the ease these people had with each other. In particular I liked Dana, her generosity, the warm attentiveness that I felt like a bright light falling on me. What I wanted to ask—all I wanted to ask, really—was, "Will you take me?" I didn't think I could ask that. Instead I framed a few questions, as fatuous, nearly, as hers.

Rules?

There weren't many. No smoking in the bedrooms, for fear of fire. Everyone cooked a group meal once a week. You had to sign up for any given dinner two days before so the chef would know how much to prepare. You couldn't have someone sleep over more than once a week or you had to pay extra rent. No sleeping with other house members, unless you were officially living together. There was much throat-clearing among the men over this, and Dana blushed richly under the freckles.

What would my room be like?

Dana would show me.

It was a *neat* room, lots of light, Dana said, leading me up the stairs. A conversation had started among the men as soon as we left the living room, and I could hear a muffled laugh below us now. Dana was saying she wished my room had been available when she moved in, but now she was all set up in her space and didn't want to switch.

The stairs opened onto a large central hallway. I quickly took in three or four rooms opening off it. We turned left and then left again along a narrow walkway between the stair rail and a wall, toward a door at the front of the house.

"It's kind of down here by itself," Dana said, turning back to me, smiling again.

The room was small, but it had windows on two sides. One looked out over the driveway, the other across the street to the similarly exhausted-looking houses there. It had three pieces of furniture— a bed, a bureau, and a nicked desk. One of the drooping parchment-colored window shades was torn. Both had faint white lines in them, lines that leaked tiny stars of light here and there.

"Duncan's room is next to you. You're lucky. You'd *be* lucky, I mean. He's quiet. I have John and Sara. They're not here right now. I love them both, but they make an astonishing amount of noise."

"Doing what?" I asked.

She shrugged. "Well, they have to laugh a lot, 'cause they're big dopers. Most any drug will do. It's a kind of principle with them, 'the expansion of their brains.'" Her fingers made nervous quotation marks. "You could offer them anything, acne medication or anything, and they'd take it." She tilted her head back, pretending to swallow. "Glug, glug, glug." Then she looked at me, her eyes wide. "But also," she said, "they screw a great, great deal."

She had a funny voice, I thought. Harsh and staccato, and somehow touching. "*I* am quiet as a mouse," she announced. "And you?"

"I never really thought about it. I've never lived with anyone." The words were out before I even realized that I was lying again. But this time it felt like the truth, I think because I hadn't considered my marriage truly living with someone. Ted and I had moved in such different worlds from the start that I'd learned nothing about myself even as a roommate, much less as a wife, from being with him. "Actually, though," I said now, "I think I am. Quiet. But if I owned a record player, I wouldn't be." I was remembering the long days I spent alone in the attic apartment in Philadelphia. Often I'd played music and danced by myself, danced until my hair was lank with sweat.

"Yeah, well, that's another rule. We can't play music in our rooms after eleven. In point of fact, Duncan is the only one who even has one—a record player. Eli did, but he gave it to the house, so it's downstairs. We all use it."

"Nice of him," I said.

"Eli can't help being nice," Dana said.

I was sent outside to the porch while they decided. I sat on the front steps and watched a group of children in the playground next door. They were tough-looking, older. Too old, it seemed to me, for the forlorn swing set and teeter-totter. In fact, they seemed to be doing something secret and possibly delinquent in the huddle they made in the corner of the play area—starting a fire, maybe. Or passing a joint. One of them glanced furtively over at me, and I turned quickly away. I busied myself looking at the house. My house.

It was sided in pale-green asphalt, with water or mildew marks of blackish gray drooping like dirty aprons under many of the windows. A wide, worn porch bent around its front half. There were gaps in the rails and splintering floorboards. The railing along the front steps had been replaced with wrought iron.

Though I tried not to, I couldn't help wondering what the people inside the house might be saying about me. I hadn't talked enough, I felt. They'd think I was depressed. Which was only fair, of course. I *was* depressed, wasn't I? Certainly quiet as a mouse, at the very least. But apparently this was just what you wanted in a neighbor. My good luck, perhaps. I tried to visualize them then, talking, but found that the only face I could conjure up was Dana's. I searched in my bag, found my cigarettes, and nervously smoked one.

I had just put it out and was about to light another, when Dana came out on the porch. I turned to her. "You're a *yes!*" she cried. "Oh, I'm so pleased, Licia."

I stood up, grinning back at her. "Me too," I said, and then realized how true that was. How relieved I was. My limbs felt longer suddenly, looser.

Dana was doing a little barefoot dance, twirling. Her hair swung skirtlike around her shoulders. "Oh, I had my merry way with them!" she crowed as she spun.

"Ah," I said. "Was there resistance?"

Dana stopped. "Oh, no! You mustn't think that! None!" she cried. "None! I just meant that I was the only one who really cared that much."

It struck me suddenly that I'd recognized this, that I'd known all along that she wanted me in the house. "Why *did* you care?"

Dana shrugged. "I was desperate for another woman, for one. I mean, besides Sara. Who's really more like one of John's vestigial organs. I feel so outnumbered all the time." And then a wide grin opened her face—you could see nearly every strong white tooth in her mouth. "And the moment I saw you, I thought, *She could be my friend.*" Her hands lifted elaborately, palms up, in a dancer's gesture. It was as if she were holding something ceremonially to give to me.

I looked away quickly, I was so embarrassed.

When I moved in the next day, there was a coffee can set on the battered old desk, filled with spry white daisies.

ALL THIS HAPPENED EARLY IN THE SUMMER OF 1968, WHEN dozens of houses like ours had sprung up all over Cambridge, all over Berkeley and Chicago and Philadelphia and San Francisco. Some were more political than ours or had a theme of sorts—everyone was into organic food or political action or alternative theater or an arts magazine. Some were, like ours, mixed, a little bit of everything. You found rooms in these houses through bulletin boards, as I had, or through friends, or political organizations, or underground streams of information. They coexisted, often uneasily, with houses belonging to mostly working-class neighbors. People who took care of their yards, who repaired their railings, who had combination screens and storm windows, who kept their doors locked at night.

Not us. The door stood open round the clock. Music blared into the street from the windows—Jefferson Airplane, Otis Redding, Pablo Casals, the Stones, Julian Bream, the Beatles, Brahms, Janis Joplin. Bikes were parked all over the porch and the scrubby front yard. Unlocked, it goes without saying.

I lived that summer like a happy dream. I worked late at the blues club every night and often stayed up several hours later than that, talking to one or another of my housemates. Slowly, I felt, I came to know them all better than I'd ever known Ted, or anyone, in my other life. The house generally rose late through those summer months—no one but Sara had normal working hours—and often two or three of us did something together in the daytime. Drove to Singing Beach, took a picnic and a Frisbee down to the river. On a rainy day, we went to the movies. Or played long, cutthroat games of Scrabble in the living room, with the windows open to the porch and the steady racket of the rain on the porch roof or dripping down on the leaves of the leggy lilac bushes.

Nearly every weekend through the summer we had a party. I remember a moment at one of them when the living room was so crowded with people—people someone knew or had brought along, people who'd just heard the noise and wandered in—that the whole room seemed to move up and down as one, a slow stoned humping to "Go Ask Alice." I felt I had lost myself in it, lost that embarrassed sense of how I looked, how I seemed to others, that earlier I would have said was a permanent part of who I was.

There were six other members of the house. Duncan was a guitarist. He was tall, elegant. Often he seemed bored by all of us. He had a girlfriend on the West Coast, an actress. Two of her publicity shots were tacked on the wall beside his bed. In them, her mouth with its shiny dark lips was open and her eyelids were lowered thickly, as though she were about to sneeze. I had trouble believing this was a person anyone would *know*, but Duncan spoke of her easily, casually, as though she were living among us too. Sheree.

He was studying composition at Berklee. He made his living giving music lessons and playing nightly in a Spanish restaurant—flamenco and, occasionally, when he could get away with it, classical pieces. He had a small, thin mustache. He reminded me of a generic movie star of the forties, handsome and rakish. I actually spent a lot of time with him, because he and I generally arrived home at almost the same late hour, usually wound up from work and not ready for bed. But he was so hard to talk to that I was always glad when someone else was awake, too, and the conversation could be more relaxed. I remember one night I saw him approaching me from the opposite end of the block as I was coming home, a tall, dark shape carrying a guitar case. I knew, even from a great distance, who it was, and the pressing question for me became: At what point do I call out a greeting? In the end, I didn't, for fear he'd be somehow offended, or contemptuous. We actually turned into the driveway simultaneously and had begun to walk up it toward the lighted house before I said, "Good night?" He shrugged in response. I didn't much like Duncan, he made so little effort socially.

When I heard him play, though, my thinking about him shifted entirely. "That's really what it was with me too," Dana confessed to me. We were sitting in the kitchen very late one night, talking. She had waited up for me after work. Duncan had come home late, and sat with us for a beer, then gone upstairs to call Sheree, collect. "I'm crazy about his music. Those fingers!" He did have beautiful hands, I had noticed them. The fingernails were carefully shaped and shone with clear polish, to strengthen them for the guitar. She frowned. "I don't know why I always have to do this—fall in love with people who do something beautifully. And it hardly matters what, really. It's the competence. It's the devotion to something. It just makes me hot."

Then why are you drawn to me? I wanted to ask. But I didn't. I didn't want to presume to name Dana's feelings about me.

Larry was the one I felt most comfortable with from the start. He taught history at Harvard and was a political activist. He was out a good deal of the time, "rousing the rabble," as he called it, mocking himself more than the rabble. His room was small, the smallest in the house. He had an enormous poster of Ho Chi Minh on the wall, and all the floor space not taken up by the bed was occupied with a bench press and scattered weights. He was short and powerfully muscled. He wore his hair in a DA, with a tumble of slicked curls trained to fall forward in the middle of his forehead, like Gene Vincent, like Jerry Lee Lewis. He liked the incongruity, he told me once, of being a commie body-building greaser hood. He had the only car in the house and didn't mind being thought of as a chauffeur. "We could get Larry to take us," we'd say, and he always would if he could. We'd cram in, rearranging the stacks of flyers, shoving the posters up on the ledge under the rear window, and he would drive us—to the North End for Italian food, to the Cape, to the movies, to the Square.

Sara and John were much as described by Dana. She'd forgotten to mention, though, that Sara was a lawyer. She'd graduated high in her class from Harvard Law School and now worked in a poverty-law office for a piddling wage. She supported them both. It was understood that John was writing a novel, but I knew, since I was home through much of the day, that he was doing no such thing. "His work habits aren't really the kind that lend themselves to the long haul," I told Dana. "In that he has no work habits."

Eli was the handsomest man in the house, and yet he left the least impression on me at the time. And I would guess that this was true for all of us. He was quiet, of course. Shy. He seemed content, most of the time, simply to observe, to watch the action, whatever the action was. And he was gone a good deal of the time, running experiments that required his presence for long hours at a stretch or at odd times of the day or night. And probably my assumptions about him—our assumptions, for I think we all shared them: that he was unimaginative, a little dull, certainly less free, less wild, less *fascinating* than we were— these made it even harder to see what he might truly have been like. I remember one night after dinner we were playing a game in the living room. It was Dana's invention. We'd all written down one adjective for each person in the house, and John collected our scraps of paper. His job was to read all the adjectives about one person aloud. The appointed guesser had to say who was being described and why she thought so. Sara was the appointed guesser, because, as Larry put it, she was the only one with "no agenda."

"What does that mean, no agenda?" Sara had cried with alarm.

"It means *saintly*, Sar," said Dana. "It means sweet."

"It means perpetually stoned," said Duncan.

Sara laughed. "Mean, Dunkey. For you, my adjective would be mean, mean, mean."

"You only get one, baby."

For Eli, the adjectives were *gentle, quiet, mysterious, gray, aloof,* and *pellucid*.

"Objection," Sara said. She lifted a legal finger. "How can someone be both mysterious *and* pellucid?"

"And who's doing these color things?" Duncan asked. One of Larry's adjectives had been *red*.

"Shh. No questions from us. It'll give everything away."

"Come on. Sara's so out of it she'd never put two and two together."

"Besides, *red*, in Larry's case, might not be a color but a political persuasion," I offered.

"Maybe this person is apparently mysterious while being pellucid, or apparently pellucid while being mysterious." Larry was smoking a cigar, and it chimneyed violently as he relaxed his draw.

"Did Sara ask for clues?" Dana said. "Are we supposed to be giving her these clues?"

"Well, it doesn't matter," Sara said. "I know it's Eli."

"Jesus, the chemically altered brain proves superior after all!" said Larry. "How did you know?"

"I knew. I just knew," Sara said. "No." She squinted in concentration. There were blurry finger marks all over the lenses of her glasses. "No. Because of *gray* and *pellucid*. They are . . . *les mots justes*." She said it again, contemplatively: *"Les mots justes."*

"Who said *gray*? Was it the same person who said *red*? Is someone doing colors?"

"I said *gray*," Eli said. "Not *red*, though."

"Eli!" cried Dana. "Why, why did you say *gray* about yourself? That makes me so sad." And in fact, her face was anguished. She was sitting on the floor by the couch Eli was sunk into, and she leaned forward now to touch his knees.

"I *don't* think I'm gray, actually," Eli said. He was quite serious, and blushing slightly at all the sudden attention. "But I was trying to imagine how all of you thought of me."

"But we don't, Eli," Dana said. "Look at your beautiful adjectives. I hope I get such adjectives. Read them again, John. All but the *gray*."

"Gentle, quiet, mysterious, pellucid, aloof."

"Well, all but the *aloof* too. The rest are heaven!" Dana said. "I'd give my right arm for stuff like that."

"Who said *mysterious*?" Sara asked.

"I did," I said. I was thinking of a moment earlier in the week when I'd come out from the living room in my bare feet after two or three of us had sat up late, talking, and I'd nearly smashed into Eli, who was standing utterly immobile in the hall, standing there and, evidently, just listening to us. Before I could speak, he raised his finger to his lips—*don't say a word*—and then turned and went upstairs. It was the first time I considered that he might be less comfortable with his role in the house than he'd seemed. More complicated, somehow, than we'd guessed.

"And *pellucid*?" Larry asked.

"*C'était moi.*" Dana smiled at Eli. "Eli the pellucid."

"*Pellucid* is a very interesting word," Sara said. "If you didn't know what it meant, you'd think it meant, like . . ." There was a long, long silence. Her eyes had gone out of focus.

John poked her. "Pellucid," he said. "You'd think it meant . . . ?"

"Oh!" She giggled. "Like really smelly, wouldn't you?"

My adjectives were *reserved, sexy, curious, fragile, blue,* and *opaque*.

"Who *is* it with the colors?"

"It could be sad," Sara said. "That this person is sad. Blue. Not a color."

"Who said *opaque*?" Larry asked. "*Opaque* is hostile."

"To *be* opaque is hostile?" I asked him.

"To say someone else is opaque is hostile. It's like saying someone is gray."

"No one said that about anyone else. Eli said it about himself."

"Sara, I know that. I know that."

"It's either Duncan," Sara said, "or Licia. The *fragile* is confounding."

"*Confounding.*" Larry's head nodded two, three times in deep appreciation. "That's a great adjective. Someone should have used that on someone else."

"I want a clue," Sara said.

"It will cheapen your victory," John said.

"Still, I want to know who said *fragile*."

"I did," Eli said. He looked at me quickly and then looked away.

"Hmm. Well. Well, I'm certain Eli doesn't think Duncan is fragile, so it must be Licia. Is it?"

Noises of assent, bobbing heads.

"Sara, you're nothing short of amazing," Dana pronounced. Her hands lifted in one of her extravagant gestures, and she offered: "Amazing, perspicacious, intuitive—"

"Orange," John interrupted.

"*You* were the color guy?" Duncan pointed his cigarette at John.

"I'll never tell."

"There *was* no color guy. Eli called himself gray, someone called Larry a commie, and someone else thinks Licia is sad."

"That's *your* theory. Only the Eli part is established as fact."

"Who said *sexy*?" Larry asked. "Who's hot for Licia?"

"Licia *is* sexy," Duncan said. "I said it."

I was astonished. So far as I knew, Duncan had never even noticed I was female. He wasn't looking at me now, either, yet he appeared to be completely unembarrassed to confess this.

"Who said *opaque*?" Larry asked again.

There was a beat of silence, just too long. "I did," Dana said.

"But you're best friends with Licia," Sara protested.

"Still, she *is* opaque. To me anyway. Licia has secrets." Dana smiled a bright smile at me, a smile that seemed suddenly false, too toothy.

"See, that's what makes her sexy," Duncan said. "A little discretion goes a long, long way." Dana looked at him sharply, visibly hurt.

"What did you say, Licia? About yourself?"

"Reserved."

"Same as *opaque*," Sara said.

"Nothing like," Larry said.

"I would still like to know this *color* asshole," Duncan said.

"Speaking of hostility."

Later Dana came to my room and apologized for calling me opaque.

I told her not to be crazy, that I wasn't the one who found it offensive.

"I do, though," she said. "I don't want you to think I'm pushing you, or bugging you, or anything."

I looked over at her, my beautiful friend, and my heart felt thickened abruptly with love. How could she imagine there was something she could give me that I wouldn't want, something she could ask of me that I wouldn't try to give?

I HAD BEEN IN THE HOUSE FOR OVER A MONTH AT THIS point, and I felt transformed and opened out—so altered it seemed nearly chemical to me, as though I were the one taking drugs. It was so much what I had wanted that I was sometimes frightened by it. By how fast it was happening. By how happy I could sometimes feel. By how radically different I seemed to myself from the good girl who'd moved so dutifully through high school and college and marriage. Whose friendships and deepest loves had all been, it seemed to me now, bland matters of convenience—someone who lived three doors down, someone in my sorority, someone I was sleeping with.

Now when I turned the corner onto Lyman Street after work and saw our lights glowing in the darkness from the first-floor windows of the house, I sometimes broke into a run, I was so eager just to *be there*.

I loved the fact that there was always someone awake, even at one or one-thirty. At that hour, intimacies sprang up easily. With Larry, for instance, one night over coffee in the kitchen. He was reading late and pleased to be interrupted, by what he called "a long, blond column of concentrated nicotine." We sat for several hours under the intermittent flicker and buzz of the bare fluorescent ring on the ceiling, and he told me his story, all about his patrician, cultured background. His parents, he said, were at the opera, the ballet, the symphony, several nights a week, "while understanding *dogshit* about any of it." He would inherit a town house on Marlborough Street eventually, and he'd made it his personal goal to look as though he didn't belong there. "I want to be the kind of person that people are always coming up to and saying, 'May I help you?' when what they really mean is, 'What the hell are you doing here, lowlife scum?' "

Duncan often arrived home close to the time I did, but because I found him so difficult, Dana began to wait up for me, or to stop in at Red Brown's and walk home with me. So there were often several people talking in the kitchen or the living room until two or three in the morning. I loved that.

I loved even the house chores, which worked to bring people closer. One afternoon Eli came back from the lab for a few hours to eat—he had to return later to watch some experimental results. It was my night off, so I was in the kitchen, cooking. Eli helped me chop green peppers and celery and onions for chili. After only a few minutes, we were both weeping from the pungent fumes. We began to invent reasons we would offer if someone came in and asked us what was wrong: we had discovered we were the wrong zodiacal signs for each other; we had discovered that worker bees could not have sex. Eli had a wonderful, incongruous laugh, loose and high-pitched and infectious.

We argued, too, that afternoon—about books, and then about a film we'd both seen a couple of years before—*Blowup*. Eli had been offended by the characters' passivity, by what he saw as their indefensible amorality. I took their side. I argued that you couldn't get hung up about guilt or responsibility for what had already happened. That what mattered was the moment, who you were now, how you lived in this place, at this time. I remember that I felt he was being unimaginative, uptight. I remember that I felt I was defending my life and the choices I'd made.

The nights I went to bed early, I sometimes lay in the darkness with my door open, listening to the noises of the others. Often Duncan was making music in his room. He played so well that I couldn't always tell if it was a record or Duncan, until—if it was Duncan—the heavenly stuff broke off abruptly, to profane muttering, and then began again. I could hear Dana's hoarse voice cracking at the end of a sentence down in the living room, or Sara's sweet murmur somewhere, or her faint cries of sexual happiness, or Eli, talking earnestly.

I was sometimes miserable, often bitterly lonely with the distance my situation imposed. At the same time, I was happier than I'd ever been. I felt I'd come to see and understand, finally, that there was a way to live among others that didn't require falsifying yourself. Somehow all the lies I'd told didn't figure in this vision. Or were canceled out by what I saw as its deeper truth.

It wasn't that I had been conscious of falsifying myself when I was living my other life. I'm sure I hadn't. I think, in fact, that I was barely conscious of having a self in that world. My mother tells me that I was a willful little girl, but I don't remember that. What I remember is later, when I wasn't willful anymore: the inner calm of knowing I was *satisfying expectations*, I was pleasing. The self isn't important in such a feeling. It was only as I began to startle and disappoint others that I was aware of myself at all—that I came to understand, slowly, that I wasn't who I had pretended to be. And now, when I was pretending to be someone completely other than myself, I felt, for the first time, at home in my skin.

How much of my feeling about the house, about my new life, connected to Dana I wasn't sure. I wouldn't have joined the house without her, I knew that. I would have settled for a very different kind of place, one where I could have had privacy, solitude. A place where everyone separated after dinner and shut the doors to their rooms. Or a place where people didn't eat together at all but kept their food in separate labeled containers in the refrigerator and pantry. One of the houses where I'd been interviewed was such a place. The labels said things like *Hands off! This is Sheila's!* and featured skulls and crossbones, *Poison* signs.

From the start, Dana had actively sought me out, nearly daily. She helped me paint my room a sort of lilac pink the third day after I moved in. She'd been sunbathing in the driveway when I carried the paint and roller and tray past her, and she appeared in my doorway a few minutes later, still wearing her faded blue bikini. "Need help?" she asked. "I'm good at this." She gestured at my supplies.

I said yes, gratefully.

Over the afternoon, her lush, solid body, freckled everywhere but on her rounded belly and long thighs, became dotted and smeared with the pink paint. She chattered as she worked, a frantic, edgy quality to her hard voice that I realized only later was there because she wanted so much for me to like her. She was offering herself to me—her history, her affection. She told me about a man she'd dated two years before—this was when she was living alone, she said—who broke her nose. She turned her face so I could see the slight bump. "They did a really good job setting it, didn't they?"

"But that's so awful!" I said.

"Oh, I hit him first," Dana said. "I hit him in the face. Many times, actually, as hard as I could." She made a fist and imitated her punch, a repeated steady downward bludgeoning. "I don't blame him at all. And he was incredibly apologetic. He took me to the emergency room himself."

She told me that she'd slept with two of the house members—Eli and Duncan. That the rule about having sex within the house had been made with her in mind. "I think Larry proposed it, in self-defense," she said, laughing. "But they all agreed I was a disruptive force." She shrugged. "I actually didn't mind. It was messing me up, thinking about Duncan all the time, about when we'd fuck again. And I kind of liked the idea of being a *force*."

"You didn't think about Eli? About . . . fucking him?" I wasn't yet accustomed to this casual use of rough language or to talking so openly about the behavior it described.

"Eli was eons ago," she said. "It didn't mean anything. We were both just lonely. We're good friends now."

She told me about a period of time after she'd dropped out of college when she and a friend made their living singing in T stations up and down the Red Line. About spending a winter on the Cape with a lover, breaking into isolated, boarded-up summer houses. "We lived mostly on that leftover, condimenty kind of stuff, you know? Ketchups and jams. *Chutney.* And then, just *every* now and then, there'd be, oh, oatmeal or dried-up spaghetti or something. We loved that, we thought of it as a banquet. I got so thin! I was beautiful! Almost as beautiful as you!"

But she wanted something from me too. My story. My sense of self. She asked me directly where I'd grown up, where I'd lived before coming to Cambridge.

I suppose it would have easy enough to tell her. Why didn't I, then? Tell her about growing up in a university town in Maine. Tell her my father had been a botanist, a sweetly distracted, cerebral man much older than my mother. Tell her that he'd died when I was ten. Tell her that my brother and I had raised ourselves in a kind of emotional silence weighted with high expectations. That my brother had met them by becoming a botanist, too, by marrying and having children. But that I had chosen not to. That I had turned away from expectations.

I didn't tell her—because I was Licia Stead now. Instead I mixed bits of the truth with half-truths and lies, so that later I couldn't remember everything I'd said and would make mistakes. Sometimes when I talked about myself, I'd catch Dana looking at me quizzically and know that I'd slipped up again.

I thought about this afterward, about the lies and what made me tell them. Partly, I think, it was in order not to talk about my life, not to have to think about it, the decisions I would have to make about it soon. But partly, too, it was because I didn't like being who I'd been, because I wanted a different history. Or maybe no history. It was, after all, that time in the world when history seemed about to be swept aside. And though I was about as apolitical as one could get, I think I embraced for myself, personally, what people like Larry were embracing politically.

Toward the end of that painting day, Duncan came down the hall and stood in the doorway to my room. "God, it's like entering someone's mouth," he said, looking around at all that pink.

"But, Duncan, that used to be one of your most favorite things," Dana said, and then she bit the air in his direction with a sharp *clack* together of her teeth.

"God, Dana!" he said, and I turned away, embarrassed and shocked that she would say something so intimate in this casual way in my presence.

But this kind of candor was, as I discovered, a matter of policy with Dana. Everyone in the house knew whom she'd slept with and when, and, often, the particulars of what they'd done together. She'd grown up in Chicopee, Massachussetts, famous, she told me, grinning, for the world's largest kielbasa. She lived in a tight Polish community, where gossip had the power to shatter lives, and her defense against it had been scrupulous and overweening honesty. No one could say about her anything she hadn't already said about herself.

She was the youngest of eight children, the oldest of whom was more than twenty-five years her senior. "I was raised by about six or seven *sort of* parents," she told me once. "And on the other hand, there was nobody in charge. My real parents had quit the parenting business by then, and my older sibs had their own lives to contend with. Every now and then someone would say, 'How are your grades this year, Dana? And who's that hoody guy who keeps coming around?' But that was about it. I just couldn't *be* bad enough to get anyone's sustained attention. Believe me, I tried."

She'd started at the University of Massachusetts at Amherst, and then quit and come to Boston. She was a part-time student at the Museum School now, in sculpture. To support herself, she modeled for life drawing classes and worked in a jewelry store, doing repairs and making rings and pins and earrings after the owner's designs. Her own sculpture consisted of odd small pieces—bronzes. They seemed to be based on various prehistoric, extinct animals. Or maybe they were entirely imaginary. In any case, to me they looked fetal, embryonic, and I couldn't decide whether I found them intricately beautiful or simply repugnant.

Sometimes I felt I was doing research at the house, research on how I could live, on what life was supposed to be. Sometimes I felt as much an observer as Eli, though I knew the others didn't see me this way. Dana was the most important source of information for me, at least in part because she willed this to be the case. But the others, too, seemed put there to show me something, to teach me.

When Duncan talked about his and Sheree's freedom to sleep with others, I needed to understand it.

"What's there to understand? I love her. She loves me. That doesn't mean we own each other, does it?"

"No," I conceded. We were both just home from work, lost in the deeply sprung couches in the dim living room, smoking cigarettes and whispering across to each other in order not to wake the sleepers above us. Our feet were nearly touching on the wooden box.

"So if she wants to ball someone else, why should that have anything to do with me?"

"Well . . . ," I protested.

"Grow up, Lish," he told me, and I thought, smiling, of the bartender, Eddie, at the Ace of Spades, saying the same thing to me.

I wondered how Larry could be so sure of his political convictions, and he leaned forward over the kitchen table, bulked up and cheap-looking in his tight T-shirt, his greasy hair, and gave me his passionate argument about witnessing the spiritual corruption that wealth brought with it.

Sweetly Sara explained to me her wish to escape the confines of ordinary linear thought, to experience other ways of understanding the universe. And then she offered me a variety of choices from her stash of pill bottles, in a variety of hues. What were they? Gee, she didn't know for sure.

And when I asked Dana about her future, she told me she didn't hope for anything in particular beyond this. "I like my life exactly the way it is. I mean, I'd like to eventually get the degree and maybe someday show some stuff. Sell it, even. God, how great, to make some money from my work! But I wouldn't change anything, even if I got rich. I mean, what could be better than this?" She gestured around herself in a long, articulated sweep of her arm, her fingers arching separately—a gesture I can never forget, for its grace, for its dancer's beauty.

But what it indicated was our nearly empty living room. Was the secondhand furniture covered with Indian bedspreads, the odd collection of possessions we shared, the fake mantel, the Scrabble board permanently set up in the corner on a card table, the records sitting in cast-off milk crates.

It made me laugh. Then, I laughed.

But later I would dream of it sometimes, those days and the house, and in these dreams the open bare rooms led from one to another through secret passages with such a sense of promise, of imminence, that I would instantly recognize Lyman Street. Oh, not by any physical resemblance to my memory of it, no. But by the sense of excitement, of possibility—of youth—that the dream itself mysteriously carried.

CHAPTER

4

THE EVENING AFTER JEAN BENNETT BROUGHT ARTHUR
to my office—the evening after I heard Eli Mayhew's name
for the first time in almost thirty years—I went upstairs,
through Sadie's room, to the attic in our house. It was really an unfinished extension of her room. You bent down and crouched your way
through a kind of large cupboard door and then stood up again in what
seemed like a photographic negative of the space you had just left—
the walls and floors dark, unfinished wood, the only light from one
bare bulb hanging, à la Philip Guston, by its own cord from the ceiling. How could it even smell different, when one partition wall alone
separated it from Sadie's talcum-scented realm? It did, though. It
smelled like mildew, a woody damp odor.

In a box there, under the syllabi and work for courses in vet school
and letters from that period, I found the photographs I had remembered. There were two, both worn at the edges, one actually folded at
one time across the middle, so that a jagged white line of the fuzzed
underpaper bisected the image.

In the first one, the house members sit lined up in two neat rows on
the steps of the porch at Lyman Street—neat, that is, except for Larry,
who forms the curved close of a parenthesis at the right side of both
rows. It was his camera. He'd set it up on a timer and come running
over and sprawled down across the steps with us.

Behind us, the out-of-focus front doorway yawns blackly open.

Also out of focus and too large, like strange floppy white blooms in the foreground, are my bare feet and John's, sticking out from the front row, along with Larry's darker and outsize motorcycle boots. Eli, also in front, has his knees bent, rests his elbows on them. We are all wearing the odd costumes of the time—frayed bell-bottom jeans (patterned fabric in the inserts of mine), loud rhythms in the shirts of John and Duncan. Dana has on a wide-striped T-shirt, Eli and John have shoulder-length hair and sideburns.

The dutiful front row—John, Eli, Larry, and I—are focused on the camera, smiling falsely as we wait for the delayed click. In the back row, though, something is happening. Sara, seated in the middle, is looking with interest at Duncan, who has turned in profile to Dana, who sits on the other side of Sara. It seems he has just spoken to her. Dana stares at the camera, not attending to Duncan, and the wind has blown her hair partially across her face, curtaining her expression. Still, you can see she's not smiling. She seems isolated, unconnected to any of us or to the activity of picture-taking.

The other photograph is of her alone. Larry had caught her sitting in the kitchen, her long legs in wheat jeans, a loose man's shirt hanging to mid-thigh. The shot is taken from an angle just above her. She's slightly out of focus, laughing, her hand in motion as a pale blur by her forehead, as though it were moving to push her hair back. Her face lifts to Larry and his camera a little helplessly, like someone surprised by the camera, someone who really doesn't want her picture taken but yields to it. What else is in her face? A sweetness, a gaiety, an openness, that makes me think of Sadie. A spirited, beautiful girl, frozen forever at almost Sadie's age. It's this picture that bears the crease—crookedly, across Dana's bosom. On the back, in what must be Larry's writing: *Dana Jablonski, spring '68. For Joey.* Larry gave it to me later, after he knew my real name.

WHEN I WAS FIRST GETTING TO KNOW DANIEL AND TELLING him my confused story, I said it was Dana who'd taught me how to love with enough recklessness and generosity to make it real. "I wish I could thank her, then," he said. Tears had sprung to my eyes.

But at the time, it was occasionally odd for me to feel so chosen by Dana, odd and uncomfortable, and I still don't understand everything that was at work in her. I wonder if perhaps even our physical resemblance had something to do with it: perhaps Dana needed to learn to love herself most of all, and loving me was a kind of rehearsal for that.

Though that's not what she said.

"Why do you even like me?" I asked her one night. "Why do you want to know so much about me?" We were walking home from a movie in the late-summer dark. The air felt dry and smelled dusty and faintly of garbage.

"Because you have so much dignity, Licia. You have just what I *want*."

"Is that why people like each other? Because they want some part of the other?"

"You don't think so?" She sounded ready to change her opinion, if that's what I required of her.

"I don't know. I'm really asking. I'd like to know."

"Well, it's why I like you. No one I've known has been so dignified. Unless they were just worn down by life, like my parents. They had this kind of exhausted dignity."

"I think you're mistaking a lot of other qualities, or attributes, or whatever, for this vaunted *dignity*."

"Hmm. Like . . . ?"

"Caution. Suspicion, even."

Dana looked puzzled for a few moments, as if giving the matter much thought. Then she turned to me in the night and smiled her open, dazzling smile. "Still, it's awfully nice to say a word like *vaunted*, isn't it?"

There was a possessiveness about her affection, though, that sometimes disturbed me. As when Larry gave me the chair. I'd been complaining about the emptiness of my room, and he appeared in my doorway one evening holding it up—a beautiful chair, such as I've never owned again. It was Queen Anne, the wood worn to a satiny finish, the seat ancient cracked black leather. It came from his parents' basement, he said. One of a set.

"Won't they mind?" I asked.

"They'll never even notice," he said. "Which is why you should have it."

"Where'd you get *this*?" Dana asked when she saw it.

"Larry," I said.

"I'm jealous," she said. There was a silence. Then she said, "God, I'm jealous. Are you attracted to him?"

"There's a rule, Dana. I'm not allowed to be, am I?"

"But you *are*?

"Larry?"

"It could happen. And I want you to love only me." She laughed hoarsely, but I could see there was a way in which she meant it. "Wait a sec," she said, and disappeared.

When she came back she was carrying a lamp, a gooseneck lamp she'd had on her own desk. She'd decorated it herself, adding two bulbous, lidded eyes to the rounded metal shade on top and, on the base, a strange flat body whose spiny tail coiled round and round itself. Now she set it on my desk and, in spite of my protests, plugged it in, turned it on. And after this I would find other gifts—in my room if I'd left the door open, or on the floor outside my door if it was closed—all extracted from the variety of things she collected and transformed and kept around her.

Her room was cluttered. A worktable—a hollow-core door over two dented file cases—took up one end of it, and the wall above this was covered with images that appealed to Dana: dinosaurs, primitive raptors, copies of old Audubon prints. There was a series of photos of the same dirty child making one face after another. Her niece, she said. There were various charcoal sketches of herself, naked, from the life drawing class—here curled on her side, there on her back with her legs spread, the dark patch shadowed and suggestive between them. She'd tacked an enormous and elaborately patterned snakeskin over her bed, and next to it was another publicity shot of Duncan's girlfriend, hung there, she told me, "to teach myself humility." She had two chairs she'd found on the street and made slipcovers for out of coarse white fabric. On them she'd drawn two lush female figures, so that you sat held in their wide laps and thick arms, nestled against the rounded drooping breasts. Each sported a tiny cushion of looped yarn where pubic hair would have been.

From her collection, she gave me over the months a decorated cigar box, a large shell you opened to find a minuscule diorama she'd constructed of life on the ocean floor, a pair of earrings she'd made, a sheer scarf bought at Goodwill. Occasionally, when she was sitting in my room, she'd pick up something of mine—an ink doodle, a Blake poem I'd copied out, a flower I'd carelessly let dry in a glass. "Do you want this?" she'd ask. "Could I have it?"

It became a kind of joke. I teased her with it sometimes, it shames me to remember it now. "Why don't you just build me a shrine in your room?" I'd ask. "Larry can take a picture of me, and I could give you things like toenail clippings. Locks of hair." She actually blushed before she laughed.

It's impossible, I think, not to respond to such fierce wooing. I suppose I could have been repulsed or even angered by it—and occasionally I was, a bit, out of fear more than anything else. But mostly I learned to love her in return. Not without caution, not without reserve. But I think I needed Dana too. In order to feel love, to risk responding, I needed someone who would throw herself against me, encircle me, and Dana was such a person. I'd grown up with a parsimonious sense of love. I'd made a marriage in which love was in many ways an afterthought. I suppose that like Dana, I wanted what I didn't have—what she had, in fact.

But it frightened me, too, and I was glad, I discovered, for the sense of distance from her that all the lies I'd told gave me. I don't know at what point I might have confided in her, at what point I might have been willing to let go of Licia Stead and introduce her to Jo. But for as long as I knew her, I wasn't ready.

ONE NIGHT DANA STOPPED BY THE BAR WHERE I WORKED TO pick me up—with Larry, which meant we'd have a ride. Cappy, the bartender, liked Dana and usually gave her and whoever was with her a free beer or two while I finished cleaning up.

The group playing on this particular night was a blues band from Chicago, with a nearly elderly lead singer and harmonica player, John Ayers. He had suggested to me several times through the evening that we get together after the show and have our own party, he'd show me what a good time was all about. I told him, finally, that I was married, I couldn't go out with him.

He saw me talking to Larry at the end of the evening and came over. "This here's your husband?"

"Yes," I said, maybe too quickly. "This is Larry. Larry, this is John." I gestured beyond Larry. "And Dana. John. Dana and Larry are waiting for me," I explained.

John looked Dana up and down, smiling, nodding. Then he said to

Larry, "Man, you are *surrounded* by beautiful women. How come you got these two women and I ain't got a one? If you was even near kind, you'd give one of these fine women to me."

Larry tilted his head. "Well, see, neither of these women is the sort you can just give away, if you know what I mean."

John laughed. "I do know what you mean. I know what you mean."

In the car on the way home, Dana said, "You're a mighty fine liar, Lish."

"What do you mean?" There was so much I'd lied about that I'd already forgotten the little lie to John Ayers about Larry.

"Larry's your husband. Snort, snort." I was in the back seat, unlacing my Frye boots. My feet ached. Dana was in front, next to Larry. She hadn't turned to me.

"Well, it worked," I said. "The guy wouldn't hear no until he thought I was married."

"All I mean is you have a kind of gift for it." She said this very quietly, and Larry looked over at her, sharply.

"And what does *that* mean?" I asked.

"Just that there are all these little contradictions all the time in what you say."

"Leave Lish alone, Dana," Larry said.

"Why? We're friends. Why shouldn't I ask her to clear some things up?" She sounded angry now, but with him.

"Like what contradictions, Dana?" I asked.

"Jesus, don't get into it with her, Lish." Larry looked back quickly at me. "No one has the right to behave like this. She's like the fucking CIA or something."

"No, I'm just wondering," I said. "What?"

Now Dana turned to look at me. "Well, like at work they call you Jo at least half the time."

"I told you." Had I told her? "My Social Security card says Josette Felicia. I hate Josette. I like Felicia, I use Felicia, but they saw Josette first. Thus . . ." I held my hands up, empty.

She turned back to the front. After a moment, she said, "And then there's the fact that you're from Vermont, and then suddenly you also have this family in Maine."

"What the *fuck* is this, Dana?" Larry slapped the steering wheel. "Maybe we're all made up. Maybe I grew up in . . . Louisiana, or Mississippi or something. What difference would it make?"

"I want to *know* Licia. I keep thinking I do know her, and then I don't."

"Don't talk about me in the third person, Dana."

She spun around. "I want to know you, okay?" Her voice was pressured. "I love you, and I want to know you. That's not a crime, is it?"

"This is too fucking weird for me." Larry was shaking his head.

"I think you do know me, Dana."

"So everything you've said is true."

"You may not have all the factual information, but you know me."

"Are you married?"

"Jesus, an inquisition!" Larry said. He was driving faster now, down the last block before our turn.

"Are you married? Was that true or a lie?"

"You know me."

"God, let me out of this fucking car." Larry spun into the driveway. The tires threw gravel.

"How can I know you if I don't know what's true and what's not true?"

"This is so crazy, Dana."

"It's not crazy."

Larry had cut the engine, and now he turned to us. "I'm leaving now. You two can stay here forever discussing this issue, but I'm splitting. Please lock up when you leave." He got out, slammed the door closed.

"I'm coming in too," I said, and started to open my door.

"No!" Dana reached over toward me. "Stay," she said, more quietly.

I turned back to her. "Dana, I'll say it again. I did lie. About some *things*. Some *facts*. But I've never pretended feelings, or thoughts, that I didn't have."

"Are you on the run?"

"What?"

"Did you do something? Some . . . political *act* or something? Something illegal?"

I sighed and sank back. "No. Nothing so dramatic."

"Then why did you lie? Why do you lie?"

"I don't know." But she didn't turn away, she didn't stop looking at me. Finally I said, "Because I wanted to escape from myself. From my life. Because I was afraid."

"But afraid of what?"

"Afraid . . . of everything catching up with me. Afraid that you might not have let me in the house if you knew the real story. I never thought it through very well. I think I was afraid of you."

She made a noise. "*No* one is afraid of me."

"That's not for you to say, Dana."

We didn't speak for a long moment. Dana's hands had appeared over the back of the seat, gripping it, and I could see her jagged, bitten nails, whitened at the tips under the pressure.

"Will you ever tell me the real story?" she said at last.

"I probably will. I will. But you'll be disappointed, it's so banal."

"*Nothing* about you could be banal to me," she said fiercely.

"Oh, Dana. I'm just a sorry, confused person. Please. That's all I am. Just . . . I'm not nice. I lied. I'm sorry. I'm not truthful. I've messed up my life." I started to cry, loud, embarrassing gulping sounds for a minute, and then I got control and was able to breathe, to weep normally.

"I'm sorry," Dana whispered. "I'm sorry. I'm too devouring. I eat people. Duncan said it, and it's true. I know it's true."

"No, it's what's wonderful about you, Dana, how much you want. How much you give. But it's a kind of high standard. For a person like me."

"I feel I've ruined everything."

I shook my head. I fished in my bag for a tissue and blew my nose.

"Can you forgive me?" She was still stretching toward me over the seat.

"Oh, Dana, *stop*." She bit her lip. "*Please*," I said.

She shook her head. "No, I mean it. I need you to say you forgive me."

"Only if you turn around and stop *looking* at me. I look terrible."

She spun around in the front seat and we sat for a minute or two, both facing forward, as though we were traveling somewhere. I blew my nose again.

Finally I said, "Someone should tell Larry we're ready to behave better now."

"Hah!" she cried in surprised delight, and then giggled. "Yeah, that it's safe to come out."

"Oh, Larry," I pretended to call, keeping my voice soft. "Oh, Larrreee, you can come *out* now."

"We've put away our *horrr*mones," Dana called.

I looked over at the house. Lights everywhere, as usual. "Let's go find him," I said.

"Let's *get* him," she said. "He should be ashamed, the scaredy-cat."

We got out of the car, slamming the doors. Halfway to the kitchen door, I remembered he'd wanted us to lock the car. Which seemed, when we tried it, first the hardest and then the funniest thing in the world to do. We were convulsed with the laughter of relief, at those buttons that kept popping up, at the endless slamming of the doors, like the sound track of a kind of vehicular farce.

There was no one in the kitchen or the living room as we crashed through the house. We found him upstairs in his bed, bare-chested, reading. He didn't look up when we came in. I sat at the foot of his bed and Dana nestled next to him and rested her chin on his muscled shoulder. He put his book down finally, and we talked in whispers until three or so, the house ticking silently around us, the sleepers dozing through our laughter.

IN MID-SEPTEMBER, THE PACE OF THINGS SHIFTED. FIRST Duncan and Dana, then Larry, started school again. Duncan's guitar students drifted back from vacation and camp, and we all began taking messages for him from the mothers trying to arrange his time at their convenience. The house emptied in the daytime except for me and John, and the oddly timed visits home of Eli.

It was hard for me. The summer had been better because of everyone's loose schedule. There was always company—someone to suggest a trip to the beach, or a bike ride, or an afternoon movie. Now I was alone most days, and the time stretched out painfully. I stayed up later, slept later. I tried to discipline myself to read in structured and yet arbitrary ways. All of George Meredith. All of Wallace Stevens. I didn't want to think of Ted or of my mother, both of whom I felt I'd betrayed. I'd written each of them once. A postcard to Ted, saying just that I was safe, that I needed some time alone. A letter to my mother, trying to explain why I was doing what I knew she would think of as a foolish and cruel thing. I hadn't sent either of them my return address, and I'd asked them both not to try to find me.

I didn't want to think of myself either, of what I would do next, *after this*. Since it suddenly seemed there might be an *after this*. Instead I tried to keep busy. I haunted bookstores, sat in cafés, drinking coffee and smoking. As the weather got colder, I went often to the Gardner Museum—for the humidity, for the scent of jasmine in the courtyard.

But of course, the truth was that I was depressed, and that waiting for me the moment I stilled was a sorrow that filled my time amply with its emptiness, that kept me very busy even as I lay open-eyed on my bed or sat at my desk staring out at the houses across the street. I tried my hardest never to still.

ONE DAY I WOKE TOUCHED BY MORNING SUN AFTER SITTING up too late talking the night before and then reading in my room. My mouth tasted of every cigarette I'd smoked. I'd left my window open, and it had gotten chilly in the night. I lay now tented to my nose, glad for the damp heat of my own breath. Someone was whistling downstairs. Probably John, making his elaborate ritual breakfast before slowly reading the *New York Times* all the way through. I was wishing for flannel pajamas, for an electric blanket, for heavy woolen layers like the ones I'd slept under as a child. I was wishing I didn't have to get out of bed to shut the window. I hugged my knees to my chest. The flesh of my legs felt smooth and cool.

Finally I found the grit to do it. I threw back the covers, stepped to the window, and slammed it shut. I pulled on a T-shirt and headed down the hall to the bathroom. I pushed the door open into humid warmth. Eli turned to me slowly, drying himself. He was naked. His body was slender and pale, hairy only on his chest and below his knees, and then the dark pubic patch. His thighs were long, the muscle a beautiful shape, and his penis swung heavily as he turned in my direction. The wet coils of his hair just touched his shoulders. He seemed merely puzzled by my sudden appearance.

"Oh! Sorry!" I cried. I pulled the door shut again and ran back through the chill to my bed. I slid once more down into the warm spot I'd left behind and closed my eyes. And saw his slow turn to me over and over, his hand ceremonially opening out the towel as though that were a form of greeting, the weighted dark of his penis moving over his white thighs.

ANOTHER MORNING, LATE IN THE FALL: DUNCAN PISSED OFF. I had just come downstairs to have breakfast in a T-shirt and jeans, and bare feet in spite of the chill, and he announced this before he said hello. It was fucking ridiculous, he said.

"What? What's the problem?" I asked.

He was bitterly pleased to explain. There were two dollars in the kitty with which to shop for his cooking day, and he had no money—"Zed," he told me, drawing deeply on his cigarette—to kick in.

Everyone in the house lived from week to week or month to month, and whatever the last few days of anyone's cycle, that person was usually utterly threadbare. People borrowed from one another in a complex sociogram of debt, and the elaboration of the payback schemes was often strained. ("Look, just give me twenty of what you owe me and the other twenty to Sara, 'cause I borrowed from her last week." "But Sara borrowed from *me* yesterday.") Only I, with my steady influx of tips, always had some cash. Most of it in ones, to be sure, but cash. Daily. Duncan hadn't yet realized this. The others had. Now I told him.

"How much?" he asked.

"Enough," I said. "Unless you're planning on champagne or caviar or something."

He shook his head. "Spaghetti and meatballs." This was no surprise. He always made spaghetti and meatballs. "Salad. Sara Lee for dessert."

"Which Sara Lee?"

"You can pick, since you're putting up the dough."

"Cream cheese cake."

"I concur."

"Can I drink my coffee? Are you in a rush?"

He made a magnanimous gesture, and I sat down. But morning chat seemed suddenly hard to make. Duncan was not the sort of person who felt compelled to fill a swelling silence. He was staring at a spot of sun on the linoleum floor now, smoke from his cigarette trailing slowly upward.

Finally I made my offering. "How are classes?"

He grimaced and swatted my words away with a light flip of his hand. I was reminded of how much I'd disliked him at first. I drank some more coffee.

"Okay, your turn," I said, after a minute or two.

"My turn?"

"Your turn to ask a question. Isn't that the way human intercourse works?"

"Don't be cute," he said.

"Don't be an asshole," I answered. I had learned to say such things.

After a moment, he said, "Well, now that we've got that out of the way." And another ponderous silence fell.

I broke it at last. "Ask me one question," I said. "Just one, or I won't give you any money."

He looked at me and then smiled. Then he laughed, a rarity for Duncan. It was seductive, I granted Dana that mentally.

"Let's see," he said. "What would I most like to know about you, Licia Stead?" He examined me unblinkingly with his cold eyes, and I felt sorry, suddenly, that I'd started this. He leaned forward and drew again on his cigarette. Abruptly he said, "Okay, who's your other self?"

I set my cup down. I could feel the thickness of the blood in my ears, my chest. I willed my face to be unrevealing. "Why, whatever do you mean?"

"Your other self. You know. Everyone here has another, better self. Not just what you *see*, for Christ's sake. Dana the world-renowned sculptress. And courtesan. Larry the . . . president of the brave new world, I suppose. I'm really a famous recording artist women can't get enough of. Et cetera." Pause. "Licia the waitress doesn't cut it. So who are you, really?"

"Ah, well," I said. "Ah. As it happens, I am but a waitress, an 'umble waitress, sir." I was flirting, I realized, flirting in the lightheartedness of my relief that this *other self* he wondered about was merely the self of ambition, not some secret past he'd guessed at. "And therefore"—I fluttered my eyelids—"probably the only honest person in this house."

"Honest, eh? So you say, so you say."

"You too? Everyone around here doubts my word."

He shrugged and looked away again, not interested suddenly. Turned off.

I didn't like it, I realized, this abrupt fading of his interest. This must be how he did it with women. On, then off—the charm of a cold person who warmed just for you, momentarily, and left you yearning for more.

It only made me angry. I stood up. "Let's go," I said. "Let's get the money."

He stabbed out his cigarette and followed me through the living room, up the stairs, across the wide upstairs hallway. The other doors stood this way and that, some open, some shut: Larry's room tidily on display, Sara's and John's messy. Someone was in the shower—the one-note tune of the pipes, the humid, soapy smell in the air.

Duncan followed me to the doorway of my room, and I went to my desk and opened the drawer. I'd had a good weekend, and I hadn't made a bank deposit for several days before that. There must have been around three hundred dollars in mostly single bills, here stacked, there just shoved in.

"What do you need?" I said. My back was to him. He couldn't see the drawer or its abundance.

"I don't know. Give me what you can." He sounded so bored, so contemptuous of all this, that I was suddenly jumpy with irritation, with the impulse to jolt him, or to bend him. I reached into the drawer and scooped up handfuls of bills. Turning, I tossed them high in the air and then spun slowly around in the fluttery rain the green paper made. I came back to the drawer, scooped and tossed and danced again. And again. And then I stood grinning at Duncan across the littered floor. A dollar slid from my shoulder, fell lightly down between us.

"Please." I gestured grandly around me. "Take what you need." As I walked toward him over the whispering bills, I could see his surprise, and his pleasure at being surprised. He was staring at me, and I could tell he would have responded to any gesture I made. We could have kissed, we could have made love there on the floor, lying on my money, messing it up. But I walked by him with the tiniest turn away of my shoulder as I eased past. I could feel a dollar bill sticking to my foot, but I didn't bend to peel it off until I'd made my grand exit and was halfway down the stairs.

LARRY'S DEPARTMENT WAS REVAMPING ITS MESSAGE-TAKING system, and he brought home a box of discarded pink tablets that bore the words WHILE YOU WERE OUT and a series of blank lines for the caller's name and message. We did leave one pad by the downstairs telephone for general use, but the others disappeared into private stashes, and soon little notes began to whisper under doors, or appear stuck onto the bathroom mirror or taped to the underside of the toilet lid.

WHILE YOU WERE OUT, the Nobel Prize Committee called to say you were *this* close, but you didn't make it again this year.

WHILE YOU WERE OUT, God called. Message: Prepare to meet me. Let's say, by the clock in front of the Coop.

WHILE YOU WERE OUT, a whole bunch of little aliens arrived in the playground on a spaceship and said they were looking for you.

WHILE YOU WERE OUT, Mick Jagger called. He's mightily pissed you weren't here. Says he can't get no satisfaction.

Nietzsche called. God is dead. Forget the meeting, forget the Coop.

Albert De Salvo called. Said he was sorry you weren't here and he'd try another time.

Santa called. Wants your list, pronto.

I came into your room and looked at all your really private stuff.

We decided to change all the locks on the doors.

"I'd feel hurt by this," Larry said—this note had been waiting on his pillow, and he'd brought it down to dinner—"if we ever used the fucking locks in the first place."

THE SOUND TRACK TO *HAIR* WAS ON AT TOP VOLUME, MAKING the speakers buzz on the bass notes. John was sunk into a sofa, stuporously watching Dana and Duncan. Duncan sat draped in a striped sheet in an upright chair while Dana danced slowly around him, legs apart and bent, her quick hands making the scissors flicker and gleam around his head. I stopped to watch, too, for a moment, and she saw me and waved the scissors. She wore thick woolly socks against the cold of the floor. It was dark out already at five o'clock. I was due at work in a little over an hour. There was a steady cold drizzle outside, and I dreaded going back out into it.

Now Dana leaned toward Duncan and said something only he could hear in the din, and he threw back his head and laughed. She looked so pleased with herself momentarily, so happy, that I could suddenly imagine them making love, the long, handsome bodies working together, swinging muscularly around each other—up to do this, turning to do that. I felt jealous of both of them. She moved now to stand behind him, and he bent forward submissively and bared the nape of his neck to her to let the scissors work.

I went upstairs to change, to soak my feet briefly in a few inches of hot water in the tub. I washed my face and put my makeup on—carefully. It made a difference in tips. I pinned my hair up behind my ears, so it fell down my back but was held away from my face. The music downstairs stopped. Someone put on something by Vivaldi, and the volume was radically reduced.

When I came down, Dana looked over at me in the mirror above the fireplace. She was standing alone in the room now—the others had disappeared. Her hair had been cut off to a length of about two or three inches all around her head. Freed from its own weight, it rose in thick waves around her face, waves that still showed the sharp line of the scissors' path. She turned around. She looked stricken, like a child who has barbered herself and is waiting for her mother's response.

I crossed the room, lifted my hands to her hair, and touched the ends. Then I ruffled it up, fluffed it this way and that. It was a terrible, cruel haircut, but Dana herself didn't look bad.

"You need to let me fix the ends," I said.

"What do you think?" she asked. She turned to herself in the mirror. "Why did I do it?" she whispered.

And I realized, looking at our reflections together, that though no one could miss how badly chopped at the hair was, the cut itself increased Dana's beauty. Next to her, I—who'd resembled her so closely—looked conventional, merely girlish in my long straight hair. Dana's bones seemed to have sprung free from some pull; their Slavic force announced itself.

"It's going to be fine," I told her. Her eyes were wide in fear. "It's going to be better than fine," I said. "Wait up for me. I know. Wash it and wait up for me. I'll even it out."

"It's terrible, isn't it?"

"Dana, did you hear me? You're going to look great."

"Am I?" she said. And then she turned suddenly. "Oh, look!" she cried. "Here it is, all my hair!" She'd gathered it and piled it on the wooden box between the couches. "Maybe I should try to *glue* it back on! Maybe I can weave a toupee!" She laughed fiercely. Then she looked at me. "No, seriously," she said. "Would you like a lock of it?"

Before I thought, I answered, "God, what for? No!"

And then I saw she'd meant it, though she looked more puzzled than hurt by my answer. "Oh!" she said. "Well, I just thought maybe."

SARA AND I WERE GOING TO BE THE ONLY TWO THERE FOR Christmas dinner. Dana was in Chicopee, John in Chicago with his parents. (Within a week or so of his return he would move out, though Sara knew nothing of this yet. I had guessed at the possibility, since I was the witness to the furtive comings and goings of the new woman by day.) Duncan had flown to the West Coast on a red-eye special to spend the holidays with his girlfriend, Larry had gone to Marlborough Street with all the enthusiasm of someone about to have a lethal injection, and Eli was working but planned to join us later for dessert.

Sara and I each had only the day itself off, but in addition, neither of us had anyplace to go. Sara was estranged from her parents, wealthy San Franciscans; and Licia Stead's parents were, of course, dead. We had planned the meal carefully, our way of staying cheerful about all this. Roast chicken, mashed potatoes, peas—frozen, of course—and, at Sara's insistence, creamed onions. "You *cannot* have Christmas dinner without creamed onions." We had stayed up late the night before, baking and decorating cookies for dessert. We'd decorated the living room, too, with paper chains we'd made and strung around the walls. We'd wanted a tree but were appalled to discover how expensive one would be.

From time to time through the day's preparations, I'd been overwhelmed by an unaccountable homesickness, and after we'd put the bird in to roast, I went to the upstairs hall and called my mother. It was about noon. Her dinner, if she was having one, wouldn't start for several hours. After five or six rings, she answered, sounding far away and therefore old and weak.

"Mother?" I said. "It's Jo."

"Josie!" Her voice rang out with a pure surprise, even joy, that unexpectedly made my throat cotton, made me sorry I hadn't written her a second time and reassured her that I was all right.

When she spoke again, she'd composed herself. Her voice was dry. "Well, I suppose I should say 'Merry Christmas.' "

"Well, that's why I called, Mother. To say Merry Christmas to you." I had composed myself too. "And I wondered how you are.

What are you doing? For Christmas?" I asked, as though this were the kind of question that existed between us.

"Oh, Jo." She didn't want to make small talk with me and this made her sound irritated. "Well, your brother's here," she finally said, grudgingly.

"Nice," I said. "And the kids?"

"Yes. Of course, Jo."

"Nice. Sounds like fun."

She didn't answer.

"Tell me how you are, Mom."

"I don't want to, Josie. I'm too mad at you, if you want to know the truth."

"Well, that tells me something about how you are." The wires between us fogged and ticked.

Finally she said, "When are you going home? What you're doing isn't right."

"But I need to do it anyway."

She made a snorting sound. "There's needing things and there's wanting things, and you're mixing up the two."

I didn't answer for a moment. Then I said, "I called to wish you Merry Christmas, Mom."

"Well, I'm glad to hear your voice. I'm glad to know you're alive. But I tell you what, Jo—I don't want you to call me again until you're back at home, where you belong. That's just the way I feel."

"Over and out," I said. I was angry, too, now.

"Goodbye, then, Josie."

"Bye, Mom."

I sat in the upstairs hall for some minutes. Sara was singing carols in the kitchen. I'd noted a tendency with her to drift toward the ones in a minor key—"O Come, O Come, Emmanuel"—or to the later, sadder, and more obscure verses of familiar ones: "Sorrowing, sighing, bleeding, dyyyyyying, / Sealed in a stone-cold tomb."

What was I smelling? Sage, rosemary for remembrance, the nostalgic herbs of family meals, of feasts of celebration with others. I felt a wave of the purest self-pity. Tears rose in my throat. And then I made myself think it: I had chosen this, I had wanted it. It was I who was hurting others in my life, not the other way around. "I, I, I, I, I, I, I," I whispered savagely. Downstairs, I heard Sara say, "Whoops!" and then, almost simultaneously, a loud, wet-sounding crash.

We finished eating about three-thirty, finished cleaning up some-time after four. We played a game of Scrabble and were almost done when Eli got home. He helped us set the table again, for dessert. While we were still sitting there with cookies and coffee, Larry arrived, loud and cheerful and smelling of "postprandial cigars," as he called them. He was carrying a liquor carton, in which he had wine and ice cream and most of a pumpkin pie. The wine was real, in bot-tles, not jugs. We searched everywhere, but there was no corkscrew. Larry remembered: he had a Swiss army knife in his room, with, he thought, a tiny corkscrew on one end. He ran up and got it, and indeed, it did have a tiny, inadequate-looking curlicue you could unfold from its red body.

On its first pass it tore out, shredding the cork. The second time it had more purchase, and it slowly lifted up what was left of the cork. We cheered. We poured the wine into our odd collection of glasses and moved to the living room, making trips back for the ice cream, the cookies, the pie. Sara brought candles in, and she set them everywhere—on the fake mantel, on the wooden box, on the window-sills, on the floor. We turned off the lights. Larry put on one of his records, a Creole mass. The wine was thick and soft, unlike any I'd ever tasted. The room glowed. The music was joyous. We compared Christmas notes. The creamed onion fiasco here, the drunken uncle on Marlborough Street. Eli's boss turning up late last night with expensive champagne for everyone still working.

I asked, for once, and Eli explained what he was working on. As he spoke, he seemed astonishingly relaxed and easy with himself. Excited, actually, and very patient. He'd be a good teacher, I thought. He used a metaphor in his explanation about seeing things clearly for the first time—about making a scientific discovery, I suppose—that I still remember. He said it was like the moment when you know you are in love, and you suddenly understand what all the feelings and the ques-tions are about, what universe they connect you to. We opened another bottle of the good wine, the music shifted to the blues. Sara smoked some dope. My mother seemed very far away.

At around eleven, the front door opened. We all looked over. Dana appeared in the hall doorway, bundled up and smiling at us. Her cheeks and nose were fiery red. "Did you know it was snowing out?" she cried. "It's beautiful!" And indeed, there were white flakes resting in the thick hair that curled around her face.

"Oh, Dana!" Sara cried. "I didn't think you were . . ." She frowned. "Interested. In snow."

Dana laughed and pointed a mittened hand at Sara. "Think again," she said. "If you dare." She came and sat on the arm of one of the couches. "This looks so nice," she said. And then she noticed the food. "Oh! Cookies. Oh, boy!"

"And we have this wonderful wine from Larry," I said. "Get a glass."

"I'll get it." Eli stood up. "Does anyone want more ice cream?" he asked from the kitchen doorway.

"Me!" Dana called. She'd gone back into the hall to take off her coat.

She entered again, to Sara's evident puzzlement—her face fell openly, stupidly, into confusion: hadn't Dana already just arrived?— and flopped deeply into one of the couches. "Guys, guys, guys!" she said. Eli set a glass down in front of her and began to pour some wine. She rubbed her hands together. "It's so good, you can't imagine, to be *home*."

THERE'D BEEN A JANUARY THAW THE WEEK BEFORE, THREE days of weather in the fifties and low sixties, followed by two days of rain. The snow melted to granular patches and then washed away, and all the bits of paper and trash, the nameless grayish stuff that had endured the winter, reappeared. But you could smell earth, dirt, for the first time in months. On the sidewalk in front of our house, a child's blue mitten resurfaced, and I had laid it on the fire hydrant.

Now it was frozen there, gripping the bolt on the top. The ground had turned rock hard again, the salted streets were rimed cheerlessly white. It was nearly ten below zero.

Tuesday was normally a slow night anyway, but on this frigid Tuesday I had only two tables at ten o'clock, couples slowly drinking beer and playing the jukebox. Four guys at the bar. No street traffic, except every now and then some sexless, bundled form moving by fast, its breath pluming fiercely. Cappy sent me home.

I passed only two people on the way, both hurrying—scurrying, really, just as I was—to get to someplace warm. The last block or so, I actually did a little mincing run, trying to speed my pace but at the same time hold my body heat inside my coat.

Lights were on downstairs, I saw. Larry's car was not in the driveway. I slammed the door behind me and stood in the front hall, moaning for a minute with each panting breath. When I was finally able to relax a little, I pulled my hat off, then my mittens, and stuffed them in the pockets of my coat. I called out, "Hello-o-o!" There was a funny house noise from the kitchen, but for the rest, everything was still. I remembered that Larry and Sara had talked about going to a movie. Duncan would still be working, Eli at the lab, no doubt. I unwound my scarf and draped it on one of the empty hooks.

I had just bent over to start to unlace my boots when I heard a sigh from the living room, a long, slightly guttural sigh of what sounded like the deepest weariness. "Hello?" I called again. No answer.

With the laces of one boot dangling, the plastic tips clicking lightly on the wooden floor, I stepped forward, around the corner into the living room doorway.

Dana lay wedged on her side against the couch. Blood was everywhere—pooled under her, smeared on the floor. Her bare feet, stretched toward me, were printed with blood on their dirty white soles. I made a noise. Dana was utterly still, her hands relaxed open. I crossed to her, I bent down. "Dana," I whispered. "Dana!" I knelt and took her by the shoulders, moved her slightly. Her head rolled back, flat, and I saw that her cheek was deeply cut. I reached to her face, and my fingers came away wet, red. Dana's skin was gray, a waxy gray, her eyes partly open. Blood sat in her mouth, outlining her teeth. I saw that her shirt was coarsely slicked red, that there were edges of torn fabric and skin like opened mouths, here on her chest, here on her rib cage. But she was warm, the blood was warm and sticky.

I was holding her face. No breath, no movement, the horrible color with all the bright blood. I was kneeling in it, Dana's blood. And what I was somehow thinking was that she was alive, she was still alive—I'd heard her, hadn't I? She was warm to my touch, she was warm, and she just needed air. She needed my breath, and she would be alive again. I bent forward, closed her nostrils with my fingers, put my mouth on Dana's, blew. And heard—a sound I would never forget, as I would never forget that one long sigh, Dana's final breath—the wet bubbling of my own breath pushing out from the slice in Dana's cheek. I rocked back in horror. Then, after a few seconds, I leaned forward again and shook her gently, as I would later shake my daughters from deep sleep. She wobbled limply, loose as a doll.

At that moment the house made a sharp noise, and I was abruptly in a terror of recognition: someone had done this, some person! I half stood, to flee, then stopped. I couldn't leave Dana here! Not if she was alive. I scrambled back and reached for her. I was making some kind of steady, crazy noise that I could hear as though it came from an animal separate from me.

But Dana's weight was appalling, slippery and utterly, leadenly, resistant. I dragged her no more than a few feet, and then my panic was suddenly absolute and selfish. I let Dana go, I heard her head thunk on the wooden floor. I was half crawling, then I managed to stand and run, grabbing the doorframe to make a wide turn into the front hall, caroming off the post at the bottom of the stairs, clutching at the front doorknob.

Outside, my own raw noise in the cold still night increased my terror. I ran toward a porch light across the street. I fell once on the sidewalk, then again on the wooden stairs going up. I grabbed the door, rattling it, turning the knob. It was locked. I banged on the glass panel, on the wood. I found the bell, but even before I rang it, a face appeared in the glass. A woman's. It opened in horror and then disappeared. Then a man was there, an old man, scared too. But he opened the door, and I stepped in and reached for him. My hands left blood on his shirt, and I felt him try to pull away, but I held him tight until my noises stopped and I could frame words. And then I said, "Help. Help us," and started to cry.

CHAPTER

5

BY THE TIME THEY DECIDED TO TAKE ME BACK ACROSS the street, there were perhaps ten police cars out there, angled wildly this way and that. Their headlights were on, and the whirling beams on their roofs strobed the blank houses with hectic light. One was parked in our driveway, one had simply driven up onto the front lawn. Its two front doors were hanging open.

I'd been talking for what felt like hours at this point to different policemen at the Davises' across the street. First to the one who'd responded to our emergency call. Then, after a while, to someone not in uniform, who was gentle but "needed," as he said, to hear me explain everything once more. And then explain it again. Things I couldn't remember: What time, exactly, did I leave Red Brown's? What kind of noise did I think I heard in the kitchen? What had Dana said earlier about her plans for the evening? And then things I couldn't begin to focus on: Did she have any enemies? Had she fought recently with anyone?

Now this same policeman—Connor was his name, Detective Connor—needed me to come back across the street. He wanted me to look around, to see if anything was missing. He wanted me to show him how she'd been lying, where she'd been lying, before I moved her.

"You okay, hon?" he asked. I was following him. His shoes made a scuffing sound on the gritty, frozen street. The Davises were standing behind the glass pane of their door, watching us. From one car or another you could hear the muffled squawk of a radio transmission.

"Yes," I said.

"So . . . you come up here, right?" he said.

We had crossed the lawn and mounted the stairs. We were standing on the porch now. His breath smoked out of his mouth and nose under the porch light someone had turned on. He wasn't wearing a coat, just a sports jacket, and looking at him made me feel even colder than I was. "You don't see anybody in the living room." He gestured at the lighted windows, where it was as crowded as a party now, with policemen both in and out of uniform moving around.

I shook my head. "No," I said.

"So you unlock the door, right?" He made a gesture with his hands at the door, showing me what I had done.

"No." I shook my head again. "No, it wasn't locked."

"It wasn't locked? It was open? The door?" His face was round and slightly simian and, now, surprised-looking.

"No, it was shut, but it just wasn't locked. We never locked it."

He made a sharp noise to himself. "Okay, so you never locked it." And then he looked at me. "Never locked the back door either?"

I shook my head. No, I whispered.

He grimaced. He had sandy, curly hair, cut short but for the sideburns. "Okay, so you open the door." And he did. The noise floated out into the night. Voices. Laughter, which shocked me. "And you come in." He let me pass in front of him, shut the door behind us.

He touched my shoulder gently. "Don't move, hon," he said, and walked away from me, to the back of the house. I could hear him talking in the kitchen, talking to several other people. As he came out again and crossed the living room toward me, he called, "The back door either," and someone in the kitchen clearly said, "Mother of God."

"Sorry," he said to me. "Just relaying that detail. That's very helpful information." He was trying to make me feel useful, to relax me. "Okay!" he said. He clapped his hands and rubbed them together. "Now. You come in, and you're standing here, right?" I nodded. "So . . . you hear anything, see anything, right away? Anything funny?"

"No. I . . . I just started to take my stuff off. My scarf." I gestured to it, looped unevenly over the hook. From another life.

"You had this on." He lifted it, felt it, as though it might tell him something.

"When I came in, yes. I stood here for a minute, actually." I backed up a little and leaned against the door. "I was so cold, I suppose I was making a noise."

"*You* were making a noise."

"Yes," I said.

"What kind of a noise? Someone in the house would have heard it?"

"Well, actually, I think I first called out. I yelled *hello* or something. In case someone was here."

"And there was no answer. No noise."

"No. Not then. So then I took my scarf off." I paused. I needed to get it right, I thought. Exactly right. "No," I said. "First I stood here, for . . . it was like a minute, making this other noise. Sort of . . . moaning. I was too cold, too cold to move. *Then* I yelled hello. And then I took my scarf off. And I started to unlace my boots. One boot." I looked down now, and there they were, the dangling laces, still untied. There was blood on the knees of my jeans, on the hem and sleeves of my army-surplus parka. I looked up. After a moment, I said, "And then I heard Dana make a noise."

"What kind of noise?"

"A sigh, sort of."

"How do you know it was Dana?"

"Well, it came from the living room. I mean, I didn't know it was her, until I came to the doorway and saw her."

"So it could have been someone else, couldn't it? If they left quickly."

"No, it was Dana."

"I'm just asking," he said. "This is just theoretical. I want you to think about the possibility that there was someone else in here with her, who made the noise and then left quickly."

"No," I said. "No, I don't think so."

"Why not?"

"Well, because why would they? Why would they make a noise? If they were trying to hide."

"Maybe they were hurt. Maybe there'd been a struggle."

"No." I shook my head. "No, she was alone. I would've heard them leave, they would have been running or something. And except for her sigh, it was very *silent* in there. In the whole house."

"Okay."

"And then the floorboards, they creak. And if someone had left, I would have seen them, see?" I pointed at the back of the living room, visible from here. "I would have heard them, and then, once they headed back toward the kitchen, I would have seen them."

He looked and then nodded. "Okay. Okay, so you hear her. And then what do you do?"

"I came to the doorway and saw her."

"You came here." He moved to the open doorway and gestured.

"Yes."

"I'd like you to come here now. I know it's hard, but she's not there now. Just come over here. I want you to show me where she was." His hand made a beckoning motion, drawing me toward him.

I came to the doorway. One of the men working looked up quickly, but the others didn't pause.

"There." I pointed past the smaller smear of pooled blood, about a third of the way from the couch to the doorway, to the larger pool, staining the floor by the couch.

Detective Connor put his hand at the back of my waist and pushed me gently forward.

"Where? Exactly."

We stepped past the smaller mess. I pointed to the bloody smear on the couch and started to cry. "Here. Her head was sort of wedged here, by this blood. Her feet were toward me. I saw them first. They were bloody on the bottom. She was just lying here, on her side."

"And you came to her."

"Yes."

"Did you realize she was dead?"

"No," I whispered. "Because I had heard her." I wiped at my eyes and nose with my hand.

"So you thought she was alive."

"Yes. I thought so. It wasn't logical."

"I understand. Here," he said. He held out a cellophane package of tissues.

I took it, tore at it. "I thought . . . She was *warm* still. When I touched her. That was it, I think. Her blood, even, was warm. I guess I thought if I could get her to breathe again, then maybe I could get help. It wasn't logical."

"No, but that's how it goes," he said. "So you tried to give her artificial respiration."

"Yes, I guess so." I blew my nose. "I turned her. I tried to blow air into her lungs."

"And then you heard the noise."

"Yes." I didn't mention, I hadn't mentioned, the other noise, the noise of my breath escaping from Dana's wound.

"Now, what kind of noise was it, exactly? From where?"

"I don't know. It was from the kitchen, I think. It could have been just some old-house noise, something the wind was doing, or the refrigerator or something. I don't remember it, really."

"But it panicked you."

"Yes. That's when I started to run. And then I realized I couldn't—that I shouldn't—leave her, and I came back. But I couldn't move her."

"But you said you did move her."

"I mean, I couldn't *lift* her. I was trying to take her with me. I started to. I kind of slid her a little, I guess. But she was heavy, and I was really scared. So I left her." And now something almost like a wail escaped me, my chest squeezed painfully.

"Okay, okay, okay. C'mon," he said. He put his arm around my shoulders. He guided me into the kitchen. "C'mon." He pulled a chair out. There were several men in here, too, and he signaled them somehow and they left. He put a glass of water down in front of me.

I drank a little, and choked. This set me off even more.

Detective Connor was patting me, hard, on the back, when Larry and Sara came in the kitchen door from outside, walking behind one of the uniformed cops. They looked terrified. Sara recoiled from me as I got up and went to them, but Larry reached out and held me, and I leaned against his chest awkwardly—he was shorter than I was—coughing and weeping.

SOMETIME SHORTLY AFTER THAT, THEY DECIDED IT WOULD be easier, better, to take us all to the police station. They'd be in the house four or five hours longer, they said, so it made more sense to ask the questions they had for us there. And they'd have to get all our fingerprints anyway, to check against whatever prints they were able to pick up in the house.

I asked if I could change my bloody clothes, and they said they would get a change for me from my room, that they would need the clothes I was wearing. I told them what I wanted, where to find things.

One of the policemen was talking to Larry now, and he must have mentioned the kitty—the money can—because someone else went outside and produced it, an empty coffee can in a plastic bag. They'd found it in the yard. Asked how much was in it, Larry and I each offered a different guess, but Sara had checked it that afternoon—she was due to cook tomorrow—and so she was certain: there was seventeen dollars and change.

"Gone now," the cop said. "Even the change."

They drove us to the station in an unmarked car. We had started with Larry toward his, parked at the curb down in front of the house, but one of the policemen gestured us away from it and toward one of theirs; and it was then that it occurred to me for the first time that we were all suspects, in some sense. As we drove to Central Square, they asked for and we gave them Duncan's and Eli's names and places of work, and John's, too, even though he'd been gone for almost a month. As though triggered by the mention of his name, Sara began to weep now.

I changed in the old-fashioned ladies' room at the station, handing each article of clothing over the door to a silent policewoman standing outside the stall. I never saw those clothes again.

WE WERE THERE FOR HOURS, MUCH OF THE TIME SPENT WAIT-ing for one another to be questioned. Duncan came in after about the first half hour, but they had greater trouble finding Eli—getting into the building and then locating him in his lab. It was several hours before they led him into the room where all of us but Larry—he was being questioned then—were sitting around a big table. When I saw Eli, I stood up. As soon as I touched him, his mouth dropped open, as though he would cry out. But no noise came. Instead his face crumpled and his eyes filled. His head swayed slowly, weakly, on his neck. "It isn't true," he whispered to me after a moment, and the tears spilled down his cheeks.

The cops were nice to us. They brought us coffee and, as the night wore on, doughnuts and Danish. Sometimes a couple of them sat in the room while another of us was being questioned. They talked to us. It was probably just a robbery gone bad, several of them offered, as if this were consolation. Dana had been upstairs, heard something, came down, and interrupted the guy looking for something to steal.

Once, when they'd left us alone for a while, we started talking together about a party the summer before to which the cops had been called by neighbors. Several guests—Dana among them, we thought—had pulled them inside, tried to get them to dance. A kind of numbed exhaustion had overtaken us by now, and we were laughing, remembering this, when one of the detectives came in. He looked quickly from one of us to another, and we stopped, instantly.

It was almost dawn when they brought us home. There were still some plainclothes policemen working in the house—perhaps lab guys, they were wearing plastic gloves—so Larry offered us all beds on Marlborough Street. Duncan said he had friends he'd go to, and Eli thought he'd better get back to the lab—he'd left in the middle of a procedure. But Sara and I, after getting our toiletries under the watchful eyes of one of the detectives, got into Larry's car and sat silently with him as we drove into Boston. The river was frozen solid again after the thaw of the weekend, and the sky was lightening to a chilly pearly gray above the city. Larry's heater blew loudly over us and dried my throat and eyes.

We entered his house from a parking area at the back, coming into a cavernous old-fashioned kitchen and then a tiled basement hallway. Upstairs, the carpeting was so plush that we made no noise. The house was enormous, and deeply dark. Larry showed us to a room on the third floor with twin canopied beds and its own bathroom. Light leaked in weakly through the layers of curtain at the windows, but he unhooked the tiebacks for us, and we were in gloom again. His room was directly across the hall, he said. He'd warn his parents we were here. We should sleep as late as we could.

Sara and I talked only briefly while we shed our clothes. As we were drifting off in the muffled dark, she said softly, "It's so hard to believe. At ten o'clock Larry and I were laughing our heads off at W. C. Fields. Now I can't believe I'll ever laugh again."

THE NEXT DAY THE POLICE WERE NOT AS NICE. THEY HAD talked to Cappy, my boss, about what time I'd left the night before, and found out he knew me under a different name from the one I'd given them. They had an arrest record on Larry, for various acts of civil disobedience. They'd learned from Duncan and from Eli that Dana had been "sexually involved," as they put it, with both of them.

They'd found dope in Sara's room and in Duncan's, they'd discovered Sara's various illegal pills. They'd found the loose cash in my room, which they saw as connected to the drugs.

All this information loomed larger, became more important, because they hadn't found much of anything else. The ground was too frozen for footprints, the smear of Dana's blood on the back door was from a gloved hand, and there were no fingerprints on the knife they had concluded was the murder weapon, one of our own dull kitchen knives the killer had left lying on the floor.

They kept questioning all of us off and on for several days. They made it clear what they thought of our "lifestyle." They asked about other sexual activities and attractions in the house, they hinted at their belief in the possibility of orgies, of drugged sexual exchanges. They telephoned both my mother and Ted, checking out my identity.

I talked to both of them, too, the second evening—tense, strained conversations. I told them both I'd be back soon. That I had to see through all that was connected with Dana's death, but when it was over I'd come home. I said that—"I'll come home"—to each of them, each time not sure what I meant, where home was. Ted's voice in response was like that of a stranger: polite, incurious. "Do what you feel you have to do," he said.

"Thank you," I said, pretending I heard something more generous than I had.

We slept in the house that second night, all but Duncan. He had come home in the afternoon to get some of his stuff, and he told us he thought he'd stay with friends for a while. The police were being hardest on him because they thought they saw some possible motivation for his killing Dana in his having slept with her while he had a girlfriend elsewhere. In Dana's perhaps dangerous or threatening preoccupation with him.

We couldn't figure that out: he had an alibi, after all. At the moment Dana lay dying, he was playing the guitar at Sebastian's in front of thirty or forty people, several of whom had already been called upon to place him there. We were all sitting around the kitchen after he'd left, talking about it. "Maybe they think he hired a hit man," Sara said, her wide eyes rounded behind her smudged glasses. I burst into a kind of loose, hysterical laughter, and she stared at me, offended, I think. She'd been serious.

I was fragile and on edge because we'd had to clean up Dana's blood earlier. This was a surprise to me. I don't know what I'd thought—that the police provided some service? In any case, I was the one who did it.

Eli and I had arrived home at the same time, and we stood together silently in the living room doorway, just staring at the terrible mess. I looked at him. He was white; his mouth hung open.

"Eli?" I said.

He turned and went back into the kitchen. He stood there, looking out the door, as I gathered the cleaning things. Just as I was going back into the living room, he said something.

"What?" I said.

Without turning around, he whispered, "I'm sorry. I'm sorry, I just can't."

While I scrubbed, I cried loudly, utterly careless of the tears and mucus flowing freely down into the pinked soapy bubbles on the floor. Eli came back in while I was still kneeling in the mess, and he stood watching wordlessly for a minute before he went upstairs. I could hear him a few moments later in the bathroom, throwing up.

I slept with Larry that second night, for comfort. In my own room, I had been unable to drop off. For one thing, I could hear Sara crying, little whimpers that opened up to whoops of sorrow from time to time. I got up and knocked on her door, but she called back, "No! Please don't . . . don't come in."

"Sara?" I called. I leaned my forehead against her door. "It's me."

"I really need to be alone, Licia," she said in a raw voice. "I just need to cry. You can't help me."

"You'll get me if you want me?"

"If I want you. Yes."

I stepped away from her door and stood in the open square hallway. The door to Dana's room was ajar. I'd looked in there only once. The police had taken various things of hers—the photo of Duncan's girl-friend, a few of her small, strange bronzes, clothing, personal items. All the papers from her desktop were gone. They'd left the bed unmade.

I knocked lightly on Larry's door. No answer. I opened it and stepped carefully over the weights to his bed. "Larry," I whispered.

"I'm awake."

"Can I sleep with you?" I asked.

In answer, he shifted over. "Here," he said. "Here." And he reached up and took my hand.

IN THE THREE OR FOUR DAYS FOLLOWING DANA'S DEATH, WE all behaved differently. Duncan pulled away, essentially moving out. (He would be the first to say he was, in fact, going to leave.) Sara talked and talked during the day, and then she shut herself away at night and could be heard weeping—a noise that, as it drifted through the walls and closed door, sounded not unlike the cries she'd emitted regularly in her life of more or less constant sex with John. Eli disappeared for longer and longer periods to the lab, seeking comfort, I suppose, in the unvarying routines of work. When he was around, he seemed silenced, stunned, uncomfortable in any room in the house but his own. Once, on my way to the bathroom, I passed his open door and saw him lying, fully clothed, across the tidy bed. The light fell on him and his eyes were open, but he didn't see me or hear me, and he didn't move.

Larry's way was to take charge. He did the shopping, the bulk of the cooking. He drove people where they needed to go—to the police station, to work, to class. He helped Duncan move his belongings out.

And I? I can hardly say. I moved woodenly through what needed to get done. I wept at odd times. I panicked at odd times, too, so frightened occasionally that I couldn't catch my breath. Sometimes I literally could not believe what had happened, it seemed a long nightmare I would wake from soon. And then I did believe, and I started to cry again, to weep for Dana.

And from the first moment I was able to think clearly about anything except Dana, I realized that my life as Licia Stead was over, and I mourned her too.

LARRY WAS THE ONLY ONE OF US WHO REGULARLY READ THE papers—the *New York Times* and the *Boston Globe* each day. And so it was he, drinking coffee between classes in a cafeteria in Harvard Square, who found the piece about Dana's death the second day, about the "further discoveries" the police had made. The headline of the *Globe* article was POLICE LINK LIFESTYLE TO CAMBRIDGE MURDER. Before he came home, he stopped and bought the *Herald*, too, because he knew it would be even worse there. And it was. "Neighbors reported being regularly disturbed by parties which lasted into the wee hours, by drunken and drugged revelers urinating or vomiting into bushes." The quantity of drugs found was vastly exaggerated. Of Dana they wrote: "The tall blond beauty had written in notebooks of her obsession with one of the house residents whom she'd been periodically intimate with, but this hadn't prevented her from having sexual relations with at least one other resident."

"I don't see how they can say this," Eli said. He ran his hands wildly through his hair. "How can they say this?" We were sitting in the kitchen, the three of us. Larry had come in as Eli and I were having lunch and slapped the papers down on the table. We'd taken turns reading them, sometimes aloud.

"God, she's dead, isn't that enough?" I said. "It's so crazy. Even *they* don't think any of this is connected to her dying."

"It'll fade," Larry said. "It's good copy for a while, and then they'll find the guy and that'll be that."

"But meanwhile it's like they're killing her all over again." I began to cry. "It's so much not who she was."

"It's not who she was, it's not who any of us are," Eli said. "I can't believe they can get away with it." He slammed his fist on the table. "There must be some laws for our protection. For her protection."

"But it is who we are. That's how we are seen. That's how this society understands us," Larry said. "You forget that. This"—he held the paper up and rattled it—"this is their truth."

"I can't think about that," I said. "Don't talk about it."

"You can't afford not to," he said.

So I suppose, over the next week or so—the papers kept it alive as long as they could—that this was some of what we all mourned and adjusted to, also, this recognition of the enormous gap between how we had understood ourselves and how we were being described. Not just a gap, actually. More a contradiction. Because everything we'd seen as making us innocent or good or open or pure—our sexual honesty, our willingness to stretch the limits of our minds chemically, our political activism—exactly these things were what were now being described as tawdry, or disgusting, or criminal.

I must confess that the smallest—in every sense the smallest—part of myself took some private credit for never having actively participated in any of it beyond a toke or two at a party. The very thing that had made me feel frightened and rigid then became now the source of a secret pride. Which brought a quick dose of shame in its wake every time I allowed it.

I WANTED TO SLEEP WITH LARRY AGAIN THAT NIGHT—THE third night—but he wouldn't let me. "It's a bad idea," he said. His voice seemed large in the dark, too loud. "I'm a horny bastard. I'll talk with you, though, if that would help."

I said it would, and so he got up and we went downstairs together. I made coffee and we took it to the living room and sat down opposite each other in the sagging couches. It was then that he told me he was attracted to me. "I have been all along, Lish," he said. He laughed. "Lish. Joey. Whoever the hell you are."

"Have you? Dana thought so. I didn't."

"How come you're so dumb?" His tone was friendly, affectionate. He was wearing pajamas and big fuzzy slippers.

"I guess I wasn't thinking."

"I'll say."

"I mean, about you or anyone. I'm still all screwed up about my marriage. I *am* married, after all."

"So you say."

"I am. I'm going back. I guess. It seems I am anyway." We hadn't turned the living room lights on, and Larry's face was hard to make out in the bluish half-light seeping in from the kitchen.

"But what are you going back to?"

"I don't know," I said. And I tried to explain it all to him—who I really was, how my marriage had been, what the Ace of Spades had meant to me, all my reasons for leaving. He was interested and sympathetic.

And then, of course, we came back around to Dana again. At one point I asked him, "Did you ever love her?" It seemed to me everyone had. "Were you ever attracted to her?"

"I loved her," he said. "I don't see how you couldn't love her. But I was never interested in her sexually. She was too lonely for me, too hungry or something."

We both hoped she'd lost consciousness quickly. We imagined the moment of her coming in to find the thief. We imagined the various things she might have said. *Can I help you? Do I know you?* Not really scared, we thought. Just, Dana. *Hi. What're you doing here?*

She hadn't struggled at all, the police said. No scratches or bruises, no cuts on her hands, which there would have been if she'd tried to defend herself, tried to grab at the knife. No flesh under her fingernails. It seemed as though she'd simply received the knife thrusts and tried to move away. We puzzled at this. I thought it was a sign of her goodness, her unwillingness to think evil of others, even of someone trying to hurt her. Larry's vision was more complex, darker. He had thought of Dana as nearly helpless in some ways, compelled not to offend and fundamentally desperate to be loved. And therefore passive, maybe even too passive to protect herself from a murderer.

We talked about how quickly it must have happened, how she'd just wakened, perhaps—her bed had been slept in. That maybe she didn't have time, really, to react in any way before she started losing blood and moved away to try to save herself.

"God, if I'd just come home a few minutes earlier," I whispered.

"And then he would have killed you too," Larry said.

"Oh, no! He wouldn't have killed *two* people."

He snorted. "Of course you're right. He absolutely drew the line at one, our boy. He was a man of some principle." He'd gotten a cigar a little earlier from his stash upstairs, and now he was gesturing with it.

"That's not what I meant, and you know it."

But I was imagining it, Dana coming barefoot down the stairs, just as I opened the front door. Her eyes puffy from sleep. "Oh, hi!" she says. "I *thought* I heard someone." And then we both hear a noise in the kitchen, the thief leaving, panicked by our voices. We go in together, together we find the kitty lying empty on the kitchen floor. And the terrible news is only that we've lost seventeen dollars and change.

Larry and I talked about perhaps passing the guy in the Square, the very guy, one of the druggies who'd lived on the common all summer, desperate now for money. Or just a petty thief, a guy who made his living testing doors, popping easy locks, scooping up what he could quickly and getting out. Someone you might sit next to at Joe and Nemo's or Albiani's. This is what the police thought now. They were going through their files, picking up everyone known for this kind of crime, checking alibis.

"It seems so amazing to me, so *scary*," I said to him as we washed out our cups in the kitchen, "that it could just be so random. That it could have been Sara or me walking in on him and dead now. I've never thought of life that way before," I said, vowing privately never again to lose sight of this.

"I think I always have," he said.

WHEN I TOLD MY MOTHER AND TED THAT I NEEDED TO STAY to see things through, I wasn't sure what I meant. The police were still talking to all of us then, pretty much daily, so that was some of it. And Dana was being autopsied, a horrible part of the incompleteness. I suppose I thought that when that was over, I'd go to her funeral, I'd meet her parents and say how sorry I was. I suppose I thought the house members would all go together, in fact, all of us who had known her so well in her real life, and loved her, and could tell her family how remarkable she'd been. I wanted them to see her as we did, as I did, to know how honest she was, how loving, how her impulse was always to give of herself, to want to comfort others. How her hands and body made a ballet out of the most ordinary gestures. I wanted them to imagine her dancing wildly by herself in our living room one rainy afternoon for the sheer joy of moving, or turning to me as we trekked across the Cambridge Common in the falling snow, tears in her eyes because it was so beautiful, because she was afraid she might not remember this moment forever.

But none of that happened. On Friday, the day Dana's body was released, two of her sisters drove up from Chicopee to collect her possessions. They'd called the night before, and we'd straightened up a bit for them. I'd forced myself, finally, into Dana's room and made her bed, pulled up the covers she'd thrown back when she went down to meet her killer.

Her sisters were both stout women, one Dana's height, one much smaller. The larger one was in her late forties, I think, and graying. The smaller one was older than that, and she in particular made me think of photos you see of Polish peasant women: her woolen coat was a little too tight across the back, and she wore a babushka, as the women in those photographs invariably do. Both of them had the high, rounded cheekbones, the slanted eyes, that had announced Dana's Slavic heritage too.

They didn't want to talk. They barely responded when I said how sorry we were, how much we loved Dana. I showed them her room, and they looked around silently at the female chairs, the snakeskin, the life drawings of Dana, naked. The larger one's lips tightened. "The police took some things," I said apologetically.

"Hmm," the smaller one said.

I trailed them when they went outside to get liquor boxes from their car. I started to help, but the little one—they hadn't said their names, just "We are Dana's sisters"—pulled the box from my hands and said, "We can do this. Don't!"

I felt as if she'd slapped me.

I retreated to the kitchen then, and smoked and drank coffee while they went silently in and out past me, banging the glass storm door behind them.

On the last trip out, the larger sister stopped in the kitchen, resting her box on the table in front of me. I tried not to look, but I saw, nestled in the clothing, two of the little beasts the police had left behind.

"We've left some things up there. Some trash," she said. Her voice was hard, as oddly ugly as Dana's had been.

"Fine. I'll put it out."

"You'll see, it's all in the boxes. It won't be much trouble for you."

"Fine," I said. She started to pick up the box again. Her hands were large also, reddened and chapped.

"Will there be a funeral?" I said. "A service?"

"It's just for the family."

"Oh, we'd want to come. We were her family, too, you know."

"It's just for the family. The real family."

"But we loved her. We . . ."

But she was shaking her head, her lips a dark, grim line. "No one, no one but the family," she said.

"But we so much want to . . ."

She set the box down. "Let me tell you. You listen to me. You stay the hell away from us. My parents are old, how do you think they feel? This about killed them. Their daughter, their baby, dies before them. This is the worst thing, the worst thing for parents. But then, no, you—you, her so-called friends—you have to drag her name through the dirt. How do you think that feels? Eh? They open the paper and it's Dana Jablonski this, Dana Jablonski that. All of you, and your drugs and your dirty ways, talking such filth about her? Who are you to say one thing about her?"

"But we didn't! We didn't talk to the papers at all."

"Ahh!" She flapped her large hand at me. "You're all . . . scum." Her eyelids thickened, reddened. Quickly she picked up the box. "Liars and the worst kind of scum," she said, and left.

I went to the door after her. I was going to say something, I didn't know what. To defend us, to speak up for our connection with Dana, for mine anyway. But by the time I got there, she had stopped outside, the big one, at least ten feet from their car. She'd set the box down on the ground, as though she suddenly found it unbearably heavy. She was shuddering helplessly, while the little one reached her stumpy arms up around her, her hands in their white knitted gloves like two little wings opening and closing on her larger sister's broad back.

AND SO IT WAS OVER. I TALKED TO THE POLICE ONE LAST time and left them with the various telephone numbers where they would be able to find me. Sara and Eli were looking for other apartments, other houses. Larry was going to stay on until the end of the month, and then he didn't know. Maybe Marlborough Street for a while.

I left in the late afternoon for an early-evening flight. Sara was back at work. Larry was at a class, and I was glad not to have to say goodbye again. Only Eli was home. He had offered to go with me to the airport, but I turned him down. My last sight of him was as I left in the cab. A light snow was falling, the start of a big storm. The sky was a sullen, pregnant gray. The front door was open behind Eli, as black as it is in the photo I still have of all of us together. He stood framed by it, his shoulders lifted against the cold, his hands shoved into his front jeans pockets. I pressed my palm to the icy glass as we drove off and saw him lift one hand in answer. I watched him until we reached the corner, but he still hadn't turned to go inside. *The cheese stands alone*, I thought, one of those irrelevant phrases from some other part of life that sometimes occur to you at highly charged moments. And then I was haunted by that nursery song off and on all through the time it took me to make my way back to my other life.

CHAPTER

6

HAT'S WHAT I WAS DOING, THEN, TRAVELING BACK TO
my old life to see if I could pick up the pieces—to see if there
were any pieces left to pick up—when I met Daniel.

We were in Logan Airport in Boston. Our flight had been delayed
for several hours because of the gathering storm. I had drifted around,
drinking acidic coffee in the restaurant, reading the *Globe* quite
thoroughly—there was no mention of Dana that day. Now the flight
had been called, but it was overbooked. A small crowd was milling
around the gate, and when the attendant got on the speaker system to
ask if anyone would be willing to give up his seat and fly out the next
day in exchange for a future free ticket, Daniel and I both stepped
forward, along with two other men—one a student type with an enormous backpack towering ominously over his head, the other middle-
aged, clearly a businessman.

I suppose I could have gone back to Lyman Street for the night, but
the idea never occurred to me. Or perhaps it occurred and was nearly
simultaneously dismissed. I know I felt I'd said my last goodbye, I'd
closed the door on that part of my life, on those people, on "Licia
Stead." In any case, I rode with the others on the shuttle bus to our
free night at the airport Ramada Inn, still thinking of, still humming,
"The Farmer in the Dell."

As we were checking in, the businessman—Dave, sporting the long
sideburns that respectable people were just beginning to wear—

proposed that we all have a drink to celebrate our decision and our future free travel. The point of this was to have a drink with me, the nubile blonde, I could tell that. But I didn't want to be alone in the hotel any more than he did, so after I'd taken my bag to my room, I went back downstairs to the bar to meet them all.

Of course it was Daniel I ended up talking to. The student fled fairly quickly, and then it was just a matter of waiting Dave out, which took a while. But finally Daniel and I were alone together at the over-varnished dark table, and we stayed there as the room emptied around us, as the bartender gave last call and started to clean up. As he finally flipped the other chairs up and rested them, legs in the air, on the other tables.

What I knew about Daniel by the time we were walking slowly through the deserted lobby to the elevator was how unnervingly beautiful I found him—pale and fine-boned, with a physical reserve, a kind of tautness, that compels me still. And that he was kind. He'd been especially kind to me, but he had also been kind to the student, and even kind to Dave. I knew that he'd been in the Peace Corps in Africa, that he'd grown up on a farm, that he was in divinity school in Boston, a worried believer who thought he could help people, could make a difference in the way they felt about their lives. What I felt I understood about him, what seemed to glow in his intelligent face, was that he was *good*, with a goodness I believed in absolutely, even then. You couldn't not.

And what did he know of me? Well, first the basic facts. That I'd grown up in Maine, gone to the University of Maine, and taught high school for a short time before I became a waitress. After that much information, Dave left, and things got more personal and tawdry. Daniel learned that I was married, that my life was a mess, that I'd been willing to get off the plane because I wasn't in a hurry to go home to my husband, which was where I had to go. That someone I loved had just died. That the world seemed a place without meaning or heart to me. I'd wept briefly, sitting at the gleaming table with him, and he'd leaned forward to shield me from the eyes of the bartender and the only other people left in the room, a couple getting noisily drunk at the bar. For a few seconds he placed his hand tenderly on the side of my face, and I had the sense that if I could only stay here with him, everything would be all right.

The elevator doors had just closed us in, he was just saying, "You know, I wish we could . . . ," when the universe seemed to lurch and the doors slid open again. I saw that we were on the fourth floor. Mine.

"God, *that* was a fast ride," I said.

He reached over to hold the doors open for me. "It was. Much too fast."

I backed awkwardly out of the elevator, and we said good night over its threshold. As the doors shut on Daniel, his mouth was opening to speak. I stood for a moment, wondering what he might have wanted to say, and then I turned and walked slowly down the dim, carpeted corridor to my room.

We saw each other in the morning, of course, jockeying in line for the plane, but it seemed easier not to talk then beyond a nod of grave recognition.

It was more than three years before we met again, in New York this time. I was the one who called him, tracking him down through his divinity school. I had thought of him often in those years. Thought of his face mostly, the incandescent skin wired with some kind of internal light; and of his cool hand, touching my face. I was working for Dr. Moran in that interval, and then in veterinary school. My life was solitary for the most part—animals and colleagues excepted—and full of hard work I'd already come to love. Occasionally, though, that pattern would shift, and I would become, for a time, wildly, angrily promiscuous. I'd use six or seven people in rapid succession. And then I'd be done and retreat again to isolation and work.

I didn't stop to ask myself why, what it was I thought I was doing, but I came later to feel it had to do with a sense that perhaps once again I was settling too soon, rushing into something I thought would solve all my problems—work this time, instead of marriage. And running from something, too, some deep fear that connected to Dana and her violent death. But I didn't examine this. What I felt then, all I felt, was rapacious, ridden by a scouring sexual appetite.

And when those waves of impersonal appetite seemed completely over, it was Daniel I was thinking of. Daniel, with whom I had spent one evening.

He was surprised, and then delighted, to hear from me. We had three or four conversations by telephone, each of which lasted several hours. I remember it, stretched out on the bed, talking in my tiny apartment. The maple branches brushed against my window with a gentle scraping sound—I watched the pale undersides of the leaves lift and lower—and we talked. We compared job markets, veterinary medicine versus the church. We talked about how we saw our careers playing out. We discussed families, children, the power of mothers in our lives. I told him about my painful, unresolved feelings about my father, dead at sixty-four, about my parents, how they'd met when my mother came straight from secretarial school to work for him. We talked about animals, how we knew them, how we felt about them. I told him about Dr. Moran and his wonderful hands, about a snake I'd actually become fond of. Daniel had been in charge of the family chickens on the farm and had hardly a good word to say about birds. We agreed on dogs and cats. We titillated each other with references to other relationships, hints of our sexual histories. My ear would hurt when I hung up.

Finally we arranged to see each other, to come to New York. We met at an expensive restaurant he'd chosen for us, though we barely bothered to finish the meal we ordered. Thickheaded and nearly speechless with desire, we took a cab back to my faded hotel near the 92nd Street Y and joined what seemed like an army of German tourists in the tiny and ancient elevator. It groaned, it rumbled. It stopped on every floor. People got off, got on. The languages changed. Years passed. I heard French, and then what I took to be Portuguese. We'd been in front, by the elevator doors, at the start of the trip, but by the time it was nearly over we'd shifted around so many times to accommodate others that we were now wedged together at the back, our bodies pressed to each other along one side. I was trembling, I couldn't bear to look at him.

"Now, this, on the other hand," Daniel said in a conversational tone, "*this* is a very slow elevator."

We were married six weeks later, and I would say we have lived happily, if not ever after, at least enough of the time since. There are always compromises, of course, but they are at the heart of what it means to be married. They are, occasionally, everything.

BUT OF ALL THE COMPROMISES MARRIAGE REQUIRES — AND IN particular, marriage to a minister—perhaps the most difficult for me has been putting my life and my concerns aside when someone else's life and concerns are occupying Daniel's mind. It isn't just that he's busy when this happens, as an architect might be, or a lawyer or a stockbroker or a professor; it's that he's taken up emotionally too.

In those days after I'd seen Jean Bennett and Arthur and heard Eli's name again, Daniel tried to sympathize with me. At dinner on Tuesday night I talked about it all, as I hadn't in years. I called up the old names from my life in the Cambridge house, and he wondered with me about the others—I'd kept up with none of them. How funny it was, he agreed with me, that it should be Eli, the one I knew least—the one all of us knew least—who had reappeared in my life. How strange it all was.

"Do you remember my premonition?" I asked him, resting my elbows on the table.

"What premonition?"

"You know—I told you—that sense I had yesterday of dislocation."

"Oh, the *ad*monition." He smiled.

"Bullshit," I said. "Now we know it was a premonition."

"Do you think so?" he said. "Well, I'm just sorry you have to feel any of it again."

We sat in silence for a moment, and then he asked, "If it was a premonition, what was it a premonition of, exactly?"

I realized I had no idea, and laughed. "Well, maybe it *was* an admonition."

Meanwhile, of course, Daniel had active grief, recent death—Amy's—to contend with. As well as a service and a burial to arrange, and all the logistical problems around that. We'd have several of Amy's relatives from out of town at our house Thursday night, so even I would be part of it at that point, though I had this aspect of my involvement in Daniel's life down to a science: the girls' beds and the guest room off the kitchen were always made up fresh. I had casseroles frozen. I'd buy a baked ham. On Wednesday afternoon I'd hit the gourmet shop for take-out food and rolls, for scones and breads for breakfast. I'd set up the ten-cup percolator, rarely used, and buy half-and-half and whole milk, extra orange juice, fruits and jams, butter and margarine. My job was to recede and leave food and comfort behind, and I'd learned how to do that without much cost to myself.

From time to time over these few days, Daniel gave me his distracted attention: "How are you holding up?" "When this is all over, we'll sit down and really talk." "This must be terribly hard for you."

Was it? Was it hard?

I suppose, in some ways.

Most of all, though, it preoccupied me. I saw Jean once more, on Wednesday evening, when she came to pick up Arthur after his round of steroid injections. There was no real change in spite of three doses, but I gave her the pills and some Valium I'd started him on because he seemed anxious. She told me I'd hear from Eli over the weekend. I was anticipating that, then, thinking of how it would feel to speak to him, to see him again; as well as thinking often about Dana. Not just Dana as she'd been in life, which came back to me primarily in ways I'd revisited over and over through the years, certain familiar *scenes*; but Dana as she'd looked when I discovered her—something I'd success-fully not thought of for a long time. Though even here I'd reviewed my own terror so often at the start that it, too, seemed oddly distant now.

Newly preoccupying, though, in a repetitive, pressured way— like the oddly riveting details and images from a dull movie you thought you'd forget instantly—were certain ancillary scenes. I hadn't recalled the cleanup, for instance: that came raw and, yes, *hard* when it returned. Or our bitterness and shame over being exposed in the papers, over having exposed Dana. I recoiled inwardly in a new way from these memories. I was puzzled briefly by their fresh power.

Until I realized that they came because of Eli, because it was he who had reentered my life and not one of the others. Because it was he who had been unable to touch Dana's blood, who had watched me weeping on my knees in the pinkish mix of soap and Clorox and blood and gone upstairs to throw up, over and over. And it was he who had seemed most shocked and upset at the useless and irrelevant exploita-tion of what had been made to seem sordid in all our lives. It was Eli's perspective that made it hard, when it was hard.

I found myself thinking, too, of my life, of what I'd made of it since then. In the first years after Dana's death, I would call up her face when I felt lost or uninspired or hopeless. I'd remind myself of how young she'd been when everything was taken from her. I'd use her loss as my scourge, a prod to rise above my own misery. How lucky I was, after all, just to have *gone on*. To be living, to have my work, my hus-band. Even to be feeling despair was, I'd remind myself, pure good luck. Grace, as Daniel would call it.

At some point, though, I'd stopped. I'd stopped feeling that intimate connection to her death. My life changed and I changed. Time folded over those events and that story. Other deaths, other griefs, replaced my grief for Dana and reshaped my thinking about how life got lived, how death got faced. How we accounted for our time on earth.

Now it had come back to me, but with some of that sense of remove I felt looking at the group photo of us on the porch steps, seeing myself there in my long hippie hair and my bell-bottom jeans. Remove, and a kind of shame for having forgotten so much I'd sworn always to remember. It seemed to me then that if there was an admonition, it was simply this: we have no right to let go of so much that shaped us; we shouldn't be allowed to forget.

WHEN I GOT HOME THURSDAY EVENING, THERE WERE THREE cars besides Daniel's pulled into the yard around the kitchen. I parked in front of the house, so everyone could get out easily, and made two trips in with the extra groceries. Before I'd left home in the morning I'd set out fruit and cookies, sherry and wine with a corkscrew and glasses, coffee cups, and the percolator, ready to be plugged in. I noted with satisfaction as I moved into and out of the house that the smell of coffee filled the kitchen. I could hear people walking around upstairs. There was no sign of Daniel.

I put cheese and crackers out now and set the oven on preheat. Then I crossed the twilit yard. I entered the open barn and went through the dark to Daniel's door, where a knife of bright light gleamed along the bottom. "Open up," I called.

In a few seconds the door opened. Daniel had his glasses on, and his chin doubled as he looked over them at me. He held a pen and some loose papers.

"Checking in before the fun starts," I said.

"Lovely." He bent and kissed my cheek quickly, then moved back around his desk and sat down.

"You're working on Amy's eulogy?" I asked. I sat down opposite him, on a daybed he used when he napped or read. The room was slightly overheated. I slid my coat off.

"Actually, Sunday's sermon. I saw a connection and wanted to make some notes." He slid the papers on his desk around. He took off his glasses and poked fiercely at his closed eyes. Then he lifted his head and looked at me. "How was your day?" he asked.

I shrugged. "Crazy. I did some really neat surgery, though."

"Ah! What?"

"A degloving. On a cat. The owners wanted the leg saved, and I got to do it. Mary Ellen assisted."

He looked blank.

"It's when the skin is accidentally just peeled off"—I gestured peeling a glove back from the arm—"so much that there's no hope it'll ever regrow. Usually you just remove the leg when that happens, but these people didn't want that, so there's a kind of elaborate but wonderfully commonsense surgery you can do—I've only just read about it before—where you open the fur on the side of the cat and bend the leg back under it." I had been excited, actually, while I did this, and Mary Ellen and I had talked eagerly to each other through the fussy procedure. "You make a kind of pocket, I guess you'd say. And then you stitch the fur back over the leg. In a little while, *voilà!* the skin attaches itself to the leg, so you can open the pocket up, release the newly furry extremity"—my voice put quote marks around this phrase—"and stitch the flaps back together, sans the leg piece. Which also gets stitched together." I sewed in the air for him. "It pulls kind of tight, but cats are stretchy guys. This one was."

"Stretchy guys," he said, and laughed. I felt a bloom of pride at pleasing him. Daniel.

Then he stopped and shook his head.

"What?" I said after a moment.

"Sometimes all that effort for an animal just seems nuts to me."

I was suddenly defensive. "Love is love, Daniel, wherever it lands."

"I know, I know." He seemed weary, old suddenly, with his pale skin, his eyes reddened where he'd rubbed them. There was a nervous steady pulse in one lid.

"What's the program tonight?" I asked. "How can I help?"

"You've done enough. More than enough, with the food and the bedrooms. Everyone's going to Amy's for dessert around eight-thirty, so we'll be out of your hair then. Till bedtime anyway."

"I will be invisible at bedtime. In that I will be in bed."

"Not invisible to me, my darling."

"I hope not. But where's the rest of the family eating?"

"Well, the immediate family's at home, with her parents. But I think quite a few are coming here—I told them we had plenty."

"We do."

"Some are headed for the inn." He shrugged. "Probably worried the minister wouldn't serve enough booze."

"They hadn't heard about the minister's wife, apparently."

He smiled. "Just as well. We need to have our secrets."

"So if everything's ready by—what? Six-thirty?"

"Sounds good."

"I'd better get going, then."

He stood and began to rearrange his desk. "I'll be right over to help."

"You don't have to," I called back as I shut the door.

The barn was a gloomy void after Daniel's warmly lighted study. I stood still for a moment, letting my eyes get used to the dark and smelling the barn's old, deep must. Piano music drifted to me from the house, the player picking out a piece Cass had done in recital once, a Mozart sonata. I went to the open doorway and looked across the shadowy yard. The windows were all lighted, and the house itself seemed flattened and two-dimensional in the twilight, as artificial as a stage set.

Someone—it was an elderly man—caught my eye, moving haltingly through the living room. After a few seconds, he reappeared in the kitchen and stood bent over the food on the table. As though it were his house. As though we had never been. As though he, and the person making music, and the woman I saw upstairs now, silhouetted for a moment in a bedroom window, were sufficient here.

I was aware, suddenly, of feeling canceled out, lost. I had a moment of what I suppose I must call grief, a powerful sorrow. For myself and the girls and Daniel. For what had been our life in this place and was already—this is what I felt—passing. Had always been passing.

And then I forced myself to walk forward through the dark yard to the back door, putting a warm smile on my face, getting ready to be the minister's wife.

IT WASN'T UNTIL BEATTIE MENTIONED THE DATE AT WORK the next morning that I realized it was Halloween. I'd done nothing to get ready. I skipped lunch with her so I could drive to the drugstore in another tiny mall, closer to town, and buy treats. The bags of small candy bars made expressly for this holiday were heaped in bins by the register. I bought two of them—forty treats in all. Surely enough, I thought. But then, just as the heavy adolescent girl at the register had finished ringing me up, I reached back and grabbed another bag of twenty. On Halloween, people drove in from the countryside and parked around the green, to move from house to house in town. Out where they lived, everyone was too widely spaced. The checkout girl—Melanie, her plastic name tag told me—sighed in irritation and started her process again.

At the end of the workday I hurried home, but I could see as I pulled into the driveway that the little halting figures in groups of five or six were already making their way in the dark, some carrying flashlights—their beams skittered and leapt wildly here and there. I'd probably missed quite a few.

Quickly I set up. A big bowl to dump the treats in. Four or five candles lighted in the front hall and on the stoop—we hadn't had a pumpkin in years, not since we found ourselves carving it alone in the kitchen, the bored girls having drifted off to TV or the telephone or homework. The bell rang almost right away, and I answered it, squealing in energetic fright at a small monster in a store-bought costume, the oldest of his troop and therefore the leader. I distributed candy to them all. Two of them were tiny children, toddlers really, who'd been utterly silent as their older siblings brayed "Trick or treat!" and who seemed not to know what to do now in front of this strange, noisy woman. ("Hold your *bag* up, dummy!") Both of these little ones wore their masks tilted back on their heads for greater comfort, like beanies with faces. Their mothers were waiting on the walk, chatting with each other, pretty young women. They called out "Thank you!" and "Happy Halloween!" as I was shutting the door.

When they'd gone, I went to the closet off the living room and recovered my own mask—Olive Oyl. I prized it for its expressionless innocence. It also made my life easier. I could just make Olive Oyl's high squeaks as I distributed treats—*ooh, ohh, mmm*—and be liberated from true conversation.

Daniel came home around six-thirty, and we had a quick supper, just sandwiches. We took turns rising to answer the bell several times. I asked him about the funeral, how it had gone.

"Harrowing," he said. Apparently the oldest child, seven, cried loudly through the whole thing, sometimes even calling for her mother. I imagined it, Daniel speaking calmly in his rich, soothing voice and the child answering, filling the air with her desperation. There could be no comfort for anyone else in the service—not in its solemn sorrow or its shared rituals or the old consoling words—with such scorching and entirely reasonable pain on display. Daniel seemed beaten, physically smaller, the sharp bones in his white face more pronounced than ever.

After supper, he left for church to go over the Sunday service with the choir, who were at Friday-night rehearsal.

As the evening wore on, the numbers of kids dropped off and their ages went up. Now I had children ten or twelve—big children, unaccompanied by adults, in elaborate costumes they'd made themselves: swathed in bloody gauze, dolled up as a French tart, swaggering in wide lapels and homburg as a thirties-era gangster.

By eight-thirty I had no candies left. Quickly I gathered up and put in Baggies all the cookies in the house, left over from last night's company. When those were gone I gave away all the apples and oranges and pears. Still the tricksters came. A few sullen teenagers rang, costumes replaced by thuggish behavior. I should have realized that since Halloween fell on a Friday this year, it would become the evening's activity of choice for many more kids than usual.

The last treats I gave out were an orange and two bananas, to three boys who'd left their unmuffled car idling deafeningly at the curb while they came up the walk. "Treat," they grunted in almost bored unison when I opened the door. There was a little silence when I handed the fruit over into their bare hands—they had no bags, of course. I was glad for my mask, for the distance it created between us.

"A banana," one of them said. "Is this some kind of fucking joke or something?"

"Trick!" I squealed in Olive Oyl's high-pitched voice, and shut the door quickly.

I blew the candles out after that, and there were no more visitors.

When Daniel came home at ten, I tried to amuse him with this story, standing in the bathroom doorway as he brushed his teeth. "Whooo," he said carefully, his mouth full of white foam.

I had thought we might talk that night, but he was tired, and we went to bed almost right away, without talking, without making love.

I lay awake for a while, listening to his damp breathing, to the cars and voices in the distance, to the occasional raucous shouting, which might have signaled a trick for the adults to clean up in the morning— eggs or soap, or toilet paper wrapped around a tree.

THE NEXT DAY, SATURDAY, WHEN BEATTIE CALLED ME FROM the exam room to the phone, she whispered dramatically, "It's that Jean Bennett again." As I followed her down the back hall, I realized by the rush of disappointment I was feeling that I'd been hoping for Eli—to see him, to talk with him. *That* had been part of the arc of expectation I'd ridden through the long week: on Saturday, my other life would come back to me.

Jean Bennett wanted to report on Arthur. Her voice sounded resigned. I heard in it, too, as I hadn't when she was in my office, that she was from the Midwest. "No better at all," she was saying. "Though he seems relaxed. In fact, he seems happy, poor old guy."

"Well, I'm not surprised, honestly. I'm very sorry, though."

"Yes. Anyway. My husband—Eli—said to tell you he'll try to see you, early next week, he thinks. He had to stay on in San Francisco for the weekend. But he'll come in Tuesday, most likely. To figure things out. I told him I didn't want to be in charge, nor did I want to be trans-lating from you to him. He said he'd call, to let you know exactly, and to see what will work with you, of course."

"Of course," I said.

"And in the meantime, should I just keep on with the steroids and stuff?"

"Yes, let's do the whole round, just in case. And if the Valium is keeping him mellow, I'd stick with that too."

"Yes," she said.

I asked her if she needed a refill. She checked. She didn't, if Eli really could see me Tuesday, so we agreed to wait and said goodbye.

After I hung up, I felt the weight of my disappointment—an empty feeling. I thought about it as I worked through the afternoon. What had I been imagining? Surely, when he came in, Eli and I would have talked mostly about Arthur, after all. But eventually, I thought, even-tually we would have come to Dana. Dana, and who we were then, and all that had happened. Surely that was so, difficult as it was to imagine how we would begin. *Remember the day after Dana was killed, when you got sick to your stomach because of all the blood? Remember the way the police went after Duncan? Remember how it felt to be the ones left alive?*

And now that it would all have to wait, I discovered how impatient I was.

"IS IT TOO LATE TO TALK?"

Daniel had left the kitchen right after we'd cleaned up, gone back to his study for a while. When he returned, he'd gotten immediately into bed. Now he was staring blankly, an opened book lying on the quilt that covered him. The light fell across his chest and over his hands on the sheet. He looked peculiarly like an invalid, which somehow irritated me. "I'm pretty tired," he said.

"But I thought we would, tonight."

"I'm sorry." He'd come late to dinner, too, after I'd called over to the barn several times. He was preoccupied, he said, about his sermon.

"It's just I've been alone with this all week." I was standing at the foot of the bed, trying not to sound impatient.

"Alone with what?" He was frowning.

"With Dana's death. With Eli's coming back."

"Oh, that." He nodded. Yes, yes, yes, yes. That.

"Oh, *that*." I tried to sound amused.

"I'm sorry. It's just . . . it seems, in the context of all this"—his hand lifted—"so . . . remote."

Now I nodded. I nodded and nodded, and then I left the room. I moved through the house, turning off lights. I came back to the bedroom doorway. He was reading. At any rate, he was holding the book upright. I said, "This is exactly what pisses me off about you, Daniel."

He lowered his book. He took his glasses off and looked at me. I was leaned against the doorframe, arms folded. "I don't think I knew this, Jo—that there's something that pisses you off about me. As in *all the time*, I assume."

"Well, there is."

He sighed. He looked away. He looked back at me. He was letting me know how tired he was. His voice, when it came, was patient and ministerial. "And is this the context in which you want to discuss it?"

"No. I'm sorry. Of course you're right." I hated that voice. I hated being talked to like that. "It isn't the context. You win."

"Oh, now come on, Joey."

"No. No, you're right." I went to our bathroom, an odd jury-rigged space off the hall where the front stairs had once been. I used the toilet, I brushed my teeth and washed my face. I came back into the bedroom and undressed, hanging my clothes on the hooks. Daniel was watching me now, the book set down.

Finally he said, "Why *do* you think you're so upset about Eli? About Dana?"

I pulled on my T-shirt. I turned to him. I tried to keep my voice steady and reasonable. "Daniel, why *not*? It's this horrible, violent thing in my past that is part of who I am, and of how I got to be who I am, and I live with it all the time in some faraway sense, and now it's here, it's in my life again." My voice had risen.

There was a short silence, and then he said, "I didn't know, either, that you *lived with it* all the time." His tone weighted the words, and I understood that he thought I was being melodramatic.

"Oh, Daniel, you know what I mean."

"I don't, I'm afraid."

" 'I'm afraid,' " I mocked.

His skin seemed to tighten. "Let's talk about this tomorrow," he said. "When we're not so tired."

"*I'm* not tired."

"Right," he said, and he turned out his light. "Good night."

Being plunged into darkness—*at his whim*, I thought—felt like being slapped. I had to force myself to breathe evenly. I shut the bedroom door behind me. I paced the house frantically, Bailey and Allie behind me. Tears seemed to jolt from my eyes.

In the kitchen, everything was tidy and still in the green glow of the appliances' digital clocks. Someone coming in here would think this was a lovingly ordered household, a place of peace and concord. *I hate this*, I thought. *I hate my life.* I stood with my hands on an old bowl left to dry on the kitchen sink. Its shape and the raised ceramic grapes on its side were utterly familiar under my fingers. *I could smash this. I would wreck things.* Bailey moaned in worry behind me. Why hadn't I gone to bed? Why was I roaming the dark house? Why wasn't I moving now? Why was I weeping?

I went to the kitchen door and opened it. The rain that had threatened and spit off and on through the day had started in earnest now. It made a steady rustling noise on the dry leaves that had fallen all week in the yard. The cool air blew wet through the screen onto my face, onto my bare arms and legs. I stood there until I was shivering, until finally I wanted to dry my tears and find the warmth of bed.

Daniel was gone when I woke. The steady sound of the rain had kept me falling in and out of sleep until nearly ten. In the bathroom mirror, my eyes were swollen from crying. I ran the cold water until it numbed my fingers, and then I filled the bowl. I held my hair back and bent over, pushing my face in. I opened my eyes wide and saw the clear blue-white of the basin through water. I stayed there until my cheekbones felt like cracking from the cold. My dripping face, when I stood up, was a brilliant deep pink. I thought, *I'll go to church.*

RELIGION HAD NOT BEEN A PART OF MY UPBRINGING, ALTHOUGH, since it was a kind of social requirement, as a little girl I went semi-regularly to church with my mother. But my father, man of science as he saw himself, thought faith was a childish comfort for the weak, and this is what I came to feel, too, probably mostly in order to be more grown up, more like him. When I fell in love with Daniel, then, I wasn't sure what my feelings would be about his work or about my own religious impulses. I was very moved on the rare occasions when I heard him preach—he was only a part-time, and very assistant, pastor in those days. I think that early on I mistook this feeling in myself for incipient faith and hoped it would grow, that Daniel and I would have this in common.

But as I learned to separate my pride in and love for him from what I did or didn't feel about the church, I saw that this wasn't going to happen. And what's more, my work, and then the girls, kept me from any kind of regular attendance. By the time he got his first church, Daniel and I understood enough about each other to make it clear to the search committee that they could not expect to be getting a traditional minister's wife in me.

That had remained our pattern in the two other churches he'd taken. I did what I could to support him, I made our home a part of his ministry, but I attended church only sporadically and I did not perform any role in its life. Fortunately it turned out that this was not as problematic as it had seemed at one time it might be; more and more as wives of ministers worked, and as ministers themselves were women with working husbands, the church used assistant pastors and lay people to perform those functions anyway. I know my not attending church was noted—at any rate, my occasional appearances were the trigger for hearty chuckles and jokes. ("Well, well, I guess this is gonna be one hell of a sermon.") But I don't think many people took offense at my removal from the church's life. They were used to it by now.

Today I felt my attendance would be a gesture of conciliation after our minor ugliness to each other the night before. A way of apologizing, of merging our lives again. I suppose also I was seeking to see Daniel at his best—as a means of kindling my admiration for him, of letting what was finest in him touch me, stir me, call up all my love.

The rain was steady as I drove over. A mist still sat in the low parts of the fields, where the grass was turning yellow-brown. Ahead of me most of the way was a car that carried four older women wearing hats, but they drove on when I turned off at the green where Daniel's church was. Another town, another church, for them.

I hadn't brought an umbrella, so after I'd parked I half walked, half ran through the rain, trying to favor my good hip. The church doors stood open, and I stopped in the narthex to take my coat off and shake it out. I entered the nave and moved to a pew about two-thirds of the way down, just at the edge of the fuller rows. I slid in and sat down. I bent my head and pretended to pray so I wouldn't have to meet anyone's eye and nod or smile. I could hear the little wave of interest and curiosity move across the few pews nearest me—hear it as the lightest hiss of whispered information, as a rustle of fabric on skin when the bodies turned slightly to take me in. I looked down at my hands, clasped in my lap—how bony they'd become!—and listened to the depressive meandering of the organ. The rain was a drumming on the high sloped roof, a moving beaded silver on the clear glass windows.

The organ focused in briefly on a melody and then stopped. Daniel rose from his invisible seat behind the pulpit, a slender man made somehow massive by the full black robe. He said, "Let us pray." And with the words "Almighty God," I gave myself over to it again, to the world whose beautiful ancient rituals he believed in and I sometimes yearned for. I rose, I sat, I opened my hymnal with the others. I recited the prayers and confessions, just another member of the congregation.

There was a moment, though, when I knew Daniel recognized me, when he realized I was there. He made no motion, gave no sign, but there was a kind of sharpening of his attention, which I felt connecting us. After that he could look away, or he could look directly at me, but it didn't matter. I felt that every gesture and word was meant for me, without excluding any of the others. I was glad I'd worn the dress I had, a draped gray silk with a white collar, which he loved.

When Daniel stood for the sermon, he surveyed the room and then he smiled. "A belated happy Halloween," he said. There was that polite titter which greets anything even approaching humor from the minister.

He often started this way, talking casually: today telling an anec-dote, an anecdote about me. "At our house," he said, "we ran out of treats." His eyes had swung to me, and they rested there as he contin-ued. The tough guys were there, and the bananas. Not the obscenity, though, and his gentle smile apologized to me for the censorship.

After this, information: he talked about the history of Halloween, the conflation of pagan rites with the celebration of All Saints' Day. Which this Sunday was, he pointed out. He defined it, talked about its traditions. The drumming of the rain on the roof intensified and slowed as he spoke. He read again parts of the scripture lessons, a pas-sage from the Old Testament about Israel living in safety in a land of grain and wine, "where the heavens drop down dew." He read from the passage he'd selected from Revelation, pointing out the startling specificity of the promises, the beauty and safety of the twelve-gated city, coming at last to the magical lines I looked up much later: "And the twelve gates are twelve pearls, each of the gates is a single pearl, and the street of the city is pure gold, transparent as glass . . . its gates will never be shut by day—and there will be no night there."

He quoted next from hymns, from popular culture, pointing out the various images of heaven, of eternal life, that surround us daily. He talked about the way we construct our ideas of an afterlife from all these promises, the way we borrow this language to console ourselves and others when someone dies, when we lose our private saints, our household saints.

"And yet," he said, and paused. "And yet it seems these images, this language, have lost their power to console." And he called up for the congregation his grandmother, a time she took him in her confidence to tell him that though she'd once believed she would meet her hus-band and all her dear departed friends after death—that they would all be in heaven together—she no longer did so. She no longer even knew, she said to him, where they'd gone.

I'd met his grandmother a few times in her great old age, a tall, skinny woman with a low-slung bosom, dressed for company whenever we visited in the same ancient, shiny navy blue dress. She had let Cassie rest on her lap while she rocked and talked to us one of those times, and after Cass climbed down and toddled off, she leaned forward conspiratorially and said, "*That* one is full of the devil." And I'd felt an unfamiliar clutch of fear, as if a fairy-tale witch had cast a spell on my child.

"If my grandmother," Daniel was saying now, "so well schooled in the Bible, so instinctive a believer, so surrounded by old-fashioned faith, came to question these promises, who among us in this more secular world can believe anymore in such consolations?" He shook his head. "No, most of us, if we believe the Bible at all about eternal life, believe it purely as metaphor. It must be *something like* a land of milk and honey. It is *like* a twelve-gated city. It will be *as though* we experienced shade and light all at once, and the absence of night and hunger and thirst and pain."

But even this has no power for most people. The little child, he said, whose parent dies cannot conceive an afterlife, even through metaphors. "And why should such a vision console someone whose feeling is, 'I want my mommy. Bring me back my mommy'? Whose question is, 'Where *is* she now?' " Most of us are like that child in the face of the death of someone we love, he said. Inconsolable, yearning, in a pain that feels permanent, that feels it will always be a part of who we are.

"But pain may be a gift to us. To us, and to that child. Remember, after all, that pain is one of the ways we register in memory the things that vanish, that are taken away. We fix them in our minds forever by yearning, by pain, by crying out. Pain, the pain that seems unbearable at the time, is memory's first imprinting step, the cornerstone of the temple we erect inside us in memory of the dead. Pain is part of memory, and memory is a God-given gift."

His speech had become more rhythmic along the way, something the girls used to tease him about. With their noses for hypocrisy, for falsehood, they didn't like him to be other than *their* Daniel. *Bogus*, they called any way of talking not his own. And from this they developed a dismissive name for any preacher who seemed to specialize in a false tone in the pulpit—a *bogue*. Said with flippant contempt: "What a bogue he was!"

But I felt a breathlessness, hearing it now, knowing he was drawing toward his point. He raised his arm, and the sleeve fell darkly away. "We *pity* the child who cries out," he intoned. "Perhaps we should pity more the *younger* child who *doesn't*. Who cannot *know* his loss, who won't remember."

He turned. The light glinted on his glasses. "For there will come a time when the lucky child who felt enough to weep then will at last be able to smile and say, 'Remember when Mommy read me those stories, remember when she danced, remember when she made my costume.' When the friend who thought she would never recover from grief, when the husband or wife who thought his own life was over, will cease to cry, will be able to take pleasure in saying: 'Remember how she used to lean her head back when she laughed?' 'Remember how he loved to garden, out there way past the last frost?' 'Remember when she cut all her hair off and was so sorry?' "

Dana! I was thinking. Remembering it now—the hair heaped on the box, her face in the mirror.

"And the funny things: Remember how he loved those knock-knock jokes—and how bad he was at telling them?" The congregation laughed lightly, as though they had known this person and *were* remembering. "Remember the time she reached for the pitcher and poured orange juice into her coffee—and drank it anyway?" More titters. I laughed, too, though I was still thinking of Dana, of the beauty revealed in the face surrounded by the lopped-off hair.

Daniel paused, a long pause. His voice, when he spoke again, was soft, nearly a whisper. "And feel the pleasure in having her *there* again. In bringing him back to *life* for those moments. A new life. Truly a life after death."

His face seemed to tighten. "Because if metaphor is one of the ways we have left to approach God, to begin to understand faith, memory itself is a living metaphor for the eternal life." He paused, then slowly said, "Loss brings pain. Yes. But pain triggers memory. And memory is a kind of new birth, within each of us. And it is that new birth after long pain, that resurrection—in *memory*—that, to our surprise, perhaps, comforts us.

"It comforts us. And that comfort—and even joy—the comfort that rises within each of us by the grace of God: that comfort teaches us something, here on earth, about eternal life. It makes us all feel something we *can* believe in about its promise." He waited a moment, looking out over the heads of his congregation, looking, I felt, into me, and then he bent his head and read, "Then I saw a new heaven and a new earth. And I heard a loud voice from the throne saying, see the home of God is among mortals. He will dwell with them as their God. They will be his people and God himself will be with them. He will wipe every tear from their eyes. Death will be no more. Mourning and crying and pain will be no more. For the first things have passed away."

He lifted his head. "Remember it," he said. "In this world, God gives us pain. But He gives us memory, too, to change that pain to laughter, to joy. To bring the dead back into our lives. To comfort us. To make us understand, by this living metaphor, His tender power." He rested his hands on the edge of the pulpit. "To show us how, in that new world, God Himself will wipe away all tears."

There was a long silence, and then he said, gently, "Happy Halloween." He raised his hand. "Happy All Saints' Day." And as he disappeared from my sight line, the organ pealed out the opening bars for the last hymn, and we all stood, and busied ourselves looking it up.

We sat for the benediction. I kept my head bowed as Daniel walked past me down the aisle, though I could have reached out and touched his robe, though I felt the air around me stir with his passage.

He stood in the narthex, out of the rain, to greet the parishioners. I shuffled slowly up the aisle with the others, chatting politely when I needed to. Those in a hurry vanished out the side aisles, but most people seemed to want the company of these last minutes as a congregation.

The air cooled and dampened as I moved back. The church doors were open to the dark day, and the rain, which had picked up again, roared dully behind all the other noises. We all tightened our coats, buttoned them. There was the smell of wet on the earth, on the fallen leaves. It was wonderfully fresh after the closeness of the church.

As I drew nearer, Daniel's face was in shadow, turned to greet the next churchgoer, and the next, the gray light falling from behind him. He was shaking each hand, commenting, receiving comment. He held on to people, he touched their shoulders, he bent to hear the fragile elderly voice, the thin childish one.

In front of me was an old couple, and Daniel took his time with them, seeming not to be aware of me waiting behind them. Yet I felt the tension in his not looking, in his not acknowledging my presence.

The old man had much to say about the afterlife, perhaps triggered by the sermon but largely irrelevant to it. He was talking loudly now of his Sunday-school teacher. "She always used to say"—and here he lifted his gnarled finger—" 'We shall gather by the river.' " Dramatic pause: "Now, can you imagine how confusing *that* was to a small boy afraid of crocodiles?!" He laughed a loud, thoroughly practiced laugh, and Daniel laughed too.

I had been feeling an adolescent's impatience, a tickling pleasurable irritation as I waited, so that when Daniel finally turned his pale eyes to me, I could have cried out. His hand was shockingly warm to my touch in the chill air. He pulled me to him quickly, kissed my cheek. The cool smoothness of his face, the way he smelled, the sense of his taut body under the robe, made me breathless, and I couldn't prevent a quick burst of giddy laughter. I stepped back. He still held my hand, and I felt myself flushing.

"Thank you for a wonderful sermon," I said.

"You, above all others, are welcome." His face was grave and smiling at once.

Then he turned away, as he needed to, and I moved on, out into the rain. But as I sprinted awkwardly down the street for the car, I felt such a wild reckless joy and excitement that I wanted to yell, to dance under the pelting rain. "Daniel!" I wanted to shout. I wanted to tell the others running, too, scattering to their cars around the green. "Daniel, my husband!"

CHAPTER

7

"MAYHEW?" I CALLED.

I wouldn't have recognized the man who came around the corner from the waiting room, but as he moved toward me down the hallway, I adjusted my memory. Flesh had weighted the tall, big-boned frame. He'd gotten solid and wider, he'd become somehow prosperous-looking. His walk was a little shambling as he came toward me with the dog in his arms. Ah! He had a slight paunch, and he was completely gray. His hair was shorn tidily but still wavy. His face, too, had thickened, I saw as he drew near, smiling at me. A handsome, jowly, middle-aged man.

"Stead?" he answered mockingly as he entered the light falling into the hall from the exam room.

I laughed. "Not now. Not ever, actually. As you may remember."

We stood a moment looking at each other, I just in the room, he just outside it. Then he said, "Here's Arthur. Let me"—and he moved past me to the examining table—"let me get him down." And with a tenderness that seemed incongruous in such a large man, he lowered Arthur onto the table, settling him with a few caressing strokes. Then he turned to me and extended his hand. His face was heavily lined, I saw, lines of intelligence and worry. The flesh around his eyes was pouched and deeply crosshatched.

"This is"—he was gripping my hand now, moving it with both of his—"just such a surprise. And, of course, a pleasure." He released me.

"Is it Dr. Becker now? I don't know what to call you." His eyes probed me, and I thought abruptly of the visual adjustments he was making too.

"Jo. Joey. Not Dr. Becker," I said. "Please." His hands had been warm and dry.

"And certainly not Lish," he said.

"No, but you knew that even way back then."

"Yes, I vaguely remember some ceremonial unveiling of the true you. Though I must say I've thought of you as Licia all these years." I noticed now that there was an ironic quality to the care, the precision, with which he spoke. Mocking. Or self-mocking.

I moved around to what I thought of as *my side* of the table. I felt I needed to speak, perhaps mostly to put myself at ease. "I have to say, Eli, it was a real shock when your wife—when Jean—said your name and we figured out it must be you. But I'm delighted . . . I guess I'm delighted . . ." I smiled at him, and he smiled back, his eyes almost disappearing into the flesh around them. "I *was* reeling for a few days, with all those difficult memories. But I guess I've found"—I shrugged—"well, I don't know: a fondness in myself for those times. What I've remembered mostly is how young and *sweet* we all were. So I've actually looked forward to this."

"Sweet, eh?"

"Oh, yes!" I said. "You don't think so?"

He shook his head. "In any case, I haven't been sure what to feel." And then he smiled again, and I realized that his smile hadn't changed. There was still something surprising in the way it opened his serious face, something youthful in it. His eyes shifted down. He gestured at the scrubs I wore, at the white jacket. "I must say it's extraordinary to see you in the costume of science."

"Oh, it's not worth wearing real clothes at this job," I said. "I'm always startled that a few vets *do*."

"Well, no, what I meant was—thinking of the past—one of the things I remember most clearly was that schism in the house. The group house. Don't you? That antiscience sentiment? The contempt in which everyone held my kind of work? At least I felt it was so. And I even had it myself. I was embarrassed, more than a bit embarrassed, about my own work."

"Were you? I guess I remember that a little." Of course I did. We had all thought of Eli as dull, as less remarkable than we were, because he dealt with facts. We, we glorious others, lived for art, literature, music, the imagination—what *might* be. He was stuck, poor Eli, with what *was.*

"I was ashamed, in fact." He shook his head. "Ah, the sixties. What a rotten decade."

"Well, often this doesn't feel much like science, actually. In fact, sometimes it seems like so much hocus-pocus. I mean, there are a few things we can cure, but a lot of it is still sort of primitive." A thought occurred to me. "I read something by Chekhov once, about what it felt like to be a doctor in the nineteenth century—how little one could actually *do* about so many things." I lifted my hands. "As with our friend here."

"So I understand," Eli said. He reached over and patted Arthur.

"Do you want to talk about the options?" I asked. The dog had been lying still on the table, seemingly relaxed, watching the discussion move from one of us to the other. Whenever Eli touched him, he lifted his muzzle and his watery gaze in trusting greeting. *Oh, it's you.*

"Jean said there was a surgical possibility," Eli said.

I shook my head. "No," I said. "No, in fact, there really *isn't* here. I probably mentioned it to her because sometimes with these back crises, if we get to them soon enough, there is a chance with surgery. But I'm afraid that by the time we knew something was seriously wrong with Arthur, the damage had been done."

He nodded. She must have spoken of this, too, she must have blamed herself.

"I'm certain—and I rarely say this, but I *am* certain in this case— that there'd be no point." I explained to Eli what I thought had happened to Arthur, what I thought the choices and options actually were.

We were standing on opposite sides of the examination table while I talked, with the dog between us. Eli's questions to me were quick, probing, always apt. His face was mobile in its responsiveness to whatever I said—his forehead deeply corrugating in a frown, his lips tightening, his thick eyebrows moving up and down to register my points. I thought abruptly of the careful mask that other Eli had worn, the cautious way he carried himself. This Eli was alive, and the energy in his face was testimony to that. Even the lines: evidence of a *lived* life. He rested his hand on Arthur from time to time, as I did. Our hands touched once, and I moved mine away, quickly.

"So what you're really recommending is euthanasia," he said

finally. He was leaning against the wall, his arms crossed. His face was grave.

I had sat down on my stool by now, to rest my hip. I shook my head. "No. No, not at all."

"Then why do I hear that?" he asked. It wasn't a hostile question.

"Because I *did* say it's incredibly time-consuming and overwhelming to most people. But I have clients who manage it. Two, to be exact. Sometimes we have one of those dogs here for boarding—Sam: Sam the dachshund—and he's a happy guy. But he drags his hindquarters around, and we have to express his bladder for him, just as you've been doing with Arthur. All that kind of thing. There's a lot of cleanup, a lot of work."

An image occurred to me. "Maybe you've seen this photo: it's kind of a famous photo, by Doisneau. It shows a dog in a cart on the street in Paris. They make carts for these dogs, the smaller ones," I explained. "You strap them in. Their hind legs. The picture is quite lovely, I think. Quite charming." I had been delighted when I discovered it, leafing through a collection of Doisneau's work in a bookstore in Boston. Two women talk animatedly in a doorway, and the dog sits in profile on the sidewalk in front of them—sleek, alert, poised to go—with his hindquarters slung easily over his tiny cart, a cart whose pretty wheels seem a winsome and somehow logical extension of his body.

But Eli's face had tightened in disgust. "No, I haven't seen it."

I pointed at him, at his face. "*That*, my friend," I said, "is why you hear this as a recommendation for euthanasia. You don't like any part of the idea."

He stared a moment, considering it, his jaw working slightly. "I'm afraid this is true," he said at last.

"Well, it's true for a lot of people. It's how they feel about damaged animals. And it's perfectly reasonable, it seems to me, when there's so much work involved for the owner. And I think . . . I mean, from what I understand, it sounds as though you and your wife, you and Jean, are pretty much at your limit with work and travel and the move. And"—it occurred to me suddenly—"do you have kids too?"

"No." Then he smiled. "Just Arthur here. Do you?" he asked, after a second or two.

"I do. Three. But they're all more or less grown and gone at this point. Three girls. Excuse me: *women*," I said. Separately, they paraded through my mind. Hello. Hello. Hello.

"And you're still married."

"Yes," I said.

"Yes," he echoed. He shook his head. "I would have bet money you were going to end up divorced."

I had a moment of confusion, and then I realized he was talking of my past, of the marriage I was running from when he knew me. "Oh! That marriage *did* end. Sorry!" I smiled. "I always feel that one doesn't even count." I laughed quickly, a funny, false noise that vaguely embarrassed me. "No, it was over right then, actually. All part of the counterlife. Or that dream we were all dreaming, or whatever it was. But I've been married to Daniel, to the girls' father, for twenty-five years or so now."

"Ah!" he said. And then we both fell silent, looking at Arthur.

"It's a very hard decision to make," I said gently. "The standard party line—I actually have a brochure I can give you—is to weigh certain factors against each other. But in the end, I think it probably rests more with what your feeling about animals is, whole versus not whole, and so forth. And how you see yourself, or humans generally, in relation to them. Big philosophical issues that translate into visceral, gut-level responses." His face had collapsed and become blank as he studied Arthur. "And then, unfortunately, have to get weighed against the kind of affection you feel for the dog."

"Yes," he said. His hands moved to Arthur again. The dog made a loving grumble of response.

"And it's hardest of all, I think, with this kind of injury." I gestured at Arthur's muzzle. "When they're not in pain and they're so normal in the front."

"Yes," he said softly.

We stood there for a moment, both looking at Arthur. He blinked and lowered his head to his paws, watching us, as though he understood we were talking about him.

"You certainly don't need to decide anything now," I said. "Or on any kind of schedule."

He cleared his throat. "The awful thing is I have decided. I'm just not ready to act on it."

"Well, that's fine too. Take him home again, get used to the idea.

Or as used to it as you can. And just call me whenever you're ready. We can keep him on the Valium, to make his life easier."

Another long silence fell. Then he looked at me keenly. "Do you do a lot of these?"

"Euthanasias?"

"Yes."

"Not enough to ever find it easy."

"Would you do it to a dog of yours in a similar situation? Do you have a dog?"

"I have three."

"Ah." He smiled. "One for each daughter."

"As it turned out. And the answer is I don't know what I'd do. I think I might find it easier than you to have an incapacitated dog around, just because of my work. But I can also think of situations my dogs could be in where I'd have no hesitation—none—about euthanasia." I had actually tried five or six years earlier to euthanize one of our own dogs myself. Lou. He was eighteen, incontinent, and so arthritic that he could barely move. He snapped when you tried to help him, it hurt so much. We had all adored him, for his beauty and strength and speed when young, for his gentleness, particularly with the girls when they were little, and for his great heart: whenever anyone in the household wept, he came and sat leaned against her, whimpering gently in sympathy. When I picked up the pink syringe of Beuthanasia, I started to cry so hard that I couldn't see through my tears to find a vein, and Mary Ellen had had to take over.

"But even that's beside the point," I said now. "It's your judgment and your feelings that matter."

"I understand that, of course. I just wondered."

Another silent moment passed. I looked quickly at my watch. Eli saw me.

He bent at once over Arthur and lifted him, just as I stepped toward him and touched his arm. "I'm sorry. I don't want to rush you."

"No. No, this is really between me and Arthur now. We don't need to take any more of your time. We shouldn't."

I came around behind him to open the door, and when he turned to me, our faces were suddenly very close. I could smell him, an expensive, lathery odor.

"I'll call you next week, then," he said. He smiled, a quick, sad smile. "That terrible line. True in this case."

I had stepped back. "I'm sorry it has to be."

He sobered. "And the Valium?"

"I'll meet you up front with it. How much do you want? A week's worth?"

His mouth tightened. "At the most," he said.

As he was standing in the front doorway to leave, a few minutes later, he turned to me, behind the counter, and said, "At some point, Jo, it'd be nice to talk about life. Life beyond dogs."

"Oh, is there such a thing?" I asked. I could feel Beattie's gaze shift sharply over to me from her computer.

He smiled again, and then he was gone.

"Who was that big fat man?" Beattie asked later. "You know, Mayhew, the one who belongs to Arthur."

"Beattie! He wasn't fat." We were moving around each other in the hallway office, she printing out billing records, I checking supplies.

"You know him from somewhere?"

"I do, actually. My deep, dark past. Why? What makes you ask?"

"Your voice was different, is all."

I thought about this, wondering if it was true.

"Well, *I* thought he was fat," Beattie said after a few moments. She wasn't looking at me. The printer ground away. "But I like 'em thin. Daniel, now. That's my type."

"You can't have him, Beattie."

Her laugh shrilled, and she walked off, trailing computer paper.

FALL SEEMED TO DEEPEN AS THE WEEK WENT BY. IT WAS colder, very cold at night, and often in the morning a frost clung to the golden grass. The brightest leaves—the cerise and pale yellow of the maples—were gone by now, and just the golden yellow of birches and the deep red-brown of oaks remained. The vistas had opened up slowly as the leaves fell and blew into bright piles that collected against the fence lines and shrubs, that pooled at the edges of the roads. Now you could take in the whole town at once, you could see past the white houses to the distant mountains beyond. All week I waited for Eli to call or appear. I thought of him often, of him and Arthur. But he didn't come in, and he didn't telephone.

Over the weekend, we had a reprieve suddenly: three Indian summer days—golden, warm. Daniel and I decided to take our Monday afternoon to put the storm windows in and clean them. We did this on opposite sides of the glass so we could talk as we went along and also point out streaks to each other. The air was dry and cool as it drifted over me in the house, but Daniel was working outside, in the sun. First he pulled off his sweatshirt, then the plaid flannel long-sleeved shirt under that. In his T-shirt and jeans, he looked lean and tough, like the bad boys I wasn't allowed to date in high school. I could see the muscles working in his arms, the cording tendons.

He caught me watching him as he rubbed the glass between us with his cloth, watching and not working. He stopped too. "What?" he said loudly.

I shook my head and grinned. I leaned forward and put my lips on the cool glass, pressed them. When I pulled back, I yelled, "You're cute."

He smiled and then raised his hand and tapped the glass by the mark of my lips. "Streak," he announced.

I made a face and wiped it away.

Ever since the Sunday I'd gone to church and then waited in bed for Daniel to come home—washed, perfumed, the space heater faintly humming on *high* so we could be naked in comfort—I'd been eager for him. Not all the time, to be sure, because our lives were so disparate and busy. But there it was, and the three times we had made love since had been with a newness, a wily attentiveness to each other, that surprised me. One of these times we'd actually tried it standing up in the kitchen, with me, in my striped bathrobe, backed up against the wall. But Daniel had abruptly cried, "Ah! no! no!" When we stopped, he said, "That was my back yelling, not me," so we'd shut the dogs in the kitchen and done it on the living room couch, with their dolorous halloos our distracting music.

And one night, when we were both tired, we spent a while laughing and arguing desultorily about who should do the work ("No, you get on *me*"), until finally I reached down between my legs and began lazily to touch myself. Daniel slid back to watch me. After a minute, he began to stroke himself, too, and we watched each other for a while, our breathing getting more and more ragged, until we both shut our eyes and arched away from each other, crying out over and over in a nicely timed duet.

It was all fun, but to me it felt a little abstract, too—a little the way I'd felt during those impulsive, driven months of hungry activity on and off through veterinary school. It made me wonder if there wasn't something about seeing Eli again—about the return of my past into my present life—that was fueling my appetite. Why does hunger come when it comes? Or need? And does it matter? Shouldn't we just be happy to have it arrive again from time to time? I didn't know, but I thought of it now as I watched Daniel at work through the glass.

Cass had called two nights before this. Her slow circle around the country was closing, bringing her back to us. She was in Pennsylvania now. She thought she'd be home for about a week at Thanksgiving, though she couldn't say for sure what day she'd arrive. Daniel and I talked about it during the intervals when I was lifting the panes from inside to set them in place or sliding them up, the intervals of only air between us.

I wanted to get all the girls home for the holiday. Daniel thought that was probably a mistake, that Cass might want us to herself, and that in any case, all three of them together often led to trouble. "If she wants to see Nora, she can easily go to New York," he said. He was perched on the extension ladder. Behind him, the sky opened up over the hills, and the dark road wound left and disappeared into pinewoods.

"But wouldn't you like to have us all together again? It won't happen that often in our lives as they get older and move away."

"I don't know," he said. I hoisted the glass up between us, and we lifted our plastic bottles and sprayed at each other. As we both began to wipe at the mist, as Daniel's composed face began to come clear, frowning in private concentration at his task, I thought of Eli Mayhew suddenly, that open, expansive quality to the way he looked now. People could change, I thought, and I wondered for an idle moment if Eli had found that true of me. And if so, how.

In the end, Daniel agreed to my issuing a Thanksgiving invitation to all the girls. That night I called Nora.

"How long will she be there?"

"It's not clear, natch."

"Natch is right." She sighed. "Damn! I have this *project* due. I wasn't even going to have Thanksgiving."

"Yeah, we were just going to have a minimal thing ourselves, just with Sadie, 'cause Daddy has that big church meal the Sunday before."

"Christ!" she said. I could imagine her gnawing her lower lip, a habit she didn't share with Cassie. "Well, I suppose I can work it out."

I was silent for a moment, feeling guilty, but then irritated at having to feel that way. "Look, Nor," I finally said. "It's not written in stone. I said *nothing* to Cass about it; it was just an idea I had."

"No, I'll come." Her voice was resigned.

"But now I feel guilty. I'm not putting pressure on you, honest I'm not."

"Mom, come on. I really *do* want to see her. I haven't for more than a year, and she *is* my sister. My twin, for God's sake."

After a beat, I said, "Brian's welcome, too, you know."

She made a light snorting noise. "I'll spare him, I think."

After I got off the phone, I thought of this response and I felt wounded. Was this how she saw us? Some difficult, O'Neill-like family she had to shield her boyfriend from?

As we walked the dogs later, I told Daniel about it. He disagreed with my interpretation. "She's just feeling what I was, that the two of them closed in together for a long weekend is a recipe for trouble."

"It doesn't have to be."

"No, but it often is."

"You'll help me, won't you, Daniel?" I must have sounded lonely or frightened to him, because he stopped me on the dark sidewalk and kissed my cheek. Actually, because it was so dark—pitch dark, as we were on a side street, away from even the feeble lanterns around the green—he missed and got my ear. We swayed together a moment. When we turned to walk again, he kept his arm around me.

Lights were off in most of the houses we passed—it was nearly eleven. The town was silent but for the odd barking of a dog. When we walked by the middle of the three Georgian houses facing the green, we looked over as one to the glowing windows of its front parlor. The room was empty, the lamplight fell on an empty chair. We turned away. A little breeze lifted my hair, brought us the smell of dry leaves, of pine. "This is so perfect," I said. "This weather." I sighed. "This is why we live in New England."

The next morning it was snowing wetly, big plops smeared against the windows. When I opened the kitchen door, the raw damp air blew in, and the dogs milled around behind me with their tails down. "Get!" I said. They cast tragic glances back at me as I shut the door on them.

"Did you know about this?" I asked Daniel when he came in for coffee. He was a weather fanatic, a holdover from his youth on the farm. There weather told you what you'd be doing on any given day.

"I did."

"And you let me be romantic about our fall night? You laughed *up your sleeve* at me?"

He shrugged. "That's just the perfidious kind of guy I am."

"I'll say."

The drops gathered into clear slush at the sides of my windshield as I drove to work. The wet glistened on the road. Feeling sleepy, I stopped off at the bagel place to pick up some coffee.

"How'ja like Mother Nature's joke?" the owner asked me energetically. Malcolm. He ran the place single-handedly.

"She can stuff it," I said.

"Joey, Joey!" he scolded, grinning. He shook his head as he rang me up.

Though normally she worked just Monday, Wednesday, and Saturday, Mary Ellen was in today; she wanted Saturday off this week for her son's birthday party. It was sometimes crowded moving around in the hallway, with all the dogs and people. Late in the morning, Beattie came back to my exam room. "Your old boyfriend called," she said. Her lips were pinched disapprovingly.

"He's not my boyfriend, Beattie."

"Didn't say he was. I said, 'Your *old* boyfriend.' "

"He wasn't *ever* my boyfriend."

"Well, he called. He's coming in this afternoon." She sniffed.

"To put the dog down."

"Yep." She stood for a moment, watching me, waiting for some response. She cleared her throat. "I ask myself, you know, what I would do. I wouldn't do that."

"Beattie," I said, suddenly irritated, "you don't even have any animals."

She turned to go. "It doesn't matter, does it?" From the hall she called back, "I know what I know."

As I went to tell Mary Ellen I'd need her later for a euthanasia, I was smiling, smiling at Beattie. These were famous lines of hers, spoken, usually, at exactly the moment when she did not know what she did not know. I was thinking, *I'll tell Daniel*—we had a store of her pronouncements. But then I realized where she'd come from to get to what she didn't know, and I told myself that the story was based in a kind of animosity to Eli Mayhew that seemed too complicated and preposterous to explain.

The snow continued wetly through the day, sometimes lightening briefly—the sun nearly breaking through and graying the sparse flakes—then thickening again, closing the world up around us. Night had fallen by four, a combination of the effect of the storm and the recent change from daylight savings time. The last two clients of the day had already called to cancel.

Mary Ellen and I went up front to where Beattie had the radio turned to the news. We all stood around listening and eating cookies that Mary Ellen had had to buy at the bake sale for her day care center. Finally the announcer got to the weather: The snow was icing up now that the temperature was dropping; there'd already been a few fender benders in the evening commute. I looked outside. It was four-thirty, and our three cars were the only ones left in the parking lot.

Beattie worriedly announced that she thought maybe she ought to go home early. Mary Ellen and I assured her this was fine. And actually, I was glad. I hadn't wanted her around for Arthur's euthanasia. Not that I thought she'd say or do anything while Eli was there, but she might make me uncomfortable somehow afterward. I was just as happy not to have to think about her comments.

We told her now we'd help her close out the office, and we all began to move easily and efficiently around each other, turning off machines, locking up medications, filing, cleaning. Then Beattie was standing behind her desk, adding layer upon layer of sweaters and outerwear, most of them baggy and vividly colored and knit by herself. As I headed back to set up for Arthur and Eli, I heard her call, "See you tomorrow!" and I yelled, "Drive carefully." The bell on the door jangled as she closed it.

After she left, it occurred to me that I didn't know whether we would dispose of Arthur's body or Eli would take it. When I was finished in back, I went to Beattie's station behind the front counter and turned on her computer. I called up Eli's file. There was usually a note as to the disposition of the body, and Beattie had made one here: Eli would take Arthur home. I went up to the start of the file, and there was the address. 11 Duxbury Court.

Fancy. Expensive. A newish development in what had been the wooded part of an old estate. Eli's home, and Arthur's grave. I thought of the trails that had crisscrossed through the land before it was developed, of how, deep in the woods, you could see crumbling stone fences that had once marked off the open fields of old farms. Townspeople had used the estate for bird-watching, for walking dogs, as we sometimes did, or just as a retreat, a nearby place to go that made them feel far away from the world. When the owner died and his family sold it to a developer, there were protests and outraged letters in the local paper. To no avail. Time marched on. And brought me, I thought, Eli Mayhew.

I closed down the computer and went to my exam room to wait.

Eli arrived just after five-thirty. When I heard the bell jangle, I stepped into the hall and called out his name. He appeared around the corner with Arthur in his arms. He came slowly down the hall. He set the dog down on the table again. His face was grim and flat, and I realized by its absence now how much animation had livened it before.

"How long does it take?" he asked. He was unwinding a long, elegant scarf from his neck. Snowdrops glistened on the shoulders of his jacket.

"Just seconds, really. Some people prefer to stay, and other people say goodbye and wait outside. Whatever feels right to you."

"Jesus, nothing feels *right* about this. But I'm staying." He wouldn't look at me, I noticed. His face seemed shut in anger or pain.

I kept my voice gentle. "I need to tell you, then, that it may not be easy. It should be, and most of the time it is—they just go to sleep. But some dogs vocalize. Some lose bowel or bladder control. Some thrash around a bit. I think what it is is that the feeling of the drug disturbs them."

"They *cry*?" he said.

"Yes. Howl for a few seconds."

He turned sharply away. "Jesus."

"Arthur most likely won't. I hope he doesn't. But I want you to be prepared if he does."

There was a long silence in the room. Eli's hands—I noticed again how large they were, but with long, graceful fingers—stroked Arthur's shiny fur, over and over. Finally he did look up at me, to say, "I don't know how you do this."

I shrugged. "Some vets won't." But that had always seemed the cruelest choice to me—when people needed it, to send them searching for someone who would do it, someone they and their animal didn't know.

"But you chose to."

"I don't *like* it, Eli."

"No," he said. "No, of course not."

We stood glumly for a minute. I was intensely aware of the bright-pink syringe lying on my table. "Do you want a minute alone to say goodbye?" I asked.

He shook his head. "I said goodbye." He looked up at me, his eyes shiny. "Let's do it," he said abruptly.

I opened the door and called Mary Ellen. She came nearly instantly; she'd been waiting too. I made the briefest of introductions—a gesture, really, and their names—and then I turned away to get the syringe while she reached for Arthur's front leg. "You can hold him, if you like," I said to Eli. When I turned back, I saw that he had bent over Arthur, his face buried in the dog's neck. He was speaking gently, saying what a good boy Arthur was, repeating this over and over. Arthur was making a soft, throaty noise of pleasure and poking at him with his muzzle.

Mary Ellen nodded at me: she was ready. I came around her in front of Arthur, set my fingers beside the vein, and injected the needle. I pulled back slightly at the start, and the blood eased in—I had the vein. Quickly I pushed the pink fluid in.

Arthur had turned to me briefly at the stick, but then he relaxed. And within a few seconds he went limp and rolled slightly farther to his side. I heard Eli's sharp intake of breath. I had my fingers on Arthur's vein now. I had felt the throbbing slow and stop. Nothing. I nodded at Mary Ellen and she left, silently. Now I set my stethoscope on Arthur. After a few seconds, I said to Eli, "He's gone."

Eli stood up. He was looking down at Arthur, who lay utterly relaxed on his side now, his eyes slightly open. Eli's eyes were red, his face was pulled into deep lines, nose to mouth, mouth to chin.

My hands were trembling. "I'm sorry," I said. I reached out to touch his arm, feeling his unfamiliar solidity under the thick fabric of his jacket. His head swayed slightly on his neck as if in response, and I remembered suddenly the way he'd looked when I saw him in the police station after Dana died.

"I know," he said, and turned again to the dead dog.

He left a few minutes later, carrying Arthur out into the heavy wet snowfall in the box we provided. I stood at the door, watching him set the box down tenderly, watching him open the car and then load Arthur in.

Mary Ellen was suddenly behind me, her hand on my shoulder. "You okay?" she said.

I turned to her. She had her coat on, and big purple boots. She would probably be late to pick up her son at day care. Her broad, pretty face was tense behind her glasses.

"I am. It's never easy, is it?"

"No," she said.

"Thanks for staying."

"You've done it for me," she said. She pulled her hat on, and some mittens. Nothing matched. "Is he a friend?" she asked. She was gesturing at the parking lot. Arthur and Eli were gone.

"Kind of," I said. "Someone I knew way back when, who just moved here."

"Beattie said something like that." She pulled her shoulders square. "Well," she announced. "I gotta go."

"Oh, I know," I said. "Go. Go." I waved her away.

"You're okay."

"I really am," I said.

"Treat yourself when you get home," she said.

"Thanks, Mary Ellen," I said.

And then I was alone. I moved around the office slowly, putting a few things away, wiping down my table. I left a note for Ned, explaining that we'd left a little early. I got my coat on.

The air outside was raw, and I was sorry I hadn't taken the time to get out winter clothes this morning. Gloves anyway, or maybe a hat. Had I not believed in the snow, after yesterday's warm sunshine? It was still melting now as it landed, but the ground felt icy underfoot. I sat in the car and let it warm up, my breath a pale shadow in front of my face with each exhalation.

The houses along the back roads home were lighted for the most part. Here and there you could see someone—usually a woman—moving around, or the bluish flicker of a TV. Daniel wouldn't be home yet. Our house would be dark. I pulled up to a red light at the intersection of Bishops Pond Road. If I turned left instead of right here when the light changed to green, I would have only a half mile or so to get to Eli's house. I imagined the way it would look—massive, many-windowed, many-terraced. I imagined Eli, carrying the box that held Arthur.

Do you do many of these? Eli had asked.

Hundreds by now. Maybe a thousand. Always with a kind of breathlessness at the last moment. A fear of it, I suppose. A fear, of course, that it might not go well, that the animal might keen or howl, as some did, or that the owner might be overwhelmed by grief. But mostly, just a kind of terror of the speed with which it happened once I gave the injection, of how quickly the line between life and death was crossed. I thought of that moment with Arthur, his utter relaxation into death within seconds, my hands on him as he went over. Eli there.

And then I realized that the Eli who floated somewhere close by this image in my mind, the Eli who bent over his dog, was the young Eli, the Eli standing alone on the porch as I pulled away in a cab from the house on Lyman Street. Consciously I tried to focus on the older Eli's face. And could not quite get it. I realized I was confusing him visually with an old friend of Daniel's from divinity school, another big, slightly paunchy man who had visited us occasionally over the years when he was on the East Coast.

The light changed, and I turned right, for home. In the headlights, the snow thickened with a dizzying motion. I drove slowly, and after I'd pulled into our driveway and turned the lights off, I sat for a long time in the dark, watching the wet flakes swirl and thinking in a confused overlay of the house on Lyman Street and of putting Arthur down—so that it seemed to me nearly as though I'd done it then, in that world, in that other life.

CHAPTER

WHEN I CAME INTO THE KITCHEN TWO DAYS BEFORE
Thanksgiving, Daniel pointed to the dirty duffel bag, the
banged-up guitar case by the back door, and said, "Cass."
"Where is she?" I asked, still stupid from sleep.

He raised his eyes and pointed his thumb at the ceiling. Upstairs.
"Sleeping, I reckon."

"Did you hear her?" I asked.

"I heard something, but I thought it was just the dogs."

I poured coffee. "Damn it, why does she do this? I have to go to
work."

"I'll stay home. I just have calls and letters, and I can do them
here."

"Will you call me when she gets up? Or have her call. Maybe I can
weasel home early somehow. Or for lunch or something."

"She'll understand."

"But it's so familiar!" I pulled out a chair and sat down opposite
him at the table. "She doesn't say when she's coming, so I can't be here
to welcome her, so she'll be hurt and I'll feel bad." I drank some coffee. "But also set up. Da *dah*, da *dah*. And off we go again."

"Don't get ahead of everything, Joey. Maybe she's mellowed." He
was smiling at me.

I looked out the window at the dooryard. No cars but our own.
"How'd she get here, I wonder."

"Somebody must have dropped her off."

"What time do you think you heard her?"

"I didn't look. More night than morning, though."

Allie came and rested her head on my thigh. Good morning. I stroked her fur, absently pulled at a burr stuck in it. "God, I wish I could stay. I'm so excited to see her. I wish I could stay. I wish I were you and you were me."

"Mmm. Me too. Then you could call all the members of the fund-raising committee."

"And you could check the stool samples."

"And you could tell the roofer we'll have to pay him in installments."

"And you could catheterize Florence Dicey's cat."

He smiled at me. "Horrible lives, aren't they? Interchangeably and profoundly horrible."

I couldn't get away all day. When I arrived home, late in the afternoon, Cass was in the tub—I could hear her singing upstairs over the faint rumble of running water. Daniel had left me a note on the kitchen table, saying he'd be back for dinner briefly at around six, reporting that he and Cass had made chili, suggesting that maybe I could throw a salad together. The table was set for three, the kitchen was neat, the dogs' bowls were full. The dogs themselves were circling me frantically, and now I stopped to pet each one and then released them into the dark night air. When I flicked the outside light on, it caught their rumps disappearing, the long bushy tails swinging with pleasure as they plunged into the black thicket under the pine trees.

I pried off my boots, hung up my coat, and then climbed the steep painted stairs, pulling on the wooden handrail. Cass's duffel was open on the floor of her room now, and her clothes were sorted into several messy piles. The bed was made. I leaned against the noisy bathroom door and knocked. "Cass?" I yelled. "Cassie, it's Mom."

The water stopped. "Mom?"

"Yes, I'm home."

"Three secs. Two. I'll be right down."

In the kitchen, I poured myself some wine. I rinsed the lettuce and made a dressing. I could hear Cass moving around upstairs. I wanted to go to her, but I felt I'd been instructed not to, told to wait.

Finally I heard her on the stairs. I rushed into the living room and met her as she emerged from the narrow stairwell.

"Darling!" I cried. She was thin, her hair was nearly shaved, but her face was innocent and open in embarrassed pleasure, and she looked pretty. I held her. Bones, bones. How mushy I must feel to her! We rocked together a moment. Then I felt her slight withdrawal. Quickly I released her. "Let me *see* you. Let me see *this* incarnation," I said.

She laughed and twirled around in a charming gesture—but a gesture, too, that let her move farther away from me. Her expression was still perfectly pleasant, but it had somehow closed up. She was much too thin, I saw now. Her jeans hung loosely off her hips and legs, bagged a little at her bottom. Her hair was bluish fuzz on her skull. She had an earring in one eyebrow and a semicircle of a dozen or so more arcing along the outer curve of one ear. She wore a tight orange top, leopard-dotted. Her breasts had gotten nearly flat, her rib cage was clearly outlined. On her feet were thick, orthopedic-looking black boots. But she had smelled clean and soapy when I held her, her eyes now were bright, and her skin, Daniel's pale skin, was clear and taut.

"The hair is an adjustment for me, I have to say, but you look great."

"Well, I had to shave it." She made a face. "It was so fucked up from the last dye job that I had no choice." She was wearing dark eye makeup, like kohl, all around her eyes. They looked, as my mother used to say, like two burned holes in a blanket.

We went into the kitchen so I could heat up the chili and pour her some wine. She began to talk, pacing, sipping, finally sitting down at the table. The talk seemed pressured, as though she needed it—a miracle, for silent, sullen Cass. I busied myself putting clean dishes away, wiping counters. I was fearful of coming too close, even of sitting opposite her, fearful of seeming to want more than she was giving. Or of wanting anything at all, really. Cass made you careful.

"I've gotten so I really really hate it," she was saying. "Just the kind of stupid interactions, the way things have to get negotiated. You know, who has power over who, who's going to decide. But it's all such crap. Like, decide where to spend the night? I mean, what are the options? Ever? We either have one place or none. And who cares? And it's, like, once Stellie left"—the other girl in the band—"I was supposed to be, like, everyone's mother. They were always confiding things. Ugh. Creepy things. Even Raimondo. Who wants to know? I'd tell them. Who wants to know stuff like the girl you once beat up, or the time you made it with a guy, or who followed you into the men's room and did what to you tonight after the show."

Sometimes I thought she wanted me to probe—I could feel her eyes skitting over to me after she said something that might have shocked me—but I stayed quiet. I made the most noncommittal of comments, or just mild noises. Olive Oyl on Prozac.

"So I think this is it for me. We have, like, six gigs after Christmas all up and down the coast, and then I'm done with it. I bail."

It suddenly occurred to me with a kind of yank of the heart—fear? pleasure?—that she might be suggesting she'd like to live at home again. "And then what will you do, you think?"

"New Yawhk!" she cried. "I'm gonna go get famous." She laughed. "And spit in all their eyes."

Whose eyes? I wanted to ask. Why? But some part of me relaxed—my life with Daniel wouldn't have to change—and then I felt mean because of that.

I was hoping she hadn't noticed my relief. But she was safely launched in another direction: "See, I met this guy in Washington, and he handles models, sort of drugged-looking models. Not, like, pretty-girl stuff—I mean, it wasn't like he was coming on to me. But he said he was sure I could do it. I guess I have that certain *sordid* beauty they want." She posed suddenly, pouting, pushing her shoulders forward, elongating her arms, deadening her face, and I saw that she was like an ad I'd seen. For what? Underwear, maybe. Perfume. I wasn't sure.

"My hair should get kind of, like, a little longer, but no problem, it will be by then, and then, if I can just get some cash together, maybe Stellie and I can cut a demo or something. That's the big dream. The modeling, if that works out, is fine, but it's more, like, kind of a means to an end."

"So you got thin for that."

She laughed roughly. "I got thin, Mother dear, because I haven't had enough *food* to eat. Because I've stayed up too late doing naughty things." I could hear that she was pleased to be telling me this, pleased to introduce me to the harsh realities of her life. "But that *is* why he offered me the job, so I dassn't fatten up much. We have to keep the home-cooking scene here pretty minimal. We want those bones to stick right out there." She tapped her clavicles with her purple fingernails.

When Daniel came home I relaxed a bit. He was much easier with her, much more able to ask her things directly. I felt, though, that the version of her life she offered him was different from what she had wanted to show to me. With him she talked about the music she'd written, the limitations of the band, what she thought she might be able to do with Stellie in New York. Once or twice she alluded to something darker, but she didn't seem to have the desire to shock Daniel, or to wound him, with what was painful to hear about in her life. If that's what she'd wanted from me.

Was it? I had never known with Cass. And the truth was she probably didn't know either. When I was most confused by her, it helped me to remember myself at her age—just that egocentric, just that lost, just that uncaring about the pain I might be causing others, because I felt I was in so much pain myself.

After supper, Daniel left and Cass helped me clean up. Then she asked to borrow my car. She wanted to go to the Sidecar, a bar two towns over that featured local bands. "I just want to see what's happening, see if anyone I know is around. I won't be late."

But Daniel was long home from his church group and we were both in bed with the light out when she came in. I listened to her moving slowly through the living room, murmuring to the dogs as she made her way. Their paws clicked wildly on the floor in their dance of excitement. She stumbled on the first step up and said, "Shit!" clearly. The floorboards upstairs creaked and groaned and marked her progress until she'd gotten safely into bed.

I relaxed then, I changed position. I spoke Daniel's name, barely audibly.

"I'm awake," he whispered back. "Reminds me of the bad old days. Doesn't it?"

Yes. Yes, it did. The times when one of the girls was out until dawn and we didn't know whether to call the police or not. The time when friends had brought Nora home so drunk that she threw up before we could get her to the bathroom. The time when Sadie called from Hadley to say she'd wrecked the car and cut her forehead open. All the times when Daniel and I lay like this, side by side in the dark, unsure, unknowing, scared as children; while the children moved dangerously around in the world, learning to be adults.

THE NEXT DAY, A HALF DAY OF WORK FOR ME, CASS OFFERED to go get Sadie at school and to do the shopping I needed done on the way. Both girls came stumbling in with grocery bags just as dusk was falling—and the first few flakes of what was predicted to be a blizzard. They were noisy and cheerful, and their speed and energy and sheer volume reminded me of the happiest days of their adolescence.

We had a light supper—chowder and corn bread, fruit for dessert. After dinner, I got the stuffing ready while Daniel and Sadie made two pies. Cass sat at the table with a glass of wine, disappearing outside occasionally to have a cigarette. We could see her through the kitchen windows under the falling snow, her breath itself as cloudy as smoke, her skull covered by a wool cap, her body huddled against the cold as she drew luxuriantly on the cigarette.

When the pies were in the oven, we all moved to the living room. Cass played us a few of her own songs—gloomy and elliptical, but with complex, even lovely rhyme schemes. It was hard to get a sense of what they might sound like in performance: she kept interrupting herself to tell us what Stellie would be doing now ("She's going, like, 'aa-oaah, ah, ah' ") or what the bass player would be up to. But when she finished we all applauded, and she flushed and suddenly looked girlish and sweet. Sadie pulled two red tulips out of the pitcher on the table next to her and tossed them to Cassie, who stood to pick them up, pressed them dramatically—elegantly—to what there was of her bosom, and then suddenly curtsied to the floor, showing us fully the smooth, shadowy surface of the top of her head.

Afterward she played some tapes for us, tapes of her band and of a few others she knew. Standing by the tape deck after the first few songs, she started to sway in rhythm, tentatively, then assuredly. Sadie jumped up and joined her. Together they moved around the room, as all three girls used to do occasionally in high school, each lost in a separate, wild response to the beat—Sadie's more a matter of bouncing, almost leaping, up and down, her arms moving like wings, elbows in the lead; Cass doing a kind of step dance in her clunky boots. They both kept their eyes nearly closed in pleasure, they wore eager, rapacious smiles. They were showing us something, marking some difference between themselves and us with their loose, beautiful bodies, with their response to the music. I loved to watch them, but it made me sad too.

Both of them were pinked and glistening with sweat when Daniel and I met each other's eyes and he announced, in the break between two songs, that we were going to walk the dogs and then go to bed.

Cass ran to the tape deck and clicked it off. "No, no, no, let us do it. Sadie, lookit the snow!" She went to the window. We all got up and followed.

Outside, the world had been transformed, all the particular shapes and structures of our yard gentled, humped. Each dark branch of the horse chestnut was outlined in white. The light post wore a jaunty, perfectly balanced cap of it. The snow still fell, slow fat flakes in the windless air. We were silent a moment.

"This is *perfect*," Sadie announced then. "God, isn't it great? I have a holiday and we get snowed in. I ordered this!" she cried.

"I worry about Nor," I said to Daniel.

"Don't. It'll all be plowed by the time she starts out," he said. "Especially because it's Thanksgiving."

"What time is she getting here?" Cass asked. I was standing right behind her. She smelled of wine and tobacco and bath oil, and faintly, too, of perspiration, a salty odor.

"Noony, she thought," I answered.

" 'Noony'?!" Sadie cried. She and Cass looked at each other and grinned. " 'Noony,' " Sadie repeated. "She said 'Noony'!"

"What's so funny about that?"

"It's the kind of thing you're always saying, Mom."

Cass began to sing, moving her splayed hands in stylized punctuation: "Noony. / By the way, it rhymes with moony. / If you'd rather, Georgie Clooney. / *But Mom said it:* / Noony . . ."

I waved dismissively at them and headed for the bedroom. But I was feeling a kind of sweet delight at their amusement—an amusement Cass would never have indulged on her own. Maybe Sadie could show Cass a way to be occasionally affectionate about my foibles, my failures, instead of always angry. Just as I shut the bedroom door, I thought to yell at them, "And bundle up! You're all overheated, and vulnerable."

They burst into laughter and drifted out to the kitchen. " 'Overheated and vulnerable,' " I heard Sadie repeating.

When Daniel came to bed, I leaned over and bit his shoulder through his flannel pajamas.

"What for?" he complained.

"For being the old progenitor here. I love what we made. I love having them home."

"Um," he said. And then he made his voice formal and raised a warning finger: "Let us see what the morrow brings."

"Oh, don't be a pill! You love it too. You know it."

"I do," he said.

Just then there was a sharp rapping at the window. Daniel slid out of bed and pulled the shade up. The two of them stood under the falling snow, waving to us. Their hats were pulled down over their ears, across their foreheads, which rounded their faces and made them look like children again. Their cheeks glowed.

Now they stepped forward and pressed their faces against the glass, smashing their noses flat and white, smearing their lips to one side, gooey monsters. Daniel feigned horror and quickly pulled the shade down again. We heard them laughing. A moment later, a snowball, then another and another, hit the glass. Then their voices faded into the storm, and the dogs' excited barking slowly moved away.

Off and on through the night I woke to the clanking passage of the plows, nearby or furred through distance. Beyond that there was only the cocooning silence of the thick snow surrounding the house. It was still falling heavily when I rose in the dark at six-thirty. I'd offered to do the morning and suppertime shifts with the boarding animals. Ned and Mary Ellen would handle the rest.

I ate a slice of toast while the car warmed up. It took me a while to clean its windows, and I had to rock it twice to get it out of the drive-way, but the roads were scraped and sanded, and then salted, too, once I got out on the two-lane highway.

Our mall hadn't been plowed yet, so I parked at its edge and trudged across it through the prairie of deep snow. The dogs heard me opening the front door and began to cry and bark, and when I turned the lights on, the din became general.

The dogs we had for this long weekend all got along, except for a male husky–German shepherd mix named Lucky. I left him in his cage for a while and released all the others. They milled around me like so many scattering pool balls, sniffing me and each other, and then moved loosely with me to the back door. When I opened it, they burst into the yard—a flood of seven happy dogs, more than usual because of the holiday—and began larking around. All but one, a fat old Cairn named Watson. He stopped by my feet in the doorway, taking in the hostile transformation of the universe. The snow was deeper than he was tall. He turned and started to go back in.

"Ah, ah!" I said. I picked up his tight, barrel-shaped body and carried him to the center of the yard, set him down where the snow was already dented from the bigger dogs' play. As he circled to find the perfect spot, he picked each paw up and gave it the most delicate of shakes, a kind of rumba of fastidiousness. Finally he did his business. Then he made a bounding yet dainty run, nearly like the hopping of a rabbit in the deep snow, back to the open door and in.

I stood in the center of the yard for a moment and tilted my head back to let the soft snow touch my face. The dogs pranced and rolled for pure joy in the pale, gray-brown light. They chased each other wildly. I made snowballs and threw them; the dogs leapt and bit at where they'd disappeared. As they played, their muzzles whitened, their paws pilled up.

I left them reluctantly and came back in. Watson trailed me around as I did my chores, watching me soberly. I shut him out of the cat room, where we had only two boarders. I let one of them out to roam and use the litter pan while I checked its cage. I put more food down. Then I went back out and worked my way through the dogs' cages. Two of the dogs had had accidents, so I cleaned up and changed their bedding. Several of them had their own food, in cans—those dishes needed to be washed. Water refreshed, kibble set out for the others.

I went to the cat room, put the first cat back and let the other one out. Then I called the reluctant dogs in. Watson greeted each one like a tiny worried mother, licking at their snow, fussing about how they smelled. Slowly I recaged them. I released Lucky and let him go outside for his solitary run while I refilled his food and water dishes. Three dogs needed medications. I put the last cat back in, called Lucky inside, locked up.

And while I did all this, I thought only of them, of the dogs and cats, of their requests for affection, of their comical or passionate relations to one another, of the performance of their bodily functions. I was taken up by them and their life and energy, by what they needed and asked of me. I let go of everything difficult or complex in my life.

It reminded me of my days at Dr. Moran's, caring for the dogs and cats he boarded and treated. It reminded me of what a comfort it had been to me, even just physically, the escape into the lives of animals. As I was driving home, I thought of all this, and it seemed to me that I'd chosen work which offered me daily the presence of a pure innocence, a forgiveness for all my human flaws. It occurred to me suddenly that this, too, might be a kind of running away. A thought I dismissed quickly. Or didn't dismiss, exactly, but allowed to be subsumed in memories that came to me now, memories of what my earlier, real running away had brought me: Dana. Lyman Street. Eli.

Eli, whom I'd see the next day.

For we were having a party—we'd decided on it after Nora agreed to come home—in order to dilute what might be the intensity of the family weekend. It was Daniel's suggestion, and he'd offered to make several of his party dishes—a mammoth pork stew, roasted chicken wings. He'd also suggested I ask Eli and Jean. What he actually said was, "And why don't you ask Eli Mayhew, since you have such a flaming crush on him? And Sadie would like having his wife, I suppose."

"Daniel! I don't have a crush on Eli!" I said. "How can you say such a thing?"

"Okay, you don't have a crush on him," he said, smiling. "Ask them anyway."

It was only later, a day or two later, after I'd thought about it and realized how often I'd spoken of Eli since I'd seen him again, that I acknowledged to Daniel that I did, in a *certain way*, as I put it, have a crush on Eli. And I started to explain the web of memory and loss and yearning I'd spun around Eli's arrival in my life. But he just grinned at me. And then laughed as I kept earnestly at it. Finally I gave up, smacking him lightly several times on the butt as he danced away from me, crying out in mock pain.

But here's what I thought: that if I had a crush, it was on an earlier Eli, one who didn't exist anymore, and the real Eli was just a vehicle for it. Or, perhaps even more complicated, that the crush—if you could call something so psychologically distorted by such a playful name—was on myself. The middle-aged Eli contained for me, of course, his youthful self, yes. But he contained *me* also. The self that had known him then. Myself-when-young. And that was what made him attractive to me. You read or hear every now and then of a romance starting up between middle-aged or even elderly people who knew each other years earlier. People who throw over long-established, comfortable marriages or sensible lives for the chance to love again in a particular way—a way that connects them with who they used to be, with how it felt to be that person. And now, with Eli's arrival in my life, I could understand the potency of that connection.

The self-intoxication you pass off to yourself as intoxication with someone else.

So yes, I said to Daniel. I did, I had a crush on Eli Mayhew. And now I looked forward to the party, to seeing him there. We'd asked the girls for names of their friends to invite, and so it would be a big gathering, fifty or sixty people, and it would include all ages, even some babies, the first of the children of Cass and Nora's friends. When I called to ask Eli and Jean, she'd answered the phone. I told her there would be a real cross-section of the population of Adams Mills, and she sounded delighted. "I feel as though we've barely even had time to look around us so far, and we've met almost no one, so this is wonderful. How nice of you." After a pause, she said, "What should I *wear?*" and we both laughed.

Now, driving home on this snowy morning, I wondered how it would go, how it would be to see Eli in a purely social context. Mentally I'd rehearsed various conversations we might have. It seemed possible we would speak of the past, it seemed possible we might offer each other some new ways of thinking about the pain and confusion of that time, some new ways of understanding who each of us was then.

And it also seemed possible—and more likely, I reminded myself—that we would make standard chatter. That Eli would become just another pleasant person I knew in Adams Mills.

DANIEL AND SADIE WERE UP WHEN I CAME IN. SHE WAS IN her bathrobe at the table, drinking coffee, a new habit for her, one that made her look older, to my eyes almost jaded. Daniel was peeling potatoes at the sink.

"Ooh!" she cried. "Cold air!" She clutched her bathrobe around her throat. "Shut the door! Shut the door!"

"It is shut, darling. It's just a little atmosphere that's attached itself to me."

"Is it awful out?" Daniel said.

"Not so much, actually. But the snow is really deep and heavy. Wet."

"Nor called," he said. "She's started."

"Well, the main roads seem fine. Tons of salt. She'll arrive coated with it. But our *yard*, Daniel!"

"I know. I'll get on it before she turns up."

I kissed Sadie's head, her smooth brown hair. She smelled of sham-poo. "How'd you sleep? Have enough covers up there?"

"Mmm. I was snuggly. But Cassie! She snored like a big fat old *man* all night long. I could hear her even through the walls!"

"That must have made her particularly popular on those nights when they all slept together in the van."

"God, the whole van probably vibrated."

"What time will Nora get here—did she say?" I asked Daniel. I moved over and stood next to him, watching his quick hands flick potato peels into the sink. He was still wearing his pajama top. His hair was wild.

"She thinks around one, unless there's some problem on the road."

"So you think dinner around two?"

"Yeah, I should think so. She'll be starving."

"But we don't want to cut it too close, in case she's late."

"I suppose that's right."

"Have you noticed," Sadie piped up in her baby voice, "that when we're all home, half the conversation is logistics? Who's going where, what time, how, who'll drive. Like that."

Daniel turned to her and grinned. "Half logistics and the other half battles to the death."

"Daniel!" I cried. "God, what a depressing thought." And I went to change out of my scrubs.

Of course, there was truth to his remark, and it was the reason he had been reluctant to have all the girls home at once. Our holidays in particular had a history of disaster. Once, in childhood, upset about some slight, Cassie had run away Thanksgiving morning. We hadn't noticed she was gone for more than an hour, at which point Daniel started driving around looking for her and I began to call friends. By noon, the turkey in the oven, Nora baby-sitting for Sadie ("Do I get paid for this?"), each of us was out in a separate car, cruising all the back roads slowly, stopping and hiking across the dry, pale-brown meadows to any place she'd ever shown interest in—Bishops Pond, the woods behind the Holt estate, the old mill site, the playground behind the school.

We'd agreed to meet every forty-five minutes back at home, and I remember waiting for Daniel's car in the driveway, watching for the little bump of her head in silhouette in the front seat, and never seeing it; Daniel shaking his head as he got out of the car to confer with me, his mouth bitten in, a grim line. At four, I came back early, certain any more looking was fruitless, and went to call the police—in Daniel's study, I thought, so Sadie and Nora wouldn't hear me and be frightened.

And there was Cass, curled up asleep in his daybed, her thumb to her mouth, her face streaked with the dirty traces of tears. She'd been in the barn earlier, she said when I woke her, but it got too cold, so she'd come in here, " 'cause it reminded me of Daddy." As though he were the one who'd run away.

On another occasion, Sadie had decided she was vegetarian, on moral grounds. No turkey for her, thank you—just stuffing and pota-toes. These she doused liberally with gravy. After Sadie had almost cleared her plate, Cass leaned over and asked, "Know what gravy is made of, dummy?"

"Cass, don't," I said, realizing only at this moment what we'd let Sadie do.

"No, what?"

"Blood and gooey fat that's dripped down from your poor, inno-cent, slaughtered, turkey-lurkey."

There was a silence. "No, it's not," Sadie said. Cass grinned even more widely. "Is it, Mom?" She turned to me.

"Cass," I said, "I could skin you alive."

Sadie shrieked and rose from the table. "You made me! I hate you—you made me eat it."

"Sweetie," I was saying. "We didn't notice." I couldn't say, *We didn't care.*

But she was running off now. Her chair went crashing against the wall as she spun away from it. You could hear her feet thudding on the stairs, her door slamming.

First Daniel went up to her, but she wouldn't let him in. Next we made Cass go up and apologize. We could hear her raised voice, we could hear that there was no answer.

When she came back down, Cass was smirking. "She's got a big sign on the door now, and it says we're all murderers and sadists."

"Hmm," said Nora, theatrically thoughtful. "I thought *she* was the only Sadie," and they laughed together wickedly, twins again in meanness.

Another time it was Nora who refused to come to the table, refused to eat with Cass because she'd called Nora a *ho*; and with us because we hadn't been willing to intervene. The charge had something complex to do with Nora's stealing a boy away from a friend of Cass's, and we couldn't follow any of it. Besides, we'd learned long since to stay out of the running conflicts between them. "But a *ho*, Mother! That's— that's terrible."

"It's just a word from a rap record, Nor. No worse than lots of others. Can't you let it go?"

But she took her plate and went up to her room, and we all ate downstairs in joyless silence. Near the end of the meal, Cass burst into tears and said, "Just say it. You all hate me. You all wish I was the one who wasn't here and Nora was the one who was."

"Shoot me now, Daniel," I said when we went to bed that night.

"Oh, no. That would be too easy." We both laughed, grimly.

NORA ARRIVED JUST BEFORE ONE, LOOKING ELEGANT AND arty in a chic way. All black, naturally—bell-bottom slacks, and over them a very short, tightly fitting jacket with a zip front, the silver tab outsize and industrial-looking. She had large silver earrings on, too, and her hair was pinned back with a silver clasp. She was slender but not thin. She had a bosom. The only resemblance to Cass initially seemed to lie in the similar, very clunky boots they both wore, though Nora's had a higher heel.

She and Cass were sitting next to each other on the couch in the living room before we ate, and I kept coming in from the kitchen to look at them. Would I even have known they were twins if they were strangers to me? I suppose, when you stopped and really compared their faces, it was clear. The long nose after me, Daniel's clear white skin, the dark brows and wide mouths. The lazy sensuality, the held-in quality that made them seem older than Sadie by more than the five years that separated them. But the differences between them, between how they'd arranged and treated what they'd started out with, were so profound that they seemed more than accidental, more than just where life had led them.

Cass had been telling Nora about her plans, and now Nora, in a proprietorial tone (it's *my* New York), began to offer to help her.

Cass was more than gracious enough in response, I was glad to hear, talking with a calculated hesitance about the place she *thought* she might live in with Stellie, about the job she *might* be going to get.

Nora had started in on what jerks those model-agency guys were—what did Cassie know about him? she ought to check out his reputation; Nora had some friends in that world, she could get phone numbers for Cass to call, and so on—when I called them to the table.

Several times through the meal I met Daniel's eye as we kept things rolling innocently, *interestingly*, along. Daniel was open and easy with them, and all three were easy with him. As they always had been. Even in arguments they listened to Daniel, "the fairest of us all," as Nora once called him. He asked questions now, lots of them, which was more acceptable to the twins than my doing so. That was *probing*, a no-no. Sadie's sweet enthusiasm about both their lives made them expansive and generous. Cass told funny, harrowing stories of the road. Nora talked about her film project, about money problems with it.

Sadie and Cass had just begun to tease her about when she might marry Brian, when she announced she wasn't ever going to, that they were planning to stop living together in January. There was a serious turn after this, talk about relationships, trial periods. They were kind to one another, speaking of their failures, though they made fun of Sadie when she tried offering her high-school love as an example of this. I mentioned my divorce as a disaster brought about by not letting couples at that time experiment with living together.

"I always forget you were married before, Mom," Sadie said.

"Me too," I answered, and Cass laughed appreciatively.

They sent Daniel and me to the living room after the main course was over so they could clean up, and I felt some tension about leaving them alone together; but when I stepped in once to see how they were doing, there was the clatter of dishes, and then I heard Sadie say, "Is it a famous recluse?" and Nora answered, "No it is not Howard Hughes." So I came back and leaned comfortably against Daniel in front of the fire.

By the time we'd finished dessert, it was after five. Sadie went upstairs to call some friends who would also be home for the first holiday since college had started. Cass picked up her guitar and began strumming in the living room. Nora went to her room, to change, she said, but maybe just to be alone. Daniel and I worked in the kitchen on food for the next day's party, and then we sat at the table to sort out what our chores and duties would be. At six-thirty I drove over to the clinic to feed and exercise the animals again. The snow had stopped, though the plows were still working here and there.

When I got back, there were extra cars parked in the plowed-out drive. I could hear the bass line of murmurous music and the sound of animated conversation pitched above it as soon as I got out of my car. Inside, I greeted them—Sadie's friends—and then withdrew to the kitchen. Cass came in and cut herself another piece of mince pie. She hunched at the kitchen sink to eat it from her hands.

"Watch it," I said. "You'll lose your skinny job."

She made a face.

"Where's Daddy?" I asked.

"Out yonder." She tilted her head.

"Are you going to retreat upstairs?"

"Naw. Nor and I thought we'd go over to the inn for a while." She began to lick her fingers.

"Oh, nice," I said. Could it happen? Had they been apart long enough, had they grown far enough away from each other, that they could be friends at last?

I took a corkscrew, two glasses, and a bottle of wine through the snowy yard to Daniel's door. "It is I," I called. "Let me in."

He was smiling as he opened the door. "You couldn't take it either, could you?"

"It *is* noisy."

"One day of togetherness, and you're hiding out here with me."

"Well, you're my pal."

"Don't forget it."

There was a book on the daybed, *Memory's Ghost*. He moved it and we both sat down, propping ourselves in opposite corners, our legs stretched out, touching. I opened the bottle and poured the wine. We leaned forward to knock our glasses together before we drank. "*En garde,*" I said.

"What are we toasting?" he asked.

"Cass and Nora are going to the inn," I said. "Together. That's toastworthy, if anything ever was."

"Ha!" he said as he leaned back again. "Maybe now that it's too late, they'll get along famously."

"It's not too late!" I cried. "It's never too late. What do you mean, too late?"

"Too late for us. Fine for them. Great for them. But too late for us as a family."

I sighed. "You're right, damn you." I drank some wine and set my glass down. "This is all pretending, isn't it?" I made a wide sweep with my hand. "We're not really a family anymore."

"I wouldn't be so absolute." He set his glass down, too, frowning. His hand reached out, pushed my skirt up over my knee, found bare flesh. His fingers were cool, he spoke gently. "Why are you always so cataclysmic, Jo? First it's never too late, then the whole thing is false anyway. Slow down, sweetheart."

I looked at him. "Daniel, Daniel, master of the Golden Mean."

"Why not? Why not try it?"

"No, you're right." I shifted slightly for comfort. "But it *is* irretrievable, isn't it?"

"It's just different, Jo. It's another thing, with its own pleasures and pains."

"But they're pleasure and pains that . . . take me up less. They're in *their* lives, and it's all more remote from us. See, I miss it. I miss feeling *in* it with them. I want to feel used more. I used to feel useful."

"You *are* useful." He squeezed my thigh.

"To what? To whom?"

"To me, utterly. To your work. To your clients and your animals. You're necessary. You're being used, all the time."

"Then why don't I feel that? Why don't I feel better?"

For an answer, he slid across and sat next to me. He kissed me, slowly. "Let me make you feel better," he whispered. "Let me use you."

I felt sorrowful still. I didn't want to make our sweet comfortable love.

But Daniel was willing—eager—to do all the work initially. He shifted off the daybed. Holding me at the waist, he moved me in two long slides so my hips were at its edge. He knelt on the floor then, between my legs, and pulled off my woolly knee socks with elaborate care, stroking my feet, my calves. I lay back, my head touching the wall, and watched him, his pale face intent on his task.

He reached up under my skirt now and eased my underpants down.

Gently he kissed the inside of each knee, and then pushed them both back and up. I closed my eyes, swung my head to the side. I felt his hands slide down the insides of my thighs, his thumbs and fingertips fluttering, finding me, circling, entering me for moisture and then circling more. The pressure was light but steady. And now he pressed his face to me, and I felt his tongue, too, and then I couldn't tell it, tongue from fingers.

I felt his hands shift around under me again, cupping my bottom. He slid me a little more toward him, opened me wider still. I let my legs fall fully back—the openness was what thrilled me, that and his tongue licking me everywhere and his fingers teasing me, coming into me. I tried to hold on to just this moment, to feel it and feel it, but I began to ride higher and higher as he played with me, and then I came, calling, with his face pressed against me, and behind my closed eyes, oddly, what I saw were field flowers, pale yellow, purple, devil's red. Flowers, as I bucked and held on to his hair, his ears.

When I'd finally relaxed completely, when my breathing had begun to come back to me, I turned on my side and swung my legs up to make room for him. He climbed up next to me on the daybed. We lay facing each other. My breathing evened out completely. I heard the metallic ticking of the baseboard heater, the wind in the pines outside.

Daniel had unfastened his pants at some point, dexterous man, and now I felt his hard, silky penis push against my legs. I reached down, lifting my leg to rest it on his hip, and helped him come into me.

We lay there, nearly face-to-face, Daniel moving in me from time to time with a gentle, wet sound. His breath was warm in my ear. "Mmm," I said, and he answered me.

"Why is it like this?" I asked him after a while.

"Like what?" he asked, pulling himself back and then slowly pushing in again. "What do you mean?"

"Sex. It's gone for so long, not happening much, or just routine. And then it comes thundering back."

"What's the alternative?" he said now, and he moved deep, two or three times, in me.

"Unhhh," I said. "I don't know."

"Always fantastic? Always hot?" He smiled. "Hard to imagine." Now he drew back and came out of me. After a moment, I reached down to touch him where he rested, wet against my belly. I held him and stroked him, slowly and then faster, my arm finally aching in its awkward position between us. Just as I felt I couldn't do any more, he rose above me, turning me on my back, and entered me again, pumping harder, watching us where we were joined. He worked, his face deeply concentrated. Then suddenly his head dropped back and he cried out, twice, three times. He slowed, and gradually I felt him soften within me. I was gripping my own knees, swiveling myself around him. He fell forward onto me finally, and we lay still together, holding each other.

After a while, he said softly, "It's circular, Jo." Then he laughed. "Cyclical, I mean. It just comes around from time to time. 'Howdy. Remember me?' "

"See, that's it." I was whispering to match his voice. "I don't want it to be circular. I want linear. I want events. I want to be blown away."

"Joey," he said tenderly. He stroked my face, put his fingers in my mouth. His hand tasted of salt and sex, his and mine.

I chewed on him, gently. "Maybe if we took lots of vitamin E," I offered after a few moments.

"Would you want it, though?" he asked. "I like its ebb and flow. I like it to stop so it can start again." He moved his hand. " 'How can I miss you if you won't go away?' "

I laughed. We shifted. After a few moments, I reached for my wineglass over Daniel's body.

Then suddenly, from the yard, we heard the voices calling, laughing. Car doors began to slam, one after another. We had a little flurry of guilty activity—sitting up, fastening pants, pulling panties and socks back on. Skirt down, hair smoothed, shirt tucked in. And then, with an elaborately slow John Wayne walk, Daniel moved behind his desk and took his seat. I stretched out demurely on the daybed, and we looked at each other and lifted our glasses again, saluting, I think, our transformation back to the people Cass and Nora and Sadie believed in.

9

TOWARD THE END OF THE PARTY, A BUNCH OF THE YOUNG people were dancing in the corner of the living room by the stereo, one of them holding a baby of six or eight months, twirling it slowly while the baby patted his face and they laughed at each other. Allie, who loved to dance, was circling them all with a herder's nervousness, barking from time to time. The talkers were talking louder to hear one another over the noise, though the music was still fairly subdued—Latin stuff.

I went to the kitchen to consolidate platters of food so I could carry them out to the living room, where almost everyone seemed to be at this point. Things had thinned out a bit, but those who had stayed seemed committed for the long haul. Mostly people I'd known for years, they were locked in conversation, in pleasant social interchange all over the room: here a group sitting in a cluster by the fire, there a person leaned against the wall, head bent forward and down to listen to someone else.

I looked up as I was working and saw Eli standing in the kitchen doorway. "I like your house," he said, looking around the huge room. He and Jean had arrived fairly early on, and I'd made the rounds with them, introducing them to people I thought they'd enjoy. I'd been pleased to see them moving easily around on their own after that, Eli at one point launched into a fierce argument with a radical friend of Nora's from high school, Jean standing in a group of five or six people including Mary Ellen, laughing.

"Thanks," I said now. "It is sweet, isn't it?"

"It's more or less what we imagined when we decided to come to New England. An old farmhouse, with these kinds of rooms opening up off each other ad infinitum. Beams." He gestured up at ours, darkened and cracked, hung with drying herbs from Daniel's garden.

"So why didn't you?"

"There wasn't one on the market when we were looking that didn't need lots of work. *Lots* of work, and we didn't want that. And then we saw the house we got, and decided new was nice too."

"Those houses *are* pretty swell."

"You'll have to come over and see it. You and Daniel."

"Daniel, yes."

He nodded. "I talked to him briefly. He's not a minister, is he?"

"Yes, he is. Why?"

"Oh, something he said made me think that, but then I thought surely not."

"Why not?"

"Why not?" He lifted his shoulders. "Well." He grinned. "I don't know ministers, that's all. I guess I'm a pretty parochial person. Anyway, I was just startled to think it might be so." He gestured at the table. "What are you doing here? Can I help?"

"I want everything on these two plates," I said. "I want to take it all out into the other room. I want it eaten up."

"Done." He stepped closer to me and started to work, too, piling all the little rounds of bread at the edges of the platters. After a moment, he said abruptly, "How does that affect your life?"

"What?"

"His being a preacher."

I looked over at him, but he was steadily working. I smiled. "How does your wife's being a political scientist affect your life?" He looked at me, too, and after a second smiled back, acknowledging the point.

I said, "He likes his job, and that's good for our life. And he's a great listener. That's nice for me."

Eli nodded. Then he stopped working and turned to watch me, to watch my hands. He said, "Look, I wanted to thank you, for your support. For your understanding and sympathy. About Arthur." His voice had changed.

I straightened up. "Oh, Eli, thanks aren't necessary."

"No, they are. *You're* a good listener too. It meant a lot to me to have you be his vet for that moment, to have you put him down. Or whatever we have to call it."

I didn't know what to say. I bit my lip. "Well, I'm touched," I managed. I reached out and set my hand on his arm. And felt again the thick massiveness of Eli, the unexpected heat. We stood there for a moment. He was looking down at me, and I was aware, as I never was with Daniel, of feeling small, of feeling very female. Then I moved my hand away. I turned and began to work again.

He said, "It's an odd kind of bond, wouldn't you say? It's as though we'd committed some kind of crime together."

"Eli, no!" I cried. I'd stood up straight. "No, not at all. You mustn't feel guilty about it. No. It's as though we've endured the death . . . the death of a friend together. That's all."

"I know. I know you're right."

I turned away from his gaze. It was too serious, too open for me.

"And we *have* endured the death of a friend, haven't we?" He was standing very close to me, and his voice was deep, intimate. "I mean Dana," he said.

I felt a kind of thrill, the near dizziness you get when someone first speaks of love. I lifted my hand to my throat and swallowed. I said, "I'm so glad to have you speak her name."

"Sometime it would be good to talk about all that."

"Yes." I turned and began to bend and reach over the table again, sliding the last wedges of cheese onto the platter.

"I've been feeling . . . pleased, Jo. I wanted you to know this. That if I had to meet someone from that time again, it should be you."

Now I looked hard at him. "Thanks. I *think* thanks," I said.

He laughed quickly and stepped back. I picked up one platter, and he followed me in to the living room, carrying the other.

He and Jean left shortly after that. At the door, she promised they'd have us to their house soon—maybe a light supper the next week, before the holiday rush started? Lovely, I said. They turned and waved under the porch light as they started across the snowy yard.

The kids had definitively jacked the music up in the living room by now, and their dancing had gotten wilder, claimed more space. Finally the adults retreated to the kitchen, those who were left—a familiar core of us, a group that had had babies at the same time, that had traded child care and sat in each other's yards at summer barbecues until there was no light left; or in one another's kitchens on winter nights, reluctant to end the evening, to drive home down the empty, snowy roads. We talked now of the town elections, of the scandalous breakup of a friend's marriage, of the lives and doings of the nearly grown-up children in the next room.

Shortly after midnight, the last two couples left, together. Daniel went into the living room and announced he was cleaning up. Several of the kids helped, and then slowly they began to drift away too. The music was soft now. As I undressed, I could hear the voices calling good night in the yard, the *whumps* of the car doors.

It was around one-thirty when I climbed into bed next to Daniel. I was thrumming with energy still, wildly alert. "It was a nice party, wasn't it?" I said.

"Mmm."

"I heard a really funny discussion with Mary Ellen and some others about Watergate at one point. Watergate! Can you believe it?" I began to recount it to him. He made no response. I stopped and after a moment said, "You're not too interested in this, are you?"

"I'm interested, Jo. Tomorrow I'll be interested. I have to sleep now."

"I can't, yet."

"Get the light, though, will you?" He was frowning, his eyes shut.

I flicked the light off and lay in the dark. My ears were ringing, as though I'd been on an airplane. And indeed I felt that way after the noise and energy of the party, a kind of traveler's speedy dizziness. I wasn't ready yet to be lying here. To sleep. I got up and shut the door as quietly as I could behind me. The murmur of the girls' voices pulled me through the darkened living room to the kitchen. They were sitting at the table, with the overhead light on. It looked like a painting, framed by the kitchen doors. They laughed as one, the same uplifted faces. Then I saw that Cass was smoking. I resolved to say nothing, though it was a house rule that she shouldn't inside. But I didn't want to interrupt what seemed their easy familiarity, I didn't want to give her a reason to be angry at me tonight.

Nora's eyes focused on me in the doorway. "Mumster!" she announced. They all looked over.

"Hey, are you pleased with your party, Mommy?" Sadie asked. She was already in a nightgown. The other two were still dressed.

"Of course. Are you? Did enough good things happen?" I pulled out a chair and sat down with them.

"Umm," Sadie said. "I'll say! I got to dance with Ivan Baloff, the hunkiest hunk of honey here."

"No way," said Cass.

"I did too. And not just once. A bunch of times. We were *hot*."

"I mean, no way was he the hunkiest hunk."

"Who was, then?" Sadie asked.

Cass thought for a moment. "I'd have to vote for Guy Talbot," she said.

"Guy Talbot?" I cried. This was one of our friends, a real mope. "But he's such a gloomy Gus, Cassie. He's like a character out of Dostoyevsky. He's always in some kind of agony." He was handsome, though, I realized that suddenly. Handsome in a way that didn't matter in the least to me.

"But see, I love that," Cass said. "I love tormented guys."

"Well, you won't later," I said. And instantly regretted it. I could feel Cass bristle, her eyebrows arched aristocratically.

"Oh, I think I will," she said coolly. "I have earlier, and I think I will *later*."

"Oh, how do *you* know, Cass?" asked Nora. She was smiling at me and Sadie.

"I know," Cass said. She turned to me. "See, I'm just not interested in what you and Dad have. In a safe life," she said. "In sweetness and light." She made a fist and brought it down on the table. The glasses and dishes jumped, and she smiled. Her lips were still a deep brown-red. "I want things to be hard," she announced.

"Things *will* be hard. You don't have to want them to," I said.

"Yeah," Nora said. "Hard is easy to get. It's when you want things to be good, when you *want* all sweetness and light, that you understand what's really hard." She was the grown-up, talking to the child.

"Well, if you mean boredom is hard, I'd agree with you there." Cass drew fiercely on the last of her cigarette, her cheeks pulling in, and began to crush it in a coffee saucer. She turned her face away slightly to blow her smoke out.

"What are you suggesting, Cass?" Nora said. Her face was flushed. "That what I wanted with Brian is boring? That Mother's life with Daddy is boring?"

Cassie's green eyes flickered from face to face. She nervously pulled another cigarette out of the pack lying on the table and began to tap it. She shrugged suddenly. She was backing away from the argument. "It's just not for me, that's all." She sounded infinitely superior.

"No," Nora said. "No, you'd rather fuck in the van in some dark alley, with three guys sitting there watching it all."

There was a long, terrible silence. I could feel Sadie looking quickly from one of us to another.

Finally Cass stood up. She stretched lazily, an unfolding of long bones. "You should try it sometime, Nora. It adds a certain zing. It ain't boring anyway." She turned at the door and pointed her unlighted cigarette at her twin. "And by the way, remind me, sweetie, never to confide in *you* again."

We heard her shoes clunk across the living room, up the stairs. I looked over at Nora. She looked slapped, white around the eyes. She caught me watching her and turned away quickly. Her chair made a scraping noise as she stood, and two of the sleeping dogs jumped up and swam around her. "She never changes." Her voice was trembling. "I should never have come home." And she, too, walked out of the room.

For a long moment Sadie and I sat staring at each other. Her hair was wet and lank with sweat, her makeup had worn off. She looked about ten years old. She raised her eyebrows. "Zowie!" she said.

"Yikes," I answered. I put my face in my hands and rubbed my eyes. "Maybe both those things are true," I said. "That Cass will never change and that Nora shouldn't have come home. Wouldn't that be awful?"

"Don't feel bad, Mom. They'll get over it." She had a little wine left in her glass, and now she finished it, leaning her head all the way back. I saw the flick of her tongue.

"What *were* you guys talking about before I so rudely interrupted?"

"Nothing, really. Just the party." She set the glass down. "Who was cute, who likes who. *Et* cetera."

"The chemistry sure hit the fan when I arrived."

"Well, it always does," she said cheerfully, as though reassuring me of something.

"It always does?" I cried.

"Yes, you know that."

"I do?"

"Yeah, it's 'cause they're both so jealous about you. That's my theory anyway."

"Of *me*?"

"*Duh*, Mom. Yes, of you."

"Why me?"

"Because you're so . . ." She tilted her head, made a face. "Elusive. You know, Dad is just always there, the same, steady as a rock and all like that. And you . . . you're different."

"You find me elusive."

"Well, *I* don't, but that's me. They do. But it's, like, neither of them can admit it? So they kind of vie for you. Or with each other. Or something."

I picked up the saucer with Cassie's cigarette butts—two of them—and took it over to the trash can. When I came back, I announced, "If I thought I caused their antagonism to each other, I'd kill myself. If I thought I seemed *elusive* to my children, I'd kill myself." I sat down.

Sadie was immune to my histrionics. "Well, you have to admit you're secretive."

"Sadie, I am not! I always tell the truth. You guys can ask me anything."

"Okay. Fine. How's this." She leaned forward. "You *lived* with Jean's husband?"

"Oh! That."

Sadie laughed, and I did, too, for a few seconds, sheepishly. "You make me laugh," she said.

"So I see."

"Well?"

"Well, that was years ago. Obviously. I was in a group house with him. That's all. A kind of quasi commune of the sixties."

"Before you were married?"

"No, I was married then, to Ted. But I'd left him for a while."

There was a quick puff of exasperated breath: See what I mean?

"I left him twice, actually, poor man."

"God, Mom!" she protested.

"Well, that first time it was a kind of experiment, when I was in the group house. And then I went back. and then I left him again, for good, because I'd learned something from the experiment. That I couldn't live with him anymore. But that *was* when I knew Eli. I was about . . . I was twenty-two. A little older than your age."

"But he wasn't, like, your boyfriend or anything." Her voice said *please don't tell me that.*

"I was married, Sadie. I didn't let myself have a boyfriend."

After a moment, she frowned and said, "So when, exactly, did you meet Dad?"

They all knew the part of the story that had me and Daniel meeting at an airport when I was still married to someone else, that had me calling Daniel three years later, when I was divorced. I'd used it too many times when they mooned over boys as adolescents, hoping to be chosen, hoping to be called. The last time, I'd barely begun the tale when Nora said, "Don't, Mom. We all know," and she chanted it: *"You were the one who picked up the phone and called Dad."*

I told Sadie a longer version now, about my confusion in running away from Ted, about my staying out of touch with him and my mother for all those months, about my return, my leaving again for Maine, my depression, and then my finding my way—to my work, to her father, to the life that brought us here in the middle of a cold New England night, to this room, this table, this story.

I didn't talk about Dana, though. I'm not sure why. I saw her face as I was speaking. She was especially in my mind, of course, because of seeing Eli and talking to him at the party, because he'd brought up her name at last. I'd thought of her earlier, too, at the moment when Cass seemed to be suggesting I'd led a boring life. Thought of her and knew I would say nothing. I would not use the drama of Dana's random, senseless murder to make myself seem more interesting to my difficult daughter.

I think that I was also aware that Sadie might have heard a great deal in the last few days from Cass and Nora about what was *hard*, as Cass put it, in their lives, and I didn't feel I needed to add the terrible lesson from my life to all that. So I didn't speak of Dana, of Dana or her death.

The house was still, the dogs and people were all sound asleep, when Sadie and I stood at the foot of the stairs and said good night, whispering. "I love talking to you, Mom." She reached out and hooked my hair behind my ear.

"Do you, Sadie?" I was surprised and moved, by her sweetness, by her willingness to touch me.

"Mmm," she said. "And thanks for inviting Jean to the party. That was great." Then she hoisted her nightie slightly, like a nineteenth-century belle lifting her long skirts, and turned, and I watched the bottoms of her grimy white bare feet winking up the ladderlike stairs.

IT WAS ABOUT A WEEK AND A HALF LATER THAT DANIEL AND I went to hear Cass and her band play. She'd hit the road again the Saturday after Thanksgiving, with the last flurry of gigs. Providence was the closest venue, and we'd promised to show up there.

After we'd found the place and parked, Daniel cut the engine, and we sat silent for a moment. Then he said, "I wonder who it is that books a place like this. How do they even *know* about them?" The street was empty, littered, completely cheerless. The neighborhood surrounding it was full of triple-deckers with aluminum or asphalt siding. Sodium-vapor light fell on everything with an unhealthy orange glow. Here and there a collapsing porch roof was propped up with long pieces of raw lumber. The plate-glass windows on the storefront next to Al Priest's, the bar Cassie was playing in, were papered on the inside with long-faded banners reading EVERYTHING MUST GO. BARGAINS GALORE! On the other side was a locksmith shop, and on the corner, a small bodega, closed for the night, with a faint fluorescent light glowing somewhere deep within.

"They were probably grateful to get the gig. Providence must be the big time for them, wouldn't you think?" I'd been feeling irritated with Daniel for the last few days, ever since our dinner at Eli and Jean's. The evening there had been uncomfortable, so much so that Daniel had announced afterward that if I wanted to see Eli Mayhew again, I should do it on my own. I blamed Daniel for the way it had gone, I was annoyed at him.

There was a raw rain falling outside—there had been for the whole drive east. Now that our wipers were off, it blurred our view of the street.

"*Here* we go," I said. A group of people was approaching, you could hear their voices drawing nearer under the rain's thrumming on the car. A girl shrieked with laughter. There were six or seven of them. A few had umbrellas, but most were in parkas with the hoods pulled forward, hiding their faces. "Come on," I crooned to them all. "Come to Cassie."

They did. They stopped at the bar, and when they opened the door, there was a confusion of music and voices that floated out to us.

"Gee, it's alive in there anyway," Daniel said.

"Let's go. At least now we know we won't be the first."

I had started to move away from the car when Daniel called over to me, "Lock it."

He was right, of course, it was a rough neighborhood, but somehow I felt annoyed with him for thinking of it and for his peremptory tone—one in a series of what I knew very well were petty grievances I could have been said to be collecting against him over the last few days: He stood up one evening in the middle of something I was saying to him and began to pick up the bits of wet leaf one of the dogs had tracked into the living room. I overheard him on the phone passing judgment on a movie we'd seen in exactly my words, without crediting me. Even the blood-specked tissue stuck on a shaving cut one morning got on the list, and the familiar, theatrical groan as he rose from a living room chair. I knew these were absurdly small-minded; I knew they weren't, in some sense, *real*. I knew anyone could have made a similar list about anyone else. About me, for instance. I knew, but somehow once I started, I couldn't stop myself.

The club was warm and cheerfully noisy as we entered, the sound like a thick substance you moved through—a combination of canned music and shouted conversation. The room was long and narrow. There was a bar running along one side, up to where, on a lighted, raised platform, the mikes and stools and drums were set up. A solitary fat bass rested against the wall. The place was two-thirds full, mostly with young people sitting jammed in at the little round wooden tables. A few people were at the bar. *Singletons*, I remembered from my waitress days.

The jukebox was playing a loud song, hard and driving and antimelodic, a male voice shouting the lyrics, in accusation after accusation. A lone young woman was moving dreamily on what must have been the dance floor, a small open area in front of the bandstand, looking seraphic, so at peace, she seemed to be dancing to a tune other than the one playing.

Daniel and I went to the front of the room, searching for a table from which we might be able to see the bandstand easily, but they were all full up there. We decided, leaning toward each other and shouting, to sit at the near end of the bar. Better than a table anyway, we concluded, if people were going to be dancing right in front of the musicians.

"What, beer?" Daniel yelled at me when the bartender came over and pushed napkins at us. He, anyway, seemed not to care that we were the oldest people in the room—a big-jawed man who hung his face out at us and nodded once when Daniel gave him the order. The young people around us deliberately hadn't registered us, as though we were profoundly handicapped, somehow difficult or embarrassing to look at.

The beer tasted wonderful, sharp and deeply bitter. I was ravenous, suddenly. I asked Daniel to order nuts or chips or something. "Which?" he yelled.

"Anything!" I shouted back.

I'D BEEN NERVOUS ABOUT THE EVENING AT ELI'S, BUT IT HAD started well enough: Jean had cut her hair, and this gave us all something immediate to talk about. She looked elegant, and I said so. It was as though she were wearing a trim, wavy cap on her head.

"I hate it," Eli said. He was helping me off with my coat in the entry hall. The floor was slate, I noted, as water from our boots pooled on it.

"Why do they do it?" he'd asked Daniel, who looked up from heeling his boots off, blank and polite. "Women," Eli explained, gesturing at Jean and me. "Why do they take what's so lovely and—chop!—get rid of it?"

I had thought of Dana then, looking at herself in the mirror over the fireplace. "Why did I do it?" she asks me.

"We do it because it's easier," Jean had said. "Same reason men have short hair." Looking at her as she spoke, I realized she was as transformed as Dana had been: everything about her could be understood differently. She suddenly had a flapper's careless glamour.

"The hell with ease," he said. "Tell you what. Grow it back and *I'll* brush it for you, or shampoo it, or whatever it is that makes it harder."

"Oh, Eli, as if you were ever even *here*."

He laughed. "I've been on the road all fall, lecturing and conferencing," he said to Daniel as we moved into the living room. I trailed Jean with the wine we'd brought.

Daniel was asking Eli about his travels as we settled ourselves. There was a fire going in the large stone fireplace. I looked around. The room was huge, wainscoted to eye level with some reddish wood. Cherry, most likely. I sat on a black leather couch, Daniel in a deep plush chair. Jean had taken the wine from me, with thanks, and was pouring for us now from a bottle already open on the coffee table. Two huge abstract paintings, full of bold bands of color, stood propped against the wall. They weren't going to fit above the wainscoting.

"I was supposed to be gathering my strength with the sabbatical," Eli was saying. "Getting ready to launch myself anew. Instead I've completely dissipated it. I've shot my wad. But it's been fun." He laughed. "Hard on Jean, though." He'd sat down in a chair next to the fireplace. "Made her so mad she cut her damned hair off."

"God, the egocentrism of the guy! Here you go," she said, handing me my glass, Daniel his. "Sometimes," she said to Eli, lifting her own glass in his direction, "a haircut is just a haircut."

Daniel laughed, his face moved into a rictus of false pleasure. He was being too polite. I sensed right away that there was something in Eli's manner—in Eli—he didn't like, maybe that mocking, ironic tone, maybe his ease around Jean and me, a kind of possession he seemed to take of us, of the situation. The alpha male. In any case, Daniel was being overcareful, solicitous. Now he was asking what Eli was doing on the road, what he'd been lecturing on—and so I, too, found out that he was working with something called nerve growth factor. Something that could regenerate damaged nerves in the brain. That the focus of his work might eventually be Alzheimer's disease, or spinal injuries.

"Transport's our area."

"Transport?" Daniel asked.

"Getting the stuff where it needs to go. Right now you have to apply it directly, because the brain has such an efficient defense mechanism against toxins—and in this case, useful drugs. And that means surgery. Brain surgery." He shook his head. "Which is hardly practical for a disease population of any size. So we're looking for alternate ways." He smiled at Daniel. "Alternate routes. I'm the transportation planner for the brain." He leaned forward and stirred the fire with the poker. "If I ever get to work again."

Jean began to speak. She had questions about the town, she said. A list, actually. Would we mind? No, fire away, I said. And she did. Where did we shop for groceries? What were the best dry cleaners? Were there good local restaurants? She'd noticed we had a piano—did we know a tuner? A dentist?

We gave her information, told tales on our neighbors. The dentist who'd survived a midlife crisis by training as a lay therapist, who stuffed your mouth with cotton and then earnestly asked you how you *felt* about your sexuality, about your parents. The eccentric chef at the tiny French restaurant, who could be heard weeping in the kitchen if things were not achieving the requisite level of perfection.

We moved around seemingly with ease from topic to topic through the evening—the party at our house, who the various guests were. My work, Arthur. Dogs in general. Dogs versus cats. Adams Mills, Jean's and Sadie's school. Throughout it all, Daniel maintained his civility, the reserve I'd noted earlier. "Do tell," he said once, and I raised my eyebrows and made a face at him. If I could make him laugh at himself, maybe he'd notice how ridiculous he was being, maybe he'd relax. *"Do tell?"* I wanted to say. But I didn't dare.

Halfway through dinner, Eli turned to him. "Jo tells me you're a preacher."

"That's right."

"That's an interesting line of work." I watched Daniel's thin smile. "I'm wondering how you got into it."

"Oh, I suppose in many ways it was similar to how you got into your line of work." I tensed.

Eli laughed. "I doubt it, but I'll bite," he said. "What do you mean?"

Daniel shrugged. "I felt compelled, I took courses, I got more interested. I went on to graduate school and got my degree. There's not much else to do once you have a D. Min."

Eli nodded. Then he leaned forward, elbows on the table. "See, it's the *feeling compelled* in the first place that I find fascinating. That really interests me. How does that happen?"

Daniel set down his knife and fork and looked over at Eli. "You're asking about a call or a revelation, I think."

"Yes, I am."

"Sorry to disappoint, but I had none. No scales falling from my eyes." Daniel's tone was dismissive, but Eli didn't hear that. It occurred to me for the first time that he might be a little obtuse about people.

"Well, what then?"

"Nothing very dramatic at all. Just a slowly increasing sense of belief, of myself as a believer, as someone who wanted to make that central in his life."

"But belief in what? That's what I wonder. In the *soul*?" Eli's voice gave this italics. He did not, you could tell, believe in the soul.

"Among other things. The soul. Yes," Daniel said. Looking back, I would remember his face then, its clarity, its wholeness.

"*Aha*," Eli said. He seemed, really, delighted. This new, middle-aged Eli loved to talk too. "But what if I told you that thought, feeling, personality—even faith—are a matter of neurons, neurons firing in specific learned pathways in the brain. That's what the *soul* is. That's all. You can extinguish any of it with a single knife cut or a blow to the head."

"I'd say that had nothing to do with what I was talking about."

"But look, what I'm saying is that God is an idea. A human idea. He resides in the particular arrangement of the matter in your brain. Change the matter and presto. God is gone."

Daniel cleared his throat. He said, "And what *I'm* saying is that I agree you might be able to eliminate my belief by altering my brain, but that doesn't mean God is gone."

"But where else does he live but in your brain? Your brain and other brains that have been deliberately structured the same way. You're a smart man, you see that. He's an idea, like the idea of life after death." His hand circled. He smiled. "Or the *virgin birth*." His smile widened.

"Eli . . . ," Jean began.

"No, he doesn't mind explaining this." Eli turned to Daniel. "Do you?"

"There's nothing to explain," Daniel said. "I'm not explaining."

"Ahh! I've offended you. I didn't mean to. Look, why not see me as a candidate for conversion." His hand rose and rested on his own chest. "I mean, here I am, a lost soul, a nonbeliever. Why not try to convince me, persuade me. Why not save me? That's what your faith is about, isn't it? Harvesting *souls*?" He was completely genial in this, but there was the quality of assumption that we could all treat this as he did, lightheartedly. A kind of intellectual joke.

I looked over at Daniel. His face was tight. "If that *were* what my faith was about, what I'd say to you is that you're not ripe." Eli missed the metaphor. He looked puzzled. Daniel went on. "There has to be some need, some desire, even, for God. Maybe just some sense of something missing in your life. And I don't think you feel that." Daniel sat back in his chair. "I'm sure, actually, that you don't."

At last Eli heard it, the dismissal in Daniel's tone. His face shifted. He, too, sat back. "No," he said. "No, you're right. I don't."

"Eli," Jean said brightly, "lives in his own universe. Some men are like that. And here's the evidence. We married four years ago, and Eli was then fifty-two and had never been married. Never even lived with anyone. Except Arthur, of course. It's a wonder he ever did marry. He would like *me* to consider it a miracle." She laughed brightly and turned to me, clearly inviting me to join her, to help her shift the course of events. She asked me now about the Holts, the former owners of the estate. We talked about their grand house, divided into expensive condos. We talked about condos versus houses, about the problems of new construction versus old construction. She was good at this, good at talking, at acting. It must be part of what Sadie admired about her as a teacher.

I followed her lead. There were stories about our house to offer. The annual spring flood in the earthen basement, the beautiful old bottles and jars of aged, mysterious fruits and vegetables in the root cellar, left at some time in the distant past. Eli, and then finally Daniel, joined us, and we all moved away from danger, back to what didn't matter so much. We made our way carefully through the evening until Daniel and I could decently excuse ourselves and leave.

THE STAGE WENT BLACK NOW, THOUGH IN THE DIM LIGHTS from the bar and the glowing jukebox we could easily see the band members coming out onto it. They picked up their instruments. The room quieted slightly. Cass moved to the front of the stage and stood with her guitar slung low, at hip level. Her hair had grown a little; it was the length of what we'd called a pixie cut when I was young. She wore a short-sleeved shirt, tiny and pale, with a row of glittering buttons down the front. Her long arms looked fleshless, skeletal—made me aware, suddenly, that wrists were *knobs*. Her hipbones jutted above her jeans in the bare space between them and the too-short shirt. Her navel was exposed.

She stamped her foot twice, the lights went up, and abruptly a wall of undifferentiated noise assailed us. A group of four or five girls immediately rushed forward and started dancing, and it was through their motions, their nervous, bouncy boxing, that I heard the beat at last and then oriented myself in the din so that I could separate out and get them all: bass, guitar, drums. A guy with a sax blatted, too, in quick, short phrases that tried to pull the beat a different way. Cassie's guitar threaded through the more dominant rhythm, offering—if you listened carefully—a kind of melody. And then she stepped forward and nearly rested her mouth on the mike. She began to sing. Her voice was a growl, a howl. Rich, though, rounded and complex. She sang a song she'd sung for us at home, sweetly, huskily. Here it was bluesy, primal.

If you didn't wanna stay with me
You coulda said so
You coulda said so
If you thought you had to wander free
You coulda said so
You coulda said so . . .

The room shouted along with her. I watched her mouth shaping the words to several more verses—the exposed teeth, the tongue, the curled inside of her lips. Her head was tilted, her eyes were closed in agony. Her fingers moved over the guitar at her crotch as though she were playing with herself, which was probably the point.

If you thought love was no good for you
You coulda said so
You coulda said so
If you didn't want to work to be true
You coulda said so
You coulda said so . . .

By now the dance floor was jammed, an undulating mass with the odd arm flung suddenly up, the heads bobbing this way and that. Cass stamped one foot, one leg, in a regular rhythm. When she rested, when the band took over, she closed her eyes and an ecstatic smile lighted her face. Or she turned and beamed on whoever was soloing a smile of such beatific affection that I was jealous of each recipient.

Now she stepped forward again. She was wailing.

Instead you raaan,

she sang,

> *sometime between dark and dawn.*
> *Instead I woke up, baby, and you were gone.*

Now a soft growl:

> *I reached for you, baby, but you were gone.*
> *You coulda said so.*
> *You coulda said so.*

The band stopped then, and she sang alone, musically, in her regretful, rich contralto: "*Yooouuuu* could have: *said! so!*" A slow broken chord on the guitar, and the lights went off.

The whistles and screams washed over them in the dark, and when the lights went up again, I saw that the flesh of her neck was silvered with sweat already, her shirt dampened under the arms. She was laughing and loving the waves of appreciation. She danced lightly under them a moment, bent her head and lifted it several times, now this way, now that. Then she turned her back to us, I heard her thumping out a beat: "two . . . three . . . *four!*" and she spun around as the noise began again. The dance-floor people were moving nearly against Daniel and me. I turned back to him and yelled, "She looks so happy!"

"What?" His hand cupped his ear.

We leaned together, and I shrieked, "She's happy!"

He pulled back, nodding. He agreed.

We sat through the whole first set. Cass sang the lead in most of the songs. There was one instrumental, and on two of the other songs the men sang. (Was that dark one Raimondo? I wondered, or was Raimondo just a white boy with a dark name?) When it was Cassie's turn, she howled and wailed and shrieked and grunted, but it was strong and powerful music if you gave yourself over to it, and her voice was the center of all of it, lifting from a growl to a clear, pure singing, and then back again effortlessly. When you watched her, it seemed it must be agony—the body hunkered to keep her mouth to the mike, her face contorted, the bobbing, skipping dance she did when she moved with the beat. But if you closed your eyes and just listened, you could hear that she was utterly in control. Her wild response to the applause after every number was a kind of agreement with it: I was great, wasn't I?

She came to sit with us during the break, a towel around her neck. The crowd parted to let her pass and followed her with eager, friendly eyes. We ordered her a beer. She let me kiss her. Her shirt was soaked, her hair wetted into little points around her face.

"You were wonderful, Cass," I told her. "I'm so proud."

Daniel said something to her on her other side, and she turned to him. He moved over and made room for her to sit between us. But this meant, in the din, that she had to talk to one of us at a time in order to be heard and to hear. Basically, she chose Daniel, and I thought of what Sadie had said to me the night of the party—that the twins found Daniel easier. In the noisy bar, an image from another life occurred to me: Daniel standing behind the glass storm door of our first apartment, holding both little girls as I went down the walk to work in my scrubs and sneakers. They were wailing, crying, and I could hear his murmuring voice under that, trying to make them call goodbye, trying to reassure them. I'd turned and made an amused grimace, which he mirrored—I could see his pale face through the glass, the squirming, miserable twins in his arms. And then I turned away. While they called to me and cried, I walked away. I went to work, and as soon as the routine of my long, hard day began, I forgot them. I forgot them. My choice, surely.

Now Cass turned back to me. "Thanks for coming, Mom."

We'd told her ahead of time we could stay only for one set; it would take us several hours to get home. Besides, she was leaving right after the show. She was driving to Concord, New Hampshire, tonight. They had a bed there, a gig the next night.

"I loved it, dear," I said. "I was so impressed."

"I think I'll be home for a few days at Christmas," she said. "If that's okay."

"More than okay."

"What?"

"More than okay," I yelled. "Great."

"Oh, good." She slid off her stool. "Well," she said. And she kissed Daniel quickly, and me, and then was gone.

The thick, snowy rain was welcome after the smokiness of the bar.

The silence of the street too. I heard our smallest noises magnified. Wetted footfall, the car door opening and then slamming, the metallic clicking of our seat belts. The rustling of our clothes. The slow tick of the battery clock on the dashboard before Daniel started the engine.

"She was really good, wasn't she?" Daniel said. We were on the highway now.

"She was. I loved watching her."

"I'm exhausted by it, though," he said. I looked over. Why did he have to say that? It made me suddenly tired, too, and before, I had felt only exhilarated.

We drove on, not talking. I nearly dozed once or twice, turned away from Daniel, looking out the dotted windows at the whir of black trees against the bruised gray sky. I had the sensation you have as a child, that I was the one holding still while they were rushing by me, going somewhere.

And then I realized with a shock that snapped me wide awake that what I was feeling was a bitter sorrow with my life, a sharp envy for Cass. That I wanted to have what she was having—to have *had*, anyway, what she was having. That I wanted to be standing at the center of *my* life in hot lights, moving in ecstasy to music that crashed around me, that came from me, that linked me to others. That I wanted to be turning and dancing and laughing under the caressing waves of applause. That I wanted to be driving with the band through the rain down some nameless country road to a place where I'd never been before. That I wanted to be making love slowly and elaborately in the parked van in a dark city alley, listening to the hitched breathing of the others while they sat back and watched.

CHAPTER

10

I HAD LISTS FOR THE HOLIDAYS, AND EVERY DAY I TRIED to check off two or three items. Get pecans for baking. Order a goose for Christmas Day. Find warm slippers for Sadie. Another day, another list: for Cass, buy the secondhand jeans jacket I'd seen at the church resale shop, with a sinuous red dragon embroidered on its back. Pick up the personal stationery I'd ordered for Daniel, and get cards while there at the shop. Drop in at Layton's for the trailing, romantic shawl in the window—far too expensive, no doubt, but then it was Christmas, and Nora had expensive taste.

Beattie and I and sometimes Mary Ellen sat together at lunch behind the counter these wintry days, with the sign in the window turned to say CLOSED. The boarding dogs sat rigid at our feet in case a crumb should fall their way, but the effect was of great attentiveness to our conversations. Occasionally when I looked at them, seemingly so riveted to our easy banalities, I had to laugh.

Mostly these days we talked about how much we had to do. Beattie was making a doll's wardrobe for a favorite great-niece, and she described this to me one day in elaborate detail—the playsuit with matching bloomers, the party dress, the wool coat and beret, the sundress. "Two tiny pockets in the skirt," she said, "and I made the most cunning little hankie that tucks into one, just the points showing, like that." She made a minuscule church steeple with the tips of her fingers.

"You are a good person, Beattie," I said. "It's store-bought for me all the way."

"Well, you're very busy," she said. She burped daintily, her hand over her mouth. She'd been eating carrot sticks, slowly, in a rabbity, swivel-jawed way. After a moment, she said, "Still, I think there's nothing like something you make yourself." Never one to avoid the backhanded insult.

"Mmm," I agreed.

"Edith, now. She's sending people that TV-shopping junk she ordered for herself. I shouldn't criticize, I'm glad to get rid of anything I can, but doesn't that seem kinda *mean* to you? Of course, it's all still in the boxes and the tissue and whatnot, so they'll never know, but it's not the same."

No, I said. It certainly wasn't.

I moved efficiently through my days. Daniel was especially busy now, as he always was in the church's Advent season. There were extra choir performances. There were almost nightly prayer meetings, as well as several community events to prepare for and stage, including a huge party where gifts were given out to the needy and elderly. There was a children's pageant, calling for many rehearsals. The girls had always loved this. First when they could be in it, as a shepherd or a wise man or an angel or, best yet, the Virgin Mary. Later because the pageant used a live sheep and donkey and there was the excitement of waiting for the inevitable and deeply hysterical accident. Daniel loved everything in this happy season, and he was cheerful through the long days in his slightly distracted way.

And I was grateful. Because for all the busyness, all the extra cooking, all the ticking off of chores to be done, what I was thinking of was Eli Mayhew, of his quick call to me the day after we saw Cass, and of next Sunday, when I would meet him for coffee. There had been some urgency in his voice, I thought, and this excited me. I wondered what it suggested, what it might lead to.

Sometimes what I imagined was simply more of what we'd glancingly already had—talk. But sometimes I let myself think that the talk would become more private over time, even intimate. He would become a dear friend, a confidant. And our spouses? Oh, they would know about and respect our intimacy, maybe even be mildly amused by its intensity, its power—Daniel's ill will was somehow easily vanquished in this fantasy. Or never considered.

Occasionally, though, my imagination offered up the more predictable outcome: an affair. I would remember touching Eli at the clinic and again at my party—the density of his body, its heavy heat, so different from Daniel. I would see again the slow turn of his beautiful young body toward me in the steamy bathroom long ago. Like a greeting.

And then I would dismiss it. Coffee. Coffee and talk on a winter Sunday morning while Daniel was at church. That was all.

I HAD SUGGESTED THE PENNOCK INN, TWO TOWNS OVER. What I had said to Eli on the phone was that it was prettier, nicer than the town inn, but as soon as I hung up I had to acknowledge that I'd chosen it mostly so we wouldn't run into people who knew us. Who knew me, in particular, since Eli knew hardly anyone yet.

When I arrived, there were only two other tables occupied in the dining room. I actually looked, I checked to see that neither held someone I knew. Eli was sitting by himself, next to the window overlooking the falls. He'd been watching for me: he waved as soon as the hostess pointed him out, as soon as my eyes fell on him.

I was late. Sadie had called just as I was leaving the house. As I sat, I was apologizing, breathlessly. I explained further as I removed my coat, as he signaled the waitress, as I ordered my first cup of coffee and he his second. I was, in fact, babbling, talking about Sadie, her adoration of Jean, her need to be in touch often this first year of college. Behind him, through the crazed, bubbled panes of old glass, I could see the gun-colored waterfall rushing down between ice-covered rocks.

He was watching me steadily, and when I finally slowed down, he said, "You're nuts about your kids, aren't you?"

I shrugged. "That's what it means to have kids, I think."

He smiled. "Oh, I don't know. A lot of people complain about them."

"Oh, but most of that is stylized, don't you think? People *like* to grouse. And of course, adolescence is tough on everyone."

"But you survived that."

I laughed. "Well, we're not out of the woods yet."

The waitress brought my coffee and refilled Eli's cup. We waited. When she'd left, he said, "I regret it." He shook his head. "No kids."

"Do you? Well, you married so late."

"I did. It was hard, surprisingly hard"—he smiled mockingly—"to find an absolutely perfect person."

"I congratulate you." I raised my cup. "She is perfection; I know this from Sadie. And it's plain, of course, as the nose on my face." I sipped the coffee. It was not quite warm enough.

"Well, as it happens, she *is* perfect for me."

"Which means?"

He looked up in surprise. He saw it was a serious question, and his mobile face screwed up in thought. "Well, I guess that Jean and I have a certain . . . distance from each other. That sounds cold, and I don't mean it to. But each of us has his life, a very separate life. We're used to being solitary, we each lived alone for so long. We leave each other room. A lot of room. It *is* distance." He lifted his hands. He was wearing an expensive-looking, loosely woven tweed jacket. "Maybe that's a privilege of the childless marriage."

"It might be." I tilted my cup slightly back and forth in its saucer and watched the surface of brown liquid shift. "Somehow, over the years, Daniel and I have become—I don't know—sort of mired in each other. I can *not notice* him too easily. It's as though we're two halves of something." I looked up at him. "You know what I liked? I liked the way Jean stood off from you a little the other night, made fun of you in a way, and spoke of you . . . theatrically, I guess. Certainly distantly. So she could make us all more comfortable when you and Daniel were headed for that little . . ."

"Explosion?"

"Oh, Daniel never explodes. *Contretemps.* Let us say contretemps."

"Well, if we must."

I laughed, too loudly. It sounded harsh and artificial in the nearly empty room, and the three women at the table closest to us looked over and then leaned in to speak to each other.

I shifted in my chair. "Anyhow," I said, "I admired the way she pulled that off. Daniel would never put up with my speaking of him so distantly in his presence."

"What would he do?"

"Oh, step forward. Speak for himself. Correct me. I don't know." I felt suddenly uncomfortable. "I'm not criticizing him. Just trying to say how things are different in our marriage." I shrugged. We both looked away, at the falling foamy water. Distantly through the window you could hear its steady thunder.

When Eli spoke again, his voice was lowered. "You must be wondering why I called you."

I looked over at him. His eyes were on me, those eyes that used to watch and watch. They seemed smaller now, less needful, more amused. It made him look less soulful than he had looked in the past, but sexier. "Well, yes, a bit," I said.

He leaned forward. "But seeing me, meeting me again, must have done the same thing for you that it did for me."

I blushed. I could feel the heat in my face, a sudden parch in my eyes. "Maybe so," I said. Perhaps he had been imagining, too, the various ways our relationship might play out.

But then he smiled and said, "It brought back that whole time, which I'd felt I left pretty much behind."

After a beat, I said, "And that's what you wanted to do? To leave it behind?"

"God, yes!" He laughed with his mouth closed, a funny snorting sound. "Didn't you?"

Well, of course I had. I had rushed from it into all that I had now. And then only slowly begun to yearn back. I shrugged. "I loved it. In a way. I mean, I know it ended so badly for all of us. But I felt so free. So *care*free. Relatively speaking. I suppose mostly what I'm saying is that I felt young. Young and passionate and a little reckless."

"See, I hated all that." His face, registering feeling so transparently, shifted, grimaced, as though he'd tasted something sour. "Feeling so at the mercy of all that."

"Did you? *Were* you? At its mercy? I never thought of you that way." I had thought of him as exactly the opposite. Careful. Steady. *Gray*. An image of his face across the dining room table occurred to me, watching us with his steady, calm eyes. Watching.

"Very much. Very much. And I wanted . . . everything." He laughed. "To be loved, but to be alone. Because I was only truly comfortable by myself. To be great in science, but not to be, God forbid, a scientist. I think I mentioned that before, how agonized I was—torn, really—about all that. I mean, I loved science, but I could tell it cut me off from the world I wanted to be in. From all of you, certainly." He looked out the window. "My problem was I could understand that, too, or at least understand where it came from, that sense of science as betrayer. I mean, with Dow Chemical and napalm and the sense of imminent nuclear disaster—everything that was in the air generally." He smiled grimly at me now and made a fist in the air. "But it also pisses me off now just to think about it—the stupid, antiscientific romanticism of that era." He frowned for a moment. "I think that might be part of why I react so badly now to people like your husband, like Daniel. Smart people who won't accept the implications of science into their thinking."

I started to say something, to defend Daniel, but he opened his hand to stop me. "Look, I'm sorry. I don't mean to get into that again. It was bad enough to have antagonized him when he was a guest in my home. All I mean to say is that I was unhappy then, when we lived together. I felt . . . tormented a good deal of the time."

After a moment, I said, "I'm so sorry to hear that." I sipped at my coffee. "I thought of you as *happy*. Content anyway. I would have said that then, I think. Content."

"Content!? With what?"

"Well, you had your work. Of all the members of the house, I would have said you were surest about that, most committed to it. And you liked the house, I thought." I set my cup down. "And we all liked you well enough."

"Stop right there. *Well enough.* That's it, I'm afraid. Who in their right mind wants to be liked *well enough*?"

I laughed, embarrassed. "Point taken." We sat in silence a moment. Someone had turned some Muzak on low, and I was aware of it suddenly, a sprightly, violin-ridden version of "Leaving on a Jet Plane."

Eli said, "Do you remember this: coming out of the living room one night and finding me in the hall?"

I blushed, because I was suddenly conflating this with the day I walked in on him in the bathroom. But I said, "Yes. I almost ran you down."

"See, the thing was, I was afraid to come in." He shook his head. His voice was pitying, tender, as though he could see himself there, as though that person were his child.

"Afraid?"

"Yes."

"But afraid of . . . ?" It seemed impossible to reconcile this large, gruff, nearly ebullient man with a younger Eli so frightened he couldn't enter a room of friends.

He shrugged. "How I'd fit in. Or wouldn't. You were all so . . . well, carefree, as you say. Laughing, giggling."

I snorted. "Stoned out of our minds, probably."

"No, here's what it was." He raised his finger. "I thought I would ruin it. I was afraid of having to feel the change when everyone got stiff, got polite. Having to feel my *effect*." He grinned. "What we in science would have called the *Eli effect*." And then he stopped smiling, he looked down. "What I thought was that Dana would be solicitous and sweet, and everyone else would be polite, and someone would make room for me on the couch, and then, because I was there— because of the Eli effect—the fun would dry up for a bit, palpably. And then, as you slowly forgot about me, start again."

"You make us all sound quite horrid. All except Dana."

He smiled quickly. "Who could be horrid too. When she wasn't being very, very good. But that's not what I mean. And you weren't. I was talking about how I *felt*, about myself. About how paralyzed I was then. Terrified, really, of any move I might make."

He was looking at me but not seeing me. I wanted him to see me. I said, "But we all were, in some way. Don't you think?" I lifted my hands. "I was. I was married, and so I couldn't really go forward with my life as a single person, which I was pretending to be. And I didn't want to be married, I knew that. But I couldn't imagine divorce—the failure of that, the ending of that life. I was raised to *keep at it*, whatever *it* was. To work harder if it wasn't going well." I smiled. "Doggedness. Doggedness is what I was raised for."

He asked me then, and I told him, about where I'd come from, about my mother, my family. About the life I might have led if I hadn't run away from it. About Ted waiting for me the whole time he knew me, and how that felt. He was curious, probing. We ordered more coffee.

He talked, too, about his family, from a wealthy suburb north of Chicago, about being raised to believe he could do anything, have anything he wanted. He spoke of what he'd done since Lyman Street—the postdoc at Berkeley, the research fellowship at Stanford, the slow turn from chemistry to the chemistry of biology, the primacy of work in his life. "For a long time," he said, "it was all I thought about. All I'd let myself think about." He spoke of the effect of this on his relationships along the way, how they were always truncated or distorted in some sense. He mentioned a British scientist he saw every few years at conferences. A woman he went out with once a month or so for three or four years, until she finally announced that it— "whatever *it* was," he said, grinning—was over. He had relaxed as we were speaking. He was slouching forward over the table now.

"Much, much water under the dam. Or is it over the dam?" I said. "I can never recall."

"Whatever. You seem happy now. Are you?" His hand, resting on the side of his face, pushed into the flesh by his eyes, by his cheekbone.

I nodded. "Lots more than then."

"When you were what? A seething cauldron of angst?" He underlined the words with his tone.

"Well, when I was a seething cauldron of something causing angst in everyone else, anyhow. My poor ex-husband. He wasn't a bad guy, either."

"Are you in touch with him?"

"No. I heard he'd remarried, but that was years and years ago." In fact, he'd remarried twice, I knew from people who'd known us both in college. He was a dermatologist, very successful, and lived in a gated community outside Albuquerque. He had children by his third wife, children young enough to be his grandchildren.

"So you don't know if he's forgiven you."

"That doesn't even matter. The issue for me was forgiving myself. And not so much because of him. In a way, forgiving myself for being alive. For being so, I guess, *thoughtlessly* alive. Dana made me feel that. Dana's death."

He nodded. "Me too," he said. He looked out the window, over the falling water. His mouth opened, as if to speak, but then he looked at me and stopped. After a moment, he said, "And you did."

"What?"

"Forgive yourself."

"Yes. With work, mostly. It was basically my salvation. Dogs and cats, horses and cows. The odd elephant."

"Elephant!"

I smiled. "I had a zoo internship for a couple of months in vet school. Great, great fun. And a feather in my cap. Of course, it was all useless knowledge in the end. How to use a sixty-cc syringe." I made its enormous shape with my hands. "A twelve-gauge needle." I laughed. "I don't see anything bigger than a big dog now. But it was fun. And it made me feel I'd earned my way back to a normal life."

"Yes, that's what one does, isn't it? After hurting other people."

"It sounds as though you held yourself so far away from other people that you couldn't hurt them."

He laughed sharply, and then his face fell into bitter lines. "That was certainly the point," he said.

"The point of what?"

"Of the shape of my life." He raised his hand abruptly for the waitress, and I looked at my watch.

"Lord!" I said. Daniel would be getting home in about half an hour. I stood up. "I've got to run. I had no idea how late it was."

Eli got up, too, pulling out his wallet. He'd walk out with me, he said. He left a tip on the table, and we crossed the empty room. The other parties had left.

While we stood at the hostess stand in the entry hall, waiting for our bill, he suddenly turned to me and said, "Look, do you mind talking about this? About the past? What was, what might have been, et cetera, et cetera." His hand made a circle I was getting used to as a gesture of his. "How one forgives oneself for being who one was."

"No. Not at all. It's kind of special, actually, to have someone to do it with. Someone who was there."

The waitress appeared, and Eli paid her. We went outside, into the cold morning. The earlier snows had melted, and the air felt dry. You could see the distant bluish line of the mountains. Our footsteps were loud in the Sunday stillness.

I said, "I think in a way I've been wanting to talk about the past with someone. Maybe you get to a certain age and you want to . . . I don't know. Revisit the important times in your life."

"I wouldn't have said so." We'd stopped now, by my car, and I turned and looked at him. "But seeing you, Jo, and now talking to you . . ." He shrugged. "That might be true for me too." He touched my sleeve. "I'd like to see you. To talk again."

"So would I," I said. I'd turned away, a little embarrassed.

"What?" He leaned more toward me, and I was so unnerved, I took a step backward.

"I'd like that," I said.

"Good. Sometime when we're not so rushed, maybe."

"Yes." A slow heat was rising to my face. I hoped it didn't show. "But of course, here come the holidays, and my life will be crazy for a while."

"I understand. Maybe you should just call me when everything has quieted down. There's certainly no hurry about it."

I looked up at him. "No."

"So you'll call." He grinned. "Eventually."

"I promise."

"Good. Good."

He leaned toward me, and we touched our warm cheeks together.

WHEN THE GIRLS WERE LITTLE, IF THEY WERE DISTRESSED IN the night I was the one who went to them, who stayed until they were calm. Daniel had more trouble even waking up, and he needed much more sleep than I, so we both accepted this. For a few years when she was around six or seven, Cassie in particular used to have nightmares. She cried out, and I would rush to her in the dark and slide in next to her. Her body would be tensed with whatever she'd imagined. ("A lady was turning around and she had big skirts on and it was *too slow*, Mom. It was so slow.") I would be cold from the sprint upstairs. She was always feverishly hot, as though she'd been exercising fiercely, even in sleep. She gave me her heated wired body, and I gave her my large, cool one. She'd nestle against me, poking me with her sharp shoulders, her bony hips, and I'd tell her stories.

Over the nights, I slowly focused on a character I invented to give her courage, a character Cassie always wanted to hear more of: Miraculotta. At first I saw this creation as a sturdy, unflappable older girl with a Buster Brown haircut, wearing, of course, culottes. In one story she traveled and lived with apes in the jungles of Africa. In another she became a fierce warrior, despite the men who said a woman couldn't do that. She was friends with animals and could understand their speech—always a great selling point with my children. The kindly chickens and ducks gave her eggs to eat. Admiring foxes donated their tails—which they could grow back—to make a beautiful, soft robe she wore in winter. Friendly elephants bathed her, sending their spray arcing high in the air. She was never afraid of them, because she knew they loved her, she was so gay, so charming. (She'd begun to change already, though I hadn't planned it.) She built her house herself, out of snow, and lived in the white glowing space, sleeping at night under a quilt she made from the down the geese had given her.

At some point in these dark nights, I realized that Miraculotta had changed so much that now I was thinking of Dana as the model for her, bringing Dana to life again in these reassuring fantasies—taking the person who'd met the most horrible end I knew of and making her the most fearless and invulnerable creature possible. After I understood this, I began consciously to tell Cassie some things that were true about Dana, giving details from her life to Miraculotta: how she sometimes slept on the roof at night to be closer to the stars; how she made her living for a while singing in the subways. Or I would embellish a germ of truth: she was so beautiful that men painted her, drew her, and these paintings had the power to cast a spell over anyone who saw them. She gave away everything she owned, and as a reward for that—though she hadn't expected any reward—the wood spirits replenished her supplies. She built little creatures out of clay she found on the banks of the river, and they were so beautifully made, so real, that they sometimes came to life. These, too, she gave away, setting them free.

One night Cassie said to me, "I know who Miraculotta really is, Mom." She was whispering, as I had been, so we wouldn't wake Nora or Sadie, asleep in their dark rooms across the hall.

"Do you?" I asked.

She nodded gravely, her eyes wide and black in the faint light. "I really do."

"Who, then? Who is she?"

Shyly she said, "She's *you*."

I was pleased and even a little embarrassed to be so admired, and whenever I told her these stories afterward, I felt a special tenderness toward Cass. But then, of course, she got older and stopped needing me in the night.

Several years later, though, when Cass's disaffection began, and then her rage at us—at me—it helped to remember that once she'd thought Miraculotta and I were one, to know in what regard she'd held me. It helped me to understand how repulsive she found me when all of that had fallen away. "You're so *limited*," she said to me once when she was about fourteen and I was telling her she could not do one thing or another. And I thought, *Well, yes*, of course I am.

But at that earlier time, I realized that Cassie was right, that she'd parsed it well: Miraculotta was me, me and Dana combined. That when I was dreaming her up in the dark with Cassie, I was talking about all the feelings I had about that time, the sense of magical possibility embodied for me in Dana's energy and passion, in the open-endedness of my own life, in the curious and momentary hallucination we all shared then—more important to me, I think, than to anyone else in the house—that we could make of our lives anything we wanted, that all the rules we'd learned growing up did not apply.

We didn't know what would happen next: that was our great gift. The gift of youth. The thing we miss, it seems to me, no matter what we've made of our lives, as we get older. When we do know what will happen next. And next and next, and then last.

And that is what I felt again after my coffee with Eli—that sense of a surprise, that heady sense of *not knowing*, that gift of a possible turn in the path.

THE NEXT DAY I DROVE INTO BOSTON TO MEET MY MOTHER. This had become an annual ritual, since by choice she stayed home for Christmas, and my brother's family came over from New Hampshire to be with her. She and I had gradually evolved what she called our "early Christmas" together: a meeting, an exchange of gifts, lunch, a day of shopping, and then always, before I put her back on the bus, a double martini for her and a glass of wine or coffee for me at the Copley Plaza Hotel. In the old days I'd brought the girls along, and the day had exhausted all of us. For the last four years, though, it had been just the two of us, my mother and I, and our pace was more civilized, our pauses were longer. She had told me when we talked the week before that the only thing she had to get done was presents for her great-grandchildren, my brother Fred's first grandchildren, now six and three. We planned to go to the Museum of Science for these. They had educational toys in their gift shop, toys my mother believed in, toys such as all toys had once been, it seemed to me—things you cut or carved or assembled and glued. Things you mixed and stirred. Kites. Gyroscopes, yo-yos. "Nothing"—and here Mother's voice on the telephone had changed, and I could imagine her drawing herself up slightly in a ladylike repulsion—"*electronic.*"

I had laughed. For beyond even her age, my mother was old-fashioned. She'd been a farm girl, from the center of Maine, and she'd come to the university to work at nineteen after taking secretarial courses, an ambitious reaching out for a girl of her background. By chance she'd been assigned to my father's office. He was twenty years older than she was, a professor of botany, and he was married, though his wife was dying. My parents' love, their courtship, was never spoken of in our house—there was always a deep reticence about anything that smacked of emotion—but I imagined it later as her listening to him, admiring him, learning from him, botanizing with him; as her slowly becoming a necessity to him, this quiet country girl with the wide, surprising smile.

And this seemed to be the nature of their love, even long after his wife had died and they had married and my brother and then I had been born. Each of them solitary, busy, mostly silent, turning to the other from time to time to say things like, "*Isn't* that remarkable!" Or, "Most interesting."

I think she didn't feel comfortable as a faculty wife—perhaps she thought of it as a kind of posthumous usurpation of his first wife's role—so my father's life did not change much as a result of this new marriage, or even when he became a father two times over. My mother continued part time as his secretary, she still accompanied him to the office each morning and went out on long walks with him. She continued to behave, generally, as though, like him, she were a middle-aged botanist.

When he died, her grief was invisible to me, except as a kind of stiffening, a further aging. She was only forty-four then. She might have thought of her life as having other beginnings. Other chapters anyway. She might have thought of remarriage. But within a few months she was back at work full time, and her life's shape seemed unaltered. As it had for all the years since.

I waited for her on the bus platform at South Station. A raw wind was blowing off the ocean, and the day was heavy and gray. A motley group got off the bus when it pulled up: some young people, a few guys in military uniforms, a fat mother with three little kids. When the driver stepped forward and held his hand out to help someone, I knew it would be Mother descending. He had made an odd motion first, as though—almost as though—he was going to take his hat off, in respect.

She emerged slowly, said something to him after she'd gotten down: they bent together briefly and then leaned back, smiling in polite collusion with each other. Then she looked around quickly, ascertained which direction she should head in, and came toward me, utterly erect, white-haired, a kind of jaunty wide beret pinned on the back of her head. She had on her ancient all-purpose coat, heavy no-color duckcloth she zipped the plaid lining out of in spring. I was startled to see that on her feet she was wearing—for the first time to my knowledge—old-lady shoes, black oxfords you laced up over the instep, with a thick heel. Her gait was slightly more widespread than usual, as though she was conscious of the issue of balance.

I called out and crossed to her, watching her face shift as she recognized me. "Why, Josie!" she said, and we held each other.

We had lunch right away, in a place we usually went to near the terminal. Despite my exclamations of interest in various dishes, she conscientiously ordered the least expensive item on the menu, as she always did, and black coffee. She asked about Daniel, about the girls, and I gave my report, offering mostly achievements and accomplishments, not so much to boast as because that was what I assumed would give her greatest pleasure. She offered in exchange information about her students, the students who boarded with her. A thin smile played over her lips as she went on about these strangers, and I was startled, as I always was, to hear how important they were to her, to feel how much more interested she was in their activities, their achievements, than in Cassie's or Sadie's or Nora's. But they, of course, were in her life every day, whereas the girls were, I suppose, a kind of lovely abstraction for her at this point, a nice idea.

And I was glad, in a sense, for her involvement with Edward and Rolf and Naomi and Susie—the names changed almost yearly. Still, it was boring, too, the tedious accumulation of detail about people I didn't know and didn't care about. As she spoke, I drifted off. I watched the passersby moving in the brisk wind outside. I looked up at the warehouse windows above us and wondered about the kinds of lives being lived there. I let myself think of Eli. "I'd like to see you again," he says, smiling at me. I smiled at my mother now, too warmly perhaps, for she gave me an odd, sharp look and then sniffed, loudly.

I asked for the check.

I had read in the paper of a program of Christmas music at two o'clock at Trinity Church, and Mother said that would be lovely, so we drove there next. I was parking at a meter only a block or so away—we had congratulated each other on finding it—when she cried out, "Oh! I wanted to be sure to tell you: Albert Moran died."

Dr. Moran. I turned the engine off. He came to me, bending over a wounded dog, covering it with his big hands, turning to say to me in his soft voice, "Our friend here has gone somewhere he should not have gone, I'm afraid." I saw him tidily tucking his napkin into his collar before opening his old-fashioned lunchbox, as black and humped as a steam engine.

"When?" I asked.

"Oh, a couple of weeks ago, I think." Mother was casual. She was used to death. It was her familiar by now.

"Had he been ill?"

"Dearie, I don't know. I just read it in the paper and thought you might like to have the information."

"I'm glad you told me."

"Though come to think of it, they said he was in a nursing home, so he might have been. Ill. But he was ninety-six. A good old age." She sounded approving. This was how it should happen, the distinguished thing.

"Yes," I said.

She was opening her door. "He was certainly good to you. I won't soon forget that."

"Nor will I," I said.

The wind was driving and powerful off the glass of the Hancock Building as we approached the church. Mother held her hat on with one hand and I hooked my arm in hers as we pushed against the blast. Her coat flapped back, showing the worn lining.

Inside the church, we turned away from each other, gasping in the peacefulness, the dim, reddish quiet. I blew my nose, and Mother savagely repinned her hat.

As we entered the nave, the lighted altar glowed, golden and radiant, in the vast space. The dark wooden pews were more than half full, and we slid into the first empty one we came to. We whispered an intermittent conversation, quieted by the hush around us, by the high, empty spaces arching above. Mother was admiring of the needlepoint on the kneelers, the names of the needlewomen or their families picked out across them. Hannah Maynard Shaw. Lilian Tappan. Edward and Rebecca Soames.

I was glad, when the music started, to sink into it and my own thoughts—a strange mixture of Dr. Moran and my work with him, of Dana, of Eli again, and now and then of Daniel. Of Mother and her curious, proud, and lonely life. Did she regret it? Any of it? Did she sense the end of it closing in on her and wish she'd done things she hadn't? Wish she'd gone places she should not have gone? Or was it enough for her to have done steadily and honorably and carefully and thoroughly all the things she'd undertaken to do? Perhaps it was. My heart ached for her, suddenly.

The concert closed with several carols, and Mother and I stood next to each other, sharing a hymnal. Her voice was thin and parched but completely on key, and at one point she ventured into a few notes of harmony against me, and we met each other's eyes and smiled.

The museum was busy, though not frantic, as it sometimes was when we came; late enough in the day so the school groups had left, we speculated. We went straight to the gift shop, and Mother started making her careful choices: a bag of cat's-eye marbles, a boomerang, a kit for building a dinosaur's skeleton. There was a painful kind of parsimony to all this, and I found it difficult to watch. I moved away from her. I spent some time looking at the literature they had on animal life.

I was standing in the doorway, watching her pay—cash: she didn't believe in credit cards—when I heard the announcement for a movie on African lions, a subject I was not without interest in, having helped to raise a litter of them once when I was working at the zoo. It would give Mother a chance to rest, I thought, for she had seemed tired on the longish walk in from the parking area. "That would be very interesting," she said, and so I took her packages from her, and we bought our tickets and proceeded through the museum behind the crowd of people also headed to the movie.

The theater was huge: an Omnimax, I saw. The pale-beige ceiling rounded vastly over the chairs like a tepid sky. I explained to Mother the way it worked, as we sat down, as we tilted back. "Why, it's just like going to the dentist," she said, and we both laughed. It felt strangely intimate to be stretched out next to her.

The film started above us, around us. A man's voice, deep and self-important, narrated. He sounded remarkably like the civic voice that had accompanied educational films of my school days. The photography was wonderful to watch, the animals with their gravity, their powerful tawny slowness and then murderous speed.

The narrative offended me, though. It was utterly spurious and imposed, involving, as it did, the repeated stumblings into danger and then rescues of the photographic crew as they tried to get in close for better shots. The deep voice vibrated, trying to pump up the excitement, as though watching the animals themselves couldn't possibly be enough.

At some point I turned my head to see how all of this was affecting Mother. She lay perfectly still, her skirt carefully draped over her knees. Her old-lady shoes touched each other at the toes. She'd pulled her hands up and folded them together on her bosom, in modesty, perhaps, at lying down in public. Her mouth was slack, her eyes had swung up to look at something at the top of the ceiling, and I could see just the glimmer of white under the iris. I realized suddenly that this was the way she would look, dead. My pulse throbbed heavily, and I felt a moment of purest terror, of unreadiness. *No,* I thought. *Not yet.* I leaned over her, horrified.

She felt me looking; her eyes swung to me and saw the terrible thing in my face. "What?" she cried out, struggling up, as frightened by me as I'd been by her. "What?"

THE HECTIC DAYS PASSED. SADIE CAME HOME FROM SCHOOL, slept late, often wanted the car in the afternoon. I took to driving home at lunch. She would drive me back to work and pick me up at the end of the day. I foisted errands off on her or we did them together late in the afternoon. We had family meals again, we had loud music in the living room at night. The house would suddenly be full of her friends, and I caught up with them: who was dropping out, who was transferring, who was in love. Daniel played carols at the piano, and we all sang along.

My chores increased; I was never alone. My life seemed to claim me utterly, in a way I would have said I was hoping for. But throughout all this, I couldn't stop thinking about Eli. I thought of the way he had bent down to touch his cheek to mine in the parking lot at the Pennock Inn, the heat he radiated physically. I thought of the way his features had thickened and even coarsened some as he'd aged, making him seem a man of appetites. Energetic.

What Daniel had called my *crush* had changed, or I felt it differently. It was no longer my past, my own youth, that attracted me to

Eli. It was the thought of Eli himself, the heavy, buoyant middle-aged man. Still, I tried to think of this as lightly as I'd thought of that earlier attraction. As a kind of joke, really, one I might share with Daniel, as I had the other one. But of course I didn't. I kept it private. A joke I shared with only me, then. Deliberately, playfully, I fed my fantasies about Eli. I allowed them to become sexual, I gave them specific flesh. I imagined us in sundering, tearing passion in hotel rooms in Boston, in nondescript motels or inns in towns twenty or fifty miles away, laboring together, slick with sweat, sore, spent.

I'd look up from addressing cards or wrapping presents or doing dishes and see Sadie slouched in a chair, her eyes unfocused, a Walkman buzzing into her ears; or Daniel reading the paper or a book; and be embarrassed at the Technicolor detail of my sexual thoughts. Be surprised they couldn't feel my heated distraction.

It was all right to imagine this, I said to myself, my own reassuring Ann Landers. As long as I understood it wasn't going to happen.

It isn't going to happen, I'd tell myself.

And then I'd imagine another scene, another inventive coupling, another spent falling away from each other in another bed.

I went further. I'd imagine Jean's death, my divorcing Daniel. Or Daniel's death, Eli's divorcing Jean. Only stories, I said to myself. Just that. Or they could both die. Painlessly, of course. A period of mourning, Eli and I turning more and more to each other.

It was all adolescent. I recognized this and even felt some contempt for myself on account of it. It reminded me of the period in my life when I was eight or nine and most in love with my father. During that time, I repeatedly imagined my mother's dying in a variety of ways and my stepping into her role, caring for my father, becoming his *sine qua non*, his necessary. And now I told myself that this, all this daze of imaginary flesh I lived in, was as little connected to what was going to happen, to what I truly wanted, as that had been.

But what I was wondering was what I truly wanted. And what if Eli wanted an affair, what if he pressed for that? Would I resist?

I had certainly had temptations in the past—a number of mild pleasurable flirtations, and twice moments when I felt I was actively, and even perhaps reluctantly, choosing not to succumb to something that both compelled and frightened me. Once, only a few years earlier, at a conference of small-clinic vets in Hawaii, I'd been drawn to a vet from Seattle named Davis Holliston, a rumpled, cheerful, profane man, kind and sexy, a master teller of jokes. He had only to start, "A duck walks into a bar," and I would be convulsed. Night after night we sat up late, drinking and talking and laughing with others. And then, finally, it was just us, and I had to decide.

And once, much earlier, we'd hired a man older than our usual high-school student—a man in his twenties—as an assistant in the clinic. I was in my mid-thirties, just starting the practice then, swamped with work and small children and the demands of the house, which we'd recently moved into, each room of which was a project waiting to be undertaken: decaying, water-stained wallpaper, linoleum flooring, obsolete, exposed pipes running from floor to ceiling. To be reminded—as I was one night when we stayed on together and he hesitantly, then authoritatively, then wildly, kissed me—that I was sexual, that I was still young, that I was attractive, even in my scrubs, my grubby sneakers: this was a revelation, an awakening, a thrill. A temptation.

I resisted it. I broke away. I wept. I clung to him. I wept some more. I went home and confessed my feelings to Daniel. For days we made time for each other, we talked passionately about our life together and what we needed to do to make it more intense, more loving again.

I had to fire Eric. He said he understood. We stood glumly opposite each other in one of the exam rooms, the moat of the gleaming stainless-steel table separating us, and talked about it, about my life, my responsibilities, about Daniel. About Eric's life, about what he would do next.

I told Beattie I'd had to fire Eric because he'd been repeatedly late for the morning opening.

"Is that so?" she said at the time. And then, some days later, "You did the right thing, letting Eric go."

"Thanks," I said, not looking at her.

"Yes, he was too forward for my taste." I could feel her eyes sharp upon me, hoping for a confidence, a confession—some dirt. But I kept my own counsel. Mine and Eric's and Daniel's.

This was it. My history. I assumed Daniel's was something like it, though he hadn't ever spoken to me of his attraction to anyone. But perhaps he'd had to say to someone what I said to Davis in Hawaii as he leaned in the doorway to my hotel room: that I'd always assumed about myself that I'd be faithful in marriage.

"Ah!" he'd said then, sounding approving and deflated at once.

I had assumed that. I assumed it still. But it seemed to me now that there might be circumstances so compelling, so out of the ordinary run of the possible, that the old rules, the old feelings, would no longer apply.

The truth was I didn't know what I would do if I had the choice, and that, too, made me feel distant from Daniel, from my daughter, from what was normally a joyous period of preparation.

CASS AND NORA ARRIVED ON CHRISTMAS EVE, FROM OPPOSITE directions and in time for all of us to go to the ten o'clock service together. Daniel was already at church, so we piled into my car. Nora and Cass were being civil to each other, having a gingerly discussion in the back seat about a band Nora had heard recently in New York, the Little Piggies.

The night was wonderfully clear, and when we got out of the car at church, Sadie and I leaned back dizzily in the frigid air and tried to identify the few constellations we knew in the glowing sky. Cass and Nora danced around us, calling out invented names to hurry us along.

"Why, it's the Little Piggies themselves!"

"Look! Look! The Jolly Green Giant!"

"And there's Pater Familias!"

"Check it out! The Lederhosen! Over here!"

"The Alma Mater!"

"Come on, you guys! Let's go!"

Inside, the church smelled of wool, of candles, of the pine boughs that decorated the altar, and of something vaguely like cinnamon. The service was short, just scriptures and carols and a quick homily from Daniel. The children's choir did a descant in their piercing clear voices on the last hymn, and it brought unexpected tears to my eyes.

At home we had hot cider with rum and opened one stocking gift each, the beginning of our prolonged ritual. There were lumpy purple mittens for Sadie from Beattie ("She made them herself," I said). A new fishing lure for Daniel, bath oil for me, a tiny moonstone earring—or nose ring, or eyebrow ring—for Cass. A pair of tortoise-shell combs for Nora's heavy hair, from Sadie.

Daniel was especially energetic and happy. He kept putting extra logs on the fire, stirring it. He sang to himself as he got us all more cider and cookies. It was the end of a long, demanding season for him, and he had three days with not a lot to do before the Sunday service. I went to bed early, but he said he wanted to sit up awhile with the girls. As I passed through the hall on my way back from the bathroom, I could hear them in the living room, a burst of laughter and then Nora's voice: "If you strained for a compliment—and I had to, believe me—you might have called it cinema verité. But it was really just plain home movies."

"*Down*-home movies, it sounds like," Daniel said, and then I heard his loose, light laugh and I shut the door.

When I woke in the morning and turned to his side of the bed, the bedclothes lay rumpled and empty. Daniel was gone, the house was silent around me. I had an odd moment of fear, and then I realized he'd gotten up early and gone to church alone. He often did this on Christmas Day, beginning it in solitary prayer before he came home to our loud and secular festivities. I imagined him there now, sitting with his eyes intently closed in a pew in the chilly nave, the gentle morning light falling on his solitary figure, on the white-painted pews, the gray floors. How sad it was, really, I thought, lying there, that not one of us shared his belief, that he was so alone in this central aspect of his life. Did we even have beliefs? I wondered. I believed in animals, I supposed—their purity, their goodness. Cass believed in music, in cigarettes and coffee and wine and men. Nora believed in getting up early and starting each day carefully dressed, carefully made up. And Sadie? Maybe Sadie still believed in us.

By the time I heard Daniel's car crunching over the frozen snow in the yard, I was up and dressed, I'd fed the dogs and let them out, I'd made coffee and started the stuffing for the goose. Daniel burst in at the door, and I heard him stomping, sniffling, hanging up his coat and shedding his boots in the back hall. When he came into the steamy kitchen, his cheeks were flushed, his hair was raked up oddly from his hat; he looked like a badly cared for child. His face lifted when he spotted me. He cried out, "Merry Christmas, my darling, my dearest, my sweet," and crossed to embrace me. His face was cold, bristly. His nose was wet.

"Oh, Daniel," I said. I kissed him lightly.

"Why pull away? Why, when I adore you so?"

"Do you?" I asked, embarrassed. I reached out and flattened his hair.

"An alternative, just a suggestion," he said. He raised his finger, as though about to conduct an orchestra. " 'And *I* adore *you*, my dearest husband.' "

"Well, of course, I *do*," I said. "Come and sit, and I'll pour you some coffee."

We sat down opposite each other at the table. Sunlight had just begun to flicker through the kitchen windows, shifting with the motion of the pine trees behind the house as it edged above them.

"Oh!" I remembered, setting my cup down. "I had a weird dream."

"Visions of sugar plums."

"No." I smiled. "No." And then I thought better of telling him. "Actually, I can hardly remember it."

But I did. It was a dream that was familiar to me, though it took various forms. Usually I was still married to my first husband, or Daniel in some way *was* Ted. This time it had been in a strange, messy house, unrecognizable, and Ted/Daniel kept starting to make love to me, sliding his hand deep into my pants, touching me. I'd woken in the night feeling aroused, bigamous.

"I like it when I can't *quite* remember dreams," Daniel said. "When I feel my brain has its own private life that I don't necessarily have access to."

"But if you worked at it, you could reach them. Freud says so."

"Does he?" Daniel said. "Well, the hell with Freud, I say. I say let the secret life be the secret life."

I laughed and raised my coffee cup. "Hear, hear."

He reached over to pat my leg. "There, there," he said.

Then we both got up, he to shave, I to finish the stuffing and to prepare our big family breakfast. As I sailed the folded white cloth into the air and it bellied out over the table, it caught the first sure shafts of sunlight falling into the room and sank dazzlingly down, like the descent of a blessing, I thought, and I willed myself to record it, to remember.

EARLY THAT AFTERNOON, AFTER WE'D UNWRAPPED THE PRESENTS and put the dinner in the oven to cook, Daniel took me ice-skating. We hadn't gone in several years, but they'd just flooded the town green and the ice was new and smooth.

I was not a good skater. Daniel was, and he glided around and around the edge of the ice, a slim, boyish figure at this distance, bent low, stroking steadily, easily crossing one foot over the other as he swept round the curves. I pushed my slow way up and back, stopping every few trips to rest my sagging ankles and tensed legs by sitting on the wooden bench at the edge of the ice. From here I could see the front of the Congregational church, and behind it, modestly peeping around its corner, our house, in its regularity like a picture of old New England. Smoke puffed from the chimney; we'd left the sleepy, sated girls still in their bathrobes by the fire.

At last Daniel skated up to me, with a flourish of sprayed ice. "Shall we?" he said, and opened his arms to receive me. I slid forward, and he took my hand in one of his and put his arm around my waist. We pushed off, and after a few faltering steps, I got his rhythm. I began to lean with him, now this way, now that. Daniel powered us, his legs pumping hard, his arm around me transferring his strength to me, giving my strokes length and reach. We rode across the smooth, gleaming ice under the bare maple branches, up toward the church with its long pointing steeple, back toward the houses facing it, their doors hung with festive wreaths, Christmas lights twinkling in a few windows. The wind we generated stung my nose and cheeks, but I was exhilarated. Up and back we went, leaning steeply into the curve at each end.

I felt young and strong, I felt I could have gone on like this forever, with just the sound of the rushing air and the skate blades slicing the ice; so that when Daniel let go of my hand and dropped back away from me to skate off again, I wasn't ready for my own sudden heaviness, the stumplike thickness of my limbs. I stopped dead in the middle of the gunmetal pond. Daniel danced by me, running, leaping, now that he was free of my dragging weight. He was showing off, spinning as he passed, landing on one skate, bending balletically.

I felt lumpen, old, and stiff. I turned around and around in the center of the pond, watching him circle me, full of a childish rage at him but also wanting to call him back, to stop him. To ask, somehow, for his help.

11

"CAN YOU HAVE A DRINK?" ELI ASKED. "ARE YOU DRIVING back this afternoon?"

"I'm not sure," I said. What I'd told Daniel was that I was meeting Lauren Howe, a friend from Maine, and might spend the night if it got too late. "I may stay over. In any case, yes. A drink."

He raised his hand, a peremptory gesture, I saw. Authoritative. A gesture that *assumed*. It excited me, this small thing, the way in adolescence seeing a boy's big hands on the steering wheel of a car had excited me. Something about their power, their control over my situation, over my life. Something foolish, even willfully foolish. The waiter came and took our order.

We were sitting by the tinted window in the bar of the Ritz Hotel in Boston. On the crowded sidewalk outside the plate glass, pedestrians hurried past, huddled against the cold. The Public Garden loomed dark and mysteriously beautiful across the street. There had been skaters on the frozen duck pond when I got out of the car, and tinny waltz music floating thinly in the darkening air.

"I'm glad you called," he said.

"I am too." Though I had felt almost frightened by the sight of him in the doorway, his face questioning the waiter and then opening in what seemed like pleasure as he saw me across the dimly lighted room. "I'd been meaning to for a while," I said, "but life's been chaotic. As I predicted."

"A nice chaos, though, as I imagine it."

"It was. It was fun. But it was a relief when everyone left." Sadie had gone back to school just three days earlier, after a long holiday break.

"I'm sure."

The drinks came and we wordlessly raised our glasses to each other. In the corner, the group of men in dark suits suddenly laughed, loudly. My bourbon tasted smoky and thick.

Eli had begun to talk, speaking of the pleasure of being in the lab again—he'd come from there to meet me—of getting things set up. He said he had stayed late in town twice the week before, he talked about the seductive quality of the solitude, about how he'd always loved the lab at night. He shook his head. "Finally there's nothing like work, is there?" he said.

I was thinking of him as a young man. The worker bee, we'd nicknamed him. I smiled. "I can't imagine a life without it," I said. "Retirement. Doesn't *that* seem improbable?"

He agreed. "Impossible, in fact," he said. He spoke of a restless irritability that had overtaken him at some point late in the fall, like something physical, "like a nervous disorder. In spite of the fact that I was doing a kind of work, dashing around lecturing and attending conferences. It's not the same, though."

I sympathized. I talked about the way I felt walking into the clinic. About the sense I sometimes had of being lifted out of ordinary life, of leaving it behind. "Of course, it's different in my work," I said. "There *is* no solitude. I mean, I have the animals, with their own personalities and lives. Their own life stories, really."

He smiled. "I suppose," he said. "Sure. Arthur had one, after all. For me, though . . ." He paused, looked out the window a moment. "For me, work has been my life story, I think." He was speaking more slowly than usual and without that lightness in tone which normally undercut the possibility of seriousness in whatever he was saying. "Or perhaps a kind of substitute for a life story. I think of myself as a scientist first, before I'm a man, really. That's why I think . . . Well, when I spoke to you about Jean, about our separateness, that's why that's so important to me. Because it frees me for what's most central." He looked sharply at me. "I've tried to make my life count, and I think I have. I think, honestly, that the world is a better place because of the work I've done. And that's everything to me."

I smiled. Why? Because this was grandiose, but also, I think, high-minded. I wasn't used to such shameless high-mindedness. Daniel avoided it, I suppose because high-mindedness combined with piety is such a deadly combination.

He saw the smile. "You think I'm being immodest," he accused. "I'm not, I assure you. Crossing this blood-brain barrier is pivotal, absolutely pivotal, to curing all kinds of diseases." He lifted his hands and began to count them off, finger by finger. "Cancer, Parkinson's, Alzheimer's, even spinal cord injuries. All of them will have treatments eventually—soon. Some do already. But no way of getting them across the natural blockade in the brain." And he began carefully to explain to me the applications of his work, its importance in various of these treatments. It made me think of the night when he'd explained his research to me on Lyman Street and of my sense then of seeing a different Eli. The Eli he'd become, I thought, watching him now. The Eli he'd grown into.

He was talking about the impenetrability of the capillaries in the brain, their lack of porousness, what he called the "tight junctions" between cells. He talked about some other approaches for getting drugs across: temporarily shrinking the cells lining the capillaries so the drugs could, for a short period of time, pass through. Or surgically implanting them. "But the most efficient way, the way that will help the maximum number of people—and will have application with the maximum number of drugs—is what we're trying to do with nerve growth factor. Essentially it's like smuggling it across," he said. "You get a molecule that's allowed to cross, one with its own transport system, and you ask it to be your *mule*." He grinned. "To carry along the molecule *you* want to get in there."

It seemed of great importance to him that I understand all this, and so I took care to be sure I did. The exchange was, for me, exciting, in part intellectually, but in part also because I sensed he might be wooing me with this. At one point he actually took his pen out and drew on a napkin the way the transport proteins ferried substances across from the bloodstream to the brain cells waiting outside the capillaries. The black ink trembled and blotted on the soft paper.

I was aware of the beginning of a kind of physical restlessness in myself, an eagerness that was not yet fully sexual but could be, I could tell. I was titillated by Eli's seriousness, by his clarity about his work, by the work itself, truly. What else? By his reference again to the separateness in his marriage. Even by the way he spoke my name as he explained things.

So it seemed somehow an interruption in everything when he suddenly sat back, looking intently at me, and said, "Do you mind if we talk about Dana?"

But then I realized that of course this was part of our intimacy too. Of course we would. When I first thought about seeing him again—when Jean brought Arthur to me—that was exactly what I'd assumed we'd speak of sooner or later: Dana, the past, who we were then.

"No," I said. "No, I'd like that." This will slow us down, I thought. Yes, let's slow down. Nothing has to happen. Nothing. "It's wonderful to think of having someone to talk about her with, actually. After all this time."

He looked out the window for a long moment. And then at me, with an expression on his face I couldn't read. He said, "Did you know she and I had been lovers?"

"Yes. Dana told me that."

"Did she?" He seemed, momentarily, surprised. "Well, she told everyone everything, didn't she?" He shook his head, fondly. "She was the second woman I'd slept with, in my meager sexual life of the time. I was terribly in love with her."

"*That* I didn't know."

"No one did. Including Dana, strangely enough."

"So you just—what? Sat on it? Kept it secret?"

"No. No, I tried to tell her. I did tell her. That's the 'strangely enough' part. Because in some sense she didn't hear me. She wouldn't hear me. She . . . Well, she was a very powerful person in some ways, you know. What she wanted was for us to be friends. Just plain old friends. That's how she thought of us. So"—he made a face—"that's what we were." His hands were cradling the squat glass his drink had come in, sliding it a few inches back and forth across the tabletop. "It was she who brought me into the house; did you know that?"

I shook my head.

"Yes." He nodded. "And at first, foolishly, I thought it was another kind of invitation." He smiled, his self-mocking smile.

"This was *after* you were lovers, or before?" I was confused. "When, exactly, were you lovers?"

He laughed, and I could feel my face lift in response. "Yes," he said. "Let me tell you my story. I guess I do have a story, after all. A complicated story, in fact."

He sipped from his drink and set it back down. He'd met her, he told me, at the Peabody Museum. He felt so socially awkward at that stage of his life that he ate there regularly in order to avoid having to eat with or talk to anyone from his lab or his department. Dana was there one day, moving behind the glass cases, a beautiful tall woman with thick blond hair reaching halfway down her back. She was alone, sketching the animals, their strange skeletal structures. "The *slow loris*," he said, with a peculiar emphasis. "The *honey possum*."

I smiled again, I'm not sure why.

She saw him watching her. She waved to him: he imitated her gesture, a slow curling in of separated fingers. A day or two later she was there again, and she came up to him this time and they talked. "*She* talked," he said. "I was overwhelmed." She said if he came often for lunch she'd see him again, that that's when she usually came in too. And so she did. Once, twice. And by the next week, she'd invited him back to the house with her and they'd made love in her room.

He paused, watching his hands move the glass again. "I don't know that she was much interested in her own pleasure. My later experience tells me she might not have been." He looked up at me. "But she loved giving pleasure, in ways that were to me, then . . . astounding." He grinned. "And even now, thinking back, certainly most accomplished. But she *wanted*, I think, to be amazing. I don't know. She wanted to do everything, every time. To use up all of herself, all of you. To a person like me . . ." He lifted his hands. "I hadn't known such feelings could exist. I stopped being able to work, which for me . . ." He shook his head. "I became obsessed. I would say temporarily deranged, in fact." He smiled, sadly.

For a few weeks they met daily, he said, sometimes several times a day. She came to the lab once at night, and they made love on a counter, and then in a closet after they heard someone in the corridor. They made love, fully clothed, Dana astride him, on a bench in the Cambridge Common.

"And then, poof!" His hand made a gesture of explosion, of vanishing. "She met someone else and I must suppose was busy about the very same things with him." His voice exaggerated the pronunciation of these words. His smile was ironic. "And quite finished with me," he said.

"That must have been hard," I said. "To have someone like Dana *quite finished* with you."

"Yes," he agreed. "And yet she wasn't, actually. No, not quite. Because she still wanted to be friends, to have coffee, to talk, to go to a movie with me sometimes." Each time she called, he said, his hopes would rise. And then he'd feel foolish, exposed—but also crass, *in the wrong* somehow—that he'd expected anything more than her sweetness, her company. He said that her inviting him to join the house was the last straw. After he moved in and realized that nothing was going to change between them, they had a terrible fight, a scene in which he accused her of tormenting him deliberately.

She wept, freely. She was astonished, sympathetic. Didn't he know she was involved with Duncan?

No, he said. "And I told her I wouldn't have believed it anyway." He shook his head. "That self-satisfied jerk."

I laughed, and he smiled back fleetingly.

He said the scene went on for a while. He was accusatory. She kept calling him darling, honey, she held him. He'd wept, finally, "for the first time since I was a kid."

After this, she came to his room occasionally if he seemed upset. Once or twice she actually tried to jerk him off, or suck him off—as though, he said, it was just a physical pressure he was feeling, one she could relieve at no cost to herself, or him. Once, in despair, he'd let her. "I remember looking down at her, at her head with that great sweep of wonderful hair lying across my legs, covering me, sort of rippling as she moved, and thinking, *How can she be doing this and not loving me?*"

I blushed in embarrassment at this, I could see it so clearly.

"I just didn't know what to do with my feelings: that was the problem. I was such a *kid*. I wanted to *marry* her, I was so in love. Anyway, finally I got her to agree that we'd talk about it again, in a year.

"She said to me, 'A year. You'll see. By the time a year is up, you'll have some wonderful new woman.' And after that, she was always bringing people over to meet me. And of course, when you moved in, she wanted me to fall in love with you. I think that's part of why she wanted you in the house, actually. I remember her coming to my room, oh, several times. Talking about you. I pretended to listen. I pretended to take her seriously." He looked at me intently. "God, how I wish I had."

I could feel myself blushing again. "Do you?"

"Of course." His hands moved forward on the table, as if to touch me. And then stopped. He looked away, took a breath. "This is all so hard to talk about."

"Oh, I know. I think the only person I've ever discussed it with was Daniel. It's so impossible to explain her, for one thing. How powerful her . . . lovingness was. Like some kind of blessing. Like a heat or light you could *feel*."

He looked intently at me. "Yes," he said.

"It must have been . . . I can imagine how hard it was to feel it go away."

"To me it was like dying," he said.

I reached over quickly and touched his hand.

He was watching me. His eyes tightened thoughtfully. "It seems, doesn't it? that you and I were somehow *meant* to meet each other again."

I laughed. I was delighted. Nervous. "Careful," I said gaily. "You're beginning to sound like a religious person."

"God forbid." He smiled. "Some entity or other forbid. Please."

And now he pointed at my empty glass. "Will you . . . ?" He left the question dangling, as if he were asking about much more.

Yes, I said, I would.

He raised his hand for the waiter, signaled for two more drinks. Then he leaned back and looked at me once more, hard. "I felt then—and I feel now, too—that if I hadn't been so overwhelmed by my feelings about Dana, I would have fallen in love with you. I remember wishing I could. I admired your generosity so much, your sense of morality. I thought of you as an adult. I was so rigid, so . . . inflexible in my own judgments. So juvenile. And you seemed compassionate and grown up."

I made a soft noise of protest.

"No, I mean it, Jo. Then, and now. People don't change that much, you know. Or they change, but some central core remains there. I felt it, I felt familiar with it—with you—when you put Arthur away."

"Euthanized him."

"Yes, euthanized him. I think I said to you what a strange bond I feel it is."

The waiter came over with the drinks and a little dish of nuts. We waited while he picked up our empty glasses. He saw the drawing Eli had made on his napkin and paused. "Do you want this?" he asked. Eli shook his head, and the waiter crumpled the napkin and put it on his tray.

When he left, Eli leaned forward again. "That's part of why I was so glad when you called," he said. "I was worried you wouldn't. But I decided to be fatalistic. I wasn't going to call you if you didn't call me. And then this might not have happened." His big hand opened in the air between us. All this.

"But I did," I said.

"You did." He smiled the warm smile that made his eyes all but disappear. "Shall we talk about that night?" he asked.

I wasn't sure, really, what he meant, but because I meant *yes, yes* to everything, I said it: "Yes."

"That was the night, the year-end night."

"What year-end night?"

"That was the end of my waiting period."

"Oh, with Dana."

"Yes, exactly. I reminded her of it a week earlier." He sat back and looked out the window quickly at a pedestrian walking by close to the glass. Then at me again. "I suppose I should have foreseen what would happen when she came up blank. No memory of it whatsoever. And then, when she did remember, she was dismissive: *Yes, fine, we'd talk. Whatever.*" His voice had hardened.

What he was speaking of was only slowing dawning on me. "So this was that night? You saw her that night? The night she died?"

"Yes. I'm getting to that."

Why hadn't this come out before? I was wondering thickly. Why hadn't he said this at the time to one of us? Or told the police?

"I came back to the house at the time I'd mentioned to her— the time I thought we'd agreed on—and there was no one there. I guess . . . well, you were at work, weren't you?" I nodded. "And Duncan, too, I suppose. And John had moved out by then."

"And Larry and Sara had gone to a movie together," I volunteered, impatient now.

"Right," he said. "Anyway, I sat there in the kitchen for half an hour or so—that's what we agreed on: *meet you in the kitchen at nine o'clock*. Actually, I went to the foot of the stairs, too, and called up a couple of times. I was getting really upset. Upset with Dana. Upset with myself, for being such a loser. I didn't know what to do, I felt so powerless, so . . . forgotten. I'd put my coat back on by now, my gloves. I was actually at the back door, in one of those frenzies of indecision— you know what I mean—not knowing whether to stay or go, and so frustrated I wanted to *do* something: throw things around, break stuff. Anyway. Suddenly, I don't know why, I had the notion she was upstairs, in her room, ignoring me. So I charged up there and banged on her door. And she was. Not ignoring me so much, but actually asleep, with the radio on. That's how unimportant it all was to her." His voice was forlorn and bitter at the same time, and I remembered that young Eli and what I'd mistakenly thought was his devotion to all of us, to the house itself, the feel and spirit of the place.

Dana told him to go downstairs, she'd be there in a minute, and he went back down into the kitchen to wait. He was, he said, beside himself by now, pacing back and forth. "That's what I felt, actually. That I'd somehow taken leave of myself. You know what I mean?"

I nodded, though I wasn't sure I did.

Dana took her time, he said. She used the bathroom—he heard the toilet flush—and finally appeared, sleepy-looking and barefoot, in the kitchen doorway.

He turned on her the moment she came in—very controlled, he said, but very angry, determined she should hear him out, should understand the wrong she'd done him.

She was smiling, trying to pacify him, cajole him. He thought her tone was condescending, he thought she wasn't taking him seriously. She came over to him, patted his cheek. He pushed her away, went on talking. He wasn't even sure anymore, he said, what he was saying, some combination of accusation and rage and profession of love and proposal of marriage. And through it all, Dana stayed serene, dreamy. As though he were a little boy. As though she could manipulate him.

He'd remembered the blow job then, he said, that sense of feeling *managed* by her. He realized that she was just trying to quiet him now too. She touched him again, smiling. "Smiling," he said, "when I was in agony." He hit her, in the face. He didn't even truly realize he'd picked up the knife, it was just to get her to stop smiling, to stop saying *sweetie*, *honey*, to stop coming at him with her hands, her mouth, her body, to stop her. He didn't know what he'd done until blood leapt to the place where he'd struck her, leapt and flowed all at once.

When he stopped talking for a moment, I was aware of my breathing.

He spoke slowly now. He said she frowned and looked suddenly perplexed. "It was as if she didn't realize it either, what had happened. She touched herself." His hand imitated her gesture, his large hand brushing his cheek with Dana's hesitant delicacy.

She looked at her hand, her bloody hand, he said, and then back at him. "And she said, 'Oh, Eli,' in this terribly, terribly sad and . . . disappointed way." Then she'd stepped toward him again, and he hit her—that's what he said, he *hit* her—again and again, in the breast, the chest, the side. Just trying, trying to stop her.

I can't say what I was feeling beyond horror at this point, but Eli must have read some sympathy in my face, and thinking it was for himself, instead of for Dana's beautiful pierced body and face, he leaned forward, toward me, and he shook his head.

"I was just so desperate. So . . . wounded."

And suddenly, shrilly, inadvertently, I laughed.

At what? Clearly at the use of the word *wounded* to apply to himself. But at everything else, too, I think: at my own misunderstanding of what I was doing here, at my stupidity. And at the horror, the way a child laughs, I suppose, when he sees a grown-up in pain. The laugh that expresses the wish that everything that's so terrifying could be made funny, that everything frightening really were a joke.

Eli looked startled. Offended, even.

And I apologized. "Sorry," I said. "I'm sorry. A kind of hysteria, I suppose."

He nodded, then, and shook his head. Sudden fatigue, like the radical pull of some emotional gravity, weighted his face.

We sat for a long moment. I felt frozen, I could hardly bear to look at him.

"So you *left* her?" My voice cracked as I asked it. I hadn't realized how dry my throat was. Terror had parched it.

"I know it seems like it, yes. But what happened was *she* left. She had this sort of stunned look on her face, and she walked out of the room, she just walked out, like that." His hand swept her away. He seemed actually puzzled, momentarily. "And then I left too. It was . . .

it was like we'd had this terrible fight and we both just . . . walked out or something."

"But you knew you'd stabbed her!"

He stared at me as though surprised by my failure to grasp something important. "I did. Of course I knew it. But you have to understand what happens to people in these circumstances. In effect, I was in shock. There was that part of me that saw that she was hurt, yes. And there was a part that didn't. That denied it. That . . ." His hand circled. "Chose to disbelieve. That said, over and over, *she walked out.* It's a classic stress response, actually. So on the one hand, I did these self-protective things: I went back to the lab, I washed up, I disposed of the gloves and coat. I started to work again. And on the other hand, when the police came and told me, I was genuinely grief-stricken." He shook his head. "I was appalled. It was as though I understood it, or felt it, for the first time, really. Dana, Dana was dead." His face had twisted.

I felt my throat clog, as though I were hearing it now, too, for the first time. After a long silence, I found my voice. "But . . . you *disposed* of the coat?" I said.

He looked startled, just for a moment. "Yes. Yes. That was easy enough to do in a chemistry building." He cleared his throat. "All kinds of bagged wastes—toxic, radioactive—are disposed of routinely, unquestioningly, by the janitorial staff daily." He was explaining, teaching me something again, and he seemed almost relieved. "There was some tension about whether it would be gone in time if the police began to suspect me, if they searched the building, for instance. But that seemed unlikely. And then they focused their attention on Duncan for a while anyway."

We sat silent, our drinks in front of us. "How fortunate for you," I said at last.

Eli's face changed quickly. He sat up straighter. "You seem to think I took this lightly. Maybe you haven't understood me. This . . . *event* shaped my life. I loved Dana. I mourned her for years. And I've worked the rest of my life to assure that who I am has some meaning, some value beyond this part of my past. Look." He hunched forward onto the table. "Remember once, back then, when you and I talked about accepting what's happened in the past? About the need to define oneself by what one gets up and *does* every day?"

I saw this suddenly, this discussion in the kitchen, the young Eli and me, sweet, stupid children, chopping onions and peppers and arguing, with tears streaming down our cheeks. But I remembered it differently. I remembered using these ideas to excuse myself for the pain I had caused the people I was closest to.

He was still talking. "And I have lived my life that way: making sure *every day*"—he slapped the table twice, lightly—"of its usefulness, of its meaning. I wrecked one life, yes. Dana's life. There's nothing I can do now to change that. But I've given, I'm giving now, to thousands, to hundreds of thousands, of other lives."

I had been made stupid by Eli's confession, unable, really, to focus on any one idea, any one thing he was telling me. But now, oddly, a thought came clear. "Does Jean know about this?" I asked abruptly. "About Dana?"

He shook his head. "No. I saw no need to tell her. It has absolutely nothing to do with who I am now, with the person she married."

I was relieved somehow.

And then more confused. "But . . . so why did you tell me?"

"You don't understand?"

"No. No, I don't at all."

"Because you *know* me, Jo. Because by now you know me again, for who I've become. And you knew me then. Because you knew Dana. Because you saw how agonized I was by her death. Because it was—it is—an opportunity for me to talk about this with someone I have found wise and sympathetic. Completely balanced, actually, in the past. Because . . . well, as I said"—he dropped his head and smiled almost shyly—"it seemed nearly fated, that you should arrive in my life at this point, perhaps the one person, finally, to whom I could tell the whole story and put it behind me, once and for all. Because of what I've done with my life. What I've made of it after that . . . episode."

Suddenly I was struck, irrelevantly, with the oddity of the phrase *put it behind me*. I was remembering Eli on the front porch the day the taxi took me away, the yawning doorway behind him. The cheese who stood alone.

"And what is it you expect me to do with this?" I asked, after a moment.

"Do?"

"Yes." I was angry suddenly. At last. "How shall *I* live with it?"

WHILE I WAS GONE

"Well, I don't expect you to turn me over to the police."

So help me, I almost smiled back at him. Instead I asked, "Why not?"

He laughed. As though I were joking. And ignored the question. "I suppose it could be said that I need a kind of forgiveness from you." His face shifted. "But I'm not sure even that's right. I've forgiven myself, after all, and as you once said, that seems the more important step. No, I think I've just felt a sense of our connection. Our connectedness, to get New Agey about it."

"I see."

He was looking at me now. Perhaps it was occurring to him for the first time that he might have made a mistake. But he must have imagined alternative responses from me when he thought about this encounter. He must have given me options in his mind—mustn't he?—other than the one he was wishing for.

I think perhaps he hadn't. At any rate, when he began again, his demeanor shifted. He leaned forward over the table. His hands came over into what might have been designated as my territory. Someone watching us from across the room would have thought the moment had finally arrived for him to start to make love to me. "Do you remember saying to me once that you'd made an unforgivable mess of your life?" His voice was ragged with intimacy, sweet reason.

I didn't answer right away, though I did remember. But I saw where he was going, the parallel between our lives, and I didn't want to consent to it. He waited, watching me. Finally I said, "Yes, I think so. I know I felt I had once. Yes."

"And that's the point, isn't it?" He smiled sadly. "The unforgivable things we've done. We've all done, I suspect. Like Daniel's notion of original sin: we're all tainted. And the only way we can forgive ourselves is by redefining our lives. That's what I've tried to do, Jo. That's what I've done. I can honestly balance what I've accomplished against the harm I've done and say the one far outweighs the other. I grant there may be others who've done less harm, but nowhere near the good. Nowhere near."

After a pause, I said, "But it wasn't exactly penance, was it? I mean, you loved the work."

He shook his head. "I don't see the relevance of that, honestly."

I wanted to leave. I was frightened of him, I realized. Not of his doing anything to me; I knew he wouldn't. But of his apparent need to persuade me of his point of view. It seemed he wouldn't let me go until he had.

He was waiting, watching me. At last I said, "I don't think it suffices to forgive yourself."

He lifted his hand. "Who, then? I can hardly get Dana to forgive me."

This more than anything, this casual near joke of everything that had happened—everything he'd done—shocked me. "I don't know," I said. I slid sideways, out of the booth. I'd kept my coat with me when I arrived, and now I was grateful for that. I picked it up. "I don't know."

I walked quickly across the room. I turned at the doorway just as I reached it, and I saw he was standing now, too, throwing bills down on the table. His eyes met mine, and I felt a reasonless panic.

In the lobby, I started toward the glass doors, toward the doorman and the people moving under the warm lights of the marquee. But nearly simultaneously, I realized that this was a kind of trap: I'd be standing there waiting for the valet to bring my car. Waiting for Eli.

Instead, then, I moved into a group of people standing by the bank of elevators, and when one of the mirror-paneled doors opened almost immediately, I hurtled forward ahead of the others. The elevator operator smiled warmly at us as we assumed our places and gave our floor numbers. Someone else said four, so I did too. When he opened the doors and called the number, I stepped off with the pregnant mother and little girl who belonged there. I took a few steps behind them down the hall. Then I stopped. They went on, but I turned and came back to the door I'd noticed opposite the elevators, the door marked STAIRS.

The instant I opened it, the plush murmurous world of the hotel's life fell away. The floor was painted concrete, the rails were iron pipe. A cold fluorescent light fell evenly, harshly, over everything. I stood next to the closed door, listening to the rise and fall of my breath, the blood thudding in my ears and my chest. I was alone.

I stood there for a while—I'm not sure how long—and then I heard someone enter the stairwell high above me, the quick, gritty tap of shoes on stone as he—she?—started down. I opened the door again to the carpeted hallway of the fourth floor, and slowly I walked around, pretending I had a purpose, a destination. I came to a seating area in the corridor and stood looking out the windows there at the massive trees in the Public Garden, the lights twinkling through them. I kept seeing Eli's face, hearing his pleading, reasoning voice. I kept pushing away the image of Dana, Dana as I remembered finding her. And now this new version of her, too, stepping forward to offer comfort and being struck, over and over. I heard myself make a noise, and sat down, quickly, trying to gather myself. A couple came out of one of the rooms down the hall and walked past me to the elevators, talking in low voices.

A few minutes later, I followed them. They'd already disappeared. I pushed the *down* button. There was a mirror on the wall behind me. I turned and looked at myself in it. I was haggard, white. I looked away. When the elevator doors opened, I stepped in.

Getting the car from the valet brought me back sharply to myself, made me feel aware of my own stupidity. My cupidity. My vanity. For what had I said when I took the stub from him earlier? "I'm not sure how long I'll be, exactly. I may stay the night." "It's possible that I'll be spending the night." "It's possible that I'll start an affair tonight with Eli Mayhew."

His cheerful innocence now was a rebuke to me: "Decided not to stay, huh?"

"No," I said. And I stepped back into the glass vestibule to wait for the car, every few moments glancing into the lobby, then out to the pavement, watching for Eli.

It was such a relief to me—first to be closed in alone in the car, then to get onto Route 2 and be headed out of Boston, then to feel the silent dark of the countryside surround me—that I was well past Lincoln before I felt the weight of all that had happened. Somewhere after the sign to Walden Pond, I pulled off the highway, onto a dark lane. I parked at its edge. As soon as I turned off the engine, I burst into ragged weeping.

I don't know how long I sat there. I stopped crying several times and then started again. I thought of Dana, of the noise of my breath leaking wetly from her cheek where Eli had sliced her open. I thought of my blindness, the shameful vanity that had brought me to Boston today, that had tricked me, exposed me. I thought of how Eli had counted on me, of how he had been so sure I would forgive him. My mouth tasted bitter and tired. I blew my nose over and over, I darkened tissue after tissue with my eye makeup. I thought of Eli's false words: he *hit* her, he had said. Liar! Fucking liar. I thought of Dana as

I'd found her, of the bloody flaps of fabric and skin at the torn edges of each wound, of the drying blood on the dirty soles of her bare white feet. I thought of the weight of her body when I tried to carry her with me.

A car turned off the road and drove slowly toward me. Instead of passing by, though, it pulled up behind me, its beams lighting the inside of my car, showing me my frightened eyes in the rearview mirror. *Eli!* I thought, and panicked. I heard his car door slam, the slow, heavy footsteps on gravel. I was fumbling for my keys, trying to start the car, to loosen the steering wheel lock, when he tapped on my window. The engine caught with a sharp whine of protest, and I was starting to shift when he bent down.

It wasn't Eli. It was a policeman. Young, hatted, his white face just inches from me, he frowned at me through the dirty glass.

DANIEL MUST HAVE HEARD THE CAR CRUNCHING ON THE FRO-zen ruts of the driveway, or seen the lights skittering over the bare trees and the barn, for he came to the kitchen door to greet me, his glasses in one hand. His face lifted in surprise and pleasure as he stepped back to let me in. "Hey, I didn't expect to see *you* for hours. If at all tonight. What happened?" And then he noticed I'd been crying and moved toward me. "What's wrong?"

I stood utterly still for a moment, I was so glad to be here—home—but also so ashamed, so conscious that what came next would change everything. Then I said, "Well, see, Daniel, the thing is, I went to Boston. . . ." I took a breath. "The real reason I went to Boston was to meet Eli Mayhew." And watched as his eager, loving expression was utterly transformed.

CHAPTER

12

I SAID EARLIER THAT RUNNING AWAY FROM MY FIRST MAR-
riage was unique in my life, that it was hard for me to recognize or
remember myself as I was then because the behavior was so for-
eign to me.

But that was not, strictly, true. I ran away once as a girl, too, at perhaps eight or nine. I didn't get far, but if intentions had been wings, I
would have landed in Florida, in Brigadoon. In never-never land. As it
was, I made several mistakes and was easily retrieved. The primary one
was stealing my brother Fred's cowboy boots.

I'd long coveted them. They were red, with white appliqués
stitched on them—crescent moons and stars. From the moment he'd
unwrapped them the Christmas before, I felt that if there were any
justice, any fairness in the world, I would have known about the existence of these boots. I would have asked for them for myself. They
would be mine, not his. Now, on this dusty summer afternoon, I
sneaked into Fred's room and found them in his closet. I carried them
to the front porch. I pulled them on and set out on my journey:
down to the corner and left onto the street that became the road that
led out of town, the place where all the journeys I'd ever known began.

The boots swam freely around my feet as I walked. It was a hot day;
my feet were damp with sweat. Within the equivalent of a few city
blocks, I had blisters on both heels. At a point shortly after that, I took
the boots off and left them in the tall grass that grew by the road. I

went on, barefoot, slowed by pebbles and glass. I was hobbling and miserable when a neighbor saw me from her car and stopped. "Dearie," she called. "You've headed the wrong way!"

I let her talk me into the car, I consented to let her drive me home. But nearly as soon as we started back, I burst into tears—at the thought of my failure, at my barefoot shame. At the enormity of my sin in stealing my brother's boots, at the fear of being punished. By the time we got home, I was inconsolable, so inconsolable that there was only sympathy for my bleeding bare feet, for my hysteria, for my having been—as they understood it—lost.

And what triggered that flight? What was the itch that time? This: My older brother had told me—it seems to me only a few days before, but it might have been weeks, or even months—about my father's previous life, his first marriage. I don't know why he chose the moment. Some smugness on my part he wanted to pierce. Some casual remark that seemed to claim ownership of our parents' history. Some minor offense to him. At any rate, he told. Cruelly, harshly, the correction being to my stupidity for not having known earlier—though how could I? no one had even hinted at it—that our father had had another wife, another whole existence, before he met our mother, before we were born. That if things had been as he first planned them, we never *would* have been born, there would have been other children living in our house, with another mother, with different rules, different notions of what was important in life.

This shattered my understanding of the universe, the feeling I'd had—I think every child has it until some point in life—that my life was somehow sacred and foreordained, the one absolutely necessary life I had to live.

Apparently not. Apparently I might never have been. Or I might have been other than what I was.

And, it occurred to me then, mightn't I yet be? It seemed suddenly that what had been the cornerstone of my existence was shifting sand. That what had been a given was merely a whim. It seemed possible that there was another life waiting somewhere out there for me. This was not exactly how I thought it out, of course. Mostly I *felt* it: a yearning, suddenly justified, for something other for myself. Better. More real somehow. More like the lives I read about in my books.

Later the boots turned up missing, causing my mother to ponder retroactively the mystery of blistered heels on a barefoot girl. A new interpretation was arrived at, and I was walked down the road, made to find the boots—rain-soaked and stiffened, curled, *ruined!*—and punished.

I don't mean to trivialize my feelings on coming home to Daniel by comparing them to that other homecoming. On the contrary. For that early shame felt deep and permanent, a stain I would wear forever, an agony I was condemned to wake to over and over, a final isolation I'd brought on myself by turning in the wrong direction, heading the wrong way, when I was confused and wounded.

Each day now, too, I woke and felt something very like that agonized wrench of childhood. Sometimes Daniel was not in bed with me. He'd gotten up, sleepless, and gone to one of the girls' rooms. Or out to his study. Then the disorientation, the pain, lay in his absence, in my aloneness in the bed. Sometimes I was the one who'd moved in the night. I'd wake with the light falling from the wrong direction, the bed turned, dizzyingly, the wrong way; and in the seconds it took to orient myself physically, I would be returning, too, with a sinking weight in what felt like my heart, to what I'd done. To all it seemed I'd destroyed. It was like waking over and over to an illness, a long fever I could not recover from.

My brother had said to me then, "I'll never speak to you again." Of course, I believed him, and what's more, I believed I deserved it. Daniel might as well have said it, though we spoke daily, we exchanged information about where we were going, about what time we'd be back. And occasionally more. Tonelessly he'd sometimes tell me he'd run into someone I knew, or report on something he'd seen, something that had happened to him—the kind of thing that would once have been the beginning of a long, meandering conversation. But these were offered so listlessly now that I understood them to be mere formalities. Just as Daniel would not stop saying *good morning* to me, or *how was your day?*—just as he would make himself be civil to me in those ways—so he would politely, dutifully offer me nuggets that neither of us had the energy to turn into conversation.

Though at odd moments, the silence between us would be broken by the quickest, the most radical of exchanges about what was truly important to us. One of us would blurt out just a sentence or two, as though we couldn't bear to keep at it any longer than that, as though one idea at a time was all either of us could express or take in. These were sometimes preceded, these cries from the heart, by an oddly formal introduction: "*Allow me, Daniel, just to say* I never meant for it to go as far as it did." And the quick answer: "I'm sure that's true." . . . "*I would ask that* you never see him again.": "Of course not." Once, in bed, long after I would have assumed he'd fallen asleep—just before he got up and went to sleep elsewhere—he suddenly said in a rough, low-pitched voice, "I don't know how to stop thinking about it."

For once, my work was no consolation; the world did not fall away when I moved among the animals. As I touched them, as I manipulated them, as I treated them and thought about them, I was still too much myself, too much the Jo who'd wrecked everything. I didn't know anymore what it felt like to take satisfaction in anything. I couldn't remember when I had liked myself or anything about my life. My very voice made me sick: its dryness, the way it cracked on certain words. I hated my need to smile at clients. I hated the sight of my ugly shoes emerging from underneath my scrub pants, the way my hands looked arranging things on my table, the way my body felt as I moved around the clinic in it. Though when Mary Ellen spoke to me quickly, privately in the hall one day, offering to pick up the slack for a week or two if I wanted some time off, I understood by the panicked rapidity of my refusal how much worse things would be if I couldn't come in every day.

A week passed since I had met Eli. Then ten days. The world froze and we froze in it. The bird feeder hung empty. We opened the door and let the dogs run at night instead of walking them. Neither of us had the energy to make our bed, or any of the beds we variously slept in. Or to pick up, to build a fire, to throw away rotting fruit or dried-out flowers or the old take-out containers that accumulated in the refrigerator. I felt I was living on pure will. Every act was a deliberate one, costly and difficult. I've said that once I felt *held* in my life. Now I was holding on to what was left of it for dear life. Dear life. While below our tepid, empty exchanges, the deep moat of silence widened between us.

OF COURSE, WE HAD TALKED THE NIGHT I CAME BACK. BUT even then I knew how it was going to be, I could feel the coming silence in the long, poisonous pauses that expanded as the night progressed. I suppose in some way I knew how it would be even as I was blurting out my confession, but I couldn't have—I *think* I couldn't have—stopped myself anyhow.

Why? Why couldn't I have kept quiet? I asked myself that often in the days that followed. Why hadn't I spared him my painful, ugly little secret and kept things *the same* between us?

I suppose the answer in part is that the weight of what I'd learned and the power of the emotional state I was in were so heavy and deep, it felt they had become me. I felt I had no choice. I didn't, in fact, think about an alternative. I suppose it was in part because I needed Daniel so much, right then, that my need made me stupid. I suppose I was so caught up with what Eli had said and the way it altered my own history that I wasn't thinking about how my confession would alter ours. But even as I spoke, *had to speak*, I was thinking: *This, this is what you've done.*

"Oh, God, Daniel," I'd said when I saw his face change, saw it go white. "Let's sit down, let's get a drink or something, and then I'll tell you the whole story." I think at first I felt that if he heard all of it, if I explained it in exactly the right way, he would see how it had been, how *I* had been in it. He would be, as he always was, so *with* me that he could feel it as I had felt it, he could help me now with my terror, my horror. And I think I hoped, too, that there would be a way made available for my words not to mean what they had seemed to mean.

He was still concerned, if not quite loving, when we sat down together in the living room, when I tried to start and burst into tears again. When I began my tale with Eli and Dana and their long-ago love affair.

But after I'd finished that part of it and his face had sagged in sympathy and horror, after he'd agreed with me that, yes, this was a murder, no matter how it was explained, no matter what Eli had made of himself later—after all that agreeing and sympathizing were over, he'd stood and put another log on the fire, and from that distance he turned and asked me, "So what does all this have to do with your going to Boston secretly to meet him?" And I understood that where the story for me was somehow all of a piece, for him it was two quite separate narratives, with two separate meanings.

Now I fumbled again to tell it, trying in a different way to call up the magic of my own past as my seducer, to explain the *pastness* in my attraction. To explain Eli as my betrayer, and to connect all of this to my horror at how it had turned out. I knew that this version wasn't strictly true. *Part* of me knew it wasn't true. But I was also desperate to have Daniel's sympathy, desperate for him not to feel what he was bound to feel. Desperate to imagine I still had the power to make things right.

While I spoke, he had come to sit at the other end of the couch. I watched his profile looking at the fire, watched it as his face pinched shut, his lips tightened in an embittered line. It seemed minutes after I'd shut up at last when he said, "You will forgive me"—those were his words: *You will forgive me*—"if I can't really focus on Eli and Dana. I know that's part of your shock and pain, but . . ." He shook his head, and his nostrils flared slightly. "Fuck it. That's how I feel. Fuck that."

We sat in silence for a long time then. I couldn't answer him. I sat thickheaded, staring into the fire. Daniel never used language like that with me, to me, and I felt the words like blows.

Finally he said, without looking at me, "Be honest, Jo. Do me that courtesy. Be honest about why you went to meet him."

It was as though I were in a nightmare, a nightmare in which the frightening thing was that I had no words. I opened my mouth and no words would come out. At the same time, I couldn't believe that there wasn't going to be some way for me to make him understand me.

At last I started stupidly to go over it once again. I may even have been using the same phrases, since my brain would not work to find new ones. I know I started to weep again, too, but that felt suddenly like self-pity, and I tried to stop.

Daniel was looking at me as though he didn't know me. He stood up and crossed the room. He lifted the screen and set it in front of the fire, and then, with his back to me, he said, "You met him to screw him. You met him to fuck him. You met him to lie down with him and wreck our marriage."

When I didn't answer, he left the room. I heard him in our bedroom, moving around, and then he crossed the living room, holding some clothing and his glasses. Without saying another word to me, he went up the narrow stairs to the second floor.

AS WE PASSED THROUGH THE LONG DAYS THAT FOLLOWED, I sometimes envied Daniel what I thought of as the simplicity of his pain, his sorrow. He had been as good as betrayed. I had been ready to sleep with someone else, it was the most astonishing accident that I hadn't. Though occasionally it seemed to me as I rewrote things mentally that *of course* I wouldn't actually have gone through with it, of course I would have stopped.

For me, the sorrow was laced with guilt. I was the betrayer, after all, and it was with a pained and startled self-recognition that I felt this as something *familiar* about myself. I had thought of it as new, as *news*, really. Something startling, something fresh I was learning about myself. It had even titillated me: I could be, I might be, a person who could betray someone.

Now it came muddled with Dana's death, with that time in my life when I'd betrayed everything: my husband, my mother, my past. When I'd betrayed even Dana—I felt that way, I remembered that feeling—by living, when she died.

It wasn't news, then. Or it was old news. Stale, sad news.

And of course, pressing in on me every day along with this sense of all I had ever done, now and earlier in my life, to hurt people who had only loved me, there was also the knowledge that I needed to decide what, if anything, I was going to do about Eli, about what he'd told me. About Dana's death.

They pushed together, they merged in my mind, they became confused equivalents, Eli's killing Dana and my casual, sleazy destruction of all I would have called *fine* in my life. In this mood, it took a conscious effort for me to convince myself that what I had done was different in any degree from what Eli had done. The idea that I had any morally higher ground, that I should be Eli's accuser, seemed ludicrous.

At other times I actually thought that if I went to the police and accused Eli, there would be relief in it for both of us. It would be like accusing myself too. I imagined that to put myself through such a thing—a confession, a full confession of how I had come to have this information, even as I was also making public the information, his confession to me—would be a necessary punishment for what I had done. What was it he had said? That we were all tainted. Yes, my heart said. Yes, I am.

And then I would swing into the mood opposite this. I would recollect my rage at Eli that evening, I would call up the image he had given me of his hitting at Dana over and over, the blood leaping to every wound. I would accuse him mentally of manipulating me, trying to trick me. There was no equivalence between us! Our betrayals, our sins, our *taintedness*, were of an entirely different order, could not begin to be compared. Once, in this mood, I hit the examining table in my office so hard that Beattie came rushing down the hall, thinking I'd fallen or dropped something.

When I was feeling that way, what I thought was that I should report him so that he—he, the murderer—could be punished. But then I'd think about everything else he said. I'd wonder if it had been true, his sense that he'd lived his life redeeming himself by his work. And if it *was* true, was that enough? And was I in charge of seeing that he was punished, thereby ending the work, the good part of his life?

Sometimes it would seem to me that what I needed to do was simply to forgive Eli, in order to be forgiven myself. But, I'd tell myself, I didn't have that power, that right: to forgive, or to be forgiven. It was, after all, Daniel whose forgiveness I needed. And Eli needed, not mine, but Dana's. Or her family's. Or society's. And I could speak for none of them.

The days dragged by. I would wake at night and move around the cold house trying to imagine a solution, and I could not, because everything was so knitted together in my mind. There seemed nothing I could do, no action I could take, no remedy, that didn't smack of self-interest or self-justification. And then even this fastidiousness, this self-examination, would disgust me. It seemed like a further egocentrism, an intolerable dwelling-with-myself. Myself, whom I felt sometimes I could not bear.

And with everything else, there was, of course, the shock, pure and horrible, of having to revisit Dana's death with this new understanding, this new way of envisioning it. Something I could not, of course, ask Daniel to help me with, though I wanted his help. I wanted him.

As one does when threatened with loss, I fell in love with him again: with the tender note in his voice as he spoke in the morning to one of the dogs; with the white oval of his face turning up at me as though I might be someone else coming into the room—or another version of myself. With the mysterious, private quality to his expression as he talked gently on the phone of someone else's sorrow; with his long, narrow feet and the delicate tick in his toe bones when he descended the stairs from one of the girls' rooms in the morning. I thought of us, silently together in the boat the day before it all began. I wanted him back. I wanted everything back.

Once, in the night, Daniel stumbled into the kitchen when I was there and, turning on the light, started at seeing me. There we stood, blinking at each other in the sudden harsh light. Each of us had raised a hand toward the other. I wanted, more than anything, to go to him, to touch him. I wanted his touch. When I thought of this moment later, I saw us as actors depicting yearning across a stage set, the black windows painted into the backdrop, the strewn table and angled chairs the props, the main characters stage left and stage right, stopped in the act of moving toward each other. It seemed for an instant he might make some gesture to come toward me or that gave me permission to go to him. It seemed so, but he didn't. His body slackened, his hand fell. He smiled, an ironic smile, a sad smile. "It's no fun at all, is it?" he said.

DURING THESE WEEKS, WE STAYED AWAY FROM EACH OTHER when we could. For Daniel, this was easier. He could let his job expand to be as big as he needed it to be. Instead of being home for dinner before an evening meeting, he went to a restaurant with Mortie, or the head of the committee on renovations, or the church musical director. He let the meetings themselves proliferate. I knew his strategy. He delegated nothing, he participated everywhere. And the church, hydra-headed, many-mouthed, was all too eager to devour him. He was hardly ever home.

Since it seemed to me that I could speak to no one of what I'd done, of what I knew, of what I was so pressingly thinking about, I had fewer options. Daniel's absence unburdened me, of course. But when he was home, usually in his study, I almost always left. And even when he wasn't there I sometimes went out, running from the emptiness of the house. I drove aimlessly down the country roads, through the dead and dying mill towns, the expensive reconstructed communities. I parked across from working farms and watched the cows. I sat for hours next to unused fields, grown over with juniper and pines, filling in with thin maple saplings and chokecherries. I became an expert on where to find small coffee shops, the kind that featured square Formica-topped tables with plastic mustard and ketchup bottles placed on them like decorations. Or on the locations of ladies' rooms on my routes—in the basements of old town halls, around the back of wood-frame gas stations. I came home after work and drove out in the late afternoons—growing longer, twilight an event now. I returned after dark to the dark house. This was how it would feel, I thought, if Daniel died. I thought, *He is dead to me. We are dead to each other.*

ON A SLOW SATURDAY IN EARLY FEBRUARY, I LEFT WORK EARLY, at Mary Ellen's suggestion. She'd stay, she said, her wide, flat face frowning in concern. I looked like I could use some time off. Daniel's car was in the driveway, though he wasn't in the house. Probably in his study, then, working on a sermon. I couldn't bear the empty silence. I decided I would walk down to the town library.

The library was a strange, octagonal brick structure, built in the late nineteenth century—one of only two brick buildings in town, the other being the post office. It had been endowed by the last of the Adamses, whose unfriendly portrait loomed behind the main desk as you entered the central hallway. I greeted the librarian, a starchy, skinny woman with dyed black hair, who'd been there as long as we'd lived in town, and went to the nonfiction shelves. I strolled aimlessly through them for a while, pulling out a book here and there, pretending to read. I actually got absorbed briefly by an account of the ebola virus.

When I'd put that away, it occurred to me I could use the computer to locate an article Mary Ellen had mentioned to me, an article in the *Globe* about the reasons for the increase in the numbers of women going into veterinary medicine.

The computer room was in an alcove off the main reading room. There were six stations, all donated, hardware and elaborate software, by the same anonymous person who'd put the local elementary school on line. I looked up my article and read it with mild interest.

Then I wondered suddenly: how far back could I go?

To exactly where I wanted to go, it turned out. It was a shock to see the photo of Dana, probably a high-school graduation shot, with her hair carefully flipped up, just so, at the ends, her lipstick dark, her face childishly fat. The stories were as I'd recollected them, but there were more of them than I'd thought. It had loomed large, this murder in a working-class neighborhood. It had scared people. What you could read under the surface as you went through the articles was that an attempt was being made to account for it. To be reassuring about it by offering details of the irregularity of the victim's life. It could not happen to *you*, the articles were saying, because you lock your doors at night, you sleep with just your husband, you live with just your family, you are responsibly employed.

There was a photo of us, too, the house members, caught in someone's flash as we moved in a group together: maybe leaving the police station? I couldn't tell. I had raised my hands slightly—they resembled two large mittens—and my face was partially obscured by my hair. Larry was next to me, looking thuggish and angry. Sara peered directly at the camera, the light glinting in her glasses, her mouth slightly open, her face stupid. Eli and Duncan and John were just figures behind us, boys with hair that was too long, too sloppy, too unkempt.

I lifted my eyes then, looking away from this. And what I saw was Eli, the real, grown-up Eli, standing in the main reading room. Seeming to survey it, really, with his air of ease and assurance. He wore a parka. His long, expensive scarf was looped around his neck. There was a shaft of sunlight between us—like a lens, an angled particled brightness I had to look through. It created a strange sense of distance, of unreality.

He was smiling at someone. Now he spoke, and Jean stepped into my line of vision and stood next to him. Together they looked around the room with a civic, proprietary air, and then they turned as one, apparently to leave.

As they turned, he saw me. She had already disappeared from the frame that the doorway had made for my view of them, but he stopped now, just inside it, at its edge. It seemed for a moment he might come over to me, he might have something to say. My legs stiffened almost involuntarily to rise, my chair slid back with a hard noise that made the other occupant of the computer room look over in irritation.

And then he thought better of it. His hand lifted just a little in greeting, and he smiled at me, a sheepish smile, as though we shared a slightly embarrassing secret—and he was gone. Off, perhaps, to survey other properties in town that he, as a taxpayer, owned a share of.

I sat there, tensed, shocked, and then, in a palpable wash of emotion, abruptly rageful. His very being—his health, his evident prosperity, his smile, his lifted hand—all of this was an offense to me. It seemed unbearable that he should exist in the same world as I did. In a world where Dana was dead. It was all I could do to turn the machine off, my hands were trembling so. I slid my coat on and went outside.

It was mild that day. The roads and parking lot were wet, the snow on the fields and lawns flattened and crusted on top with its own melting. There was the sound of dripping everywhere, and the smell, every now and then, of pine, or of earth. I walked slowly home, trying to calm myself. My coat flapped open in the gentle air, my boots struck the gravel road edge with a cheerful sibilance. A few cars passed me. The air they stirred pressed my coat to my side and lifted my hair slightly.

In the house, I shed my coat. I went and sat down in the living room. It was silent but for the steady whir of the humidifier—which, I noted now, was empty. I took the water chamber to the kitchen to fill it. Its opening felt vaguely slimy when I lifted the cap off, so I scoured it with soapy hot water before refilling it. When I'd replaced the chamber and turned the machine on again, I came back into the kitchen and looked around me. Everywhere, I saw the signs of our sorrow, of our carelessness about our life together. It had to stop. It had to stop now, I thought.

I put on an apron. I unloaded the dishwasher and then reloaded it with crusted plates and pans. I wiped the counters and the table. I scrubbed the sink and bagged the trash, hauled it outside to the storage bin. I went into our bedroom next and stripped the bed. I took the sheets and the dirty clothes to the basement and started a load of wash. When I came back up, I moved along our row of hooks, gathering the clothes we'd thoughtlessly worn over and over through the past weeks. I threw them down the basement stairs and they landed, arms and legs spread awkwardly. I picked up the old newspapers lying around and bagged them for recycling. I stacked the scattered books. I gathered the pens and pencils, the glasses cases, the odd dishes left here and there. I was aware suddenly, above the slosh of water, the hum of motors, of my own panting, angry breath: it was as though I were doing all this instead of hurting someone, breaking something.

I had to talk about it, I realized. I thought I knew what I was going to do, but I still wasn't sure if it was right. I needed to talk to Daniel.

Without giving myself time for second thoughts, I left the house and crossed the yard through the melted, melting snow. The barn smelled richly of humus. I knocked on Daniel's door, and as though he'd been expecting me, his voice called out instantly and without surprise, "Come in."

I opened the door and took a step in. He'd pulled his glasses off. He was holding them a few inches away from his face.

"I need to talk to you, Daniel," I said.

He made a gesture of consent and set his glasses on his desk, on top of a yellow pad filled with writing in his neat, vertical hand.

I shut the door behind me and came over to the chair that faced him.

"Please. Sit," he said when I hesitated, and I did. The room seemed dim after the bright sunlight outside. Daniel was working just by the ghostly light from the windows.

"I think I've decided what I'm going to do," I said.

He shifted quickly sideways in his chair, as though bracing himself.

"About Eli," I said.

"Ah," he answered. A little smile flickered at his lips and then was gone. I understood it. He'd thought I was speaking of something else—of us—and he was amused, bitterly amused, at his mistake.

"I feel it's step one, getting that done," I apologized.

He shrugged.

"Daniel," I said. "I have to begin somewhere."

"Yes," he conceded. And after a moment, "Well, what's your decision?"

"Well, I haven't absolutely decided. I just think I have. I need your opinion." His face tightened. "I want it, anyway."

"What do you *think* your decision is, then?"

"I want to turn him in."

He gestured. *So?*

"But it feels like revenge, or anger, to me. And I'm not sure I have the right to that. Or I'm not sure that's right."

"Why shouldn't you be angry? He *killed* someone. He killed someone you cared for deeply." Daniel spoke dispassionately, minister to parishioner. For once, I was grateful for the tone.

"But I'm not sure that's entirely the source of my anger."

He nodded. *Go on.*

"He shamed me too. He exposed my foolishness. He embarrassed me. He wrecked things between us."

"Jo. *He* didn't wreck them."

"This is how I *feel*, Daniel. This is what it *feels* like I'm doing, to me. I know I'm to blame. I know that. But what I worry about is that doing this, turning him in, is a way to—I don't know—deflect that. Find a way to blame him. For all of it."

Daniel looked at me, steadily, coolly, over his desk. Then he was done with that, and he stood up and went to his window. In the summer, all you could see out there were woods. But now, with the leaves gone, there was a flickering view through the pines to our neighbors' house—the battlers. The shitheads.

After a long moment, he turned back to me. His face was shadowed by the light entering the room from behind him. His voice was dry but gentle. He said, "I may not be without mixed motives here, too, you realize."

I hadn't thought of it. I hadn't thought of all I might be asking of him, though I'd thought of some of it. In any case, I said, "Yes," now. And after a few seconds, "Yes, but I trust you, more than I trust myself, to sort that out."

He breathed heavily, once. Then he said, "Thank you." I couldn't get his tone. I waited.

"I can't think . . ." His voice was burred, and he cleared his throat. "I can't think that presenting the truth to the authorities is exactly revenge. Revenge will be theirs, if they exact it. You'll just open Eli up to those processes, whatever they are. You will, in effect, render unto Caesar what is Caesar's—this crime against Dana. Against us all. And Caesar will do with it what he may."

"But it's likely to be very . . . involving. Very prolonged. If there's an investigation and a trial and all that. It's likely to be . . . costly. To me. To us. Not just to him."

"It's the least of it, Jo," he said dryly.

"But what I worry is . . . I worry, too, that somehow I'm seeing this as *my* penance, my way out. Because it will be painful for me. And part of me wants that. Some public pain. But it's so unfair, it's so unconnected to me and you together, and it will involve you. You understand that. It will involve you. It'll make it go on and on."

"I wouldn't worry about it."

"But I do, Daniel," I cried. I stood up. My hands rose, opened. "I don't want to compound and compound my injuries to you."

"You've already done the worst thing."

"Oh, Daniel," I pleaded. "I didn't sleep with him, after all." I stepped toward him, pleading. "I didn't, in fact, sleep with him."

Now that I was closer to him, I could see his face in the shadows. He was smiling, sadly. "No, you didn't. But what a strange position you put me in, Jo. In effect to ask me to be grateful the man was a murderer. To be grateful it turned out he killed your friend. Since that's what it took—isn't it?—to keep you faithful to me."

DANIEL CAME OVER LATER AND FIXED HIMSELF A SANDWICH for dinner, in spite of my offers to make something—hamburgers or pasta. He was almost finished with his sermon, he said, and he wanted to keep at it a little bit longer. I watched him carrying his plate across the yard, watched the open barn door swallow him.

I thought about leaving, about taking another pointless drive, but instead I went into the living room. I sat there for some time, feeling numbed, flattened. Then I came into the kitchen and sat at the table, picking at the tasteless bits of chicken and lettuce Daniel had left out. I had no appetite for fixing a meal for myself.

It was five-thirty by now, but there was still a lingering gray light in the air, the days were that much longer. I noticed that the dishwasher light was on—the load I'd run earlier this afternoon. All right. I'd finish that job anyway. I crossed to it and started to unload it. Behind me I heard Daniel open the back door. I turned and watched him come over to me. He set his plate and glass down. Neither of us spoke.

I went back to work, bending to the dishwasher, collecting a stack of plates to put away. I could tell he hadn't left the room; in my peripheral vision I could see that he was standing by the table, his hand resting on a bowl of fruits and vegetables that had sat there untouched for days. I didn't know what to say to him, how to break the silence that grew and grew.

I reached up and had just opened the cupboard door to put away a few plates, when I heard and then felt the loud, shocking *splat* of something exploding with great force next to me on the wall. I saw it: seed, juice, pulp—a tomato. Then I noticed the red dabs freckling my arms and hands. I could feel wet splotches of it on my face.

I turned in amazement to him, and he looked back, startled, too, it seemed, his eyes widened. We looked at each other for a few seconds. He lifted his shoulders slightly. "It was rotten," he explained, and left the room.

I stood, stunned, not knowing what to feel, what to think. Finally I turned and ran the water until it came warm. I rinsed my hands, splashed my face. I wet a dish towel and dabbed at my sleeves, my hair.

My heart was beating recklessly. How he must have looked—Daniel—
watching me, picking up the tomato! The hateful force with which he
must have thrown it!

Automatically, I started to wipe the drooling mess from the wall. I
was imagining Daniel on the pitcher's mound in some dusty infield. I
was seeing his windup, the leg lifting, the toes curled in, the slight, elegant kick, and then the wonderful force of his lean body pushing forward through space behind the unfurling throw. He'd been a pitcher
on his college baseball team and toyed briefly with the idea of trying
to turn pro. Until five or six years ago, he'd still pitched every spring
for the town league.

I was mystified now, and somehow oddly moved, too, by what he'd
done. By what he'd not done. Because I knew he hadn't missed me. If
what he'd wanted was to hit me, to hurt me, he could easily have done
that. And he hadn't. He had chosen not to do that. I held on to that as
I cleaned up what was left of the mess. Daniel: he had chosen not to
hurt me.

13

Two days later, on Monday, I drove into Cambridge. I felt nearly happy, I think simply to be taking some action, though I had no clear idea what might result from it. Anything seemed possible, even the idea—I'd entertained it several times—that this was what Eli had actually wanted when he confessed to me: somehow to have it all come out at last. The possibility of a trial had occurred to me, too, as I'd mentioned to Daniel—something prolonged and difficult, calling everyone back to that time. I didn't care anymore. What I felt was a strange kind of passivity about the results. I would do this, and whatever happened would happen, but I would be moving on. I could turn to the next thing, which was, of course, me and Daniel. Somehow it seemed that whatever it was I should be doing about that wouldn't be clear until I had acted on what Eli had told me. Until I was finished with it.

I didn't tell Daniel that today was the day. I don't know exactly why I didn't. Perhaps because I knew what he would say? ("Oh. Fine," and then the turning away, slightly wounded.) Because it was, in some sense, *private*, my doing this? Because I was, as Sadie had accused me of being, an elusive person, secretive by nature? I'm not sure. But I sat there in my bathrobe drinking coffee, not saying anything, and I watched Daniel leave, having offered me the briefest possible explanation of his own Monday: "I have some stuff to do at church." (Was it because of his chilliness then?)

Outside, he walked halfway across the yard, looking slouched, weary, old. But then something shifted for him—perhaps he was simply far enough away from me—and he stopped. His body arched back a little, he lifted his head, as though taking in the sky, the gently falling snow, and his arms rose slightly from his sides for a moment. When he walked on, he seemed taller, younger. I was glad for him, glad for whatever had lightened in him. And because of that I was glad, too, that I hadn't said anything.

The snow was dry and powdery as it blew in delicate, serpentine waves across the road. I didn't need the wipers. It was after ten by the time I started out, and the rush hour was well over. The drive in was easy and fast. Too fast. I felt unready when I got to Central Square. I parked in the metered lot down the block from the big stone station and walked slowly back to it. The snow made a light hissing noise as it landed, as it brushed against the buildings.

Inside, the police station looked unchanged but for the bright fluorescent lights. I told the man at the desk I needed to find the ladies' room and talk to someone in homicide.

"In what order?" he asked, and I smiled back at him.

"A. Ladies' room. B. Homicide," I said.

There were other officers moving around behind the desk, speaking loudly, casually, to each other, calling to fellow workers entering or leaving the building. I had thought I'd feel conspicuous, but as the desk officer directed me, I realized I was in some sense almost invisible to them. Anonymous anyway. What hadn't they seen, after all, that would make a middle-aged suburban woman in any way striking? or even interesting?

Upstairs, things had been rearranged. The ladies' room was so different, it struck me that perhaps it wasn't even the same one I'd stood in those years ago, handing my bloody parka and clothes over the top of the stall door to the brusque policewoman who handed me back my clean things. And the homicide unit was housed in a comfortable, colorful room full of blond wood, the officers working at computer stations in modern swivel chairs. When someone approached me at the counter, I gave the name I'd gotten from the desk officer and waited while he was summoned.

Officer Ryan was a youngish man, certainly under forty, though as I followed him across the space behind the gate he'd led me through, I noted that his hair was thinning on the crown of his head, a circle of pale white emerging from the dark whorl. ("I think I have some new information about an old case, a murder that you handled here," I'd said after we introduced ourselves. He had a soft face, doughy, with a fat lower lip. He'd pushed it forward in response to me and nodded a few times. "Fair enough," he'd said. "Come on in.")

Now we went into a room that seemed too large for just the two of us, a rectangular room dominated by a huge oval table and perhaps fifteen chairs pushed in around it at various angles. He gestured. I pulled out one of the chairs and started to sit.

"Can I get you something?" he asked. "Coke? Coffee?"

"No," I said. "No, I'm fine."

He shrugged and sat down too. He folded his hands in front of him on the table, thumbs touching, and began to bounce his chair gently up and down. "So, Mrs. Becker—it is Mrs?" he said. "When did this homicide occur?"

"It's Doctor, actually. Dr. Becker. I'm a vet."

Again he made that adjudicative nod, with the thrust lip.

"But please call me Jo, in any case," I said. "It was 1969. It happened in 1969."

"And what's your connection to it?" His eyes were dark and liquid, so dark I couldn't really tell their color. They moved constantly, to my face, to my hands, to the window, to his own hands, back to me. Resisting the tension this called up in me, I slowly explained Dana's death, and who I was to her then, and the course of the investigation that had followed.

"I don't remember this one," he said when I was finished. "But I'm sure there are guys around here who do. So it was put down in the end as a B and E gone bad?"

"An E without the B," I said. "There was no break-in, because nothing was locked. We were trusting souls. Or we believed in being trusting souls." To his unreadable quick glance over, I shrugged. "It was that time."

He nodded and bounced for a moment, jittered his eyes around, waiting for anything more. "So," he said. "Before I pull the box, what's the new information?"

"The box?"

"The file on this. Before I look it up."

"Oh. Well. It's a confession, really. From the person who did it."

He stopped bouncing abruptly, and his eyes settled on me.

I cleared my throat. "I recently met again . . . or rather, one of the old house members, one of the people the police talked to back then, moved into my town recently—I live out toward western Mass., the middle of the state, in Adams Mills. And we, this man and I—his name is Eli Mayhew—became reacquainted. And then, I don't know, it was a few weeks ago, he told me he'd killed her. He killed Dana."

He had leaned forward, elbows on the table. Now he scratched his ear. "Yeah," he said. This news seemed to have slowed his metabolism. "Well, that's pretty amazing."

"I know," I said.

"Exactly how did that happen?" he asked. "That he told you that?"

"I know it sounds crazy just to say it like that. I was more or less dumbstruck myself."

"So he just up and blurted it out one day?" He was watching me carefully now, with a kind of stilled attentiveness.

"Well, it was slower than that, of course, more gradual. We . . . well, I was his vet. He brought his dog in to me to be put down, and we made the connection—who we were, how we knew each other." I realized I was using my hands nervously, but I couldn't stop myself. "And we saw each other socially a few times. I mean, as couples, my husband and his wife too. But there was always this kind of reference coming up to that time, and to Dana." I shrugged. "But I suppose that's not really all that surprising. It was such a traumatic thing, and we were both so young and marked by it. But he wanted to get together alone too. I mean, there seemed to be something more to it, for him. We saw each other a few times. Alone. Without our spouses. And the last time we met, he told me he'd done it, he killed her."

"Just like that?"

"Well, no, of course not just like that." I smiled at him, stupidly. Then tried not to. "It was all mixed in with a kind of . . . justification of his life since then, I guess you'd say. See, he's a research scientist now, a very distinguished and well-known man. And so some of what he was in effect saying to me was that he'd made up for it. He'd lived his life in such a way as to . . . balance it out."

Detective Ryan sat back and started bouncing again. His hands, folded once more, rested on his belly now. He frowned suddenly. "*Where's* he work?" he said.

"Beth Israel. I don't know the university appointment. Harvard, maybe? I don't know, actually."

After a pause, he said, "He explain his motivation to you?"

"Well, yes. They'd had an affair. He and my friend. Dana. The police knew this at the time. They'd been sleeping together. But much earlier, actually. I'm sure it's all in the file. And then she'd left him. Broken it off, I guess you'd say. But they were to have talked about it, they'd arranged to talk about it after a long time on the night she was killed. He . . . he was still very much in love with her—he told me this—and . . . well, she'd even forgotten about this appointment, to talk, and then, when she did come downstairs and he started to speak to her, then she was . . . well, he described it as patronizing. Condescending. He was terribly upset, and he just struck out at her."

"With a kitchen knife." I had told him this earlier.

"Yes. He just, I guess, picked it up. They were standing in the kitchen together."

His face moved, his lower lip jutted out. Suddenly he nodded, once, as though, yes, he'd gotten the picture, he understood it all. He looked up at me. "So how did you respond when he told you all this? *When* was this, you said? A week ago?"

"Three weeks ago now."

"Oh. Three weeks."

"Yes."

"So you waited 'cause . . . ?" His thumbs rose up from his folded hands.

"I was in a kind of shock, I guess. I haven't been sure what to do. It was so long ago. That it all happened. And he *is* a different person now."

"So you more or less bought his . . . justification, like you said. For a while."

"No. No, it wasn't that. I didn't *buy* it, as you say. But it seemed . . . a difficult thing to do. To turn him in, essentially."

"You were getting to be friends."

"Yes!" I was relieved. "Yes, I liked him. I'd liked him then too. But it seemed to me also—to come here—like playing God or something."

He nodded and bounced, nodded and bounced. This was, I suppose, the moment when I could have spoken of my attraction to Eli, when I could have said, "Well, more than *liked*—I was drawn to him. I thought he was to me too." But I didn't. I didn't say anything like that. A door had opened and quickly closed. And once it was closed, it seemed irrelevant. I didn't. I was glad, I think, not to have to.

It was a mistake, a lie. But I didn't say anything. I let the moment pass.

He shook his head now. He was smiling. "Well, this is how it happens. A lot of times, you'd be surprised."

"What? What happens?"

"People need to talk. They talk about it finally. It's kind of amazing, actually. They *tell*. You'd think, it's been thirty years, they'd get used to living with it. They'd even forget they ever did it, maybe. But no, it seems to be the kind of a thing that sooner or later, they have to tell it to someone else." He seemed pleased, even amused, by this. "But this one is a long time. A *long* time." He shook his head.

I wanted to contribute to his pleasure somehow. It was the first response he'd had that I could read. "Well, we all dispersed," I explained. "We went our separate ways and didn't see each other again. Till now. So this . . . so our meeting really triggered it."

"Yeah," he said. He pointed at me suddenly. He'd stopped bouncing. "Did you give him any indication what you were going to do, that you were coming in here?"

I shook my head. "I . . . I *asked* him what he expected me to do. I indicated to him, I guess, how uncomfortable it made me to know this. But I didn't say . . . I didn't say anything about what I was going to do."

"So how did you leave it, exactly?"

"I didn't, really. I just walked out."

"Walked out of . . . ?"

"The Ritz. We'd been talking at the bar in the Ritz."

"The Ritz." He pouted. "That's pretty far from western Mass."

"Well, he works in town. And I was in for the day."

"And you haven't spoken since."

I shook my head again.

"So your guess would be that he does not know you've come in here."

"No, though he will figure it out the instant you contact him. If that's what you'll do. Is it?"

"Yes. I imagine so." He nodded several times. "What we'll do is, we'll pull the box, go over everything and see how it comes together with this new information, and then we'll try to talk to him."

"What do you mean, *try*?"

"Well, we'll see. Maybe he'll be very willing, maybe he'll come right in and tell us the same thing he told you. And maybe he won't.

Maybe he'll be more defensive, want to have an attorney present, be very careful about giving us any answers at all. Maybe he'll deny it." He lifted his shoulders. "And so forth. We'll have to see how it all comes together."

I felt included in his *we*, somehow. "Do you think . . . will I have to testify against him? In a trial?"

"I don't know. We'll see what we've got, and take it to the DA if it looks likely, and he'll take it from there. But we've got some baby steps first, so we don't want to get ahead of ourselves here. There are a lot of possible ways for him to respond, and a lot depends on that." He shrugged. "At this point, I really don't know much."

"But you will *pursue* it."

"Oh, yeah, of course. Yeah, don't worry about *that*. No, this thing is in motion now."

"Will you let me know . . . will you keep me informed about . . . what happens?"

"When there's anything to tell you, we will. And you can call me, anytime. Anything else comes up, or you remember anything else, you can call me." He had stood up now and was extracting a card from the wallet he'd taken out of his back pocket. As he handed it to me, he said, "And if he gets in touch again, anything threatening, or frightening to you, you call. Right away." He pointed at me again, thumb cocked, gunlike.

I nodded, feeling an overwhelming rush of gratitude, of relief. They would take care of me. *It would be taken care of. It would go away.* It was in their hands now.

On the way home, I drove down Lyman Street. I had to circle back twice through the warren of one-way streets to figure out how to get onto it, but I would have known the house anywhere. It was remarkably unchanged, though most of the other houses around it had been improved, or rebuilt elegantly, or drastically modified. Several of them were painted in luscious Victorian colors, three or four tones to a house, the differences emphasizing sculpted details or patterned shingling, bits of dentiled or curved trim that had in our day been covered in siding.

Our house still wore its ugly asphalt, though the mildew had been cleaned. The porch rail had been ripped out and entirely replaced with too-skinny, too-flimsy-looking wrought iron. The snow had stopped falling now, but it lay in wind-driven ripples against the foundation of the house, against the thick bases of the shrubs and the stubby irregular clumps of frozen crabgrass on the lawn. The first-floor windows were uncurtained and blank. On the second floor, though, what looked as if they could be the same crooked, tattered shades were hanging. The idea that this had once been a place of warmth or cheer or fellow feeling seemed laughable.

WHEN I TOLD DANIEL THAT NIGHT WHAT I'D DONE, HIS HEAD dropped forward, his neck bent, as though I'd struck him.

"I see," he said finally. He was sitting opposite me in the living room, his hands full of white envelopes. He'd started to go through the mail. I hadn't known when I'd tell him, exactly, or why, but there was something about how closed off from me he'd suddenly seemed, sitting there with his mail, that made it feel essential to cut through to him with whatever I had. Turning Eli in was *what I had*, then.

Daniel sat back and set the mail down on the table next to his chair. He stretched his long legs out toward me. He was in stocking feet, old brown socks, worn thin at the heel and the ball of each foot. His hands rose to his face, and he gouged at his eyes fiercely with his thumbs for a moment. "And what happens now?" he asked, suddenly looking directly at me. His eyes were reddened.

"They can't quite tell me, it seems. They'll reinvestigate. They'll talk to Eli. They'll see what happens."

"But it will open it all up. There'll be a trial."

"There could be, yes."

His chest rose fully once, and fell.

"Daniel, I'm *glad*. I'm glad it's done."

"Done, Joey?" he said. He seemed to be faintly smiling. "It's just beginning." He looked at me briefly, and then he got up. He went into the bedroom.

After a minute, I followed him. I stood in the doorway and watched him. He was undressing, not looking at me. At last I said, "Daniel, it would have happened whether or not I'd . . . been attracted to Eli."

He looked up at me. "What? What would have happened?"

"I would have gone to the police with this."

He shook his head, his mouth a tight line. "You never would have known about this, any of it, if you hadn't been attracted to him. Your *attraction*—your word, not mine—invited it, invited this . . . confidence of his."

He'd taken off all his clothes now, and he'd turned to me. His pale, nearly hairless body was as lean and corded as it had been in his youth, with long, shapely muscles. The flesh was looser, though, and his penis, too, hung more loosely. Sometimes when I looked at him, I was reminded of older male animals—lions, tigers—and the sagging swing of their genitals. To me this had always been sweet. Now I was filled with such longing for his nakedness to mean something for us, for his body to feel *mine* again—ours—that tears came quickly up, a hot pressure behind my eyes.

I sat down on the bed. "Daniel," I said, my voice tremulous. "What can I do, what can I say, to make things better?"

He shook his head, his lips tightened. "That's the wrong question, Joey. That's not how it works."

"How does it work, then?"

"It's something about how you have to *be*."

He left the room. I heard him cross the hall. Then there was a short silence, and I heard his bare feet padding back. He stood in the doorway. "Why did it have to be another secret, Jo?"

"What?"

"I don't understand why you couldn't have said to me this morning, 'I'm going to talk to the police today.' Why is it always necessary to hold something back?"

"What difference does it make? Would it have made?"

He looked at me as though he didn't know who I was. Then he turned and went into the bathroom. The door shut. In a few moments I heard the tumble of running water and then, rising from the basement, the heartbeat throb of the old pump.

WHEN CASS WAS AT HER MOST DIFFICULT, I OCCASIONALLY panicked, convinced she was using drugs or in danger of getting pregnant or about to run away. I spied on her. I went through her room when she was at school. I dug deep in her drawers, checked all her pockets for hidden stashes. I read letters and notes she kept in her desk or in a box in her closet. I felt so guilty about this that I talked to several other mothers about what they did—not to Daniel; I knew what he'd think of me. We divided about in half as a group, the other mothers and I: those who never sneaked around, those who did. It didn't make me feel any more comfortable about it, but I excused myself. Even when I thought about those trusting, honorable other mothers, I excused myself. I told myself that they didn't have Cassie. Cassie, who could look you coolly in the eye and deny what you knew, absolutely knew, to be true.

Once, I saw her driving a friend's car, one hand draped out the window, waving a cigarette around. She was fourteen at the time, and not only did she not have a license but I had no idea when and where she'd learned how to drive. I had intermittently suspected she smoked—she often smelled of cigarettes—but I had tried to deny it to myself by blaming the fast crowd she was with. Sitting in cars, sitting in teenage bedrooms around town with all that smoke, of course she'd stink.

When I asked her casually about it one day—had anyone been teaching her to drive? maybe she'd like lessons?—she looked at me steadily and said no. When I told her then that I'd seen her, she got furious. She said I'd tried to trap her, trick her, she accused me of not trusting her. She said I was dishonest, because I'd been so indirect, "so fucking devious." And around we went.

The most painful episode for me at around this time was finding a journal she'd been keeping. I was a sort of bogeyman in this book, a nightmare figure of falsity and hypocrisy and self-satisfaction. She wrote: "God, I hope I will never be as unconscious of how stupid I seem as Mother is, constantly trying to be so *nice* to all my friends, laughing and ridiculously flirty for someone her age, while she's meanwhile grilling everybody about me, about where we go, what we do together, etc. etc." And: "Mother just left my room—*my room*, which she acts like she can come in whenever she wants. Big fucking stink: I was late getting back last night, so now I must be punished. 'What do you think would be appropriate, Cass?' Well how do I fucking know? Why doesn't she just say what she thinks, why isn't she honest enough just to be angry and invent her own goddamn punishment? No. There has to be this fake *talk*. Doesn't she realize????? we are ENEMIES!!!! Meanwhile, she's sitting on MY bed, touching MY stuff. There is nothing about her that doesn't disgust me."

It was painful, of course, to read this, but in the end I'm glad I did. It helped me know how to be around Cass. I had thought that what was most important was that she feel loved, that I continue to behave as lovingly toward her as I could. But it seemed she needed from me an austerity that honestly matched the distance between us. I began to provide it.

None of this made her warmer then, or easier, but it did feel oddly more comfortable to me not to pretend to any warmth, not really ever to wish any longer for ease. Simply to give up for a while and have my love be utterly a private, unexpressed thing, waiting for a signal from her that some aspect of it might be welcome. And perhaps in some way all of that restraint helped allow for our long, slow rapprochement. I don't know.

I felt similarly chastened now in my relations to Daniel. I think what I had hoped was that by pretending things were better between us I could make them become better. I think I did hope that there was something I could do or say that would make a difference. But the lesson I was learning was that everything I did partook of me, of the things in me that had made him turn away in the first place. I saw that I couldn't, for the moment, try to change things with him. That when I did, I would inevitably do it in my own unwelcome way, and that would only make things worse. I would be secretive, because that was something that was part of me. I would sweep too much of his pain aside, because I so wanted it to be over, because I tried to make things happen at my own pace. I would attack him, hurt him, wound him, disgust him, with my wish for things to be as I wanted them to be again, too fast.

What I was beginning to understand was that simply to act was to affirm my inescapable self, to make exactly the kind of mistake I *would* make. It seemed that for the moment, to Daniel, I was all of a piece, full of a kind of odious integrity.

Well, all right. Having children teaches you, I think, that love can survive your being despised in every aspect of yourself. That you need not collapse when the shriek comes: *Don't you get it? I* hate *you!* But you do need to get it. You do need to understand and accept being hated. I think this is one of the greatest gifts children can give you, as long as it doesn't last.

Cass had taught me well. I turned away from Daniel now. I taught myself passivity.

I was waiting anyway. Waiting for the police to call me back. I didn't know what form the next step would take. I thought maybe Eli would call me. I'd stand at the mailbox in the gently falling snow and scan all the return addresses quickly, looking for . . . what? The district attorney's office? The Cambridge police? Homicide? It occurred to me Eli might write me. Or Larry. Maybe they'd be in touch with Larry. Or Sara. Mightn't they be called in for questioning? Or Dana's sisters.

What I most often imagined was the need for more questions to be answered. Was this what a grand jury might do? I didn't know. Or I imagined Eli in a rage, threatening me, coming at me somehow. Or, less likely, Eli sorrowful—perhaps even redeeming himself to me by recognizing that what I'd done was right. I ran over the various alternatives in my mind, the dramas that might come next. I held my breath when the phone rang, I sorted hurriedly through the mail each day. It seemed to me I'd imagined every possible thing.

I hadn't thought of Jean. I hadn't thought of Sadie.

I STEPPED INTO THE KITCHEN AND HEARD DANIEL'S VOICE AT its chilliest: "And I don't think you're being fair." It stopped me. So categorical. So cold. Whom would Daniel ever speak to in this way? I set down the heavy box I was carrying—a new humidifier; the old one was corroded with our mineral-rich well water—and started to take my hat and coat off, listening carefully. Some unpleasantness at the church, is what I thought.

"I *admit* it seems nuts. But some things are nuts. Period. . . . Yes. Yes, I do. . . . Yes, I support her completely."

I hung my coat up.

"Well, then, we're both nuts."

I stood still, listening. "Sadie, no one is doing this *to you*. You happened to be in the line of fire, but . . ."

And suddenly I understood. There's been some fallout, some third-hand effect, on Sadie. Via Jean, of course. I stepped into the kitchen. Clearly Daniel had been waiting for me since he'd heard the back door open. He pointed to the phone, then raised his shoulders and lifted his eyebrows questioningly. I nodded and walked over to him.

"Sadie?" he said. "Sade? Mom's here now. You want to talk to her?"

He covered the phone with his hand for a second. "Repercussions," he said.

I nodded and took the receiver from him.

She began before I even said hello: "Mom, what are you *doing*?" Her voice was almost a shriek.

"Slow down, sweetie, and tell me what—"

"This stuff with Jean's husband. I mean, you're accusing him of *murder*?"

"He accused himself, Sadie. He told me he did it."

"*Mom.*" The tone was that of an adult to a child with an overactive imagination.

"How did you hear about it?" I asked.

"Because you've ruined my *life*, that's how! Because the whole special project I was going to do with Jean is down the toilet, that's how."

I kept my voice calm. "Because she's mad at me."

"Because she's not sure she can separate this stuff in her head, so she told me she'd rather not do it. Or I had to find someone else. But I don't *want* anyone else." She paused for breath. She lowered her voice. "This was *two credits*, Mom. This was my whole semester. It was going to be part of my senior thesis eventually."

"I'm sorry, Sadie."

There was a silence.

"Can't you stop it? Can't you undo it?" A little girl's voice.

"I don't see how."

"God, Mom. By going to the police. By saying you made a mistake."

"But I didn't make a mistake."

"*What.* Mr. Mayhew is a murderer."

"He told me so. Yes."

"Mom, he's a famous scientist. He's a . . . he's a *doctor*. I mean, why would he say that to you?" She stopped for a few seconds. Then: "Did you have a lot to drink?"

"That's an insulting question, Sadie."

"God, this is so crazy!"

"I know. But it's real."

"But how come you never . . . I mean, it's like you invented this whole thing. I mean, I never even knew you had a friend who was murdered . . . ?"

"But I did," I said. "She was . . . she was my friend."

"Yeah, well. Thanks for sharing."

"I am sorry, Sadie. For everything."

I listened to her breathe for a moment. Then she said, "Mom, look. Isn't it possible you misunderstood him? Isn't it possible you . . . I mean, *had* you had a lot to drink?"

"No. No and no."

"Well, what am I supposed to *do*?"

"I don't know, sweetie."

"So you believe it, you honestly believe that Mr. Mayhew killed this . . . this friend."

"I do. And I'm really sorry—sorrier than I can say—that it has had any effect on you."

We were both silent. She spoke first. "I am just so blown away by all this. It's like I can't . . . So you won't . . . you won't change your mind."

"I can't, Sadie."

"Well, there goes my academic career." Her voice was flip, brittle, but I could hear she was near tears.

"Sadie, if I could do this any differently, I would."

"Yeah, sure. Thanks a lot, Mom," she said. There was a muffled *clunk*, and the line went dead.

I was frozen for a moment, holding on to the phone. Then I hung it up. I turned around. Daniel and I stood looking at each other, over the clutter of mail, of grocery bags of food on the kitchen table, over the dancing, joyous dogs, who had finally assembled to welcome me home.

"Well," I said, trying to sound normal. My throat hurt. "I guess the police have been in touch with Eli."

14

Dear Sadie,

I know you are still angry with me, and though that's painful for me, I can understand it. I am only sorry that you are in any way touched or affected by all this business, which is so unrelated to you, finally. It is unfair. It seems unfair to me too. What I find myself hoping is that at some point your deep admiration for Jean will, not diminish, but be tempered enough by time and experience to allow you to consider the possibility that despite her understandable shock and anger at what's happened, she is simply wrong about Eli Mayhew. That he did in fact say to me what I reported to the police he said to me. That he did in fact do the thing he said he did, which was, in a moment of rage and passion and deep hurt, to kill someone dear to me, someone whose very sweetness and gaiety and affection were, I think, a kind of torment to him.

This is a long story, Sadie, and perhaps one I should have told you. It's never been clear to me exactly what you girls need to know of my past, or your father's past, what stories are the right ones to tell and what are better kept private. Certainly everyone, maybe even you, too, Sadie, has done things that seem shameful. I probably didn't tell you many of those about myself, unless they were funny somehow. Why? Maybe because I didn't want to condone my own behavior by claiming it. Maybe because I wanted to think of certain things I'd done as being not really who I am. Also because I was ashamed, I suppose. Because I wanted your love and admiration.

This story, the story of Eli and my lovely friend, was different. It seemed to me too frightening, too awful in its message—that we are never safe, that evil can descend on us at any time—to inflict on you or Nora or Cass. (At least this is the message I'd always taken from it.) I wanted to spare you such news about life.

Now there's a different message, I guess, something having to do with our inability really to know or guess at the secret depths of another person. Perhaps that is what you are feeling about me now, too, since you are so certain of my perversity, or my craziness, in doing what I'm doing. Who the hell *is* she?

But that is what I've felt about Eli too. I wouldn't have believed, either, that he did what I now say he did. But he told me he did, and he explained it very, very well, Sadie, in ways I couldn't have invented. It fit with everything I knew about what happened—and I was the one who found my friend, seconds after she died. Her name was Dana, and she was beautiful and lighthearted and loving. You remind me a little of her.

I suppose I am trying to defend myself to you. But I'm also asking for your forgiveness: in ways that are very complicated indeed, I do bear some responsibility for this chain of events. I hope that you will at some point feel again that I'm a trustworthy part of your life. That you do *know me.*

Lovingly,
Mom

I walked to the post office to mail this. Somehow I couldn't bear to leave it in our box with the flag up. It seemed too private. It seemed too awful that I should have had to write it at all. But Sadie hadn't called in more than a week, in spite of three messages I'd left for her and at least one call I'd overheard Daniel making, trying to intervene on my behalf.

I waited up for Daniel that night. I wanted to tell him about the letter. I wanted to talk, if that was possible. He was late getting home.

At ten-thirty I decided to walk the dogs. It had been so long since either of us had taken them out that they were hard to roust. Finally, though, we were gathered by the door, they were leaping on me, mauling me in their excitement, and we stepped outside into the dark.

I hadn't realized how cold it was. The temperature must have been near zero, the dry stillness was almost frightening. The sky was vast, and the stars were somehow more distant than usual. My breath froze and pinched in my nostrils. By the time we were halfway around the common, even the big dogs were ready to turn back. Shorty, lagging behind me, would stop and stand painfully for a moment, with one paw, then another, lifted, trying to offer it some relief from contact with the biting-cold ground. I carried him the last half block or so home. He was shuddering in my arms.

In the house, I undressed quickly and got ready for bed. When I came back into our room, all the dogs were curled up on the coverlet, waiting for me. I had to shove and bounce them around to make room for myself.

It was just after eleven. This was very late for Daniel. Perhaps he'd gone out for a drink with someone after the meeting.

What meeting?

I couldn't remember what he'd said when he went out, what he was supposed to be doing tonight. It occurred to me that if Daniel were a different person I might worry about that, about whether he'd found someone sympathetic to listen to the sad tale of his wife's betrayal, of the ugliness she'd brought into their lives. Shorty had begun to snore gently.

I turned the light off. In the dark, the silence of the house and the empty village outside seemed to change. I heard, suddenly, the ticks, the creaks of the old wood shifting in the cold. I heard the onrush of a car passing, the slow rise of the wind. One of the dogs whimpered in his sleep, licked his chops. His feet twitched as he chased something, killed it, in a happy dream. I was recalling that other world in which it had thrilled me, in a way, the surprise of thinking that I could be a person who would betray Daniel. Now I wondered if Daniel could surprise himself, could surprise me, by being such a person too. Would he let himself do such a thing? I didn't think so. And then I wondered: Is it by will, then, that we are who we are? Do we decide, do we make ourselves, after a certain point in life?

I tried to call up the moment when I had decided I could be such a person. It seemed to me I hadn't quite got there, not really. That I was still just playing with the idea of it when the ground shifted under me.

But perhaps to play with such an idea was already to be a certain *kind* of person.

I must have dozed off. A growl on the bed woke me, and then I, too, heard Daniel moving carefully through the house. The old pine boards croaked, the hinges on the bathroom door squealed faintly. I looked over at the glowing digital clock. Eleven fifty-two. The dogs shifted eagerly, but none of them got up. Too lazily comfortable where they were. Too warm.

I was going to say something to Daniel when he came in, but I heard his whisper first, speaking gently to each dog, bending over them, luring them off the bed one by one. I lay still, silent. I was loving him too much, the solicitous, elegant quiet in everything he did, peeling his clothes off in slow motion, laboriously hanging his shirt on a hook. The hissing intake of his breath when the coins in his pocket jingled faintly as he stepped out of his pants. If I spoke, he would become the other Daniel, the Daniel who had not yet forgiven me, who would be polite, stiff, only carefully responsive. In the dark, I lay still and watched the shape of my Daniel, the real Daniel, sitting slowly, carefully adding his weight to the bed. I imagined that as tenderness toward me. He whispered to one of the dogs, somewhere on the floor.

I was loving him, I was loving his voice. I was taking from him what he couldn't give to me. I felt his slow slide into the flannel sheets, the little shudder of pleasure at the warmth of the pockets the dogs had made. He smelled of toothpaste, of wine. He shifted toward me, perhaps to take heat from my side of the bed. I lay utterly still, happy—joyful—with what I was stealing.

THE POLICE CALLED ME AT WORK THE NEXT DAY. DETECTIVE Ryan. Could I come in? No urgency, he just wanted to go over things, see where we were now. I explained that my next day off was Monday. That was fine, he said. "Like I said, this is just to catch you up, more or less." We fixed a time for Monday morning and hung up.

It preyed on me through that day, a Wednesday. It was my surgery day, though there wasn't that much to do. We had a teeth cleaning on an ancient Lab—anesthesia was the issue there, not cutting—two spays, and the removal of an extra toe that seemed to be bothering a mixed-breed puppy. Mary Ellen was assisting me. One of the spays, a cat, was pregnant, and we lifted out the tiny, beautifully intricate embryos and carefully set them aside. Mary Ellen wanted to take them into her son's day care center to show to the kids.

While we were working, I was thinking about it, I heard Detective Ryan's loud voice. I pictured the homicide department's cheerful office, the hum of machines, of people working and talking. "You can only go one step at a time," Daniel had said to me over breakfast that morning when I told him about the letter to Sadie.

Well, yes. But I realized now, pulling the sutures on the shaved flesh below me, that I wanted to take this step, this next step available to me, before Monday. I wanted to take it now. I'd stopped myself from trying to force things, with Sadie, with Daniel. But any step out of all this that was made available to me was one I wanted *already* to have taken.

As we were washing up, I asked Mary Ellen if she could cover for me the next day. When she said she would, I went to the front desk to talk to Beattie. She called up my schedule on the computer and we reviewed it together, deciding who could be rescheduled, who would need to see Mary Ellen tomorrow, whom Beattie should telephone. She was, as she always was in this kind of situation, helpful and efficient.

When we'd mapped it all out, she sat back and looked up at me. "Business or pleasure?" she asked. She wore two spangled barrettes in her dry, thin hair, one above each ear.

"What?"

"Your day off."

"Oh." I laughed. "Exactly neither," I said.

She called after me. "That's right. Don't tell *me* anything."

I stepped back into the doorway. "Beattie, you don't want to know." A lie, if ever there was one. She sniffed. She knew it too.

I CALLED THAT EVENING AND LEFT WORD FOR DETECTIVE Ryan that I'd be in in the morning, but when I arrived at the counter in the homicide department the next day, he was out. "I left a message," I said. "Last night. Maybe he left some kind of message back for me?"

"What is this regarding?"

He was an older man, much older than Detective Ryan. His hair was yellow-white, thick and curly. His face, too, was white, almost unnaturally so. Parchment color.

"It's about an old murder case. Dana Jablonski. That was the victim's name."

"I'll ask around," he said.

I watched him move from desk to desk, stopping to laugh at one or two. He disappeared into the part of the long room I couldn't see from my side of the counter. I stood there for some minutes, my hip beginning to ache. Finally another man, this one truly young—a kid, I would have called him—came up and said, "Mrs. Becker?"

"Yes," I said.

"I'm Detective Lewis. I know something about the Jablonski case. What were you coming in for?" He smiled at me, a kind of goofy, pointless smile. He had big teeth, oversize for his mouth.

"Just to get caught up, I guess. I don't know if Detective Ryan had any more questions for me or not. I told him I'd come in Monday, but then I didn't want to wait that long. I'm sorry if this is an inconvenience. I *can* come back Monday if this won't work."

"No, it's okay. Why don't you come in, sit down." He opened the partition to allow me to pass. "I'll go over what we've got and be with you in a minute."

"Are you sure it's not a problem?" I was already stepping in.

"No problem. I was working on it with him earlier. I just need to catch up, and I'll be right with you." Over a white button-down shirt, he was wearing a shiny green Celtics jacket.

He led me once again to the room with the large table, and I pulled out a chair to sit down. "Can I get you anything?" he asked from the doorway. Part of their training, apparently.

I shook my head. "No. Thanks." And he was gone.

It was nearly fifteen minutes before he returned. "Got it figured out why he called you, I think," he said, sitting down himself, several chairs away from me.

"Good," I said. There was something too large about all his features, I saw now—lips, nose, eyebrows, ears—as though his face hadn't grown into them yet.

"Basically," he said, "I think Detective Ryan wanted to let you know that we most likely won't go anywhere with your information."

I was breathless for a few seconds. "But why? I mean, he thought you would, I think."

"Yeah, but . . . well, see, it would need to jive with something else. It would need to"—his hand flapped back and forth—"open something up. And the thing is, it doesn't. What it's come to is, it's your word against his." He looked at me with a keen and curious disinterest, and shrugged.

"So he denied it. That he'd told me he killed Dana."

"Dr. Mayhew. Yeah. He denied it. Denied he said it, denied he did it." This seemed somehow to please him. "He was pretty adamant."

I thought for a moment. "But he would be, wouldn't he?"

"Yeah, but the thing is, when we looked back at what we had in the box, nothing jumped out, if you see what I mean. What you said he said to you doesn't make anything make more sense. Which is kinda what you look for. For corroboration." He flashed his big teeth at me.

I was genuinely puzzled. "But it *does* make sense. I mean, there were no fingerprints, and he told me he was wearing gloves. That connects. And he could so easily have gotten rid of stuff in the lab, which is what he told me he did."

"Yeah, but none of that's conclusive in any way. None of it's news. I mean, we all knew way back then—you knew too"—he smiled again—"that the killer was wearing gloves. And, I mean, anyone could have pointed out at any time that Dr. Mayhew had the means to get rid of stuff. It's nothing new, you see what I mean?" His voice was boyish also, there was an energy, an enthusiasm, in it that was startling to me.

"But he told me," I said. My voice, by contrast to his, sounded dry and weak.

"And he says he didn't tell you."

We sat facing each other over the big table. His mouth was slightly open.

"But why would I make all that up?" I asked at last.

"Well, that's a problem, but it's not our problem." The teasing half smile lifted his face again.

"But he has much more reason to deny it than I do to invent it."

He shrugged. "Maybe."

I was irritated. "Well, of course he does. Why would I want to make all this . . . trouble for myself if it weren't true?"

"Well, it's trouble for you, but it's trouble for him, too, isn't it?"

"Well, why would I want to make trouble for him, then?" I could hear that I was beginning to sound frazzled.

He lifted his hand. "You tell me."

"There *isn't* any reason. In a way, I barely know the man. I have no ax to grind here."

"Maybe you do, maybe you don't."

"I don't. I assure you, I don't. Why on earth would I want to put anyone through this unless it was true? What kind of monster of ill will would I have to be to do such a thing?"

"It would be ill will, all right." He sounded almost amused.

"But I have no such ill will. I have no reason for it."

He let a little silence accumulate between us before he said, "Tell me something."

"Of course," I said.

"Were you ever, like . . . attracted to Dr. Mayhew, Mrs. Becker?"

And suddenly it was clear to me what Eli had said, how he'd defended himself. And even in that moment of clarity, with its accompanying sense of danger, I was aware also of being pettily annoyed, of wanting to say, "Look, *I'm* the doctor; he's the mister." For a moment I was speechless, but finally I said, "Is that what he told you?"

"Well, you know, we wondered, too, so we asked him why he thought you would go to all this trouble. It was an idea he had, let's say."

I shook my head. "It's not true."

"So you were not attracted to him."

Detective Lewis had blue eyes, bright blue below the heavy eyebrows, and they were steady on me now as he waited.

"I was attracted to him, but I didn't seek revenge on account of it."

"But you were attracted."

"I had been, yes."

"Were you disappointed in your attraction?" He was smirking, his lips tight over the big teeth.

"How elegantly you put it," I said. "No. No, I wasn't. My attraction ended when Mr. Mayhew confessed to me, when he told me he'd murdered my friend."

"So you weren't pissed off at him that he didn't respond to you."

"Not by that time; no." I shook my head.

After a pause, he said, "Did you ask him to meet you at the Ritz Hotel? Did you call him?"

"That is true, but—"

"So you were still attracted to him at that point. At the point at which you called him."

"Why are you talking to me this way?" My voice was shrill. "I'm not accused of anything."

"Well, you are, kind of. You made some serious charges against Dr. Mayhew, and it's possible you did that vindictively."

"I didn't." He was still looking at me, and I thought suddenly of how he must see me. Old. Desperate. Disappointed. I had dressed drably, I realized now—I suppose to seem responsible and reliable to Detective Ryan. This guy would be seeing it another way.

He shifted now in his chair. "What were your expectations, Mrs. Becker, when you went to the Ritz Hotel to meet Dr. Mayhew?"

"I don't know."

"You don't know."

I shook my head.

"But maybe one possibility was beginning a relationship with him. Maybe?" I didn't answer. He sat back. "Why did you choose a hotel, Mrs. Becker. You chose it, am I right? You suggested it?"

"It's a famous bar. I don't know Boston that well. I chose the Ritz bar."

"There was no notion in your mind that Dr. Mayhew might spend the night with you?"

"Look, Detective Lewis," I burst out. "Having lascivious thoughts is one thing, and making up a terrible lie about someone else is another thing. And I didn't. I didn't make this up."

"Hey, Mrs. Becker, this isn't even my case." His big hands rose. "All I'm saying here is we ended up with two people with profoundly different versions of what went on, and why, and our job is to sort out plausibilities. If there'd been one thing that made your story more plausible, we would have gone ahead. But there was nothing. And it flies in the face of some evidence we *do* have."

"What? What evidence?"

"He had an alibi, did you know that?" Lewis was slouched now. He was enjoying this, I saw. "Every one of you had an alibi, someone who would vouch for you. In his case, someone in his lab who saw him at just about that time. And he had test results coming in that he recorded over that whole period."

I shook my head. I hadn't known. How could Eli have arranged it? Half-lit scenarios began to play in my mind, but even as I started to construct them, I knew that to offer them up would be to seem more desperate, defensive. I knew it would be useless.

"And then there's the money," he said.

What I thought of instantly was the money I'd kept in my drawer. Which I'd had to explain then, several times. My "unusual system of banking," one of the cops had called it. I must have looked confused or blank, because he said, "Money was stolen, if you remember. I think you must have forgotten that."

I saw it then, the cop coming in from the backyard, carrying the plastic bag. The red-and-green Medaglia d'Oro can in it, empty. Larry, Sara, nodding: Yes, that was it.

I cleared my throat. "But it would have been the easiest thing in the world for Eli to take that to cover up for himself."

"Did he tell you he took it?"

"No."

"But he was so candid with you about other things." He couldn't keep the sarcasm from his voice. "I can't believe he wouldn't have explained that too."

After a long moment, he shook his head. He was smiling again. "I don't think so, Mrs. Becker. See, it just doesn't pull the pieces together."

I'm sure I looked defeated, done in. His voice, when he spoke again, was not unkind. "Look, what I can tell you is that we still think your friend's murder was a break-in that went bad. And we still think maybe someone will talk about it, maybe even someone in jail for something else. Though as time passes—and we know this too—it gets less likely. What we don't think is that Dr. Mayhew was involved. That's what I can tell you."

I was silent, looking out the window at the pale sky. Then I said, "So you think I'm a pathological liar."

He smiled once more, that false, vulpine smile. His head tilted. "Just out of curiosity, Mrs. Becker," he said pleasantly. "Why the fake ID back then? All the lies to your roommates?" And when I didn't answer: "Hey," he said, "we checked it out. We called him. He came in, more than once. We poked around. You can't ask for more than that." He lifted his hands.

"I guess not," I said at last. My voice was small.

"So," he said, pushing his chair back. "That about takes care of it, I guess."

"Yes," I said. "Yes, I guess it does."

I was trembling, with a kind of rage, I think, as I walked back to the car, and when I got there I sat for a while turned sideways in the driver's seat, my feet on the ground still, light-headed in a way that made me feel I might at any moment throw up.

When it passed, I was slowly aware of a pure relief, a relief so intense that I gradually began to feel nearly giddy. It was over. That's what I was thinking. It was finished. I had acted. I had done the right thing as I saw it, dreading what it might lead to, and it had led to nothing. To air and freedom. To my life coming back to me. I could begin again.

I started the car. I drove across Cambridge toward Route 2. I was going down Brattle Street, between the rows of widespread, splendid houses, the vast yards opening on either side of me. I was thinking again of Dana, as I so often had in these weeks and months; but this time with such ease and familiarity that it seemed I could hear her hoarse, ugly voice speaking to me. Sudden tears spilled from my eyes. I signaled and pulled over to park.

When I had gained control of myself and could see clearly again, I looked around. A fence ran along the edge of the sidewalk next to me. It was made of tall, solid spikes, square, their white paint gently peeling here and there. The grand posts that interrupted their progress every ten feet or so were topped with elaborate and improbable wooden urns. The yard behind the fence swept up to a Georgian house. It was gray, with black, listing shutters. In front of it, an elderly woman—at first I thought her a man, but then I saw the wisps of hair drooping down from under her cloth hat—was slowly, nearly ceremonially, clipping branches from a large, scraggly shrub. Forsythia. For forcing, I supposed. Or perhaps she was just pruning. In any case, I thought of it as such an enviable occupation, and she was so absorbed in it, so engaged, that I felt a rush of odd elation. It seemed to me possible that I could peacefully come to be that old, that I would have my everyday chores to do, that I might do them in the pale sunlight of early spring. I was released to this, I thought. I was back in ordinary time.

What did it matter what Eli had accused me of? The people who believed it—Detective Lewis, Detective Ryan, even Jean—were people I didn't care about. Of course, I cared about Sadie. But Sadie hadn't heard every ugly twist, she hadn't heard the worst of it. And she and I had time, all the time in the world, I thought. I started the car, I drove on again.

I stopped in the big supermarket on the highway between Adams Mills and Shirley, and did a thorough shopping for what seemed like the first time in months. In every wide aisle there was something I could use, and it was with a sense of nearly physical pleasure that I pushed my cart up and down the sections and slowly filled it. The abundance of ordinary things, their convenient arrangement here, seemed for the moment a personal gift to me. As did my ability to notice this, to be grateful for it.

At home, I went in and out many times, hauling all the bags. The dogs were happy to follow me, each trip an adventure, the more the better. They nosed at the bags, they chased each other off, barking wildly in pleasure—their life returning to them too. They continued to argue and chase each other around the kitchen as I put things away, as if they could sense the change in the air, the change in me.

I'd bought ingredients for risotto for dinner, and when I was through putting the food away, I chopped the shallots and mushrooms, I set the broth out in a pan, measured the rice, poured olive oil into the heavy enamel skillet. I set the table. I washed lettuce and made a dressing for salad. I imagined us sitting at the table, talking. But if things were still stiff with Daniel, if he didn't want to talk, that was all right too. I had time there also. Time and Daniel's nature, which was forgiving, which was generous. I remembered that when I'd been so overwhelmed by my feelings for Eric, our clinic assistant, Daniel had wept with me and held me, as though my being tempted were a thing, an event, that had happened to us both, was causing us both pain. Which we would suffer through together.

There was still a faint light hovering in the yard when he drove in, though I'd turned the lights on inside a while earlier. The dogs whined and ran to the back hall to wait for him. I could hear his voice as he spoke to them in greeting—light, loving. I felt the cold air drifting in. And then he stood in the doorway and nodded, a half smile, polite and obligatory, on his face.

"Hi," I said. I'd tossed the shallots into the olive oil when I saw him pull in, and now I was stirring them. They hissed.

"Hi," he answered. He stepped toward me and stopped partway across the room. I had turned sideways to greet him as I worked, and now he noticed what I was doing.

"Hey, what's for dinner?" he asked, and he was unable to keep the lift from his voice.

"Risotto."

"Risotto!" And it was only then that I remembered the first time I'd made risotto for him—just after news of its culinary chic had reached our corner of the universe. It was a weekend night, and Sadie was out, or I never would have tried it. Daniel was dubious. "You can call it risotto, but it sure looks like rice to me," he said, putting on a tough-guy voice.

"Ahh," he had said with the first bite. "Very soothing." And with the second, "Wonderful. Like baby food for adults. Thank you for making it." He'd been in and out of the kitchen as I cooked, he'd seen how long it took. Now he leaned over the table and kissed me, a kiss that expanded slightly and startled us both. We sat back, and he looked at me with the slightly stupid gaze of someone in the throes of a sexual impulse. "In fact," he had said, "I think what I would like here is for you to feed me." I laughed, but then I picked up his spoon and lifted it to his opening mouth.

Surely I must have been thinking of that when I bought the rice, must have been recollecting some part of it: the half-eaten dinner, the eager stumbling across the living room, the dogs whining outside the bedroom door at the noises we made, at this inexplicable interruption in the meal, their favorite human activity of the day.

Now he started toward the living room. "Well, let me freshen up, as they say." He went out the door. And then reappeared. He'd remembered. "Hey. What happened with the police?"

"Well, there's some good news and some bad news," I said, stirring the pan. "I'll tell you when you come back."

He'd pulled on a sweater when he returned. He asked if I wanted some wine, and I said yes. He opened a bottle and poured us each a glass. As he held mine out to me, our eyes met, and there seemed to me for the first time in weeks to be an openness in his gaze, a willingness to see me, to see who I was. "Well," he said, "here's to the good news, whatever it may be. We need it."

"Indeed," I said, and lifted my glass to him, too, before I drank. I set it down. I added more broth to the risotto. Daniel went to the table, pulled a chair out, and sat down. Allie came and sat between his opened legs, resting her muzzle on his thigh. He stroked her head. He looked up at me, watching him. "Tell me," he said.

Tell me! My heart leapt. It was like being touched. I smiled at him. "Well, it's over, essentially," I said.

He looked confused for a few seconds, and then he said, "They're not going to pursue it?"

I shook my head. "Nope."

"But how come?"

" 'Cause he denied it. I guess I knew he would, especially after Sadie called. But anyway, he did. Never happened."

"So that's it."

I nodded.

"God, that's a relief." He drank and set his glass down. One hand rested gripping the stem, and he twirled it for a moment. He looked at me and frowned. "Still, I would have thought they'd somehow at least investigate it anyway."

I shrugged, stirring. "There wasn't really anything to investigate. No new evidence or anything like that. And there's still stuff that's not explained by what he told me. I mean, as they pointed out, I didn't come in there and solve it for them. *So.*"

"So in effect they said there was nothing they could do."

"More or less."

"Well, that surprises me somehow, I guess."

"Well, it ended up being my word against his, pretty much."

"So?" He sipped his wine again, and I stopped stirring to sip mine. "I mean, he's the one with the reason to lie. Doesn't that give it a little weight? Your account?"

"One might have thought so. One would have been wrong, I guess."

"I'm insulted on your behalf, madam." He was almost smiling. It was like the dawn breaking for me.

I smiled back and curtsied quickly. "Thank you," I said. "But it *is* the insult that sets us free of it."

"I suppose. So how did they present it. Just 'Very sorry, we can't proceed on this basis'?"

I turned away to add more broth to the risotto. After a moment, I said, "Well, they weren't quite that pleasant about it."

"What do you mean?"

I adjusted the temperature down a bit.

"Jo?" he said.

"Well, Eli had offered them a reason why *I* might not be truthful."

"Which was?" There was impatience, the beginning of indignation, in his voice.

"Which was . . ." I looked at him. "This, by the way, is the bad news, Daniel." I tried to keep my voice light. "Which was that I had been angry at him, at Eli, because he *disappointed* me." I tried to make the word sound comical. I made a face.

"He disappointed you."

"Yes."

He looked quizzically at me, the one sharp frown line between his brows.

"Sexually," I explained. "Because he didn't want an affair and I did. This is what he told them."

"So you accuse him of murder? I mean, people get disappointed all the time without that happening."

"Well, he made me seem very . . . aggressive, I think. Maybe he said I'd been in love with him in the past too. I don't know, I'm sure he elaborated." I set the spoon down and turned to face him, to tell him everything. "And they knew that I'd called him, that I'd chosen the Ritz. The point *there* being that it's a hotel, not just a bar. Convenient. You see."

"I see." He looked down at Allie's head, still resting on his leg. He scratched her ears contemplatively. I went back to work, but I watched him too. He looked up, finally. "You *were* the one who called him, then," he said.

"Yes."

"And you did choose the Ritz."

"Yes."

"Because it was a hotel?"

"I think I thought of that, yes."

"And *were* you disappointed, then?" His eyes were so dark, suddenly—can the pupil expand in pain? in anger?—that I couldn't read his face.

"What I was disappointed about, Daniel, was who he turned out to be. What he'd done. That . . . superseded everything, once he'd told me."

He looked down again. His hand was motionless on the dog's head. Now he removed it. He sat frozen for some long seconds.

"Daniel," I said. He didn't look at me. I'd stopped stirring. "I told you this. I told you all of it, Daniel. We don't have to do it all again. This is nothing *new*." My voice was pleading.

At last he said, "No." He sounded as he'd sounded for weeks until tonight—until his ease earlier tonight: exhausted. He seemed smaller, abruptly. Caved in. "Though I didn't know," and I heard him trying for a dry tone, a rueful distance. "I didn't quite know—did I?—that you were the aggressor, the arranger. *The one who chose the Ritz.*" His voice italicized it.

I thought briefly, rejecting it nearly as fast as the thought came, of defending myself on the tiny bit of territory left to defend: Eli had called first, had asked me out first, had invited and was waiting for my call. Rejecting it because it made no difference, really. Because it wasn't an important distinction in the end.

Because I'd seen move across Daniel's face, when he realized why the police didn't believe me, the shadow of doubt about it, too, the momentary possibility that he didn't know me at all. That I was the person *they* thought I was, the person Eli had said I was—who invented it all, who lashed out, who lied. Who lied because she was *disappointed.*

And in spite of my horror at seeing it, I felt such hungry, pathetic gratitude when it passed that there was no struggle, no pride left in me. And so I answered him, finally. I said, "No. No, you didn't."

15

THERE WAS, OF COURSE, THE REST OF LIFE GOING ON AT the same time—things to do, things to respond to.

Nora won a grant to finish her film, and in celebration, she cut her hair off.

"I can't imagine it," I said on the phone. "What do you look like?"

"Well, here's the thing." She gave a snorting laugh: the joke was on her. "Of course, I look like Cass."

After a pause, visualizing it—a fuller, rounder Cass—I said, "Well, isn't that what we all want to look like, a rock-and-roll star?"

Now she laughed fully. "Yeah, I suppose. Except, get with it, Mother: they don't call it rock and roll anymore."

And one day in early March I was putting some things away in the attic, when I found an envelope I'd left there in the fall. I recognized it immediately: it held a copy of a picture Beattie had taken of me at work, a picture of me that was, for a change, very good. I'd had it blown up, planning to give it to Daniel for Christmas.

But I'd forgotten. In my distraction about Eli, I'd forgotten it was here. I sat on a trunk now and opened it. Beattie had spoken to me as I was putting a file away. I'd just lifted my head to her, my hair still falling slightly forward, and I was beginning to laugh at the animal snout she wore on her face—a pig's—when she snapped me. Looking at it now, at my happy smiling face in another world—the gift I would have given to Daniel—I could have wept.

Spring arrived once, for two days. I left the back door open, and the dogs trailed freely in and out, tracking mud into the kitchen. I sat in the thin sunlight on the back stoop and watched them, imagining an end to winter, an end to our terrible time.

The next day, of course, there was a freezing rain. I couldn't unlock my car door and had to call Beattie, whose car spent its nights in a garage, to come pick me up.

Sadie wrote us a postcard saying she wouldn't be home for spring break, that she was going to New York, "to be with my sisters," as though these were people with no connection to us.

Daniel went away to Philadelphia for four days for church meetings. In his absence I felt such a lifting off of sorrow, of my oppressive sense of guilt, that I began to wonder if perhaps it might not be better for both of us to live without this strain—to separate. To divorce. It made my heart pound unevenly to think of it, but I forced myself to. For surely he, too, was more himself at work, or out in his study. Surely he, too, was happier in those moments when he'd forgotten my existence. I imagined a life alone, in some small apartment; I'd leave Daniel the house, of course. I imagined the ease of solitude, of meals eaten standing up or while I lay on a couch, reading. Of not having to notice, always, what I was saying, how he was reacting; what *he* was saying, how I was reacting.

But then he returned and our life went on. Three days gone. A week. I measured the time in the faint waning of my consciousness of my misery, and wondered if this would one day be enough: simply not to be consciously miserable anymore.

IN EARLY APRIL, ABOUT TEN DAYS AFTER DANIEL CAME BACK, my mother fell. What she broke was her foot, not the dreaded hip, but she'd be on crutches for at least a month. I took a week off from work to go to Maine and help her.

Daniel drove me to the airport; one of Mother's boarding students would borrow her old Buick and pick me up in Bangor. We were as polite and careful with each other as usual on the drive into Boston. I commented on the yellowing sweeps of the willows, on the odd batches of crocus or squill here and there. Daniel smiled or nodded, and in turn told me about the resolution of a crisis they'd been having at church, a kind of political struggle over deacons. For a while I closed my eyes and rested; let him think I was sleeping if he wanted to. As we drove through the city, though, slowing, stopping, starting, I sat up, looking around.

We were entering the airport. Suddenly Daniel said, "It'll be good for us, this time apart."

I looked at him. "We just had time apart. When you were in Philadelphia."

He smiled thinly at me. "Ah, yes. But that was my time away. My busy time. This time apart we can think."

"I thought then."

"You had time to."

"Yes," I said, not wanting to consider what he might think about while I was gone. But then we pulled up to the terminal, and there was all the distraction of where to park, whether he should bother to park, whether he should even get out of the car. In the end, we double-parked, and he did get out, to embrace me quickly, the lightest touch of his cool lips on my cheek. Then I walked away, into the terminal, out to the gate.

As I flew north, I moved into what seemed like another country, an earlier time of year. You could still see snow lying under the trees in the woods, and the rest of the landscape was bleak and colorless except for the deep green of the pines.

It was Susie who picked me up, holding a card against her chest with my name printed on it in big letters so I wouldn't miss her. "That was clever of you," I said, as we walked to the car. "I was wondering how I'd recognize you."

"Your mother suggested it," she said. She was short and plump, with dark, curling hair. I was trying to remember what Mother had told me about her. Math? Or physics? Something unusual for a woman, as I recalled it. "I was wondering how I'd recognize you too."

"How is she doing?" I asked.

"Oh, she's her same old self, really. In the hospital I think they had her doped up, and she seemed, like, really old?" She had the same verbal tics as everyone else her age, whatever the specialty was.

"She *is* really old."

"But, like, disoriented? And irritable. That's what struck me, I think. How irritable she was? I never think of her as complaining. She's so . . . like, *brave*, don't you think?"

"I do," I said, realizing that this was true.

In the car, I asked her to tell me about herself and the other students. She was chatty and seemingly comfortable. It was math, her field, but she'd hit a wall, she said, and didn't know if she'd go on.

"It's like there are different sizes of the 'gift,' you know what I mean? and I always thought I had this really huge gift? But now I look around me at all these math boys. . . ." She shook her head. "I don't *think* so."

I commiserated on having to think about starting over at her age, which was . . . ?

"Twenty-four."

"Twenty-four," I said.

When we came into the house, Mother's voice floated down the stairs. "Yoo-hoo!"

"Yoo-hoo yourself," I yelled back, and Susie laughed.

I went upstairs and dropped my bag outside Mother's door. "Josie," she said, reaching her arms up. She was white everywhere: her skin, her turtleneck, her hair lying in a long frizzing braid on one shoulder—except for the cinnamon-colored streaks in it, reminders of her long-ago dark auburn. She was dressed: the turtleneck under a cardigan, navy-blue slacks with one leg rolled up over the cast. There was a big woolly sock on that.

I leaned over and kissed her, smelling her talc and the light camphor odor from the heavy woolen blankets she still used. My bed would have them, too, layered one over another, their very weight seeming to press you nightly into uncomfortable sleep. The girls had always complained of this on visits to her. "I woke up with *dents* in me," Sadie had said. Sadie.

We talked for a few minutes, and then I went to change and unpack. When I finally sat down next to her bed and poured her some tea out of the pot I'd carried up on a tray—tea with lemon, and arrowroot biscuits, the old familiar afternoon snack—she threw herself back dramatically into the pillows and said, "It's my own damned fault. If only I'd been wearing sensible shoes."

"Why, what *were* you wearing? Manolo Blahniks?"

She squinted at me from behind her bifocals. "What's that?"

"I was being silly. They're spike heels."

"Well, no." She smiled. "I had on those shoes I wore to Boston."

"Mother! They don't come more sensible than that."

"Well, but I mean I should have had on flat heels. I should have had rubber soles."

"Oh! *Snow* tires."

She laughed. "More or less. It was vanity. And now I pay the price."

I laughed too. "Well, sooner or later we all pay that price, I guess."

"But this is serious, you know."

"You'll be fine in no time," I said dismissively. Her doctor had assured me this would be the case.

"No, don't say that. I mean, I know I will, this time. But it's the beginning."

"It's the beginning of exactly nothing," I said.

"Josie, my girl, it's the beginning of the end, and you know it. Slow or fast, it doesn't matter from here on out. It *is* the beginning." She raised a hand against my protest. "And don't you pretend it isn't the first thing you thought of."

"Mother, it's not."

"Well, the second or third thing, then."

I set my cup down. "Listen, lady," I said. "I'll admit it, the thought occurred, *way* down the list. But the moment I talked to the doctor, I stopped thinking about it altogether." This was almost true. "You're going to be fine. He says so. I know it. *Susie* knows it."

She huffed, a little sharp exhalation from her lips, and then she took a neat bite from her cookie. When she'd swallowed, she looked at me. "It's not that I'm afraid, I want you to know that. The only thing I worry about is dementia. And leaving home. I want to die at home."

"Now, *that* is premature."

She ignored me. "I want you to know something," she said. "I've signed one of those living wills. I know it's not binding, but I've signed it. Fred has it. He's the executor." She pronounced it murderously: exe*cu*tor. "I'll have the lawyer send a copy to you too. But I wanted you to hear it from my lips as well: I *want* to *stay* at *home*." She smacked the bedclothes with her hand on the beat. "I'd rather die sooner at home than later in a hospital. Those two nights were plenty enough for me, thank you. It was like being already dead. It was more like hell than anything I've ever lived through."

This was her mood, then. When I talked to Daniel on the phone that night, I called it "cheerful morbidity" and made him smile. I could hear it in his voice when he spoke again.

THE DAYS AT MY MOTHER'S HOUSE PASSED SLOWLY, MIND-
lessly, and I was relieved—even happy, in a way—for that. We played
checkers, Mother and I, and gin rummy. She beat me, because, as
she said in disgust, I didn't even try to remember what cards had
already been discarded. The first few days, I had her walking up and
down the long upstairs hall for ever lengthier intervals. The second
afternoon, I persuaded her to come downstairs, sitting down first at
the top and sliding the crutches along with her. I stood a few steps
below her, moving backward as she descended, encouraging her
progress, but I didn't help. After she'd struggled to get herself up, to
get her crutches tucked under her armpits again, she said, "Good
thing they built these old houses with sturdy newel posts," and burst
into tears.

I tried to do a chore or two for her each day. I went shopping, and
made her about a week's worth of dinners, which I froze. I bought her
a small backpack to haul things around in. She wore it reversed, hanging off her front, so she could get at it more easily. I did several big
loads of laundry, since it seemed it would be a while before she could
easily manage the trip to the basement carrying anything. I returned
her library books and got her new ones.

I went to the store and bought a jigsaw puzzle, and we started it on
a card table I set up in front of the fireplace. It was pleasant, the idle,
pointless, unfreighted conversation about color and shape, about who
was working on edge pieces, about where our separate clusters of
pieces might fit together. One day late in the week, as we were working on it, seemingly out of the blue she said, "I feel bad. Taking you
away from Daniel for so long."

"It's not very long, Mother."

"Still. It disrupts your life."

I smiled. "We've been *having* a disrupted life," I said. She looked up
sharply. "It's been a hard time between us. Actually, it's not a bad time
to be apart for a while."

"Well, hard times happen, Josie." She was watching me now.

"I know," I said.

"Do you? I used to worry that you didn't know that. That that's
what made you so . . ."

"So what?"

"So restless, I guess. Like the time you ran away from that hapless Ted."

"But you see, Mom, it all worked out for the best."

She sighed, testily. "I suppose so."

We fell silent again. The puzzle was a Monet haystack, the pieces were covered with blurry pastel brush strokes.

Suddenly she said, "You know, Josie, there's something I've always meant to tell you, and it's bothered me that I didn't. I don't know that it makes any difference now, but I feel I should. I feel I *ought* to do those things I've neglected to do."

I raised my hand, to ward it off, I suppose, whatever intimacy *it* was going to be. I didn't want it. I wanted everything I knew about my mother to stay the same.

"No, now you listen to me. Sit still and listen." And abruptly we were not working on the puzzle. I looked at her. Her lips were pressed against each other firmly: resolve. Then she began. "It's about your father. You know, your father and I . . . well, he was married once before. Before he and I married."

I looked away sharply. I was shocked. Had she imagined—how could she have imagined?—that I'd never known? It was true that we'd never spoken of it, but there was so much we'd never spoken of. Sex. Childbirth. Anger, love, sorrow . . . All these were encoded or contained in the language of everyday life. Or simply never referred to in our family. I thought I was going to laugh. In relief, I suppose. This was all there was. This, this was the most terrible secret in my mother's life, the one she had to tell before she died. How wonderful. How extraordinary.

"His first wife died," she was saying solemnly. "I'd known him for some years by then. Working for him, don't you know. She died awfully slowly. She was ill for years. She was ill—they didn't know it, but she was ill even before they were married, so right from the start they were coping with that. By the end, her whole insides were eaten up, more or less." She gestured at her own belly.

"I suppose that's some of it. You just didn't talk about cancer in those days. That made it kinda . . . private. And then I think your father and I were . . . I suppose I'd have to say ashamed. It seems odd now, from this great distance, that we would be. But we were happy together, even before she died, you know what I mean. . . ."

I nodded, quickly.

"And that shamed us. We . . . we really didn't speak of it, even to each other. How happy we were. At her expense. We just . . . well, what we felt, I suppose, was that we couldn't help ourselves. I know I couldn't. I just . . . well, I fell in love with him. He was so shy, don't you know. He asked for so little for himself that it broke my heart, really. I just . . . I just began to do the things for him that a wife would do. I'd pack him lunches when he went botanizing. Sometimes I'd even go along. It was lovely." Her face had softened. "I'd take a book and sit on a blanket and read, and *off* your father would go, and come back every now and then to show me what he'd found."

I thought of Daniel and me, in the boat. "It *sounds* lovely," I said.

"But that, that early happiness . . . well, it cost us something. Later. There were things we never . . ."

She sat straighter. "We paid a price," she said firmly. "Nothing is free, is it?" Her voice was stronger now. She smiled at me, a little vaguely. "Well, he told Freddie. And I was to tell you. But you were littler, and the time never seemed just right. And then, so suddenly, he was gone. And you were so devoted to him, it seemed a terrible thing to me to do anything that might hurt his memory."

I was wondering again that she could have thought I didn't know this, especially after Fred was told. Did she not understand the hard currency of painful knowledge that siblings paid each other off in? Did she not understand how everything slowly—or quickly—rises to the surface in family life?

"Well, that's my secret," she said. She was waiting for my response.

"And it's not so awful, is it?"

"I hope not, dear."

"No. It isn't."

"It doesn't change anything, does it?"

I shook my head.

"I hope you can think of your father and me . . . well, we're the same, aren't we?"

I reached out and touched her hand. "Mother, of course." She let my hand rest on hers a moment.

"What was terrible, I suppose, was the not telling it."

"It didn't hurt me, Mother."

"Well, so you say, Josie. But you don't really know, now, do you?"

"No, but I suppose it's part of who I am by now." Of course, I didn't mean the not knowing, since I had known. I meant the *not speaking*, the keeping of the secret. And I meant what the secret itself gave me so young: the seductive sense of another self, another possibility.

And what if we'd been utterly open? Made jokes about the first wife? What if we'd been that kind of family? Well, I would have been different, surely. But not because I knew the secret. For it wasn't the secret—the secret that wasn't a secret anyway—that led to the austerity in our lives. It was the austerity that led to the secret. And what I had been marked by, probably most of all, was the austerity. It had made secrets in my life too. Or silences, anyway, that became secrets. That became lies. I thought of Dana, who loved what she thought of as my dignity. And had never known my real name. I thought of my daughters, who found me elusive. In some sense, I suppose, unknowable. Of Sadie, who couldn't believe in me now. Of my husband, whom I'd betrayed. Who seemed to have been willing to think, if only briefly, that I was capable of even worse than that. Who was so cut off from me now that I had wondered if we shouldn't end our marriage.

I ought to ask her a question or two, I realized. "Did you know her?" I asked after a moment. "Daddy's wife?"

"Early on I met her a few times. But she was very ill by then. Not herself." Idly she picked up a puzzle piece and moved it around in the air over the clumps of attached pieces she was working on. "Well," she said, "maybe by then being ill was what *being herself* meant. I don't know. All I know is your father felt he'd lost her. He'd lost her already, years before she died."

Then she said, "Look here, isn't this something that goes with your stuff over there?" and held the piece out to me.

That night I sat up by the fire after my mother had gone to bed. The students were drifting in and out of the kitchen, getting late-night snacks and drinks, coming in to talk to me briefly, and it struck me with some amusement that my mother was, in a way, living the life I'd run away for so many years ago—unencumbered, free, in an easy, relaxed household among other unencumbered, free people. I called up her face, her iron-blue eyes, her age-freckled skin with the finest of lines distributed evenly on it everywhere, like a delicate mesh laid over her features. I marveled again at her innocent secret, at her impulse to tell it. After all these years, I thought. And then heard Detective

Ryan's pleased voice talking about Eli, about killers who've gone free: "They have to tell," he'd said.

Well, apparently so.

But why? What is it that comes from the telling?

Some of it must be relief, of course. A secret weighs on us, a terrible secret weighs with a terrible weight.

I thought about Eli and saw him again in the library: the raised hand, the shy smile—which I had read as corrupt, and corrupting, as an attempt to include me somehow in his guilt. But what was it he had said when I asked *him* why he had told, why he had chosen me? "I need a kind of forgiveness from you." It was what Mother had needed: why not Eli?

So maybe I misunderstood him that day in the library. Maybe he was saying only *please* through that dancing slice of light, and in return he saw me saying only *no*. Maybe my turning away from him then is what hardened him, what made it possible for him to defend himself to the police by accusing me. Because I had judged him, refused him. Because he no longer saw me as the generous, mature person he'd understood me to be.

I thought of my mother, asking me, "We're the same, aren't we?" *It hasn't changed us in your eyes to know this.* And the comfort she seemed to take in knowing that it hadn't. I thought of my blurting out to Daniel what I'd done, my hope that he could somehow love me still.

It seems we need someone to know us *as we are*—with all we have done—and forgive us. We need to tell. We need to be whole in someone's sight: Know this about me, and yet love me. *Please.*

But it's so much to ask of other people! Too much. Daniel makes it easier on those around him: God is the one he asks to know him as he is, to see him whole and love him still. But for us others it seems there must be a person to redeem us to ourselves. It isn't enough, apparently, to know oneself. To forgive oneself, in secret.

I crushed the fire into embers and replaced the screen. And as I mounted the stairs and undressed, as I slid under the cold, heavy covers ("Flat as a pancake till morning!" my mother used to say), I felt, I think for the first time, a kind of pity for Eli Mayhew.

I SPENT THE AFTERNOON BEFORE I LEFT PULLING THE SODden leaf mulch off Mother's flower beds in the front yard. I worried that it was too early, that there might still be a frost, but she was firm: "Oh, it's always too early, no matter when you do it, they're so pale and puny. Too early and too late at the same time. It could get cold again, but on the other hand, it's not good for them to grow very long in the dark. One of those chores you just hold your nose and do it and hope it comes out all right. Anyway," she said, "I always do it by tax time, and that's nearly upon us now."

It was the first slightly warm day we'd had, and I sat in the pale sunlight on the damp ground. The plants were up—she was right—poking their snub noses out of the wet dirt, often having pierced the leaves, so that I had to pull each one off carefully or risk splitting their fragile tips. They were white and looked oddly naked, their secret growing suddenly exposed like this. They seemed at first to shrink and recoil, to dry up a little in the light and air. But even as I worked, they were greening slightly too.

The sunlight bore down on my back and warmed me, though my legs and bottom were cool and damp. I took off my mother's gardening gloves after the first few minutes—they made it hard to do the delicate work around the shoots. I shifted from side to side, and then up to my knees, as my hip started to ache. But I loved it also. I felt—for the first time, I think, since I'd heard Eli's name, since I'd met him again—content to be doing what I was doing. I felt innocently *useful*.

That night I had a dream. Something in it startled me, and I woke myself, making a small noise, jumping under the heavy layers of blanket. It came to me that it had been about Daniel, though I couldn't remember what was happening. But I had reached out to touch him just before I woke, and I could still *feel* it, Daniel's cool cheek under my fingertips. How real it was! I thought.

And then I recalled the dogs in sleep, the way they suckled and ran and tore at other animals, so real their dream life was to them. Did they know the difference when they woke? I wondered. Or were they like demented people, who count as experience what they've merely dreamed?

As I lay there, I realized I was doing just that. Because I was happy, happy with just my dream of Daniel, the vague sleeping memory of him. I'd brought him to life, lying in the dark in my mother's house. I'd felt him and touched him, he'd come back to me. And for that moment in my half-sleeping, half-waking state, the joy that gave me felt like enough.

ONCE THE PLANE HAD LANDED AT LOGAN AND WE'D SLOWLY filed off, I headed downstairs along with the rest of our troop, toward the baggage claim area, dragging my rolling bag behind me. Ahead of me on the escalator, a little boy of about four was trying to tell knock-knock jokes to his mother, getting them wrong every time, jumping from "who's there?" directly to the punch line. She laughed politely at each one, though, which was enough for him. "That was a good one," he'd say. "Wasn't it, Mom? *That* was a good one."

I crossed the wide stone floor downstairs to the wall of windows and revolving doors. Outside, I could see the cars parked and double-parked, waiting. And then I saw our car. Leaning against it, with his back against the driver's side—turned away from me—was Daniel. I negotiated my bag into the revolving door and made it through. The noise outside was deafening—a plane starting its takeoff.

The dogs were in the car. I could see them barking and jumping wildly around, perhaps in response to all the noise, perhaps at the people passing by, too close to their territory. Daniel was turned almost in profile to me, watching a group of travelers boarding a bus pulled up to the middle island of the drive-through area. The scream of the plane was so intense now that he didn't hear me come up next to him, he didn't sense me standing there.

Without asking myself whether I should, whether I could, I lifted my hand to his face and touched it to the flat of his cheek. He startled and turned to me. After the slightest pause, his arms rose in what seemed a nearly automatic response to embrace me.

We pressed together, hesitantly at first. Then I felt him suddenly grip me hard—Daniel!—and pull me fiercely against him. His hands slid up and down my back, I felt his tensed strength. The moment went on and on for me, dizzying in its timelessness. I was drinking in with my body the feel of his, and I was breathless with relief, with the sweet familiarity of our touch. *This*, I thought, holding him. *This: here.* Slowly my breathing evened.

But before we stepped apart again, I made myself register consciously the expression that had passed for a moment over his face as he moved forward to hold me: a sadness, a visible regret.

At what? At this giving over, I suppose. This capitulation. To me. To us.

And I haven't forgotten. I think of it often, and I find a kind of tender sorrow rising in me for him. For the distance he had to cross, the place he'd had to come from, to yield to me. For his giving up some hardness in himself—maybe a hardness that had surprised him or pleased him in a way—to be what I knew again. To be the one who had to forgive me.

SO WE RESUME IT, SLOWLY PICKING UP THE ONGOING CONversation that was our life together. We talk. We talk. And the words make our silences easier—they're the current that runs under them.

We make love, too, a little shyly at first, as though there were something embarrassing or shameful about starting again after not having done it in so long.

And there come more and more those other moments of touching, the ones I have most deeply yearned for, I realize. Daniel's hand, resting on my shoulder as he looks over it to see what I'm doing, what I'm making for dinner. On my arm: "Here, I'll carry that." On my thigh— a claim, an assertion: You're back. I'm back. We're home again. I know you.

Summer comes, and we walk again at night, trailing the dogs on the worn paths. In the cottoned dark, the words seem easeful, seem like the spoken version of our bodies' bumping or touching, all part of the same remaking of what it means to be together, to touch each other, to love.

Still, there are things that startle me. New things. Some small, barely worth noticing, perhaps. I am talking at the dinner table one night, happy to be back in our old pattern, maybe going on too long; and I see that he has gone away, that his face has closed in and clouded, somehow. And because I can't bear to ask—to be told— what's wrong, I chatter on, ignoring it, until he comes back, until the moment of darkness passes.

Others more dramatic: Leaving late for work, I'm sliding behind the steering wheel of my car when I notice Daniel. He's deep in the barn, in shadow, just stepping out of his office to come to the house. He's seen me in the car, and he's stopped there, waiting. He doesn't realize I've seen him. *He doesn't want me to see him.* Maybe he's been thinking about all of it again and he doesn't want to have to talk to me, to have to be loving. Maybe he just wants to hold on to something he's been thinking about, working on. At any rate, he stands still, barely visible, a pale ghost in the shadows, and he waits for me to be gone.

So I go. Because this is my task, as I see it, and I'm trying to learn it well. I'm trying to accept the changes I made when I didn't intend to. I'm trying to allow for this ordinary distance between us. To let him not want me sometimes. Sometimes not to need him. So that when it comes, I can love it more: the approach, the turning back to what we do want most in each other, what we do need.

I SEE ELI AROUND TOWN EVERY NOW AND THEN. ELI ALONE, or together with Jean. Once, they were jogging by the side of the road as I was driving by. This was early in the summer, one of those long June evenings when the sun sits forever at earth's edge and day goes on and on in its warm last light. I didn't recognize them at first. They were just silhouettes ahead of me, a man and a woman, not young, but strong, fit, in good shape, their stride matched perfectly, the legs lean and muscled. Closer, I saw they were my age, and I envied them their bodies, the nice high kick behind each stroke.

And then, just before I pulled abreast of them, I knew who they were and I turned my face away. In the rearview mirror, the sun was full upon then. They were like costumed twins in their bright running clothes, their skin daubed orange in the light, their matching short hair silvered. I watched them grow smaller and smaller on the road-side. They hadn't noticed me.

I saw him by himself once at the hardware store. I was bent over a bin counting out galvanized nails, and I looked up and there he was, in shirtsleeves and old khakis, his hair grown out a little, standing at the counter asking about paints—oil versus latex. I turned and went into another aisle until he'd left.

But it reminded me of something. I stopped in at the library on my way home, though Daniel was waiting for those nails. I went to the computer room and called up again the newspaper image of all of us leaving the police station after Dana's death. There we were, young and grief-stricken and angry.

Eli and I were the only ones not wearing coats.

He walked by our house on the Fourth of July, as did half the town, following the parade. I'd been sitting on the front steps with Shorty, the door open behind me. When I saw Eli, Eli and Jean, I stepped back into the darkness of the front hall to wait until they'd passed, until that part of the parade—the antique cars, the firemen throwing candy to the avid children—had gone by. They were with another couple I've seen around town a bit but don't know. They were talking and laughing, Jean and the woman carrying mugs of coffee as they walked along in the dappled sunlight under the old, wide trees. They're making friends, then, settling in. My wish that they move away will, apparently, not be granted.

But perhaps this is all to the good. Perhaps it's best to live with the possibility that around any corner, at any time, may come the person who reminds you of your own capacity to surprise yourself, to put at risk everything that's dear to you. Who reminds you of the distances we have to bridge to begin to know anything about one another. Who reminds you that what seems to be—even about yourself—may not be. That like him, you need to be forgiven.

I tell myself it's all to the good, anyway.

Still, when I see him, I always turn away, as if I don't recognize him. As if I don't know who he is. And so far, he does too.

A NOTE ABOUT THE AUTHOR

Sue Miller is the best-selling author of *The Good Mother, Inventing the Abbotts, Family Pictures, For Love,* and *The Distinguished Guest.* She lives in Boston.

A NOTE ON THE TYPE

This book was set in a modern adaptation of a type designed by the first William Caslon (1692–1766). The Caslon face, an artistic, easily read type, has enjoyed over two centuries of popularity in our own country. It is of interest to note that the first copies of the Declaration of Independence and the first paper currency distributed to the citizens of the newborn nation were printed in this typeface.